Surreal South '11

SURREAL SOUTH '11

edited by
Laura Benedict
&
Pinckney Benedict

Press 53
Winston-Salem

Press 53
PO Box 30314
Winston-Salem, NC 27130

First Edition

Cover design by Kevin Morgan Watson

Cover art, "Crow Carrier,"
copyright © 2011 by Stephanie Bracciano,
used by permission of the artist

Printed on acid-free paper

ISBN 978-1-935708-46-9

Acknowledgments

"Before I Offer Myself to the Birdmen" first appeared in *The Cincinnati Review*, Issue 7.2.

"Bitter Soul" first appeared in *Cooweescoowee: A Journal of Arts and Letters*, Fall 2002.

"The Castle of Horrors" first appeared in the collection *One Last Good Time* (Press 53).

"The Easy Payment Plan" first appeared in *New Plains Review*, Spring, 2011.

"Eyes That Melt Wings" first appeared in *Sex and Murder*, Issue 4.

"Interstate Nocturne" appeared in an earlier version online in *Tertulia Magazine*, Fall 2010 and in *Pif Magazine*, December 2010.

"Monsters in Appalachia" first appeared in storySouth, Issue 30, Fall 2010.

"The Veil" first appeared in *The Distillery*, Volume XIII, Number 1.

Contents

For Kermit,
Defense Minister of the Surreal South

Introduction

Demons. Angels. Weird and difficult girlfriends. Serial killers. Hired killers. Zombies (of the human, canine, and Frankensteinian/mechanical/motorcycle-helmet-wearing sort). Taxidermists. Birdmen. Aliens. Pig Hole and the Pigwoman. A black velvet portrait of Elvis. A guy who fistfights monsters. Exorcism. Sex (quite a bit of sex). Ghosts (lots of ghosts). Monsters (lots of those too).

Looking over that list of (just some of) the contents of *Surreal South '11* makes us, the editors, giggle with pleasure. And tremble with fear. And kvell, just a bit.

This is the third and, in our humble opinion, the best, densest, and most exciting edition of the *Surreal South* anthology series. When we began this series, with the original *Surreal South* in 2007 (we did not know then, though we hoped, that it would be followed by *Surreal South '09* and now this third volume), we wished to put together a book that in some sense bridged the gap between work that is perceived as "literary" and work that is perceived as "genre." The first category is, as we take it, defined primarily by the excellence of its execution and the loftiness of its ambition. The second category is demarcated by its accessibility (indeed, its addictive quality) and its concentration on plot and pacing.

One of us is a self-described "thriller-writer chick" and the other is a professor of creative writing and the author of a number of "literary" (which in this case means little-read but, we think it is fair to say, well-respected) volumes of fiction. The two distinct professional realms in which we dwell steadfastly refuse to recognize each the merits of the other. Successful genre writers frequently deride literary fiction (not entirely without reason) as dull and precious; and the "genre" story continues to have next to no place (among professors, anyway; students love to read and continue to write them, despite the risks to their scholastic careers) in the creative writing classroom.

And yet: We love each other. We live in the same house, and have, for over two decades now. We have successfully procreated. We like and respect each other's work. And when we read, we pay very little attention to these labels, "genre" or "literary." We look, in our reading lives, for fiction that possesses all the merits of both categories: challenging language, seriousness of purpose, readability, and—best virtue of all! and rarest—the storytelling charisma to carry us away from the challenges of our quotidian lives into some other world altogether.

It also doesn't hurt, we've found, if the fiction contains ghosts and monsters.

This volume of profoundly weird stories is, we believe, an almost-perfect nexus of the literary and the genre. The stories it contains offer brilliant prose and unabashed plots. They are highly intelligent and compulsively readable. And they all celebrate ghosts and monsters. We really like ghosts and monsters. We're betting that you do too. We're betting that enough folks like southern ghosts and monsters that, after this one, there will be a *Surreal South '13*, and a *Surreal South '15*, and on and on like that, and that those books will be (if such a thing is possible) even bigger and denser and better than this one.

And now, if you're brave enough: on to the stories.

Laura Benedict
Pinckney Benedict
Carbondale, Illinois
October 2011

SURREAL SOUTH '11

Resurrection

The algae bloom filled the back pond where the cattle stood confused and lowing, knee deep in greenish muck and strangling fish. On Monday the water was clear, and now late Tuesday of a chilly mid-November, catfish and carp swam near the surface, opening their big ugly mouths to gulp air. Maybeth dug through the shed until she found a bucket of the stuff Ed used to treat the water, and slung some in. When she waded out in galoshes she saw colors shifting in the slime, blues and yellows, and tried to clear a spot with a stick to get a better look. She caught sight of the edges of fish, a fin here, a whiteness of a turning belly there, except not like she had never seen before, at least not around Wesley, Arkansas. Television shows, sure, or pictures that Ed showed her from a fishing trip he took with his friends from work to the Caribbean. He'd been dead almost three months now of lung cancer and being reminded of his fishing trip pissed her off anew. He took that vacation without her because he said he deserved a break. "From what?" she'd said. She was the one that did most of the work around the house and got his dinner in front of him every night. He always demanded the same meals: cornbread and beans, chicken and dumplings, greens, buttermilk and biscuits. Ed's habits dictated hers, and any attempt at a new dish, chicken parmesan or lasagna, was met with indignation. She had waited on him and washed up while he ate just like her mother had for her father. He watched bass fishing shows on TV and forked food into his mouth without even looking at it. She thought about those bass, twisting in fear at the end of a taut line, as she gazed

1

into the water now. One thing didn't look like a fish at all. More like a gray doormat. When she poked at it with a stick it came to life, a spiked tail drifting behind it as it shifted back under the algae. Flies and gnats flitted about her face. A honey bee landed on her arm and she swatted it away.

When Maybeth returned to the house there were three copperheads on the back stepping stone as if for sun heat, even though it was in the 40s. She sidestepped to the woodpile for the axe, but the snakes made a slow escape under the house. Standing there with the axe, staring at where the snakes had been, she felt sorry for herself. She had the whole of the evening ahead of her, her favorite shows, some leftover spaghetti, and all the pleasure was taken out of it by this onslaught of filthy creatures. She thought about calling her son, Ed Jr. A blessing, they had said, because late in life she had finally had the child doctor's had told her she never could. When she called his response always made her feel a nuisance though. "What is it now?" he said whenever he answered his cell phone. She wanted to call from a number he wouldn't recognize just to hear him say hello like he cared what the other person on the end of the line thought. Sometimes she could get him to come out if she told him she was cooking his favorite - chicken and dumplings. He lived in Fayetteville with his college girlfriend, a good twenty miles from the 175 acre farm he wanted her to sell since Ed smoked himself to death. He said it was too much work, and so far out no one would know if she was dead in the yard until the buzzards were circling, and hinted she needed special care.

"We are concerned about you all alone out there," he said. He had also been testing suggestions she might be going senile due to her new purchases and lifestyle changes.

"Who's we?" she said. She knew his girlfriend was concerned about getting married, and concerned about animal rights, and that she and her son were concerned about how much the farm was now worth, but doubted they shared any concern about her wellbeing.

She liked the quiet of the isolated hilltop, and the rocky drive that led to the house kept any but the most determined from coming up. With Ed gone it finally felt like hers. Ed Jr. called it "Dad's" farm, and she knew he wanted her to sell it because he now thought of it as his.

Maybeth rested the axe against the porch, and stepped from her mud-heavy galoshes into some new, purple house shoes. She stoked the fire in the woodstove, poured herself a cup of jasmine tea, and drew a bubble bath. With Ed gone, she had quickly settled into a routine of her own choosing, eating when she was hungry and what she wanted, spending leisurely evenings reading by the fire, watching television shows that he would not have allowed, declaring them useless or vulgar. She loved the heated embrace, the real-life biography of a distant princess, the competitive highs and lows of weight loss or high fashion. In those shows people got what they wanted, or at least learned valuable lessons about love and life. She sat up to her chin in lavender scented bubbles with a water-warped romance novel until the bath cooled. Then she watched TV in a kimono she had recently ordered from a catalog, her dinner before her on the coffee table with a glass of chilled Muscadine wine. Each husky rattling in the walls reminded her of the snakes beneath the house though, and she wondered how she could possibly kill everything quickly and neatly to give herself some peace.

The next day she was woken by the buzzing of insects both inside and outside the house. Wasps beat themselves dully against the windows, and flies crawled on the kitchen counters. She whacked at them with a rolled up newspaper but they proved too fast or she was too slow, and somehow no smashed bodies lay under where she struck, no matter how many times. "Fine," she said, and shoved the old paper into the woodstove. She slipped into her work boots and kimono to walk down to get today's paper at the road, but saw the copperheads were back on the stepping stone, joined by a rattlesnake and a cottonmouth. Maybeth hollered and was immediately embarrassed at the noise she had made. The snakes didn't move at the sight or sound of her, but when she lifted the axe from where it leaned against the rail they slipped like oil back under the porch. Maybe she would have to call her son, she thought. He'd only tell her there weren't snakes this time of year, and drop another heavy hint about Razorback Retirement Village, a cinderblock structure by the railroad tracks where the poor and homeless went to die.

She kept the axe in her grip and looked out towards the algae-choked pond, the gathering of cattle, and thought she saw a pig between the legs of the heifers. No one she knew had any pigs right now, but if they did she knew they were good at getting out and causing problems. She sighed heavily, feeling the weight of everyone else's needs and pigs upon what could have been a good day. As she was leaning the axe back against the railing, she saw a fluttering in the old, leafless oak at the edge of the yard. The gnarled limbs held a barn owl, unblinking in the morning daylight, a rooster preening his wings, and clusters of squirrels. Beneath the outstretched limbs of the oak paced a coon and several hens, and behind in the tree-line there were slight movements in the brush. Briars rustled and she thought she heard the sound of breath, as if an exhalation from a large animal. Maybeth felt a coldness inside her, and for some reason she could not name was glad she had not called her son. "Get!" she yelled, waving the axe at the leafless tree and all the creatures there. The coon stopped pacing and stared at her, and the rustling in the woods beyond silenced. She stepped down into the yard and searched for a stone, forgetting how closely the snakes lay under the porch. She was a good aim and hit dirt about two feet from the coon, who sat up on his hind quarters and looked at her. "That's it," she said. She went to get the .22 in case he was rabid, and when she came back with the loaded gun, two other coons had appeared like they were forming a gang. She took a shot that bit bark behind the first coon, still sitting upright and watching her, but he didn't move. From the wood's edge she heard the crackling of hoof steps on dry brush, and a snort of muzzle-blown breath.

"What?" she said, and waited as if the coon could speak. She lowered the gun.

Maybeth had no pleasure in killing. Used to be the only thing she could get Ed to take care of was disposing of unwanted animals.

He'd get the shotgun or a hoe and kill whatever was a pest around the house. He seemed to enjoy the defense of his territory as much as he did hunting. A definition of what made anything his and his alone was the blood he spilt that crossed his boundaries. Once she had watched him mercilessly sink an axe into a trapped coon's head rather than waste a bullet. So many carcasses he had skinned on that porch, flinging bits to his hunting dogs, and then dumping them in her sink for her to cook for his dinner. The flesh and bone lay in limp postures as if alive. She imagined the squirrel's body mid-leap upon a high oak branch in search of an acorn, or the fish twisting into the sun-dappled water looking for a Jesus Bug as she rinsed their meat under the faucet.

Maybeth decided to ignore the animals watching her until she could figure out what to do about them, and quickly went through her chores before locking herself into the buzzing house. She spent the rest of the day cooking new dishes to take her mind off of it, teacakes and baked rigatoni, shooing away insects. Later that night she struggled to concentrate on her book and bath while the sounds of tiny claws and teeth scraped the insides of the walls.

The next morning was clear and chill when the dog showed up. Ed had been buried three months to the day. It was the dog that confirmed the growing coldness she felt with each new animal that appeared.

"Copper?" she'd said, knowing it was crazy the moment she said it, Copper being dead since Ed put a bullet between his eyes when he said the dog's arthritis got too bad. Maybeth had thought Copper looked fine, just a little stiff, and suggested a vet's visit, but Ed wouldn't hear of spending money on the worst hunting dog he'd ever owned. He'd been a good companion to Maybeth though, following her through the fields as she fed livestock and watching her as she cooked. She made a special grave for Copper, and to mark the spot she planted a rosebush that Ed later mowed down. Now the dog came loping across the yard like it always did, and ran right up on the porch to sit by the door. She let Copper inside the house where she could get a better look at him, and instinctively dialed her son.

"Copper's back," she said.

"What?" he said.

Maybeth forgot he hadn't known Copper, and had only seen pictures of him with his dad when they were first married. She stayed silent, uncertain how to explain her long-dead dog had reappeared and was sitting in her kitchen

"Are you O-K?" he said. He paused between the O and the K, as if he were talking to a crazy person.

"Nothing," she said. "Just a neighbor's dog that run off."

He sighed then, and in a fit of generosity offered to come out with his town girlfriend for dinner. "You could make us chicken and dumplings," he said. His bony gal fidgeted and whispered to her son whenever Maybeth turned her back the two times he had brought her out to visit. She was a Vegan and wouldn't eat anything anyway.

Copper nuzzled his soft head against Maybeth's leg and she felt for the knot on his skull from when he'd been hit by a truck and lived. It was still there.

"No," she said. "I'm fine."

After she got off the phone she watched Copper, looking for some ghostly sign, as if expecting him to convey a message from beyond.

"What do you want?" she said.

He stared at her, licked his lips, and turned abruptly to gnaw at his hindquarters. She reached out and rubbed his head again, and held a long ear between her fingers briefly to feel for heat.

"Let me get you something to eat, boy," she said.

She fried up bacon and hamburger and sprinkled cheddar cheese on top. Copper ate it in big, jowly bites. He lay down comfortably by the wood stove, licked his balls and fell asleep. He looked so peaceful there, and the plate was really empty, that she was surprised not to find him anywhere in the house the next morning, the doors all still firmly locked. But, there lay the empty plate all the same.

After Copper, she saw even more animals coming up around the house. One night Maybeth heard a scratching at her back door and opened it to find Sheba the cat. Maybeth had hoped she would come back when she vanished a year ago, but knew this was not a true return as the orange and white cat rubbed against her legs. She had suspected Ed of disposing of Sheba one weekend she had gone to the grocery store. The cat was sitting in the window when she left, but when she had stood on the porch and called for Sheba that evening and wondered aloud where she might be, Ed seemed a bit too satisfied. "Told you cats weren't loyal," he'd said, and demanded his supper. He had hated the way Sheba ignored him but came running at the sound of Maybeth's footsteps, who cradled the cat like a baby while she sipped coffee. She was reluctant to give the hungry cat any food, but poured her a bowl of Meow Mix. When Sheba was gone the next day she knew what she had to do.

The house was now surrounded. Deer crept up close to the septic tank and stepped lightly amongst the snakes and chickens. Possums, a few groundhogs and plenty of armadillos rooted about the porch and oak tree. The coons were the pushiest and took up residence on the front porch. She could see them peering into the windows, placing their black, elegant fingers against the glass. Maybeth didn't consider raising a gun to anything again. She emptied all that was left of the cat food onto plates and set it out on the porch and under the oak. When next she looked outside, the plates were licked clean and no coons hovered at the windows. The possums and armadillos were gone as well.

Maybeth sprinkled chickenfeed in the yard and placed out eggs by the porch. The snakes disappeared with the chickens and squirrels, but the owl wouldn't go until she lay hunks of raw meat on top of the septic tank. The deer were satisfied with a bale of alfalfa, and the lone pig Ed had told her he hit in the head with a sledgehammer when he was just ten years old made do with a bucket of slop. She also put out plates of honey and milk, butter and bread, cornmeal and greens, anything she could think of that would satisfy. Into the green muck of the pond she slung fish food she got at the store, and some fertilizer cleared the water up overnight.

She felt she had the run of her own home again. No wings beat against the windows. Nothing scraped its claws in the gaps between the walls or wore its teeth upon her pipes. Nothing stared at her unnaturally from the treetops or field edges, or placed its muzzle against the glass to wait for her response. Everything that Ed had disposed of seemed at peace now. She relaxed back into her newly formed habits, picking beets from her winter garden, taking bubble baths and eating canned peaches or rigatoni alfredo if she felt like it for dinner. She was making pesto lasagna one quiet night when she heard the kitchen chair scrape behind her.

The woman, bony and long, sat at the Formica table, holding a baby. She had stringy blonde hair that looked wet and a pink, thin scar across one pale cheek. The baby wiggled slightly in its sodden blanket, a white hand reaching out towards its mother's scarred face.

"I'm so sorry," Maybeth said. "What did he do to you?"

"I never knowed what you looked like," the woman said. "He said you was fatter though."

Her voice sounded almost normal, but with a hollow echo to it as if from deep in a well. There was a flatness in her eyes that had been less apparent in the animals, and as she coughed and pushed her damp hair back behind an ear, Maybeth felt the room go a little colder. The baby fussed, a wheezing, airy wail coming from the blanket. Maybeth didn't want to see its face.

"I'll take some hot coffee if you got any," the woman said.

Maybeth busied herself making a fresh pot, and asked the woman again what had happened to her.

"Don't matter," she said. "Nothing to do with you."

Maybeth pulled lasagna noodles from the boiling pot, laying them across waxed paper to cool, rather than stare. When the coffee was ready she set a cup before the woman, who looked at it as if she didn't recognize what it was. She drew in a long, slow breath and sighed like all she'd ever known was disappointment.

"I like sugar," she said.

When Maybeth set the sugar bowl before the woman, she lifted a cube first from the china bowl and offered it to her fussing baby who instantly quieted. She smiled slightly then, and added three cubes to her cup.

"Thank you," she whispered. "We won't bother you no more. Just let us sit here by the fire for a bit. You can leave the pot."

With that the woman seemed to collapse inside herself, sinking sleepily into the chair while tightly cradling her baby. She did not look up or speak again, and Maybeth poured herself a cup of coffee and left the two of them there by the woodstove. She wrapped herself in a shawl to walk out and stand on the porch. She looked into the chilly darkness and allowed the coffee mug to heat her hands. She did not want to turn around and see the woman and child still sitting there in her warm kitchen, and did not know how long she had been standing there before she smelled the cigarette smoke. When she saw the lit end glow and subside, glow and subside with each ghost breath beneath the old oak, she turned to go back in. She knew she would find an empty mug at the table and nothing more.

She only had to wash the dishes before she smelled the smoke again in her kitchen.

"I knowed it was you," she said.

"I'll take some of that coffee," he said. "And a cigarette if you got it."

She turned to see Ed, sitting at the table before the heat of the stove. He looked ready to take up a plate and go sit himself before the TV as any other night.

"You know I don't smoke," she said.

"Well then coffee will do," he said. "And I'll take some cornbread and greens too."

"I don't have any made," she said.

"Then I'll wait," he said.

She mixed up the cornbread and poured it into a hot iron skillet, bacon grease sizzling with contact, and put it into the stove. With no fresh greens around, she opened a can of mustard greens and put them in the microwave. She watched him before the stove, smoking the stub of an old cigarette. As the last embers died, she sorted through the drawers in the kitchen until she found a stale pack of Marlboros.

"What happened with you and that woman?" she said. "Did you harm the baby too?"

"Didn't have nothing to do with you," he said. He reached his long fingers for the pack. She saw he had the same rough beard he never bothered to shave all the way, and his third finger was still blackened from dropping a log on it.

"What do you mean it didn't have nothing to do with me?" she said.

He shrugged his thin shoulders, frail, almost transparent now, beneath his favorite shirt. She pulled the pack back to her chest, cradling it there against the heat of her beating heart, and then put it solidly back in the drawer, slamming it shut.

"What?" he said.

The cornbread was almost ready, and she turned off the oven and checked the greens. It could all wait until she had her bath. She set the water running while she hummed and arranged her book and poured in the lavender-scented bubble bath.

"It's time to eat," he said.

She ignored him and settled herself into the bath with her book. She could hear him muttering around in her kitchen, and could smell the faint scent of cigarettes over lavender. When she got out and put on her kimono, he was sitting there in the kitchen, as immobile as a boil.

"About time," he said. "What the hell do you think you're wearing?"

She added the cornbread and greens to her leftover rigatoni, and sat down before the TV. Ed, angry, joined her on her couch. She ate her dinner, drank her Muscadine, and watched a movie where things worked out for the heroine.

"Why don't you quit watching this stupid shit and get your fat ass in there to fix me a plate," he said.

Maybeth heard him, but felt him getting fainter and fainter.

"Get it for yourself if you want it," she said.

She propped up her feet in her new purple house shoes, and thought she heard something about these as well, but airily distant from her and her concerns. Something about the size of her feet and the color looking whorish. By now his words sounded like they were choking on his own breath, throttled by smoke she could just barely still smell, an echo of dissatisfaction she could comfortably ignore.

John Hornor Jacobs

Old Dogs, New Tricks

Six dogs were dead and two maimed, whining pitifully in their pens, when the truck came over the hill, headlights shining up into the pines and then dipping down, illuminating the mat of needles covering the forest floor. The truck wound its way down the path toward the pit, rumbling and coughing through the trees. It stopped with a clatter near the kennels and Issac Douglas climbed out of the cab and walked to the back.

The men watched, standing around the pit, smoking in the guttering kerosene light. Issac reached into the bed of the truck and grabbed a crate, sliding it out and onto the gate. Dressed in khaki work-shirt and pants, grease marring the elbows and knees, Issac lit a cigarette and drew on it heavily. His khaki clothes hung loosely, cinched at the waist, giving him the look of a withered navy officer.

Cigarette jutting from his mouth, he lifted the crate with a grunt. With the quick step of someone carrying a heavy load, he walked the crate over, setting it down with a thump, leaving a faint trail of smoke in the dark.

The dogs began howling and slavering, biting at the metal grills of the kennels.

"Hush now, dogs! Hush!" A man cried, kicking at the line of portable crates. The sound of growls grew frantic, more desperate. One of the men threw a bucket of water at the pens and the dogs quieted.

Turning back to the pit, the men—rough men all, field hands and laborers—leaned on the plywood and corrugated tin sides.

Kerosene lanterns hissed in the dark, throwing yellow pools of light onto the clay floor and the faces of the spectators. The men laughed and joked; money changed hands. One man, wearing a vest embroidered with the words *Arkansas Warrior Kennels*, adjusted a digital camera on a tripod, whistling.

Billy Cather, belly spilling over belt and sweating through his shirt in dark patches, hollered, "I got two on Luther's terrier! Two hundred! Need a match. Someone match me!" A man raised his arm, waving, and joined Billy. They spoke for a moment then shook hands.

Cather walked over to his truck. He fished a beer out of a cooler and popped the tab. Returning, he passed Issac.

"You got another watch for me, Ike? I'm starting a collection." He slurped his beer.

Issac sat on his crate, staring into the light of the kerosene lanterns with an abject, blank look. He pulled on his cigarette and blew a huge plume of smoke.

"Ain't right what you did," he said slowly, not looking at Cather. "Ain't right."

"What the hell you talkin' bout, Ike? This is a goddamned dog-fight, not the Salvation Army."

"That watch been in my family four generations. Grandaddy had it in the East Indes, and Daddy had it too in the Merchant Marines."

"Maybe your land-locked ass shouldn't have put it up on a bet. Ain't nothing as sorrowful and nostalgic as a gambler down on his luck."

"I told you I'd give you money for it last week. I'd buy it back. You know I don't have no thousand dollars. Ain't worth that anyway. It's gold plate."

Cather laughed. "You said it was priceless last week." He leaned over, trying to look into Issac's pen. "When did you start raising, Ike? You don't have no kennel."

Issac blinked slowly, not looking at the man. "I got a dog. Been training him all week. Found a little something to help in Daddy's knick-knacks from overseas."

Doubling over, Cather dropped his beer and held his gut in an exaggerated pose of laughter. He hawed like a mule, making his voice project across the hollow. Men encircling the pit turned to watch.

Gene Corso walked over and asked, "What's the gag, Cather? We're about to start another match."

"Ike here says he's got a dog. To fight. You better adjust your book for him, cause his dead Daddy been helping him train the thing."

Corso squinted at Issac, cocking his head.

"That right, Mr. Douglas? You got a dog you want to fight?" He was over-polite, which felt to Issac like another form of rudeness.

Issac nodded.

"Well, we've got an empty slot. Miller took a pass, we need a dog for filler. So, you're welcome to fight if you got the entry fee. Hundred dollars."

Fishing in his pocket, Issac withdrew a wad of dirty bills and peeled off five twenties. Corso took a small black ledger from his back pocket, pulled a pencil from the spine, and flipped it open.

"Issac Douglas. Entry fee paid. Dog?"

"Dog what?"

"Sex? Color?"

Issac remained quiet, staring at the kerosene lanterns. He flicked his cigarette away, toward the trucks.

"Don't rightly know if it's male or female. I didn't check. And...after...I wasn't gonna get close enough to check. But it's a terrier."

"Fine. I'll mark it as terrier, sex...unknown. That's a first. Color?"

"Sorta gray, I guess."

Cather laughed again. "Now that's a breeder for you. Don't know color. Can't sex a dog. You sure there's even a dog in there, Ike? Sure is being quiet. Maybe you accidentally put in a possum instead?"

Corso moved back toward the pit, bellowing, "Entrants! Get your dogs to the gates." He looked at his ledger. "Cullum's brindle versus Alexander's black. Match starts in five!"

Men moved to the pens, grabbing individual crates and pulling them to either side of the pit. The crates jerked in their hands, dogs growling and shifting their weight.

When all was ready, Corso picked up a large electric torch and turned it on, shining it into the pit. The clay circle gleamed wet and red in the light. Two men, one for each dog, perched at either side, leaning forward, ready to unlatch the crates and loose the dogs.

"Ready?" Corso's voice pitched upward and the crowd fell silent. *"FIGHT!"*

The men threw the latches and leaned back, away from the circle of clay. Two dogs erupted out of their crates, feet scrabbling. The animals, thick and low-slung, met in the center, bodies twisting, jaws wide. Rearing on their hind legs, they slammed into one another, both making harsh, grinding sounds deep in their throats. The men screamed into the pit, faces flushed, shaking fistfuls of dollars at the combatants.

"Come on, *come on*, *COME ON* you goddamned...get that son of a bitch!" Cather hopped up and down, his belly flopping. His face turned red with screams.

Blood streamed down the bodies of the dogs. The black dog, slightly larger than the brindle, moved decidedly slower, answering the other's attacks sluggishly. The brindle latched onto the black's withers, making the other dog yelp, a high-pitched cry. Cather winced. Issac watched on implacably. The black shook and rolled the brindle off his back, fur flying. Blood poured out, streaking down its heaving flanks.

The dogs broke apart and circled each other once before slamming together again. The black mustered strength from somewhere and whipped to the attack, taking the brindle's haunch and giving it a ferocious shake. The brindle yelped, a hoarse sound, and latched onto the black's neck. The black released the brindle's leg and opened its mouth as if to howl, slinging ribbons of saliva and blood, but no sound issued. The brindle bore the black to the ground, the black's legs splaying out gruesomely, and they lay still for a long while, the brindle on top and the black's chest rising and falling slowly until it stopped altogether.

"The brindle wins!" Men whooped or groaned, depending on their bet. "Next up, Jessup's spotted versus Douglas' grey!"

One of the men moved into the pit and leashed the brindle, yelling "Off, 'Yota. Off. Damnit Toyota, OFF!" Men laughed at the dog's name. The dog allowed itself to be pulled away, back into its crate.

The losing entrant climbed into the pit. He was a big, barrel-chested man in a t-shirt and overalls. Tears streamed openly down his face as he kneeled by the black dog and picked it up in his arms, cradling it like a baby. The crowd hooted at him.

"Ain't no place for tears." The man wearing the *Arkansas Warrior Kennels* vest stood near Issac.

Issac nodded, glancing at the larger man.

"Can't get attached, you know? There ain't no happy endings in the pit."

"That's what they say."

"How you been training? Treadmill? Tires and hanging?"

Issac turned back to look at the lanterns and the crowd, ignoring the man. He raised an arm, holding his wad.

"Cather! I got five hundred for my watch! Five hundred against Jessup's spotted. You put up my watch."

Cather turned and wiped his mouth. He walked back to Issac, squinting at the smaller man.

"Let's see your money."

Issac fanned his wad. "It's there, Cather. Five hundred."

"All right. Five hundred." He stuck out his hand. Issac took the other man's hand in his and shook it, one hard pump and then let go, as if the touch of Cather's flesh was distasteful.

Cather laughed. "This is gonna be easy money. He's been training for a week, he says!"

Issac squatted, put both hands around his crate, and lifted. He manhandled it over to the gate, the men in the crowd moving aside for him to pass, and set it down with a harsh exhalation of air.

Jessup moved his dog with the help of another man, carrying it easily, to the opposing gate. Jessup reached over the lip of the pit, put his hand on the latch, ready to unleash his dog. Corso flipped on the electric spotlight, pointing it into the pit.

Issac grinned for the first time, his mouth showing gaps between teeth, and black gums. He stepped on top of the crate and then jumped into the light of the pit. With a flip of his wrist, he threw open the door. He took three steps back, then waited, smiling.

A dog staggered out, rib-cage and pelvis prominent, the flesh hanging in drapes on its decaying form. Maggots feasted at its eyes, flies swarmed around its anus.

"Get out of there, you damned fool!" Corso pointed the light on Issac's face. Issac stepped quickly toward the wall, hiked a leg up, and levered himself up and out of the pit.

Jessup, unknowing, threw the latch. A blur of teeth and fur exploded out of the opposite crate. The spotted terrier crossed the pit in a flash, barreling into the gray, desiccated dog. On instinct, the spotted took the gray's neck in its mouth and wrenched a huge hunk of flesh away. For an instant, the spotted froze, its mouth full of corrupted flesh. It shook its head, trying to puzzle out the scent of the dead thing. The grey took a feeble step forward and its teeth closed on the other dog's snout. Jessup's spotted thrashed, pushing away with its hind legs. Issac's gray held it fast in its jaws. A muffled whine came from the living dog, and blood burbled around the gray's lips, where its flesh met snout.

The spotted tried to roll itself away, out of the grip, but as it twisted, the gray pivoted its head, turning it further than any dog should be able to. The spotted whined deep in its throat, muzzled with the jaws of its opponent.

Men around the pit fell silent, watching the bizarre match. The spotted twisted and raked its captor with claws, ripping them down its body, splitting the skin and exposing muscles and bone. No blood came from the gray dog. It remained unnaturally still.

Then, without warning, Issac's gray brought its jaws together with a hard crunch, the sound loud and clear above the hissing of the lanterns. It was as if the spotted terrier's snout had collapsed in the other's mouth. The spotted slumped, like a marionette with its strings cut.

Issac walked over to where Cather stood. Men all around turned away as the dead dog began taking bites out of the spotted, nose mangled and oozing crimson.

"I want my watch, Cather." Issac pointed at his gray feasting on the other dog. "Ain't no arguing. That's a win. Gimme my watch."

Cather shook his head, spitting. "It's a goddamned trick. It's *unnatural.* That dog's sick or something. It weren't a fair match."

Issac took two steps closer to the larger man. The gray ripped a hole in the spotted's stomach and wormed its head inside the body cavity.

"Gimme my Daddy's watch, Cather. You can't renege. Ain't gonna let you."

The larger man turned to face Issac. "I say it was a trick, Issac. You cheated, somehow."

"Didn't cheat, Cather. Show me the damned rules, anyway." Issac wiped his hands on the front of his shirt, then brought them to his sides, balled into fists. He was a slight man, but lean. His eyes were bright.

"No. I ain't got it here. I ain't turning over that watch on a trick. And I ain't got it, anyhow."

Issac thrummed with tension. His jaw went hard and muscles popped and twitched in his cheek. When he spoke, it was through clenched teeth.

"Last chance, gimme my Daddy's watch."

At that moment, someone yelled, "Jessup's dog! It's getting up!"

They turned back to the pit. Jessup's spotted was having a tough time rising with the gray's head buried in the stomach cavity. But the gray's head slipped from the opening, covered in bile, blood and bits of flesh. The other's entrails slid from the opening and pooled on the clay. And in a strange imitation of life, the gray shook, like a dog coming from the water, but this was no longer a dog. Blood, flesh flew in radiant arcs caught in the lantern light.

The things that had once been dogs peered at the men gathered around the pit. Then, without indication of thought or instinct, the dogs threw themselves at the wall. The gray smashed into a bit of corrugated metal. It rang with a tinny reverberation. The other hit plywood, cracking it.

The gamblers fell out, running away from the pit, racing toward their trucks. They screamed and cursed, calling on Jesus. Some scrabbled at the kennels to get their dogs.

Cather turned to run, but Issac grabbed his arm, yanking him around.

"My watch, Cather."

"What did you do? What did you *do*?" Cather's face was white, his eyes enormous. His stubble-lined jowls shook as he spoke. "They're fucking *unnatural*." He tried to pull his arm away, but Issac held on.

"You ain't going nowhere, until you give up my watch."

Cather swung at the smaller man, fist smacking into Issac's cheek. Issac gave a little *ooof* as he fell, but nothing more. He hit the earth, rolled. He gained his knees and stood again, spitting blood into the mat of pine needles on the ground. He wiped his mouth.

Men reached their trucks now and the sound of engines filled the night air.

"You ain't going nowhere, Cather," Issac said. He uncoiled, his fists lashing out at the larger man. Quick blows fell, one in the gut, one in the side as the big man tried to twist away, then Cather doubled over. Issac grabbed his hair, lifted his head, and smashed a fist into the man's face. Cather reeled backwards from the blow, hit the lip of the pit, and toppled over. He screamed, a warbling high-pitched sound, then went quiet.

Trucks sped away out of the hollow, clutches grinding, dogs in the truck beds howling. In a line, their headlights passed over the lip of the hill.

For a long while it was silent except for a wet, smacking sound coming from the pit and the hiss of the lanterns overhead. A small, red light continued to burn on the front of the camera. The doors of the portable kennels stood open, and Issac realized the dogs had either been released or led away, a last, and rare, act of kindness by their masters.

He tightened his belt, took a deep breath, then walked over to the pit, looking into it.

Only a grisly red hole remained of Cather's throat. His mouth gaped open in surprise and his eyes stared at the pine trees rising all around, ringing the pit in darkness.

The dogs were indistinguishable now, each covered in gore and human bile. They worked at Cather's gut, taking bites and pulling opposite directions until the flesh and clothes tore with wet, ripping sounds. One dug its head under Cather's sternum, found something inside the man, and began tugging at the corpse.

Issac watched with a blank stare, hands hanging limp at his sides.

The other dog bit into Cather's pectoral and wrenched a huge piece of flesh away. His shirt tore with a bright ripping sound. Issac noticed a faint glimmer of gold flip into the muddy clay of the pit.

His watch gleamed, falling from Cather's shirt pocket. It came to rest near the foot of one of the dogs. Its crystal face was shattered, either from the fall or the activities of the dogs, Issac couldn't tell. Even in the light from the lantern, the jagged ring of broken glass and missing watch hands were clearly visible, fob chain curling around the broken circle.

Issac stared at it for a long while, until the dog pulled one last morsel of flesh from Cather and placed a foot on the watch-face, shoving it deep into the mud.

"It weren't supposed to play out like this," he said. "Ain't fair, goddamnit." His voice sounded hoarse in the night air.

Both dog's heads pivoted toward Issac, in unison, staring at him with unblinking eyes. They remained still, more still than any dog could.

Only when Cather began to rise did they move, throwing themselves against the wall.

Issac backed away from the pit with a hard, anxious face. He watched as the undead man rose from the clay circle, his grisly head rising above the wood and tin side. His dead eyes fixed on Issac, and he moved forward, arms out.

When the plywood cracked and Cather began pulling apart the walls, Issac turned away, running for his truck, cursing.

The circle lay broken. Cather and the dogs stumbled forward, following Issac's smell, out of the pit and into the night.

The Castle of Horrors

Jane Tanner, dead almost three weeks, tried to murder him again, this time with a pirate's sword. Russell, who worked security at the Castle of Horrors, was seated in his corner of the Texas Chainsaw Massacre room when Jane rushed him. There was no need to dodge out of the way. Jane's control with the sword was, as usual, awful. Her wild swing missed him by several feet.

"Next time I'll eviscerate you!" she hissed.

He sighed, and reminded her that the weapons were only styrofoam props that the actors used to scare the patrons. She frowned as if this were news and tried ramming the sword into her own chest. It went straight through her body and dropped harmlessly to the floor.

"Dammit," she said, "you're right. That didn't hurt at all." She sat down on the carpet to sulk. "I'm still going to kill you, though," she said.

"I know you are, Jane."

"Make your kids orphans, like you made mine."

She always remembered that part. Other particulars confused her: she'd forget that the Castle of Horrors wasn't the entire universe. She thought Russell's name was Bronco.

But the fact that her two young children were all alone, and that Russell had caused it to happen? No confusion there.

"I don't have any kids," Russell said.

"Ah, but you would, if I let you live."

"I don't think so. I never really planned on having them."

"Not yet," she said. "Soon, though, you and Claire would have gone on to have four children." Claire was the name of the woman whom Russell would supposedly fall in love with. "Three sons and a daughter." Her eyes narrowed. "Don't look at me all skeptical." She smacked Russell on the leg. This was progress for her—a week earlier, her hand would have passed right through him. "I know these things."

"Whatever you say."

"Don't whatever *me*, Bronco. Don't condescend. I'm from the goddamn beyond."

He was a man born to work security. Six-six, two hundred and eighty pounds, with thick hands and the kind of severe gaze that made people aware of their full bladders. But eventually you get tired of tossing drunk assholes out of the Pink Pony strip club. You long for a little happiness. Besides, when you get a DUI and they take away your driver's license, you need to find a job you can bike to, and you need to do it fast. Especially when you already owe back-rent.

His piece-of-shit car barely sold and got him only enough cash for the month's utilities and a halfway decent mountain bike. Things looked bleak. But when one of the regulars at the Pink Pony started bellyaching about losing his security gig at Smitty's Arcade, Russell's ears perked up. The arcade was part of Happy Land, built on the old Breakneck Beach fishing pier. Despite living just a mile inland, Russell hadn't been to the pier for years. But he had fond memories of climbing down to the sand underneath the pier to smoke weed and watch the waves.

"So why'd you get canned?" Russell asked.

"Now that's a fair question, Russ." The man set his beer on the bar. "So you know how, like, I'm *here* a lot?" He belched. "Well, there you go."

The next afternoon, Russell rode his bike to the pier. The life-giving sun warmed his face as he walked the midway. These last six years, since eking out the high-school diploma, he'd worked in a number of dark bars, and he'd almost forgotten what it was like to hear the surf and smell the Italian sausages frying and feel the salty breeze on his face. Today was Saturday, and the amusement pier buzzed with families who actually seemed to be enjoying themselves.

He walked into Smitty's Arcade in high spirits, remembering how as a kid he'd blown countless quarters here playing Skee-Ball, pinball, this-ball and that-ball, games where you'd race a car or shoot aliens, and, if you were skilled enough, get to type in your initials—or if she was watching you, the initials of the girl you had a crush on.

Yes, he could definitely work here.

Except, he couldn't.

"Who the hell said I was hiring?" asked the manager, once Russell had tracked him down behind the prize counter.

"Guy named Goober?" Russell said.

"That putz? Yeah, I fired him like three months ago." He took a small stack of tickets from a boy, counted them, and exchanged them for a spider ring. "Look, I heard the Castle might be looking for somebody. You should check with Angie."

Ten minutes later he was in the employee-only area behind the Castle of Horrors, hearing from Angie Bailey that, yes, she was hiring.

"You're really big," she said. "I mean, Jesus." Angie herself was barely five feet tall and looked like a wet bird.

"Yup," he said. "That's my talent."

Angie led him through the walk-through haunted house, his enthusiasm for landing this new job undercut by the fact that once again he'd be working in a dim, dreary place. Take the Texas Chainsaw Massacre room: the room was pitch dark except for the black-light illuminating five mannequins seated at a dinner table. One of the mannequins had on a scraggly blond wig. Her wrists were bound to the chair, and her painted-on eyes were enormous; her terror looked absolutely genuine. There must have been speakers hidden somewhere, but the screams seemed to come from the mannequin. The others at the table—her captors—screamed in mocking response. And then, just like in the movie, they began to laugh while she went on screaming.

"What are they made out of, wax?" Russell asked.

"Plastic," she said. "Pretty realistic, though, don't you think?"

"A little too realistic."

Angie smiled. "This is where you'll be stationed." She nodded toward the dinner table. "Say hello to your co-workers."

As Angie led him through the Graveyard, the Nightmare Tavern, the Rabid Swamp and the rest of the Castle's many rooms, Russell met his real-life co-workers, the dozen or so employees who dressed up like monsters and vampires and famous killers and roamed around terrorizing the patrons.

Once they were through the Rat Tunnel and back behind the Castle again, Angie gave Russell a time sheet and some tax forms. "I'll see you tomorrow," she said, and went back inside.

There was a girl leaning against the pier's railing, smoking a cigarette. She had on a wig of long, black hair with a silver streak running through it. Ghoulish theatrical makeup made her face sinister and shadowy, and fake blood covered her skimpy costume.

"I take it you're the new security," she said.

"That's right," he said. "So who're you supposed to be?"

"Lizzie Borden." She smiled, but it was impossible to see her real expression behind all the makeup. In this way, she could have been any of the girls at the Pink Pony.

"You like working in there?" he asked.

"Are you kidding? I love it." So there was the difference. She flicked ashes off the pier. "Trust me, before long it'll feel like home."

To celebrate, he ordered a slice of pizza and a twenty-ounce beer. He hung around the midway and even slapped down two dollars to toss Wiffle balls at colored cups and maybe win a giant stuffed zebra. He didn't win the zebra, but he won a Chinese finger trap.

"Look, it's nothing personal," Russell explained to his boss that night at the Pink Pony. "It's just this DUI. Plus, I fucking hate it here." He hadn't realized how true it was until he'd said it.

"Hey, come on now," his boss said. "You owe me better than that."

When he'd first started working at the Pink Pony, Russell had just turned twenty-two and still had no clue how to hold on to a job. His worst habit was falling in love with the dancers every two seconds. Then one of his big-time crushes, a part-time nursing student with a baby at home, got beaten up in the parking lot one night. In the days that followed, Russell became overzealous in his bouncer duties. His boss had been patient, though, drilling it into Russell's head that he couldn't exact revenge on every smug musclehead who strutted into the club.

"You got to detach yourself," his boss had said at the time. "Detachment—that's a life strategy I just gave you, son."

It had been wise counsel, and maybe Russell did owe his boss better. But the boardwalk was pulling him. "Everyone's always smiling all the time around here," Russell said now. It was true: a strip club was the smiliest place on earth. "But I haven't seen a single happy person in years. Do you see what I'm saying?"

Earlier, he'd given his Chinese finger trap to a kid who kept chucking his Wiffle balls at the wrong cups. The kid's smile had been the real deal.

"When the summer ends, you can't come back," his boss said. "I'll have a replacement by then. You understand?"

Russell shrugged. "There's always a bar looking for a guy my size, am I right?"

His boss looked at him a moment, face frozen, then flashed his teeth like a game-show host. "You just burned a bridge, my friend." He was a thin-necked man in his fifties who went around shooting his customers with an imaginary pistol, like they were in on some joke but deserved to die because of it. "Burned it right up."

The Texas Chainsaw room was located on the second floor of the Castle. Russell's job entailed sitting in the corner, in his black jeans and black t-shirt, and watching the customers enter one end of the room and leave the other.

Talk about an easy gig. The setting did all the work. Even the bravest customers felt queasy walking through the cemetery, the Rat Tunnel, ducking under Lizzie Borden's swinging axe. Their eyes were worthless, especially during daytime when their pupils were tiny pinpricks from the sun. So they'd creep through the Castle, snapping their heads from side to side, bracing themselves.

Still, Russell was needed. Every so often there'd be a kid out to vandalize the displays, or some asshole out to impress his girlfriend by harassing the actors. When this happened, Russell would get word on the walkie-talkie he wore on his belt. He would melt out of the walls, just one more of the Castle's illusions, to find the troublemaker and escort him to the nearest fire exit.

No question, a good summer job. Only the actors had it better, getting paid to roam the Castle and freak people out. Now *that* looked like fun. But Angie ran a tight ship with inviolable rules: she taught her actors how to scare people during the day versus at night, how to scare a group of children versus a group of children with a parent versus a group of teenage boys versus teenage girls versus teenage coed versus a guy/girl couple versus a group of older guys. She'd been the manager here a long time and had it down to a science, how to give everybody a thrill without sending anyone to the hospital or their lawyer, and she'd made it clear to Russell on his first day that he was *not* one of the actors. He should never try to frighten the patrons, just like the actors were taught never to play security guard.

He obeyed the warning for nearly a month. Then one of the actors radioed him about that damn group of drunk teenagers. One of them had just shoved Lizzy Borden into a wall.

They're in Frankenstein's Lab right now, squawked the radio. *We need you to get them out of here, Russ.*

Will do, he radioed back.

Rowdy teenagers were a dime a dozen, but most of them knew better than to assault the employees. No, these were a particular breed of assholes, the ones who in a couple of years would come to the Pink Pony and stick their hands where they don't belong and follow the dancers out to their cars at four a.m. with their box-cutters and steel-toed boots.

Frankenstein's Lab was just a couple of rooms away from the Texas Chainsaw room. Rather than go after them, Russell decided to stay in his corner, where he would be invisible, and wait. He would eject them from the park, but first he would give them a taste of what real fright was about.

Half a minute later, they entered the room.

From deep inside himself, Russell released a thunderous bellow and leapt.

When he landed, he found himself facing not a group of teenagers, but rather two small children and a young woman about Russell's age who, seeing Russell, dropped her purse, opened her mouth as if to scream, and then, as if thinking better of it, curled into a crouch on the floor. Before Russell could ask why she was crouching on the floor, she rolled over onto her back.

The two children stood in place, clutching each other. The little girl's hair was in pigtails. The boy had on a NY Giants t-shirt that came down to his knees. They looked like nice kids, the sort you wished were yours, except their mouths looked too big for their faces because they were howling. Their howls blended with the room's screams, which then became hideous laughter. Russell crouched over the woman, still wondering where the hell those rowdy teenagers were. He looked into the eyes that were looking into his, and he thought he saw the woman grimace a little, like she'd just remembered something unpleasant. Then she stopped grimacing, yet her eyes were still wide open, and Russell had the creeping feeling that the woman who was staring at him had just died of fright.

She had.

No one that day learned exactly what had happened in the Castle of Horrors. Everyone figured: scary place, heart attack, end of story. Also, Russell might have implied that he'd watched the lady collapse from his chair in the corner of the room.

The police, the actors, they all treated Russell kindly, what with him being the first on the scene, the one to radio over to Angie that she needed to call 911. He knew a little CPR, and he explained—truthfully—how he had tried the mouth-to-mouth thing, the chest-pumping thing, until a cop who'd been patrolling Happy Land's midway came and took over.

He left out the part about the woman's breath smelling like pepperoni pizza, and how he kept worrying about crushing the dying woman's ribs with his fat, useless hands.

You did your best, Russell, everyone was telling him once the EMTs had carted the young lady away. Trailing behind them was Lizzie Borden—in real life Stacey something, a local college student—with an arm around each of the dead lady's kids. Despite her heavy theatrical makeup and fake blood, they clung to her like she was their closest kin.

You tried, man.

They all said this, except for Angie. She didn't accuse him outright, but as he was leaving to go home—the Castle closed early for the day—she called him aside. They were in the employee-only area behind the Castle. They walked over to the edge of the pier. The tide was out, and crisp waves were breaking on the beach, perfect for body-surfing. Russell realized that despite living so close to the ocean, he hadn't been swimming for years.

"I'll only ask you this once," she said. "Is there anything you feel like getting off your chest?"

He waited a moment, watching the waves, the sea gulls trailing after a party boat that must have had a good day fishing. "Not that I can think of."

She nodded. "Then go home. Get some sleep. I'll see you tomorrow."

He went home but didn't go to sleep before drinking all the booze in the apartment, right down to the sample-size mouthwash he'd gotten the last time he'd been to the dentist. He paced his basement apartment, shouting at the walls and reliving the afternoon—he couldn't get out of his mind how frightened the woman had been, and then how dead—and he considered calling morgues, finding out the woman's name, calling her husband and apologizing. But he knew he wouldn't do that any sooner than he'd return to the Castle of Horrors. That place was finished for him now. Another bridge badly burned.

Bed was a comfortable place, he decided, where you couldn't kill anyone. He would have liked to stay there forever, but he only lasted a week.

What finally roused him were the three harsh raps on his front door. The meaning, unambiguous. Sure enough, the eviction notice had been slid under his door. His landlady, who lived in the apartment upstairs, must have taken his failure to leave the house as a show of bad faith. At the bottom of the typed letter, she had scribbled: GET OUT, YOU LAZY BIG OAF!

He showered, put on his black clothes, and rode his bike over to Happy Land, where he sought out Angie in her office and pled his case: *All fucked up from watching the lady die…sort of went on a bender…slept for a week…evicted…no home, no money, no one to turn to…* It wasn't so much a case, he realized, as it was a summary of his sad existence.

Angie listened, expressionless. Her office doubled as the Castle's sound room. From it, she controlled the music and sound effects for each of the Castle's exhibits. In the sound room itself, where the guests never went, Frank Sinatra was crooning about how the best was yet to come.

"I need to know if you plan on pulling any more disappearing acts," she said.

"Not a chance," Russell said. "Actually, I was wondering…" He had practiced on the ride over, but now his request sounded foolish. She'd never go for it. "I know we've got this bathroom back here, with the changing room and shower and all." He waited, to see if she'd get the hint. He pressed on. "So I was wondering, if I were to buy an air mattress…if, you know, temporarily, I could…" He coughed. "It would be like having free security all night long."

The song ended, and then Sinatra asked to be flown to the moon. An entire verse passed before she said, "Temporarily."

"Really?" Russell said. "Damn, thanks a lot." Angie was pushing thirty, with a hard face and small, suspicious eyes. In a slasher flick, she'd be the stern, not-so-good-looking girl who was still alive when the final credits rolled. But the rumor was that she had started screwing the sixteen-year-old custodian, so maybe that had softened her up a little. Russell struggled to put his gratitude into words. He wasn't used to forming sentences having to do with generosity and kindness.

Before he could figure out what to say, Angie stopped the CD mid-song, fixed her gaze on him, and said that she would be reducing his pay. "And I suggest you get your ass back to work, as in pronto, before I change my mind."

The dead woman's full name was Jane Elizabeth Tanner. The obituary, taped to the wall by the time clock, said it all: devoted mother, revered seventh-grade science teacher, volunteer at the ASPCA.

She would be missed by family, students, and puppies.

Russell was thinking, as he walked through the Castle toward his station, that he would need to forget all about this Jane Elizabeth Tanner. It was terrible, what had happened, but now he needed to put it out of his mind—especially if this was going to be his temporary home.

As he entered the Texas Chainsaw room, a woman sprang out of a shadowy corner and ran at him with an outthrust hatchet. As he sidestepped, the hatchet slid out of the woman's hands. He was about to restrain her when he recognized who it was and stopped in his tracks.

She had on the same Seton Hall sweatshirt as the last time he'd seen her. Same pair of tapered jeans and white canvas sneakers. She stood just a few feet from him, breathing heavily, looking like an overstressed mom in a supermarket parking lot who'd forgotten where she'd left her car.

"Oh, hell no." Russell squeezed his eyes shut and opened them again. She was still there. "I did *not* sign up for this." He watched her—part horrified, part fascinated—as she walked over to the hatchet, picked it up, and came running at him again. "Hey, cut that out!" he said, even though the weapon was only a prop.

"Don't tell me what to do!" But she didn't get far with the hatchet this time either; it slipped through her hands, which were translucent. So she went to slap him on the arm. This he allowed, but her hand went right through him and he didn't feel a thing.

She looked down at the floor and started sniffling.

To make her feel better, he rubbed his arm as if she'd bruised it a little.

"I see what you're doing," the deceased said. "Don't make fun of me."

He stopped rubbing. "Listen, I just read the obituary. I really feel like shit. I mean, I *really* feel—"

"*You* feel? Who the hell cares how you feel?" She went over and sat down on Russell's chair, leaving him to stand awkwardly beside her. "My God, I teach all year, then I spend the summer doing oil changes, rotating tires, working with sexist jerks and never seeing my kids...but I'm making ends meet, you know? I'm making it work. So I decide to call in sick and take them to Happy Land— which is no Six Flags, as you and I both know."

Sometimes the strippers at the Pink Pony would spill their guts like this to Russell. They called him a good listener, but he didn't see how standing around awkwardly and not saying much constituted good listening.

"But my kids," she went on, "they're good kids, you know? So they thank me like we're on some great vacation. And do you know what, Bronco? It *was* great. Best day since I can remember, because I was spending it with my kids. And then *you* had to—" She looked over at the dinner table, where the screaming audio loop had just started again, and then back at Russell. "How could you do this to me? I mean, what kind of sick—"

"It was an accident," he said. "I thought you were a group of delinquents."

"Do I *look* like a group of delinquents?"

Just then, three girls, all around twelve or thirteen, ran into the room holding hands with one another. Seeing them, Jane cowered into a tight ball.

The girls raced through the room and out the other side, barely glancing at the dinner table scene and totally oblivious to Russell and Jane. They were trying to get through the Castle as fast as possible. This was common, kids not wanting to *be* here, but wanting to *have been* here, so afterward they could buy the t-shirt that says "I survived the Castle of Horrors at Happy Land" and show it off to their friends.

"Anyway," Russell said once the girls were gone, "you must

have had some congenital heart thing." Jane had uncoiled herself and was panting from the close call. "No one's supposed to get a heart attack at your age."

She waved his words away. "What are you, a doctor? My kids are orphans now."

"What about their—"

"Dead. Five years. Hit and run." The obituary hadn't mentioned a surviving husband; Russell had figured she was divorced. "God, I hate people." She got out of the chair and went to pick up the hatchet, which was still lying on the floor beside them, but her hands kept passing through it.

His whole shift, Jane didn't leave him alone for a minute. When she wasn't trying to kick him in the shins, she was taunting him with the sweet, sweet life he would not be allowed to live. Only when someone else came into the room—patrons, or one of the actors—did she let up. She was afraid of scaring anyone, of doing to them what Russell had done to her, and so she would dart underneath the dinner table and hide there trembling until the coast was clear.

Otherwise, she prattled on breathlessly: Russell would have fallen in love and gotten his heart crushed big-time by an amateur bowler, but then he would have met Claire. They would have married in Vegas, but their drive-through wedding would not have been Elvis-themed. They would have seen Venice but not Rome. Their son would one day have thrown a baseball through the kitchen window, and instead of becoming angry Russell would have taken photographs.

His wife would have aged gracefully.

He would have known happiness.

None of this sounded like him at all. "I think you might have me confused with someone else," he told her.

"I don't think so," Jane replied. "But it doesn't really matter. You'll be dead soon anyway."

Then she'd detail the methods she was considering. Russell figured she must have been a good science teacher, because she knew exactly which chemicals would do the most damage to his private anatomy.

At ten p.m. the park closed for the night. The appeal of sleeping overnight in the Castle had diminished significantly. Russell wished he hadn't sold his car. And the boardwalk benches were too short for him. There was always the beach, he supposed.

Angie stood at the picnic table behind the Castle, by the pier's edge. She was painting a second coat on some new Styrofoam knives. The northern half of the sky was rust-colored from the New York City night. To the east, lights from a smattering of boats looked like stars that had dipped below the horizon.

Russell was about to sneak out for the night when she caught his eye. "Listen—while you were away, there's been some minor damage to a couple of the displays. It's happening overnight. I'm thinking rodents might have found a way in. Anyway, keep an eye out, will you?"

He nodded, imagining Jane alone in the Castle at night, finding her way around. "Will do."

"You're a good man, Russ."

He was glad that she looked back down at the knife she was painting, because his strained smile must have been straight out of the Pink Pony.

When she wasn't detailing either Russell's life or his death, Jane fretted about her kids. She believed they were alive but couldn't understand where they were. Each night, after the Castle closed and Angie shut off the building's many soundtracks and the employees all went home, Jane would stomp through the silent rooms for hours, calling their names. Backstage, lying on his twelve-dollar air mattress between the washing machine and the costume rack, Russell would stuff toilet paper into his ears, squeeze his eyes shut, and imagine himself thousands of miles from Breakneck Beach, riding the gondolas with Claire.

And when Jane's carrying on became insufferable, he would track her down and remind her what everyone else already knew from reading the paper: her kids were living in Piscataway with her sister and brother-in-law. They were well cared for. Usually, this news quieted her down long enough for Russell to return to his mattress for a couple hours of sleep before her frantic searching would begin all over again.

Lizzie Borden, a.k.a. Stacey Nowicki, paused from eating her meatball sub. "Some of us are going out after work. Feel like coming along?"

Russell and Stacey ate lunch together sometimes. Russell would go out to the midway for sandwiches or pizza, and the two of them would eat at the picnic table behind the Castle. Stacey was a theater major at Jersey Central College with unrealistic dreams of starring on Broadway. This was the first time she or anyone else at the Castle had invited him anywhere.

"Where to?" he asked. Today was Sunday, and the park closed early.

"County fair. It'll be a hoot."

"Stacey, we work at an amusement park. It'll be the same as being here."

"We *work* here. There, we'll hang out. Eat funnel cake. Go on some rides. They've got one of those salt-and-pepper—"

"Thanks," he said, "but no." A county fair was about the last place he wanted to go.

"Why not?" She grinned. "Are you afraid of the rides? Is big Russell a chicken?"

"That isn't it."

"Then tell me why."

It was easy to dismiss Stacey as immature. The cigarettes hadn't taken a toll on her voice yet, and with the wig off and her actual hair short and stylish, she certainly looked young, even with the ghoulish makeup. But he hadn't forgotten how she'd soothed those kids earlier in the summer, how steady and reassuring she'd been. He decided to trust her.

"I can't stand watching all those families having a good time," he said. "I used to. But when I look at them now, all I can see is the mess in their future. I see the father in the hospital, or the mother in the morgue."

She put down her meatball sub.

"Is this about that woman who died?" she asked.

"You could say that. Look, Stacey, it's really not worth talking about."

"Oh, I see—you're the strong silent type, is that it?"

He smiled. "I guess you could say that."

She picked up her sandwich again. "Well, maybe don't be a type. Maybe just be a guy." She chewed on her sandwich contemplatively. "One thing's for sure, you need to get away from this place."

He did the opposite, choosing to avoid the midway entirely during the day. The sight no longer gave him any happiness—all those families only made him claustrophobic. The smells burned his nose. The light stung his eyes. Nobody asked him along on any other outings, and Stacey started to eat her lunches with a twerp named Lizard who was always bragging to everybody about what a great bassist he was.

Preferring the Castle's darkness, Russell began to work extra hours without pay. He'd spend nights in the Castle or, when he couldn't sleep, walking the desolate pier. It wasn't the summer job he had imagined, and when Labor Day approached he should have been glad to leave. But where would he go? On Tuesday the park would close for the season, and he hadn't done one damn thing to line up a new job or home.

So when Jane forced him out of bed with her moaning one morning at four a.m., he tracked her down in the Wicked War Room, shook her by the shoulders—she was a lot more solid these days—and yelled: "For God sakes, Jane, shut the fuck up already! Your stupid kids aren't here!"

There were a thousand nicer ways to have said that, but he was feeling the panic of having no options and hoping that a rare night's sleep might spark some ideas.

"Then where are they?" she yelled back. "I demand you tell me!"

They'd been through this so many times. Russell would say "out there," pointing to the world beyond the Castle, and Jane would think he was pointing to the far end of the room and rush over there only to be disappointed all over again.

"I can't explain it to you," he said now, exhausted. "They're out in the world."

She glared at him. "This *is* the world, dummy."

He was about to correct her when he realized she had a point. Other than for groceries, when was the last time he'd gone beyond Happy Land's main gate? The season was over; it was time to leave. But then who would talk Jane down from her terror each night? And who would she bully around?

When Angie arrived several hours later, he asked to speak with her alone in her office. Then he asked if he could stay.

"I don't know, Russ," she said. "I mean, the place will be barren. And I know I'm no Freud, but maybe you shouldn't be living at the scene of the crime any longer. You don't look so hot these days."

He figured as much. The actors seemed to be avoiding him, and they didn't spook easily.

"It's just that I'm going to try to get a job at Bazookas, and I can bike there from here." He shrugged. "Besides—"

"I know," she said. "Free security."

He had no intention of working at Bazookas. He would stay right here, in the Castle with Jane. He owed it to her. He had taken her life, taken her away from her kids, and the least he could do was keep her company until she killed him back.

There was no opportunity to tell Jane his plans until late that evening, when the Labor Day crowd had thinned and they could be alone in the Texas Chainsaw room.

"Listen," he said, "If I were to stay here with you after everyone else was gone for the season, would you want that?"

She looked down at her canvas shoes. "Do whatever you want. It doesn't matter to me one way or the other."

"Okay," he said. "Then I'm going to do it. I'm staying right here. It's you and me."

She looked up at him. "Seriously? You'd do that?"

He thought about his old boss shooting him with a finger and saying, "Detachment!" But his boss had never killed anybody. And leaving would be like killing her a second time, only worse, because the suffering would go on and on.

"It's done," he said.

She made three lightning-fast loops around the dinner table while the sadists and their captive screamed madly. Then she came back over to Russell looking sad again.

"How long exactly are you planning to stick around?" she asked.

"As long as it takes." It couldn't be long. Jane was much better now at handling the props—they rarely melted through her hands anymore—and it was only a matter of time, he figured, until she got hold of an actual weapon. He'd even caught her the other day with a cigarette lighter she'd lifted from one of the patrons. She couldn't get the flame going. *Smokey the Bear had better be on guard,* he'd joked, trying to keep things light. But the point was, she'd get him eventually.

Which was why it surprised him, just a day later, when the woman so hell-bent on killing him made so basic a mistake. Every morning, he walked to the Sandy Soda for provisions—coffee, beer, microwavable lunches—as soon as the main gate unlocked at 8:55 a.m. Granted, Tuesday was the beginning of the off-season, and at 8:55 the gate remained locked. He'd had to scale the fence to leave the pier. Still, she should have known he'd be out running his errand.

Such a basic mistake, he was thinking as he stood in front of the Sandy Soda with his bag of groceries, watching the first plumes of black smoke rise above the Castle. Like Russell, she had apparently screwed up. Like him, a simple miscalculation meant the difference between life and death.

The Breakneck Beach pier fire would briefly make national news, the five-acre conflagration burning totally out of control, fueled by gas lines that ran underneath the pier and powered all the restaurants, the rides, the arcades, the Castle of Horrors, and everything else in Happy Land. The wooden pier jutted hundreds of feet into the Atlantic, and the winds that September afternoon blew at gale force, rendering useless the drifting Coast Guard boats and their puny hoses. There would be nothing to do but let the pier consume itself. After thirty years, the pier and everything on it would vanish in just a few short hours, plucked like a bad tooth from the mouth of the Jersey Shore.

Russell stood in front of the Sandy Soda, a block away from Happy Land, as fire trucks and police cars and ambulances began to congregate at the base of the pier. The flames rose higher against the kind of sky that New Jersey saw maybe five days a year—a sky without haze, the blue so deep and rich you want to eat it. The wind was cool, autumn-like, and blew the smoke up and over the water. There was no soot where Russell stood. Instead, the air held traces of fall fish—striped bass, weakfish—that were migrating down from the waters off New England. Russell sniffed the air and wondered where it might blow him tonight when it was time to find a bed.

The first news vans arrived, stopping in the Sandy Soda parking lot. Crowds were gathering. Cameramen shot tape and reporters interviewed onlookers. Then one of the TV reporters and her cameraman approached Russell. The reporter was tall and suspiciously pretty, the first one to get killed off in any slasher flick. It surprised him when she came over and said, "Russell?"

"That's me," he said, and tried to place her. She didn't look like any girl he knew, though any girl he knew would almost certainly be unrecognizable in broad daylight.

She smiled. "Becky Rossi? Breakneck Beach High?"

The name rang a bell, but not the face and definitely not the body.

Becky held out her hand to shake. "I do this now—you know, TV news?"

"I don't have a TV," he said, shaking her hand. "But I totally believe you."

She asked if he minded being interviewed.

"Sure," he said. "Okay." The cameraman positioned them so that the pier fire made the perfect backdrop.

"You might want to put your groceries down first," Becky said, and he did. "So do you still live in town?"

Russell shrugged. "You could say that."

When the taping started, Becky introduced him as "long-time local." Then she said, "Can I ask you what the Breakneck Beach Pier has meant to you over the years?"

He turned to watch the blaze. The Castle was engulfed in flame. The pier was going fast, and he thought about Jane and wondered what was going to happen to her. Could a dead person burn to death? Would she go homeless? Find her kids? He hoped the pier's destruction might ease her suffering, especially if she believed he was inside. He faced the reporter again. "Mainly it's meant heartache and sadness. I'm pretty relieved to see it go."

"Oh." She signaled for her cameraman to stop taping. When he lowered the camera, she said, "I don't think we're going to use that."

"Sorry," he said. "I don't get interviewed too often." He wished he'd shaved. It'd been a while. At least his clothes were clean. Still, he wished he looked better. She was awfully pretty, and he could imagine getting his heart crushed by her. "Listen," he said, "so if I were to ask you to go bowling with me tonight—you know, like on a date—would you do it?"

She glanced over to the fire. "I've got a big story to cover. It could take a while."

"I know…but after?"

She frowned. "Probably not."

"Oh." It was tempting to leave it at that, end the conversation, which was what security guards did. They said a word or two and then crossed their big arms and watched to be sure there was no trouble. "So you don't bowl?" he asked.

She cocked an eyebrow. "Well, sure I do. I'm actually really…wait, you *know* this, Russell." He must have had a confused expression, because she added, "Um, we were on the *bowling* team together?"

So that's where he knew her. His four weeks of high-school athletics, before getting kicked off the team for buying beer at the bowling alley's bar. He recalled a quiet girl with frizzy hair and an overstuffed backpack. She had seemed smart, but not like someone who needed to brag about her achievements on a t-shirt. And he remembered one other amazing thing.

"You nailed a 7-10 split in practice one time, didn't you?"

She smiled. "Oh, *now* he remembers."

They stood there and watched the Castle's roof cave in. The cameraman scurried closer to the pier for a better shot, but Becky lagged behind, and it felt almost as if Jane, despite everything, had arranged this exact moment—for him to be standing in the Sandy Soda parking lot, saying to this reporter named Becky Rossi whose hair was whipping in the wind, "Come on—two games. I'll even spring for hotdogs."

Becky looked toward the pier, then back at him. "The thing is, I live in Hoboken now." She opened her purse and got out a pen and notepad. "Why don't you try calling me at my mom's house later. She still lives in town. And if I'm still around tonight. . . ."

Soaring high above the old pier, the ghost of Jane Elizabeth Tanner watched the present burn brightly into the future.

Robert Hill Long

Out of the Whirlwind

Y ou'd say a live hyena is better than a dead lion, wouldn't you, Jack? Go on, admit it—nobody else in this flea market but your round Jenny by the Hummel figurines with little boy blue and the nut-brown maid snorting a basket of nosegays, and the proprietor snoring on receipts by the door. Sunday afternoon in Indiana, oh boy: the church takes its chicken-grease hand out of your pocket, and lets you go on a drive and Jack, you fancy yourself some wheelman in that pimp-colored LeBaron. Watch out, honey, the sign on the curve says 45 but I'm going to crank it up to 54. I can hear that polka beat in your forehead vein as you wink at her wide lap that never lets you lay in it anymore, and swing to the right.

You thought I was dead as Indiana Sundays. Jack, women watch me die every night and curse themselves that they're not ambulance drivers, that they're stuck in bed beside some State Farm agent who gets a hard-on only when he totes up net sales. Yeah, the Porsche crumpled like a cigarette pack, the way I liked to crumple them after lighting up the last one. Crush it, toss it away and move on. I moved on through the windshield into a million images, including this one. They rent my bible at every video store between Bangor and Anchorage, and every leather bomber the acne-boys try on in Speedway, Lubbock, Cheyenne, has a prayer to be me sewn into its lining.

You stand beneath my black velvet altar—mortgage paid off, lord of the used car lot, with a son who *likes* military school—and laugh at my surroundings, all these salt-and-pepper pairings, rooster and hen, duck and drake, buck and doe, har har, and a couple of longhorn skulls Georgia O'Keeffe wouldn't bother painting. But these are my temple guardians, Jack: don't turn your back on me, or you'll feel a horn ram through your liver and poke out the front of your Pendleton. Round little Jenny comes here to pray, no matter how loud she sings at church. When you're sneezing over the case of pocket-fobs and folding razors, she turns to me and her lips shape the words, *Please, now*. She *will* pay what they're asking to have my cigarette mouth and tipped-back hair hanging over her in that bedroom which is just hers now.

When I was a face on five thousand sixty-foot screens, you drove a '48 Pontiac that shook like epilepsy and burned a quart of oil a day, bought off a carnival midway shill who needed a fix that would last him from Indianapolis to Milwaukee worse than he needed blown head gaskets and squirrel-chewed upholstery that stunk like the last junkie to die on its floorboards. You couldn't get the dimmest girl to climb in that thing; your drive-in your date was your hand. Only way you could get a girl to replace your right hand was to drive to Sunday revivals and pretend to get saved. You spewed Jesus hallelujah from that corn-stubble head in four different tents before a girl even looked twice—and even that got you no satisfaction until you set her up with a ring, a lawn, a tract house and a light-switch to shut off before she lifted that flannel tent she slept in high enough for you to crawl in with your hard little flashlight in hand.

What did you produce, Jack? A flat-headed boy with a throat full of corn syrup who'll join the Marines and get vaporized by a roadside bomb east of Eden, and a pack of lies about the sanctities of small town life that you hand out to visitors at church, donut shop, and the car lot that wears your German cough of a name. Pflug. Ladies and gentlemen, Jack Pflug will pat your back and sell you a Pontiac in which a carney junkie expired. One of these days, Jack Pflug, the Lord of Tornado Alley is going put a question to you, and you'll have to declare all you did, and watch it get sucked up the black funnel of God's behind.

What else? You drive Jenny (who's gotten cluckier, a neglected pullet) on Sunday roads red as capillaries in the map of your face to hunt for curios. Now that you've located my shrine, I'll tell you who I am in the other world only because I want to see your heart blow like truck retread along the road home, because that's what your heart always was: bald, black, and burnt, with a big hole in the middle. I'm Noah, the new Noah, and this comatose curio joint is the next Ark, and you've shown a firefly-glint of intuition in finding it this close to the time we're pulling out of here. For that, I will reward you with the sound your heart's going to make when it goes—something between a dove's wingbeats in shotgun season and a Ford sedan smashing a Porsche over the San Andreas Fault. Now get out. I've got lawn flamingoes clamoring to audition for the perfect two, I've got ceramic dwarf lions, zebra salt-and-pepper shakers. See that Joe DiMaggio trading card, and the Marilyn Monroe smile-mosaic made entirely of dried beans? I'm taking two of each kind, and as far as humans go, it's Marilyn and Joltin' Joe. Even these longhorn skulls and plaster chickens are way past you, Jack: you're a burger with ketchup cooling on the aluminum rack. Some sixteen year old boy with a Marlboro cough, undershot boots, and an I-70 speeder's conviction that hell is Sunday in Indiana is going to shell out 99 cents soon—tonight, tomorrow night, next year—to eat you in three bites before he climbs back into his ragtop Firebird, wild to be me, in the black velvet night I own.

Josh McCall

The Easy Payment Plan

The first time Victor Fogle entered the shop he felt only uncomfortable. The store stunk of mothballs and on the display cases were women's underthings: step-ins and slips, girdles and utility bras, mysterious boxes of self-adhering flesh-colored fabric. He had no reason to be there, no girlfriend, no female relatives for whom he might claim to be shopping. But he had seen the cage in the front window and opened the door without thinking. The chimes jingled and behind the counter stood the clerk, a thin man with folds of loose skin hanging from his neck.

"Is it for sale?" Victor said.

"This is a store, ain't it?" the clerk said, looking up to examine his customer.

Victor was shy, he could admit that, but he didn't consider himself lonely or pathetic or at all like those kind of people who surrounded themselves with pets. But it was no normal pet inside the cage. It was a flox and one saw them infrequently—once behind a restaurant's checkout counter, once among the mules and heels of a fancy shoe store, a few years back in a grainy flyer posted to his neighborhood bus stop.

"I'm sure it's expensive," Victor said. The clerk told him how much and Victor shook his head. It was more than he had.

"In that case," the clerk said, fanning his hands as if he were about to perform a card trick, "there's the easy payment plan."

"I never pay on installment," Victor said, already backing out of the store. He worked for a liquidator and knew what kind of trouble credit could get one into.

"Who never pays on installment?" the clerk said, following Victor to the door. "You think it over. I'll hold it for you."

That night Victor woke to a strong odor of camphor. He thought it was in his hair, then his sheets, and when he could not quite locate the source he opened his windows and went outside. Gray clouds scudded across the moonlit sky. The backs of a half-dozen houses faced his yard, their windows dark as deadlights. Three summers earlier he had planted boxwoods along the property line and now the shrubs came nearly to his waist. He looked forward to the day when they would rise as high as his head. A streetlight hummed on a nearby corner. A drop of rain fell against his arm.

A married couple were his nearest neighbors. They were in their fifties and tonight he could just make out the foxglove and primrose he watched them plant last spring. Raindrops pinged against their aluminum carport. A book lay face-down on one of their deckchairs. He looked up at the house and saw that the car was missing, stepped through a gap in the shrubs, walked over to the deckchair, and reached for the book. A door opened and a young woman he had never seen before stepped out onto the patio wearing a long t-shirt and neither shoes nor socks.

"Oh," she said. "It's you."

"Excuse me?" he said.

"What are you doing with my book?"

"I'm sorry." He held the book out before him. "It's going to rain. I didn't want it to be ruined." There was something strange about the woman's mouth, and when she stepped off the patio and took the book from him, he could see that her top lip was deeply scarred just below her nose.

"Do you know it?" she said, holding out the book so he could see its cover.

He leaned forward to better make out the print and noticed that the woman smelled exactly like an old sleeping bag. He took a step back from her. "No," he said and before he could catch himself added, "Is it any good?"

"It's awful. In fact, it's so bad I want to throw it away. But every time I think I've had all I can stand, it gets better for a few pages."

He had never met anyone who smelled like this, never met anyone with a harelip. It was confusing and he wanted to go back inside his house.

"Don't you think things should be interesting all the way through and not just now and then?" she said, thumbing through the pages as if she might actually read him an excerpt.

"It's late," he said. "I should go."

Once inside, he bolted the lock with one hand and grabbed the edge of the curtain with the other. Through the window he saw the woman standing in her yard, her bare feet half-hidden in the damp grass. With her pink tongue she licked the scar on her lip, then looked up at the sky, stepped backwards under the awning and vanished.

He had nearly forgotten about her when one night in July someone knocked at his kitchen door. The late news had just ended and Victor turned down the volume on the TV and waited, telling himself it was only the wind. On the third knock he went into the kitchen, latched the chain and opened the door just enough to see who was outside.

"You don't happen to have a key to my house, do you?" She wore a white organdy dress and dark lipstick that accentuated her cleft lip.

"Why would I have a key to your house?" he said.

She explained that she'd locked herself out and that she knew her parents left a key with one of the neighbors but she couldn't remember which one. It didn't seem reasonable to Victor that she'd think that neighbor might be him. He didn't even know her parents' names. He shook his head no.

"Then could I use your phone?" she said.

When he pulled back on the door it caught against the chain. Embarrassed, he pushed the door shut, almost catching the woman's hand in the jamb. "I'm sorry," he said, unlatching the door and letting her in. She had her hair up in a way that made her look older than before and as she brushed past him he smelled lavender and pine trees. She ran her fingers across the countertops, touched the coffee pot, the toaster oven, the refrigerator handle.

He watched her, his eyes following first the imaginary line she drew on the appliances, then the curve of her arm and shoulder, the way her dress caught at her waist. By the time she'd turned and said, "My name's Julia. What's yours?" he had already looked away, at the walls, the light fixture, the black-and-white tile.

"Victor," he said.

"I should have gone with them, Victor. They have a timeshare in Winstona. We used to go there when I was a kid. There's a waterpark. Do you like waterparks?"

Victor started to re-latch the kitchen door but changed his mind. "I don't know," he said. He had lived in the house for eight years and had never known his neighbors had a daughter.

"I should have gone," she said. "I mean, I don't want to say I'm bored because I hate that word. But I don't know what to do with myself. There're a lot of hours in the day. You know what I mean?" She lifted herself onto the counter and now Victor could see that her knees were pink and that she had a scrape on her right shin. He again became aware of her perfume and wanted her to leave but didn't know the right way to ask.

"Do you have a job?" she said. "A girlfriend?"

"I work in the James Axelrod Building," he said. "I'm an auditor for a liquidating company."

"What do you liquidate?" she asked.

"You know," he said, "assets."

Julia slid off the counter, turned her back to Victor and fidgeted with the coffee urn. "I sometimes wonder what you do in here," she said. "I never see you outside."

He went outside but not often, usually very early in the morning or late at night. But he didn't want to explain this to Julia because then she would ask why and he would have to give her a reason. He had never really thought about the reason he avoided the others in the neighborhood, though probably it was because he knew how people could infiltrate your life, asking about your weekends, whether you were dating anyone, eventually inviting you over on the weekends, setting you up with their friends. All of which presumed you were lacking something, that you needed their attention, their help.

She turned around and asked to use his bathroom. He sat in the living room and listened to the running water and what was almost certainly the sound of her vomiting. Later he would go into the bathroom and smell the acrid odor and see orange splashes on the floor beside the tub. But for now he thought of her pink knees and her perfume and decided that he'd offer to let her sleep on his couch. But he never had a chance. "I think I should go," she said as soon as she came out.

"Don't you want to call your parents?" he said.

"That's okay. I remembered that the latch on the living room window doesn't work."

She left by the kitchen door and he watched her turn and slide through the shrubs, saw the hem of her dress catch on the boxwoods. She pulled it loose and then in the starlight he saw her lift a window at the back of the house. Two pale legs pedaled in the open window and then she tumbled head first into the house.

The leaves turned and the world grew dry and brittle. Limbs broke and fell onto the house, squirrels raced along the gutters, but no matter how many times he went to the kitchen window, his heart caught in a vice of longing and fear, the deckchair remained empty and the neighbors' windows dark.

He could not stop thinking of her. He would come home in the afternoon and think he smelled her perfume, wake up in the morning after having dreamed of her all night. He would imagine he saw her on the bus but it would be some other woman with unmarred lips and he would go into the office and find it hard to concentrate.

Eventually he found himself back in the shop on Teeter Street. The cage sat on the counter by the register, inside it the flox curled into a ball of brown fur. When Victor leaned forward he could just make out the rise and fall of its breathing.

"It's still for sale?" Victor said.

"Every day." The clerk opened the cage door. "You want to hold it?"

Victor said no and the clerk shrugged. There was something troublesome about the storekeeper, something that made Victor even more nervous than strangers usually did. It was not just that the man was brusque, but that he seemed too disinterested, too confident, as if not only did he know that Victor would return to the shop but also that he would agree to almost any terms. The proof came a moment later when the clerk quoted a price.

"That's more than before," Victor said.

"But less than it will be tomorrow."

"Fine," Victor said. The actual cost no longer seemed so important. "You mentioned an installment plan."

"The easy payment plan."

The clerk gave Victor a pen and then stood so close that Victor could barely concentrate on what he was signing. He read the section on the accrual of interest and was about to ask for a clarification when the clerk took the flox from the cage, placed it in a cardboard box, and gave the box to Victor. With his free hand Victor reached for his wallet.

"No," the clerk said and winked. "The first payment's easiest of all."

At home Victor sat the box at the foot of the couch, opened it and let his hand hover so near the flox that he could feel the brittle tips of its fur. Soft, periodic breaths puffed from its mouth. He picked it up and was surprised by its heaviness. The flox stirred, untucked its face and feet, and pressed its tiny claws into Victor's palm. Its ears stood up and its bright eyes wandered around the room before finally resting on Victor's face. Finally Victor admitted that there had been something lacking in his life, which in retrospect should have been obvious enough by the way he had longed for Julia. The flox, as if by some form of magic even more powerful than that of puppies or kittens, made the longing vanish and only then did Victor understand what had been haunting him all these weeks: a kind of lonesomeness, a kind of heartbreak, its object little more than a ghost. But the flox was no ghost.

And it never drifted from his presence. When he cooked, it sat beneath the kitchen table, and when he bathed, it lay on the rug in front of the toilet, studying him, cocking its head to one side and then the other, wiggling its nose as if the scent of shampoo and soap held information the flox could decipher. It ate little, only the vegetables he chopped up and gave to it, and if it craved anything more it was only to be near Victor, to curl up on his chest or in the crook of his neck. When he held it, the flox's heart beat loudly and regularly. I'm not lonely, Victor used to say. I'm not sad. But for the first time in his life he could now say something positive, that he was happy, and he was surprised that the change depended on so little.

Victor paid the second and third installments—really the first and second—by check. He would have preferred to pay in cash but he was never sure in advance how much each payment would be. He also put aside as much money as he could spare and thought that by the fourth or at most the fifth payment he could pay what he owed in full, which he was anxious to do. The debt seemed a kind of intrusion, like a mother-in-law or a lover's annoying best friend, a troublesome third thing best avoided.

At night he kept the animal in its box. Otherwise he was afraid it would climb into bed with him and he might roll over and kill it. The flox, however, did not like the arrangement and spent most nights clawing at the cardboard. Victor considered buying a metal cage. They made them in all sizes and he told himself that a large one would not seem so much like a prison. But he knew this was not true because it wasn't more space the flox wanted but to be nearer to him. In that case, he wondered, how awful were its days locked up in the house alone?

The night before the fourth payment was due Victor lay in bed thinking about this dilemma when he heard a noise in the apartment and thought the animal had finally scratched its way out of the box. Fine, he told himself, the decision's made. He kept his eyes closed and waited. The sound grew nearer and louder and Victor thought about how the blind are supposed to have heightened senses of hearing and touch. This is what it must be like for them, he thought, listening to the scuff move from one room to another, now in the kitchen and now the living room and now the hallway outside the bedroom door. He was so excited that it took all of his effort just to keep his eyes closed. Then something moved at the edge of the bed and Victor sat up.

"I scared you," Julia said.

"What are you doing here?"

"The door was unlocked."

Victor, who never left the door unlocked, turned on the lamp. She wore jeans and a heavy coat and he could see that her eyes were red and the scar above her lip inflamed. "What are you doing here?" he repeated.

"I've been fighting with my parents. I told them I'm not going back to school."

"School? That's where you've been?"

"Of course," she said. "Where did you think I was?" She put her hand on his arm. "I'm sorry I scared you," she said. Victor tried to move away but she grabbed his wrist. "Did you miss me while I was gone?"

"You can't just come walking into my house in the middle of the night," he said.

"You missed me," she said.

"We don't even know each other."

"We have a connection."

"I don't think we have a connection."

"Yes we do," she said.

The next morning Victor took the bus into the city and found the clerk behind his counter flipping through the pages of a ledger. "Already it's that time?" the clerk said and winked but for once the familiarity did not bother Victor. He asked how much he owed and when the clerk quoted him an amount even less than his last payment, Victor explained that he wanted to know how much he owed in total. "I'd like to pay off the balance," Victor said.

"But this is only the fourth payment," the clerk said.

"I know and I'm happy to cover the interest for the last three payments as well."

"That's not how it works." The clerk closed the ledger and began searching through papers stacked on the counter. "Interest is a function of time and this is only the fourth payment." He held up the contract Victor had signed.

"I understand how interest works," Victor said, "and there's no reason I can't pay the full amount now."

But the clerk refused to accept the remaining payments in advance and Victor left owing only slight less than he had when he woke up that morning. Soon, though, he began to understand that it was not the debt that bothered him but what the debt signified, namely that the flox was only partially his, that his ownership of the small animal was incomplete and thus precarious. Julia's presence in the house emphasized this fact in more ways than Victor was ready to acknowledge.

Most days he came home to find the young woman on the couch reading a magazine or watching the TV, the flox on her belly or chest, gnawing at a button, its dark eyes on her almost perfect face. He told himself that the loss of the animal's attentions was a small price to pay for Julia's presence in his house, though he also sometimes wondered if their affection for each other wasn't perhaps a little too physical, the flox burrowing into her crevices in a way that made Victor feel awkward and self-conscious. Of course, he forgot all of this when he and Julia made love, which most nights they did quietly and slowly as if they were trying to sneak up on their pleasure, as if pleasure were a prey easily startled. The flox now slept on the bed between them—Julia had insisted anything else would be cruel—and when they made love, it moved out of the way, though not always off the bed and occasionally Victor would reach for Julia's hatchet-shaped hip and instead find the flox.

One day he came home and found her on the couch in the living room. She wore a blouse and a skirt that he had never seen before and when he asked about them she said she had gone home to get clothes and while there she had run into her parents. The flox lay on her stomach, its face pushed below the hem of her blouse. A long muscle ran the length of her outer thigh and it excited him to know that he could put his hand there if he wanted. He started to ask about her parents but instead said, "Tell me what you were like before we met."

"I was not very happy," she said.

"But what did you do?" He had never before wondered these things. Instead, Julia had seemed to materialize as if from a vacuum at the moment he first saw her, a thing with no real past, with no weight or existence outside the radius of his own desire. But of course this wasn't true. She had parents—and perhaps friends? previous lovers?—a past now all the more apparent and troublesome because it was entirely opaque to him. "Did you have hobbies?" he said. "What did you study in college?"

"What do you imagine I did?" she said, unfastening the bottom button of her blouse so the flox could burrow deeper beneath the fabric.

"I don't know," he said. "But isn't it odd that I never saw you before that night we met in your backyard? And yet somehow you knew who I was."

"Do you know that most divorces happen right after the holidays?" she said. "I saw that on TV today."

"Do you want to introduce me to your parents?"

"It's because we're stingy and short-sighted," she said. "We don't want to be alone during the holidays but then as soon as they're over we go and ruin the memory."

"Do they ask about me?"

She opened her blouse, scooped out the flox from the folds of the fabric and held it out as if she were going to present it to him. "They want me to go back to school in January," she said.

"I thought you were never going back."

"I'm not. So they said they'd rent me an apartment here in town."

"Oh," he said.

She released the flox and it squeezed itself between her leg and the cushions.

"Julia," he said. "Can you put it down? Just for a minute?"

"I have put it down." She picked up the flox and put it on the floor. After a moment it climbed back onto the couch.

"Here," Victor said. He took the flox from her and put it in its box.

"Don't do that," she said.

"What did you tell your parents?"

"What do you think I told them?"

"I don't know. That's why I'm asking."

"Guess."

"How am I supposed to guess?"

"Guess."

"I don't know."

"I told them I was happy living here." She took the animal from its box and again let it rest on her belly. "It's so uncomplicated," she said. "That's how we have to be, Victor. Uncomplicated."

"You think you can trick me?" the clerk said. "How long has it been? You can't rush these things. There's a schedule. It doesn't work that way."

"Today's the thirtieth," Victor said.

"What?" the clerk said, checking the calendar hanging from the wall. "I don't believe it." He laughed, flicked out a hairy wrist and told Victor how much was owed.

It was a large amount, much more than Victor thought possible. He objected and insisted that the clerk had made a mistake.

"Don't forget there's interest," the clerk said.

But Victor now felt as if he were the victim of some elaborate swindle and insisted on reviewing the account. The clerk stared at Victor as if he had never before been questioned in this way and did not know how to respond. After a moment he banged his hand on his register and the drawer rung open. "Fine," he said. "Pay as much as you like. The rest we'll carry over until next time."

"What difference will that make?" Victor said.

"You're going to argue with a man who lets you set your own price?"

Victor did argue but the clerk wouldn't relent. He agreed that it was fair of Victor to question the sum owed and insist on reviewing the account, but only if there was an imminent dispute, which there wasn't since Victor could pay any amount he wanted. Therefore there was nothing to argue about. The clerk followed a strange, winding logic so frustrating to Victor that he eventually surrendered and left the store.

It might have been funny the way the tiny familiar followed at Julia's heals, the click of its claws on the linoleum, but the flox in its enthusiasm knew no boundaries and one day Victor found Julia on the couch giggling, the flox beneath the folds of her skirt. This was too much, he tried to explain. Indecent. Unnatural.

"It's just an animal," she said. "It wants to be where it's warm."

He tried to explain how it was more than that, how there were many other ways to keep the flox warm, how this was something else. But what, he could not say and in the end he rested on the argument that it was unsanitary. But Julia, like the clerk, followed her own logic and again Victor found himself surrendering.

Later that week the temperature dropped below zero and as if the clocks themselves were half-frozen the days began to creep forward in increments of minutes and seconds. Once it amused Victor to look down at his spreadsheets and see how something as solid and heavy as a car or as cumbersome as a truckload of jungle gyms could in an instant become a series of weightless numbers. Now he felt as if he were in a dream and even the simplest tasks were impossible to complete.

Christmas came and they exchanged gifts. She gave him a scarf and silver cufflinks that were tarnished and obviously secondhand but handsome nonetheless. He gave her a bracelet and a green sweater that brought out the pink in the scar above her lip. They made love, which they had not done in weeks, and when they finished she said she regretted the distance that had come between them. She said it was "unfortunate" and she hoped they didn't carry it into the new year. He said he hoped so too, that, yes, the important thing was not to carry old problems into the new year and before he knew it he was telling her about the easy payment plan and how it was anything but easy and he didn't think he could afford to pay for the flox. "Maybe we should return it," he said.

"You can't return it," she said. "It's not a handbag."

"I don't have the money," he said. "And besides, we don't need it anymore." Something moved beneath the sheets and he felt a familiar thump-thump against his shin.

"What do you mean?" she said.

"We have each other."

"And what about the flox?"

"Like you said, it's just an animal."

This was an argument Victor did not intend to lose. And the debt was not the only thing he didn't want to carry into the new year. The next morning he went out into his backyard and looked at the house where Julia's parents lived. Ice hung from its eaves and, as it had been for months, the space beneath the carport was empty. He pushed through the shrubs, patted the snow from his pants, then went to the backdoor of the house and knocked. When no one answered, he tried the knob and found it unlocked.

Photographs hung from the living room walls, all of them of the couple he used to see working in their yard. There were porcelain knickknacks on a shelf and a basket filled with months-old magazines. Down the hallway were two bedrooms. In one he found an ashtray filled with coins and more pictures, again of the couple but this time with various other people, presumably relatives. In the second bedroom he found a sewing machine and exercise equipment. Nowhere was there any sign that Julia had ever lived in the house.

He returned home to find her on the couch, the flox curled up in her lap.

 "What were you doing out there?" she said.

"Where did you come from?" he said.

"What do you mean?"

"I mean that's not your parents' house. You don't live there."

"I live here," she said, but he didn't really hear or understand what she meant. Instead he took the flox from her, put it in the cardboard box it had come in, and left. He expected her to try to stop him but she didn't.

When he arrived at the shop the shutters were pulled. It was early and for an hour he waited on the curb until, finally, a light in the store came on. A minute later the front door opened. "Now I'm sure you're at least a few days early," the clerk said.

"I'm not here to make a payment." Victor held up the box. "I want to return the flox."

"No, no, no," the clerk said, turning away from Victor and entering the store. "There's no returning."

"I'm willing to forfeit the first five payments," Victor said, following the clerk inside.

"Forfeit as much as you like. But there's no returning." The clerk crossed his arms and refused to even look at the box on the counter.

"I don't want it anymore," Victor said.

"That means nothing. We have a deal. A contract."

"And what if I refuse to pay?" Victor said.

"There's no returning and there's no refusing."

"I can't afford it," Victor said. "I don't have the money."

"It's not so much. Only what you didn't pay last time."

"Last time I didn't pay a lot. And what about the next payment? How much will that be?"

"The last payment?" The clerk scratched his chin. "The last payment varies."

"What do you mean it varies?"

"I mean it's not always the same."

"That makes no sense," Victor said. "Show me the contract."

The clerk reached beneath the register and almost immediately came up with a thin sheath of papers. Victor took the contract, walked a few feet from the counter and found himself unable to make sense of the numbers. "I don't know what any of this means," he said.

"Come," the clerk said, and Victor laid the papers on the counter. The clerk pointed at a page. At the bottom was a figure. "See," he said. "This is what you owe now." He ran his finger up the page. "And this is what you paid last time, which was nothing at all, remember?" He flipped the page back. "And the time before, and so on."

"And the last payment?"

The clerk flipped to the last page, which was blank. "I told you," he said. "It's not figured. I'm just a storekeeper. I don't have time to think about next month today."

Victor did not even bother to argue. An hour later he returned home with the flox but Julia was not there. He put the animal on the floor and immediately it scurried beneath the couch. Later he asked the children in the neighborhood if they had seen a young woman with a harelip. He explained what a harelip was and they stared at him dumbly and some ran inside to their parents.

That night he lay awake wondering if the flox would climb into bed with him. The house was quiet, nothing but the sound of wind outside his window and the occasional click of the refrigerator cycling on. Much later he heard a shuffling in the living room and a creak that sounded like the kitchen door opening. He closed his eyes and listened to the muffled sounds moving from room to room. It must be her, he told himself. And if it was Julia he promised to be like the flox, uncomplicated, needful of nothing more than food and warmth, a heartbeat with no future or past, just the constant drum of now, of a love neither precarious nor fearful. If it's Julia, he said.

Terrible Angels

Sometimes they're there, sometimes not. Tonight they are, standing next to the television set, a distraction as Francie watches *Wheel of Fortune* with her dad, a bowl of popcorn between them on the couch—light butter only, to protect the ticking heart, he always says—and she knows he can't see them, he's oblivious shouting vowels and consonants at the screen.

"*A*, you moron, just buy an *A!*" he yells, the couch cushions sinking beneath his weight as he leans forward. "Jesus Christ, Francie, am I the only one in the whole goddamn world who knows it's *aardvark?*"

He's not. She knows it too. But she's lost interest in Pat Sajak's clever jabs, the way his subtle goading provokes the contestants to buy more and more vowels. She's watching her grandparents instead, who have been standing by the television for over five minutes now. They never speak when they appear, and sometimes it's just one of them, her grandfather or her grandmother, though tonight they've come in tandem. They look just like she remembers, not having aged to the way they'd look now, if they were still alive.

"Well, look at that, Francie. Mr. Bowtie Surprise finally solved the puzzle."

Francie forgets her grandparents for a moment, just long enough to cringe at her father's habit of assigning people arbitrary names, of labeling them according to clothing, or mannerisms, or the type of sandwich they eat for lunch.

"His name is Ron, Dad."

"Well, old Ron there is wearing a mighty big bowtie."

Her grandfather laughs, though no sound comes out. He's always liked her father, though she can see her grandmother scowl, roll her eyes. Her mother would have too, if she were still around. But she's not, and Francie wonders sometimes, when her grandparents appear in the backseat of her car, or next to her in line when she's picking up a pack of cigarettes at the 7-Eleven down the street, if the ghost of her mother might ever come as well, and if it did, whether her own ticking heart would burst and cease.

"How 'bout those SATs, sweet? Tell me again when you're taking those."

The game show has cut to commercial break, her father looking over at her. He picks at the bowl of popcorn, stuffs a few puffed kernels in his mouth.

"Two weeks."

Her grandmother looks up when she says it, frowns.

"You ready? Nervous? Laying awake in anticipation?"

"None of the above. I haven't really thought about it yet."

And she hasn't. It's the fall of her senior year and she's taking the SATs for the second time, later than most. She signed up the spring before but had failed to show, the test only three weeks after her mother had died. She'd told her dad she was going, but had picked up Marcus instead and they'd spent the day lying in a wheat field, smoking pot, identifying tricycles and snow globes in the clouds above.

"I'll drive you to the test myself." He grabs another handful of popcorn, smiles over at her, pats her hand. "We can even do some flashcards, you know, verbs, nouns. Isosceles triangles. All that brainy shit."

Francie knows he'd have offered this before, that he's not just making empty promises, not trying to be the dad he never was, now that her mother is gone. He'd helped her study the first time around, though now, she thinks maybe he'd been distracting himself too, a way to forget the world as it was.

The game show returns on screen, her father sits forward again on the edge of the couch. Ron has advanced to the bonus round, and stands before the five letters of the word WHEEL, ready to choose the hidden prize.

"Pull the *L*, Bowtie!" her father shouts, then lowers his voice. "The *L* is always the RV, Francie. The *L* is the one we want."

Francie tries to feign interest, tries to pour every ounce of her brain into which letter Ron chooses, to ignore her grandparents' presence. But as Ron pulls the second *E* and her father winces and mutters *Good job, Bowtie*, her grandfather lets go of her grandmother's hand and walks in a float, comes and sits in the armchair beside Francie. She gasps a little, puts her hand over her mouth so her father won't see.

"I know, what a moron, right? He should've picked the goddamn *L*!"

Her father gets up to grab a beer, to return the now-empty popcorn bowl to the kitchen, to leave Francie on the couch to stare at her grandmother, at her grandfather, wondering why they are possibly here.

In the afternoon quiet of the kitchen, as Francie sits reading her SAT prep guide, the sound of a car engine permeates the double-paned windows, roars up, settles in the driveway. Francie knows it isn't her father, knows he's working the second shift at the construction plant today and won't be back until well after dinner. When she gets up and looks out the front window, she isn't surprised to see Marcus's hunched figure, bulked in a hooded sweatshirt and too-large jeans, moving toward the door. He's smoking a cigarette, and his face is lowered against the wind, his dark hair falling across his forehead.

Her grandparents haven't shown themselves today, sometimes they go for days without turning up, just long enough for Francie to pretend this was some fluke of imagination, a rare incident she'll never have to explain ever happened. But when she opens the door and lets Marcus in, they are both standing behind him on the doorstep. Her grandfather holds a jug of milk, her grandmother a bag of chocolate chip cookies. They both smile, great big smiles that make Francie's stomach plunge.

She shepherds Marcus inside, pulls him in so quickly that maybe, she thinks, her grandparents will stay outside. But as Marcus heads into the kitchen, to grab himself a Miller Lite without asking, Francie watches as her grandparents move through the doorway, milk, cookies, smiles all intact.

"This SAT shit again?"

Francie walks into the kitchen, where Marcus leans over her prep guide. He's already opened his beer, which sits on her book, as if the book were a coaster.

"No more of that this afternoon." He slides over and sneaks his hands around her waist. She can see the guide over his shoulder, a circular watermark bleeding onto the chapter she's just begun, the chapter on geometry.

As she lies down on her bed and Marcus pulls off her shirt, Francie looks up to see her grandparents perched near the ceiling, elbows on their knees, hands no longer holding cookies or milk.

"Can you close the blinds?" she asks Marcus, and once he does the room swallows itself in darkness, so dark she can't see her grandmother or grandfather or Marcus's hands moving toward the zipper of her jeans.

Later, after Marcus has drunk three more of her dad's beers and finally gone home, Francie heats up a plate of leftover meatloaf and sits back at the dinner table. She is halfway to her first bite, fork suspended mid-air, when she stops, sets the fork down, mouth as open as her eyes. On top of her SAT guide, where the watermark had been two hours ago, now sits a plate of three chocolate chip cookies, one glass of milk. And alongside this snack—tangible, not ghostly, she touches it to make sure—is a twig-and-twine grappling hook, the kind she once made in her grandparents' backyard.

In the car the next day, as Francie and her dad sit in traffic, she looks over at him and turns down the volume. They are on their way to dinner, someplace nice he's said, because he hasn't seen her since Sunday, because he's worked the night shift all week.

"Hey, remember those grappling hooks?"

"What grappling hooks?" He's half-singing along to Roy Orbison, an old tape he's kept in the car for as long as Francie can remember.

"Those hooks I used to make, at grandma and grandpa's."

"Those branch and string contraptions you used to build? The ones you thought you'd catch raccoons with?"

"Those are the ones."

"My God, Francie!" He laughs and looks over, his face like a kid's before a glowing birthday cake. "I haven't thought of those in years!"

"Did you keep any of them?"

"What? Oh no, France, I didn't keep any of them. But goddamnit, now I wish I had." His eyes settle back on the road, though his smile hasn't disappeared.

Francie hasn't thought of them in years either, even forgot she'd ever made them until the one had appeared, had sat there like a question mark on her open book. Her grandfather taught her how to make them, had held her hands beneath his as she tied the string tight and let the claw-shaped branches fly into the trees. Once it's secure you can climb, he'd said. You can perch up there and wait for raccoons.

She never had. The branches were too delicate, the trees too high.

"You know, you weren't a mean kid," her father says. "You talked a big talk, told your grandpa you were hunting. But we all knew you were just waiting to squeeze one of them, catch a fat raccoon and tuck it into bed with you. Like a big stuffed bear!"

Francie doesn't know why, but this is something she doesn't want to hear. The inside of the car has gone completely quiet, so quiet it hurts, and she reaches over and turns up Roy Orbison, to drown this all out, to blink everything back.

"What made you think of—oh, mother*fucker!*" Her dad slams the breaks, flips his middle finger at a white minivan cutting into his lane. "Go on! Go right ahead! The whole goddamn lane's just for you, asshole!"

Francie looks out the window, at the strip malls and banks along the road, relieved her grandparents aren't in the car, glad she doesn't have to watch her grandma roll her eyes again.

"Sorry, sugarbud." Her dad stares at the minivan's bumper. "Christ, what was I saying?"

Over dinner, where her father orders her a glass of red wine, to *let loose!* he says, before the big test next week, Francie feels him peek at her over his plastic menu.

"I noticed some of my beers were gone the other night. You been drinking, to sustain your hard habit of study, or has that boy Marcus been by again?"

"He comes by sometimes. Big deal, dad. I'm almost eighteen."

"Oh, right you are. A big adult!"

Francie rolls her eyes, sets her menu off to the side of the table.

"Look, France, you can do what you want. It's not you I'm worried about. I just think that boy's a goddamn loser."

Other girls would be annoyed by this, Francie knows. She imagines her friend Holiday hearing it from her own dad, envisions her flipping over the table, storming out like a bad sitcom sketch. And though she thinks she could do the same, her dad would actually apologize if she did, she feels the will to do so deflate from her lungs. Her father is not her enemy. He is not her enemy, and he is right.

"You don't even know him."

"Oh, and you do? Ha!" He sips his wine, for emphasis, she thinks. "Look, sugarsnap, all I'm saying is you deserve better. That boy's nothing but a lump of mush."

Francie waits for her food, and for an indignation that never comes.

Later, after they've had dinner, after she's finished the math section on proofs and has moved on to the verbal chapters, she lays on her bed and looks up at the ceiling, at the place where her grandparents had been. Though she hates when her father is right, hates the haughty jest in his voice, she knows too that when she thinks of Marcus it is not with infatuation, not even with lust, but with the slow palpitation of an irregular heartbeat, a heart not even challenged by the strain of movement.

She hadn't even known him before her mother died. But after a policeman had come to their door, after the impact of collision shattered her mother through the windshield and her own life in a moment passed through some irreversible door, she woke up as if in a haze, sitting at her desk in homeroom after the funeral, had looked up sleepy-eyed and there he was.

When Francie's phone rings, she half-expects to hear her grandfather's husky voice on the other end of the line.

"So you have to sleep over this weekend," Holiday says instead, her voice almost breathless. "Julie Sussman's having a party. Will said he'll kick Marcus's ass if he shows up."

Will is Holiday's boyfriend, a tall, lumbering fellow who never talks, and Francie has always been distracted looking at him, his forehead too large for his face.

"What?"

"Oh, come on, Francie. Like you haven't heard."

Francie narrows her eyes, focuses on the mobile of aluminum airplanes still hanging from her ceiling, airplanes her mother made when she was five.

"Marcus slept with Alicia Traver. He's been telling everyone you're too fucked up to date. You know, because of your mom and all."

Francie stares at the mobile. The last part hurts the most, not the first.

"So you're sleeping over, right?" Holiday is indignant, her voice disclosing all of the rage that Francie herself should feel, if she could reach deep into her chest and pull out a glowing ember that burned. But when she thinks of Marcus, of his stooped shoulders and stringy hair, she thinks of only mush, her father's words, a pile of gray nothing that has smothered the burn to cinder.

"Sure. I'll sleep over."

As she hangs up the phone and crawls beneath her covers, she sees her grandparents peeking in her bedroom window, and a pail of sidewalk chalk hanging from the airplane mobile, where minutes before there had been none.

On Saturday afternoon, after Francie has plowed through the guide's chapter on analogies, she takes the pail out to her driveway and grinds the chalk into the pavement. She draws a hopscotch grid, the boxes big and angry, and skips through them like she once did in her grandparents' driveway, stomping her feet heavily against the asphalt.

"What're you doing there, bud?"

Her father stands on their front porch, a beer in one hand, a bag of cheese puffs in the other.

"Nice lunch, Dad."

"Well, it sure as hell beats hopscotch, Miss Skip To My Lou."

Francie picks up another piece of chalk, drags it hard along the pavement, her hair hiding the scowl on her face.

"Look, little britches, I'm just checking in. You seem down these days."

"Marcus cheated on me."

She doesn't know why she says this, since she's not sure it matters, or if it even qualifies as cheating. Marcus was never really her boyfriend to begin with. But she refuses to look at her dad, at the self-satisfied look that will color his face, and digs the chalk into the ground expecting him to admonish her, or make light of the situation somehow, or at least tell her that Mr. Lump-O-Mush was nothing but bad news anyway.

But *oh Francie* is all he says, his voice tinged with the filaments of sympathy, and when she looks up again he is standing right beside her, his eyes on the scribbles she's sketched into the asphalt.

"I'm sleeping at Holiday's tonight."

"Alright."

Francie stands and drops the chalk. They both regard the hopscotch grid awkwardly. Her father sets his beer, his cheese puffs in the grass. He begins hopping through the boxes, and Francie feels the gurgling urge of both laughter and tears welling impossibly within her. But before she allows either to erupt, she jumps through the boxes behind him, and they hop together without eye contact or words, without her grandfather or grandmother hovering above to watch.

But in the driver's seat that night, as she and Holiday head to the party, Francie looks up to switch lanes and spots her grandfather peeping at her from the backseat, his image just barely visible in the rear-view mirror. The sight doesn't shock her, she anticipates his presence everywhere now, and she ignores him until they arrive at the party, until the doors slam and the car is locked tight.

"You ready for this?" Holiday asks, heels shaky, clicking against the walkway to the house. She's already had three beers, which is why Francie has driven.

When they walk through the door, Will is already inside, holding a cup of beer and waiting near the doorway.

"Marcus is out back," he says, before they even take off their coats. "Where the fuck have you guys been?"

Francie stares at his face, at his hopelessly large forehead over the top of Holiday's thick hair as she stands on her toes to kiss him. Will puts his arm around Holiday, beer hanging limply in his hand, and motions them both toward the back of the house. Francie feels her body go numb, her face fall blank, but she cannot stop herself from following them through the crowded living room, the beer boxes that litter the kitchen, on out to the backyard where Marcus stands smoking a cigarette.

It doesn't take long. Before Marcus turns around, Will hands Holiday his beer, slams his empty fist into Marcus's jaw. Francie watches the half-smoked cigarette fly from his mouth across the patio, landing somewhere in the grass, out in the dark. Will grabs Marcus by the elbows, holds him pinned and facing Francie, a small line of blood leaking from his two front teeth.

"Here it is, France." Will's breath steams from his mouth. "Your chance to get this fucker good, give him what he deserves."

Francie stares out at the grass, wonders where the cigarette went, whether it could smolder into flames and set the whole house ablaze.

"Come on, Francie, kick him in his fucking nuts!" Holiday yells, her eyes swimming wildly between all of them, hands gripped like claws around Will's beer.

Francie looks at Marcus's shoes, at the softness of his belly exposed by the angle of his elbows, and for a flashing moment she feels rage, not for love, but for the indecency of what he's done. But when she sees her grandfather hovering just behind Marcus, off in the dark grass, watching her from behind a set of patio furniture, she thinks of nothing but her mother, a strange memory at this moment, the memory of her mother testing the water for her bath once when she was four, making sure it wouldn't scald her, filling the tub with rubber whales and toy ducks, the kind that kicked through the water if their levers were wound just right.

"Let him go."

Will looks at her, body rigid, struggling against Marcus's strained arms. "What the fuck did you just say?"

"I said let go. You heard me."

Before Will can protest, before he and Holiday tell her how much Marcus deserves this, how they've waited three days to catch him here and make him pay, Will shoves Marcus onto the grass, and Francie walks back inside.

"Hey, where are you going?" Holiday sounds annoyed, her voice garbled by beer, and Francie wonders whether she will even remember this tomorrow, after Will has driven her home, after she's vomited the night across her bedroom carpet.

"Home."

They do not stop Francie as she walks back through the kitchen, the living room where Julie Sussman pulls a keg stand off her own couch, and out the front door into her car where, as she turns the key in the ignition, she sees a pogostick in the rear-view mirror, laying across the backseat.

Her father is not watching the television when she walks in the front door, as she half-expects him to be, but she hears music wavering from the upstairs office, the muddled sound of Patsy Cline.

"Is that you, butterbean?" he yells down the stairs. "Early night?"

When she walks into the office, he sits in front of the computer playing solitaire. He's changed the card deck to the haunted house pattern, along with a three-card deal, though Francie prefers the beach.

"What's that you got there, a party favor?"

She doesn't know what he's talking about until she feels the pogostick in her hand, resting at her side.

"Something like that." She thinks of the pogosticks her grandparents kept in their garage, how she'd once spent a whole afternoon with her grandmother bouncing up and down their street, until the sun sank behind the trees, until they went inside for pot roast and ice cream floats.

"Dad?"

"What is it, sweetpea?" His back is turned to her, his eyes on the screen.

"Can we watch a movie?"

He takes his hand off the mouse, looks at her, and for the first time she sees something sad in his face, something not unlike the way his entire body had collapsed once their guests left the house after the funeral, after he'd scraped the last of the deviled eggs and ranch dip into the waiting, open trash can.

"Sure, France. We can watch a movie."

He makes popcorn while she changes into her pajamas, and when she meets him downstairs in the living room, he's already settled on the couch, the title menu for *Mary Poppins* cued up on the screen.

"Mary Poppins?"

He peeks at her over the back of the couch. "You got a better idea?"

As he hits the play button and grabs a handful of popcorn, she sits down next to him on the couch, reaches for the popcorn too.

"Can you still take me to the test?"

"Sure, sugar beet."

She thinks of the pile of flashcards she's made, a series of analogies, vocabulary words.

"Can you help me tomorrow?"

He nods, grabs another handful of popcorn, his eyes on the television where Mary Poppins is sitting on a cloud, high above London.

"Next Saturday, if you want, we can get lunch after the test, maybe even a couple of blizzards from the Dairy Queen. My God, look at Miss Umbrella float on down to town like that!"

Her grandparents do not appear again that night, but the next day, while she and her dad sit in the living room going over flashcards, a knock rattles the door and her grandparents are both suddenly there, sitting on the loveseat, holding hands and smiling.

"Who could that be on a Sunday?" Her dad looks out the peephole, then his body stiffens and he lowers his voice. "It's that goddamn mistake for a human being, France. You want to see him, or you want me to break some kneecaps?"

Francie ushers her father into the kitchen before she lets Marcus in, but can still hear her father grumbling *mush* to himself, just loud enough so she can hear through the closed kitchen door. She lets Marcus into the foyer, doesn't offer him a seat. Her grandparents are on the couch, and she doesn't want him to stay.

"I just came to say sorry." His hair hangs across his cheek, not long enough to hide his bruised lip, crusted teeth.

Francie says nothing, stands uneasily as her grandparents shift on the couch cushions, both of their faces expectant and eager.

"So I figure none of this really matters," Marcus continues, "and that if you wanted, you could be my girlfriend. Like, for real."

Francie looks at him, her heart slowed to a dull murmur, nothing more. She glances over at her grandparents and they are laughing, with silent, wide-open mouths.

"So?" Marcus asks. "You want to?"

Francie feels her own laughter bubbling up, a laughter that could have been loud and free, like her grandparents' might have been, had their vocal cords produced audible sound. But she swallows the gurgle back, suppresses the urge so he will leave, her face passionless, indifferent to make him go.

"No," she says. "No, I don't."

Marcus looks up, his eyes cracked with hurt, a hurt that no longer penetrates, its shards small and useless at Francie's feet. He stands for a second, his mouth open as if to speak, then he seals his lips and turns, baggy jeans dragging on the walkway as he goes.

When Francie closes the door, hears her dad yell *That's my butterbean!* from the kitchen, she's too distracted to be annoyed, by the exhilaration of making Marcus go, but also by the emptiness that suddenly bounces from the living room walls. Her grandparents are not on the couch. They've disappeared as quickly as they first came, without any remnants to prove they might have been here, no cookies, no milk, no grappling hooks strewn across the couch.

"Dad?"

"You want a turkey sandwich for lunch?" The sound of his voice fills the room.

"Sure," Francie calls, then grabs her flashcards and takes them to her room.

Her grandparents are not there either, not in the windows, not on the ceiling, no pails of chalk, no pogosticks along the floor. But as Francie sits on the edge of her bed, knowing this might be it, that she must grow accustomed once more to their faces only in yellow-edged photographs, a sight once normal, slid now to strange, she leans back and her hands brush something rubbery, something plastic, something inflated.

She turns to find a pair of orange floaties, the water wings she once wore, though she knows these are not remnants from her grandparents' house, but from the baby pool that once graced her own backyard. They are the water wings her mother placed carefully on her arms, puffy rings encircling baby fat, protection even in two feet of water, in case Francie ever slipped.

Francie does not know if these floaties will stay, or if they will disappear by the time she tucks herself in for bed, as the chalk, as the pogostick, as the grappling hooks have all done. But she curls herself around them and lies hugging them on her bed, until she almost falls to sleep next to them, until her father at last calls her down for lunch.

A. K. Thompson

The Taxidermist

When Derwood saw two large, dead dogs at the side of Rt. 51, south of Coldwater, Mississippi, he pulled his truck over, and put it in park. He looked in the side-view mirror at the dogs, one liver-spotted, the other black, laying there in the dirt. He walked up to the dogs, noticing that neither looked like it had been run over. The hides were perfect—shining in the sun, slick with lanolin. Their faces were quiet—not smashed or contorted like the coon, skunk or possum he usually passed.

Road kill has its seasons, but dog is not one of them. Derwood had carefully selected dozens of varmints over the years to mount in his shop for practice, or to make a quick buck on eBay. He'd even fashioned a few squirrels into combat Marines or hillbillies, complete with mini M4 carbine assault rifles, fatigues, tiny corncob pipes, and overalls. He once made a raccoon sitting in a small lawn chair, smoking a cigar with a 6-pack of Bud Light ponies at his side.

But lately he'd become bored—tired of the same old buck coming in, carried by the same old redneck, lip swollen with chew. It was good money, of course, but he was beginning to feel more like a factory worker than an artist, and it was getting to him.

Derwood knelt down and ran his hands over the liver-spotted dog, dug his fingers deep into the fur—the skin still gave—a fresh kill. He shifted on his heels and did the same to the black dog, then brought his hand to his nose. The smell was rich—waxy and damp. He rubbed his hands together, the oil from the fur coming off in small, dirty beads.

He walked back to the truck, put it in reverse, and carefully backed up to the dogs. He let the tailgate loose and loaded them both into the bed. While he was driving home, past the Shiloh Baptist Church, he thought of all the different poses he could put the dogs into. They could fight. They could sleep. They could sit—tall and obedient as a good dog should—forever.

There were no standard domestic dog mounting forms, so he'd have to work clay onto a coyote form to get the wise arch of a dog's forehead, the thickness of the snout. He put the dogs into his walk-in freezer, and set about organizing his tools.

Scalpel
Bone-saw
Pliers
Hand vise
Knife

Once he had the station set he brought out the black dog, and put him on the stainless steel table. He pulled the work light over the dog, rolled him onto his back, and took-up the scalpel. He ran the blade, like butter, from the dog's groin to its neck. The usual bitter-sweet smell came into his nose. Carefully balancing the dog on its back, he reached over and set the scalpel down and picked up the knife. He reached his hand way up inside the chest cavity and got hold of the trachea, then guided the knife along his own arm, and cut. With the trachea in-hand, Derwood let the dog back onto its side, stood back from the table, and pulled the innards out into a waiting garbage can. The lower intestine held, so he cut around the dog's genitals, including the bung, and let the rest of the entrails fall, like so much meat, into the can.

When Derwood began to skin the dog he noticed something missing. Bruising. The flesh was clean—pink and smooth. It was more than unusual for an animal to be hit by a car and not have contusions. He shrugged this off, pinching the bridge of his nose then rubbing his fingers hard into his eye sockets. He hadn't slept in two days.

He broke the foot joints and tail, then pulled the skin from the dog. The head was careful work—running the sharp scalpel along lips and eyelids, peeling back nose and turning out ears.

No longer a dog, the carcass lay on the table, well-muscled and straight. Derwood stood over the dog—looking far more fierce than it had with its skin, and thought better than throwing it in the trashcan. He decided he would burn the carcass, along with the other dog, out back after dinner, and returned him to the freezer.

Having skinned his first dog, the liver-spotted mutt was much easier work. Anatomy is a funny thing—the slight variations between fox, coyote, now dog—nuances into just how similar every creature is on the inside.

Would this *Haruspicy* tell the same story over and over?

Derwood wondered about this every time he dumped organs into the trash can. He had read an article in *National Geographic* some years back about the ritualistic reading of entrails. What fortune lies in all that mess?, he wondered. The way a heart falls—atrium or ventricle side-up—every heart was different. In size and color. The way a small intestine curls on itself. Not once did the organs look the same, but he left it up to the junkman, who came, and went every Monday morning to collect the red biohazard trash bags, which went to the city incinerator, along with other dead things—medical waste, pieces of people mostly—arms and legs that didn't work anymore.

Derwood finished fleshing the hides, then salted them heavily. He opened his mini-fridge, grabbed a Bud Light, and lit a cigarette. With the smoke perched between his lips, Derwood turned the hides over in his hands. When a sharp knock came on the door, the cigarette fell from his mouth onto the liver-spotted dog's hide, singeing the rear end.

"God dammit!"

"Jesus, Der, what's wrong?" Larry said, holding up a handle of Jack Daniels.

"You scared the shit outta me," Derwood said, quickly carrying the dog hides to the freezer.

"Well God-damn, I'm just coming by the say hello."

"Well, hello."

"You want some of this?"

"Naw," Derwood said, holding up his beer.

"Suit yourself. Say, where you been lately? Folks are asking about you down at Porky's."

"Shit, work, you know? Deer season and all."

"Yeah, I figured, but you ain't missed a dart night in months, then all of the sudden you stop showing."

"Working, man. Just look at all the mounts I got drying out in the barn."

Derwood lead Larry outside, glancing back at the freezer door, padlock in place. A 30-by-14-foot wall was completely covered in buck mounts—antlers towering, casting shadows across each other's faces, glass eyes glistening.

"Shit, Tate County done good this year, huh?" Larry said.

"No kidding, I ain't been this busy since, well, ever."

"Most of 'em shotgun or bow?"

"Eh, a decent mix."

"We've got some damn good marksmen in this town."

"Amen, keeps beer in my gut, that's for sure."

"Say, anyone ever let you keep the meat?"

"Only one guy, you know Kelly? He told me he only had $75 to put toward the mount and offered the deer for the balance. That's a good deal far as I'm concerned."

"Hell yeah it is. Yeah, I know Kelly, he's a good guy."

"Hank Wells shot that big guy over there with the drop tines," Derwood said, pointing his beer bottle toward a monster of a buck. "Made Boone and Crockett for non-typical this year. Not bad, huh?"

"Not bad at all. Say, buddy, I'm gonna head. We was just wondering about you, not being at darts and all."

"Alright. Tell Frank and Cheryl I said hello."

"Sure thing."

Just as soon as Larry's truck was out of the driveway, Derwood exhaled so hard he bent over and stared blankly at the dirt. He didn't know why he had been feeling anxious lately, swallowed up by some force much larger than himself—like a weight was fixed to his chest. Sleep just didn't seem to come when he crawled into bed at night. The buck mounts had been done and drying for two weeks, but when Derwood went out and got in the truck to drive over to Porky's bar, he just sat there, unable to put the truck into drive. So he had been staying home, sitting out in the barn, watching all of the bucks watch him, drinking beers, talking sometimes—to who, he did not know.

Derwood was driving along the river, heading home from the grocery store when he saw an entire family of geese hit on the road—the row of goslings a skid mark chasing the center line. He slowed the truck down and saw a gosling at the side of the road, its head bobbing up and down, little paddle feet kicking at the asphalt.

He pulled over and walked up to it—green shit squished out of its ass. He knew the thing wouldn't make it, so he snapped its neck like he used to do on the farm growing up, and tossed it into his truck. When he was skinning the little goose, which weighed about five pounds, he remarked to himself how soft and downy the coat was. He looked close into its face, the small grey beak, the black peppercorn eyes. He examined the awkward, skinny wings, the dinosaur legs. He cut away the beak and legs, and put the hide with the others he had accumulated in the last week: tabby cat, skunk, opossum, crow, squirrel, red-tailed hawk, a doe, along with the unborn fawn he discovered inside of her, and the two dogs.

Derwood did not know why he was doing this—collecting road kill, taking the time to prepare each hide, padlocking the freezer, sleeping in the shop at night instead of his house, dreaming of a beast, sketching the nocturnal creature that looked nothing like any animal he'd ever seen.

That night, after a few bottles of beer, Derwood was sitting in his chair listening to the radio out in the shop. He was sketching again, trying like mad to get it right—the creature he saw in his dreams. The floor was covered with scribbled images, some up-close of a feathered foot, large claws extended. A few drawings were of eyes, a strange mix of feline and horse, large and sharp. He was no artist on the page, but could mold a hide better than any taxidermist for counties—won awards even.

He turned his head slightly, not taking his eyes off of the paper when he heard a voice. Finishing the pencil stroke, he looked over at the radio. Some show was on, a woman babbling about her misbehaving children, the host provided a there-there, then played some sappy song. Over the music he heard the voice again. Derwood turned off the radio.

"Hello?" he said.

"Larry?" he said.

He waited, listening hard, but nothing. Then, just as he was bringing the bottle to his lips, he heard it again, like it came from behind his shoulder.

Nothing wants to die.

"Jesus Christ," he said, dropping the bottle. "Who's there?"

Drown this unholiness.

"Who's there?"

They call me Un-go-ya-yen-ni. Have you met the beast?

"Who the fuck is this? Where are you?"

Language, young man!

"Yessir."

So he has shown himself to you?

"I've been having terrible dreams. I can't drink enough beers to make 'em go away. Where are you?"

I am every place, soldier. Do not wonder about such stupid things. You have not dreamt. You have not slept.

"What do you want?"

Of what I want I cannot speak—you must understand that it is what you want, not I, that is important.

"But I don't want anything. I want to play darts at Porky's."

Foolish man, always thinks he knows what it is he wants. You will search forever.

"No, really, I just want to play darts and drink those dollar drafts."

Alcohol ruins the great spirit. You must welcome the beast. Only he can set you free.

"What in God's name are you talking about?"

God has no name, only the name on your lips. Soldier, you know, yet you do not understand. I leave you now with your talking box. Find the beast, or all is truly lost.

"Who is this!?"

A strange sleep fell over Derwood—the soundest sleep he'd had in over a month. First, it was butterflies, then a donkey, then a vast bridge, a long-eared mule on the other side, then blackness. Only coal-dark sky.

Derwood woke up laying on the cold tile, depictions of a strange beast covering every inch of the floor. Eyes, ears, claws, paws, feathers, tails with fur, without, whiskers, the hard pads of a dog's foot. Beer bottles were scattered across the floor.

A single fly buzzed at the mouth of a bottle.

Derwood watched the fly, one eye open, the other closed tight against the floor.

He waited like a cat after a bird. As soon as the fly entered the bottle, he clapped a hand over the top, watched it buzz inside. He un-locked the freezer and set the bottle in the back.

The fly never flew out—it fell in to a deep, deep sleep. Then, the fly had the most marvelous dream.

It flew, with wings the size of a pelican's, over stretching fields of cotton, until it was sucked into the trenches of Appalachia. Through green canyon after green canyon, the fly flew. Really flew.

Not buzzing, but flying. As it should be. A fly should fly. Not hover or buzz or get caught under the sharp snap of a swatter. He flew, miles of fresh cow and dog shit beneath him, a buffet of warmth, too many good places to raise-up a family to choose. He understood what it meant to be a fly, flying. Defiant insect— ungrateful thing of many hairs and eyes.

He was the only fly that ever flew. He flew, through a suffocating humidity, into the swamp lands of Louisiana, and was snapped up quick by a bullfrog's tongue. No fly ever flew again.

Derwood began work in the morning—understanding now that he could never draw the beast. He had to make the beast: create the thing from scratch. Piece it together, one hide at a time. Needle and thread—the baseball stitch his father had taught him, the man who spent his savings to go to taxidermy school, only to find out he was allergic to deer, and wear rubber gloves and a mask his entire working life.

Derwood cut hide, piecing together the animals that kept to night. Cutting the dogs in half, he stitched the liver-spotted to the black, in the middle. The black dog's tail would forever wag, the spotted dog's haunches forever braced.

Derwood cut the head from the doe and stitched it to the neck of the dog. He molded the hides around the Styrofoam body of a coyote. *Coyote went into the mouth of the giant without knowing, but rescued the tick. This is how the tick became flat, pinched in the giant's jaws as Coyote pulled him from the certain death of his species.*

Derwood piled clay on top of clay to create the ridgeback of the beast. He pulled the hides tight, and fixed feathers into the ears of the doe. He took the feet of the Hawk and Crow, drew thick wire through each, and fixed them into the paws, thick rows of claws and talons woven through fur.

He took care to mount the gosling and fawn with tenderness— the two, playmates, brothers, forever. They lay in gentle repose, the fawn's neck curled in with the gosling's—their softness soaking into one another, coiled beneath the beast—a terrifying protector. Derwood stitched the whiskers of the cat and skunk into the face of the doe. He took the opossum's tail and stitched it into the coarse black hair of the Labrador's tail. He took up the squirrel, and stitched the small body onto a form—its anguished face caught then in the doe's mouth, which he filled with canine teeth.

Last, he fitted eight glass eyes into the forehead of the doe. She was all-seeing. He imagined he could see through the eyes— tiny lenses that told of the future, and of the past. Mirrors created from buck eyes, the stinging yellow of a coyote's stare.

All at once the eyes began to blink; like the sputtering engine in his old Ford, they fluttered until they were in synch—lids and lashes from the many faces batting. The eyes stared into Derwood, deep down into his very center, reading his insides, seeking some truth. A calm overtook him—a rasping grunt breathed heat onto his face. The squirrel fell from the jaws of the beast—slick teeth snapped at the sodden air. Derwood opened his mouth, took in the hot breath as if molasses had filled his lungs, and dropped to the ground.

Now you know, came the voice, *Nothing wants to die.*

The voice was soothing.

Sleep, soldier. You have done well. The bridge is yours now to tend. The animals have at last un-died—the hunting grounds restored.

The beast stood, immaculate, undaunted. Babes at its feet, a crowing in its breast, a fierceness un-matched by any wolf in its many eyes. Derwood slept soundly at the foot of his creation, and in the morning woke to find nothing but a spatter of blood leading toward the door. He caught a glimpse of hair pinched in the door, and heard a soft kicking. When he opened the door a fawn's tail came free, and it ran, bleating into the woods. A rush of nothingness touched Derwood. White ash drifted from the sky, and lit on his nose. His eye lids pulled down tight, searching the morning's horizon for the smoke of a fire, but there was none.

A Father's Place

Nine months after the memorial service, men from Kelfton & Knute showed up at our trailer, and Mom let them in. They squeezed into the kitchen, a mad scientist guy in front, two much bigger guys in sunglasses right behind him, and a fourth guy mostly hidden behind the big two. My brother Leo and I were there because Mom had decided to try home schooling. After Dad died, Leo's problems with "authority figures" at Lumberton High had just gotten worse, and I was getting picked on a lot by rich girls who had the latest cell phone.

"Allow me to introduce myself. I'm Dr. Thaddeus Wajsniac," said the man with the Einstein hair. The big guys with him didn't smile or anything. "You better sit down, Mrs. Galbo."

Mom must've sensed something was up because she took a seat at the table. Leo and I did, too. I should point out Mom was always suspicious of K & K and would never just do what they asked. The big guys pushed the guy behind them to the front.

"This is your husband," Dr. Wajsniac said. The big guys stepped apart.

Whoever he was, he had on a black motorcycle helmet with a black visor and, like the big guys, wore a suit and tie. But he *was* about Dad's height. I could see our three confused faces reflected in the visor. Mom didn't budge, though, so we didn't either.

"My husband was blown up," Mom said. "His body was never recovered."

"Actually, that's not entirely true." Dr. Wajsniac lifted the man's right hand and gone were the fingertips that Dad cut off in a construction accident in Flagstaff, Arizona. Dad used to travel around a lot, doing different jobs, and was always hurting himself. He'd gotten blown up washing dishes for K & K's cafeteria services in Iraq.

I thought *now* everyone would get up and hug, and I think the doctor thought so, too, the way he kept holding out Dad's hand, but we just sat there.

"Let me see his face," Mom said.

Dr. Wajsniac let out a long breath. If it was that bad, if Dad's face was like totally wrecked, I wasn't sure I wanted him back, but then the doctor lifted the visor, and Dad had a gas pump face, a flat mask with a bunch of LED readouts. It wasn't gross at all. "That one's for pulse, that one's respiration and that one's blood pressure," the doctor said. "Of course, the transmitter also displays this information." He patted the pockets of his white coat until he found something that he put on the table. It was a TV remote with a tiny screen. "I would keep the visor down," he said, flipping it back.

"You're kidding me," Mom said. "You Klefton people think we're stupid."

"I assure you, this *is* your husband, alive and well thanks to many skilled and caring hands and futuristic technology, not to mention my personal involvement and expertise. Processors inside the helmet keep his heart and lungs going, and the other organs…well, organs play follow the leader."

"What about his brain?" Mom thought she had him there.

Dr. Wajsniac cleared his throat. "The head was never recovered, Mrs. Galbo."

"What?"

"I'm afraid…" He tickled his throat with his finger, like only Mom might get it. Obviously the bomb had blown off Dad's head. "We air lifted the victims to a special surgical center, but I was able to re-animate only your husband, whose condition made him the perfect candidate for a new top-secret program. He can't see, hear, smell, taste or talk, but you do get touch." The doctor put a hand on my dad's shoulder. "His life force is remarkable."

"Luke, *I* am your father," Leo said.

The big guys just stood there, and between them and Leo's comment, nobody was laughing. Even when Dad was alive, he and Leo hadn't had the best relationship.

"Yes, well, we'll leave you to get re-acquainted," Dr. Wajsniac said. "Have a nice day." You could see he wasn't a bad man, just not used to dealing with people who thought their husband/father was blown up only to find out he's got a helmet instead of a head. We'd even had that nice memorial service, Dad's Kelfton ID enlarged to an 8 X 10, sitting on a bed of flowers on a table at the front of the funeral home chapel. That picture hung in the living room now.

"What are *we* going to do with him?"

The doctor checked his pockets again and pulled out a giant shot, setting it next to the remote. "He's self-sufficient," he said, opening Dad's tie and untucking a black bib from his collar. "Make smoothies and inject them here. Sit him on the toilet and he will go out the other end."

"He's a Frankenstein," Mom said. "*Your* Frankenstein. Klefton's Frankenstein. You won't palm him off on us. We're keeping the insurance."

"Mrs. Galbo, you don't seem to appreciate what a miracle he is. Consider the program that enables him to walk—balance alone is very tricky business. We spent a lot of time getting that right, didn't we?" Dr. Wajsniac tucked Dad's bib back in and fixed his tie. "Or the spinal interface, without which he'd collapse like a marionette."

"Extreme Makeover, Father Edition," Leo said.

"The kids don't understand," Mom said. "He was never more than a paycheck." He was a lot more than that, but Mom was still angry. They used to argue all the time about his never being home. Mom wanted a father for her children. Dad wanted food and shelter for us.

"Perhaps in time I could've created a head prosthesis.... But no, no, I've been told we've had him long enough."

The big guys pushed my father down into the only empty kitchen chair.

"For your safety and his, don't spread it around," Dr. Wajsniac said, going out the door. "There will be quality of life issues, nosey people who don't understand. Say he's missing part of his skull, and there's brain damage due to an IED."

They left us with what was left of Dad.

"Improvised explosive device," Leo said, "in case you were wondering. I'll be in my room."

"They want the insurance money back," Mom said.

The doctor was at the door again, alone this time. "I left my memo pad," he said, shaking his head, but it was in his hand. He tore out a page and handed it to Mom. Then he said, "We watched a lot of late-night TV together," and gave Dad a long last look, like they were old buddies. He said good-bye again. The note read, "If there's a problem, call this number."

The sun sank down, and Mom and Dad were still sitting at the kitchen table. Mom stared hard, but Dad was sure acting like he wasn't going anywhere—a first, I guess. At the memorial service she'd told us that he'd always meant well, that when he'd lost half an eyebrow as an electrician's assistant in Maine or his bottom front teeth on a drill rig in Texas or a piece of his ear to a mean pony when he was a preacher to the Lumbee here in Robeson County or, this last time, got blown to bits washing dishes in Baghdad, he'd always managed to "send home the bacon." Dad left a piece of himself wherever he went, she'd said, but his heart was always with us.

Actually, it was in Epping, New Hampshire where Dad got zapped, but Mom was doing her best.

I went to my room, did a page in my *We, the People!* workbook, went to the kitchen for Hi-Ho crackers, made up other excuses to check on them. I eyed the remote. Would she mind if I pressed a button? She clapped her hands in front of his visor—made me jump! Dad didn't move, though. She knocked on his helmet. What happened if he got angry? She pinched the back of his hand like she was trying to pull chicken from the bone. I knew it was probably necessary, but I couldn't watch. If an actor was inside, he was paying a big price. Leo stayed in his room all this time.

"What if he has to go to the bathroom?" I finally had to ask.

Mom stabbed a button on the remote like she was flipping off the TV. Bam, Dad's head hit the table.

"Mom!"

"Well, I don't know! Do you see any instructions with this thing?" She examined the remote this time before aiming it. Dad's head popped up. She pressed another button and he stood straight up, the chair falling back.

"Maybe you should get your brother. He's much better at gizmos."

"Leo!" I shouted.

Dad started turning in place, like one foot was nailed to the floor. He went around a few times before Mom figured out how to stop him. He turned right, toward the wall, then left. Several bumps later, Mom had him clear of the table. She was sort of laughing but not really enjoying herself. I think she wanted to show any secret cameras that she was nobody's fool. Dad wasn't going anywhere without her.

I reached up and flipped back his visor: 120, 90, 88, 24. Were those good signs? I was following along, trying to figure them out when Mom drove him right into the doorframe. The readouts flickered.

"You're purposefully trying to wreck him!"

"Sorry," Mom said, tears in her eyes. "This takes some getting used to."

I took his hand, the one with the stubs. I was the one who'd passed the Red Cross babysitting course, who knew the stories of Dad's injuries, who loved him best, so I should be the one to take care for him. "I'm taking him to the bathroom myself." I pulled, and he came along like a little kid.

"What's going on?" Leo asked in the hall.

"Dad needs to use the bathroom," I said.

"You're going to pull down his pants? This I've got to see."

Mom barged in, pushed me out of the bathroom, and slammed the door.

"He's a robot," Leo said. "A failed experiment Klefton is

dumping on us. I bet once they realized he wasn't military, they wanted to scrap the whole project."

"He's still our father."

"I take that back. He's a big vegetable, and we're the Osbournes. This sucks."

There was peeing, a lot louder than Leo's ever was.

We were a family again.

After Mom adjusted, she got to be pretty liberal about what I put in Dad's smoothies. Nothing seemed to upset his system, except for the Bunny brand vanilla ice cream and Windex shake Leo gave him. (Mom made Leo clean up the blue vomit that came out the nutrition port, which cured him of trying to poison Dad again but didn't stop him from throwing lit matches at Dad's helmet.) So I got out my Red Cross book and read about healthy snacks like carrots and ranch dressing or cheese cubes and grapes cut in half. I would spread a napkin over Dad's port and poke the syringe right through.

"I'm running out of ideas on what to feed Dad," I told Mom one day as she was pouring over bills at the kitchen table. Dad's death benefit meant Leo could buy every computer gadget ever invented, and she'd been letting him. "He'll support me in my old age" was her reason.

"I have no idea," she said.

Everybody likes pizza, so I blenderized a Gino's Supreme, mixing in a little plain yogurt to improve the consistency. I recorded the readouts before and after, but there was no change.

A few days later Mom said, "Remember, your father loved his sweets. He had a knack for finding those old stores where they sell candy by the barrel. He brought back some peanut brittle, and I chipped this tooth."

Mom had it capped, but you can still tell.

She put two fingers to her lips and plucked them away. "Savor this morsel from the wider world," she said, imitating him. "Taste what I have tasted. Ow!" Dad was sitting on the couch, and I hoped he knew we were laughing *with* him. He really did talk like that.

So I took over the shopping in order that I might feed Dad greater variety. I visited all those sections in the Food Lion— Mexican, Italian, Oriental, Kosher (Leo had his expenses and I had mine)—and I'd serve us the normal form and Dad the liquid version. Mom would ask, "What's on the menu tonight?" and Leo would say, "More beans, I hope," and we knew he was talking about how Dad let it rip constantly. (What the lit matches were for.)

Of course, with all my good home cooking, Dad started to develop a spare tire, so we bought a Schwinn 835P treadmill, and Dad took right to it. ("The zombie never bought me a Schwinn," was Leo's stupid comment, but how could he complain with a room full of computer junk?) You only had to put Dad's hands on the rails and feet on the track and hit the switch. He could go and go—there was definite improvement in his coordination. Leo would sneak in and turn up the speed, and I'd find Dad sweating and panting but hanging in there, pulse 160, respiration 30. I'd help him through his stretches and Mom would stick him in the shower with a plastic bag over his helmet but not too tightly.

One time after his shower, Mom said, "I've got it from here," and led him in his 100% Egyptian cotton terry robe to the bedroom and closed the door, and after that Mom spent more of the money, which was getting low, to buy him a black leather motorcycle jacket and chaps with fringe, and she stopped using the remote.

Of course, the suit not only accentuated his thighs, which had noticeably increased musculature, but also his upper body, which was lagging behind. So Mom came to the expert, and we consulted catalogs and ended up trading the Schwinn for a top-of-the-line cross country machine, the Alpine Intimidator, and Dad started working his arms and chest. (If Leo had said something, I would've put Dad's hands around his neck and showed him how to squeeze.)

Once Leo kicked back the kitchen chair I was about to sit Dad in, and he landed right on his butt. "I'm not going to let you kill him," I said, helping Dad back to his feet.

"See if he can get up by himself," Leo said.

I gave Leo a dirty look.

"Sock puppet," he said.

Worried that maybe Leo was right, I took Dr. W. up on his note—a lot.

"How's our patient?" he'd ask when I called.

"Weight 84.09 kilograms, output 50 cc so far today. Regular BM, doctor."

Because I kept excellent records and used metric, he always wanted to know. He also liked to hear about me and Mom and Leo and how we were getting along. It like amazed him that we could function at all. Six weeks after Dad's return, I had a "spontaneous gesture" to report.

"I swear he reached up to scratch his nose."

"How far did his hand rise?"

"Ten centimeters, at least."

"You don't think it was a spasm?"

"No, doctor. It appeared controlled."

"I see, I see. You better let me talk to your mom."

It was exciting to think Dad was getting better and Dr. W. wanted to question Mom about it. She was on her bed with her community college books, preparing for the day the money ran out, but I also think she just liked having them open around her. I handed her the cordless.

"Yes? What is it?" Her face fell.

"What?" I asked. "He doesn't think it's significant?"

"Where?" she asked. "There's no hope then?"

Mom hung up. "Let's have a family meeting. Get your father. Leo, too."

We'd never had a family meeting before. Mom had to threaten to break down Leo's door before he'd come. I sat next to Dad on the couch and held his hand, the bad news mostly for him, I was guessing, and because it was the only way I could stay seated. Leo stood in the hall.

"The good news is they found Dad's head," Mom said. She

looked at us and not him. "Somehow it survived the blast. The bad news is it's unsalvageable."

I squeezed his hand.

"And this is what a family meeting is for?" Leo asked. "This kind of useless information?"

"They didn't even realize it was his head. Someone had put it on a stake in the sun for a long time. Dr. W. says the damage was too extensive."

I felt a cry starting to come on. Dad squeezed my hand back.

"Shish kebob brain," Leo said. "Sand blasted."

"Shut up!" I told him. Dad squeezed even harder.

"Dr. W. says there's no re-attaching it. He said to give up this hope, which I didn't even know *was* a hope until for those few seconds when I thought we'd get back the rest of your father. I guess I have been waiting for his head to show up. But we've gotten back all of Dad we're going to get, and I don't even know if he would've wanted us to have this much. It's not like they asked him." Now she looked at him, but it was like he was a piece of furniture. "I've homework to do." Mom wanted to cry in peace.

Leo stepped toward her. "You can remarry, Mom," he said. "You can move on."

She shut her bedroom door. Dad's grip was getting painful.

Leo turned toward me. "This family was headless a long time ago," he said, giving Dad's helmet a nasty slap and going to his room, too.

More surprised than sad, I pulled my hand out of Dad's. It was like he could hear.

One night, I heard Leo talking to someone in his room.

"How again?" he asked. "OK, I see them."

I heard latches snap.

"Mother of mother boards." Leo's voice was different, not all defensive. "The green connectors? Uh-huh."

I got up and whispered through his door, "Leo, let me in or I'll scream my head off." Our bedrooms were at one end of the trailer and Mom's at the other.

"Go away."

"I mean it."

I heard the snapping sound again and he opened his door. Dad was sitting in a chair in the middle of the room, kind of like in a barbershop, but with floor-to-ceiling computer stuff.

"Who are you talking to?" I asked.

"Nobody."

"Hello, Lisa," a tiny voice said, and at first I thought it was Dad, speaking through his helmet. Then I saw a headset on the desk.

"That had better not be some kind of cell phone," I said. When I'd asked for one ages ago, Mom had replied, "What for? You expecting lots of personal calls? We can't afford it."

"It's wireless, retard," Leo said. He put on the headset, listened, said, "She'll ruin everything," and handed it over.

It was Dr. W. "I've been helping Leo with his father," he said. "I think you'll agree your brother is very angry."

"Yes, doctor."

"He needs these sessions, Lisa."

"I know."

"So with your permission, may we proceed?"

"I'll monitor his vitals." I gave the headset back to my brother.

The snapping had been Leo removing Dad's helmet. He took it off again.

"What are we doing?" I asked. It was weird to see Dad without a head, no top there at all. It dangled behind him on some wires.

"I got the idea from the Intimidator's monitor. Body temperature will indicate different emotions. We just need a way to read them."

"You think Dad has real emotions?"

"We'll have to find out." Leo took a new helmet out of a box I noticed had "K & K" on it. The new helmet didn't look any different.

"This one will tell us what he's feeling?"

"Hold," he said, and I held the new helmet while Leo's hands went into Dad's neck. He pulled out a tan wafer-thingy and replaced it with a silver one. He unplugged the old helmet and plugged in the new.

"Now what?" I asked, putting the old one in the box.

"Uh-huh," Leo said into the headset, looking confused. "I'll have Lisa do it"

"Do what?"

"Hug him and tell him you love him."

"Hug him, like around his body?" Typical of the stupid brother syndrome, Leo could switch Dad's head but not hug him. I pushed Leo aside, knelt down and gave Dad a hug. "I love you," I said. Dad was pretty stiff. "What's supposed to be happening?"

"There should be a change in his helmet."

"I love you, I love you," I said, pressing my heart against his.

"Bogus," Leo said after a couple of minutes. "It's a total failure."

"Is that what Dr. W. thinks?" I asked.

"Yes, sir," Leo said, hanging up. "He said to keep trying."

A few days later K & K was back at our door, but with another man in Dr. Wajsniac's place. This man, Mr. Farrar, was with the two big guys from the first visit.

"How's your father?" he asked, making himself comfortable at the kitchen table. Right away I knew he didn't care.

"Total vegetative state. Major degeneration of the synaptic pathways," I said.

"Sounds like you know your physiology, young lady. May I see him?"

"There's nothing to see. He's among the animated undead." This was one of Leo's terms.

"I'll get him," Mom said. Since the day she'd learned his head was a goner, she'd kind of given up. She and Dad both went around in a trance. She'd stopped griping about K & K or worrying about the money.

"My daughters are home schooled, too," Mr. Farrar told me as we waited. He was probably some kind of spy and knew all about us—or *thought* he did. That's when I decided I was going back to the junior high. I'd find the other girls who lived in trailers, whose fathers worked odd jobs or were at Fort Bragg and we'd fight back.

It took Mom a minute to retrieve Dad because he'd taken to wandering from one end of the trailer to the other, ending up behind a door or in the closet or standing in the tub or in front of a window. Mom stood him before Mr. Farrar, who turned his chair out to take Dad's hand. The big guys moved in close.

"Good circulation," Mr. Farrar told them. He opened and closed Dad's visor. He pulled out a stethoscope and listened to Dad's chest. "A machine," he said. "You do excellent work, Lisa."

"It's not work," I said. "He's my dad."

"But an Alpine Intimidator and living tissue do not a father make, do they?" He folded his stethoscope. "Who would've guessed the soul resides in the head and not the heart?" He caressed Dad's hand, stared into his visor. "It was to be the helmet of salvation."

While he was doing that, I noticed a glowing red spot, like in those commercials for non-aspirin pain relievers, on the back of the helmet. Leo walked into the kitchen, and I noticed he saw it, too, a real migraine.

"What's up?" he asked.

"I finally meet the infamous Leo," Mr. Farrar said. "How highly Thaddeus speaks of you."

"K & K wants the spinal interface," Leo said.

"Merely to make a copy. There's but one." Mr. Farrar looked at Dad with a lot of fake kindness. "We'll return him even better than before."

"Don't let them, Mom," I said. "They had Dad once already." The red spot was getting bigger and brighter, spreading around the helmet. I wanted her to see it, but she was staring at Dad's lunch smoothie.

"We'll never see him again," Leo said. "They're liars."

Dad's headache was hard to miss now. Mr. Farrar put both hands on the helmet and looked it over. "The customization…your idea, right, Leo? Most impressive." He snapped his fingers, and one of the big guys handed him a remote just like ours, which was under the couch or someplace. There were dark prints where Mr. Farrar had had his hands on Dad, and they looked painful.

"Leave him alone!"

"Permission for what?" Mom said, snapping out of it.

"He's doing a tremendous service to his country."

"He already gave one life," Leo said. "How much more service do you want?"

"Leo, I understand your reluctance to release your father, but he's property of Klefton and Knute. We don't need permission."

"I'm wondering how a terrorist got his hands on my husband's head," Mom said. "Inside the Green Zone. Then staked it in the sun. What haven't you people told us?"

Mr. Farrar ignored her, pointing the remote and firing. Dad didn't budge. "Did you check the batteries?" he asked.

The big guys nodded.

"No matter. He's easily steered."

"Yeah," Leo said, "that's what they did to those government contractors. They save that treatment for black-op types, not dish...." And Leo looked at Dad, and I looked at Dad, and I'm sure we were wondering like Mom what Dad had really done all those times he'd gone away.

"Whatever he did for you, he's their father," Mom said, turning to face Mr. Farrar. "You can't have him."

One of the big guys put his hand on Dad's shoulder, but Dad grabbed it, and the big guy dropped to his knees with a grunt. The other big guy tried to break Dad's grip on his buddy but couldn't. I heard bone crunching.

Dad's helmet was now very red, like hot-burner red. Otherwise, he was his usual low-key self.

Mr. Farrar looked fascinated. "Shoot him," he said.

Leo said, "Go ahead. You'll fry your precious interface."

Mr. Farrar pointed at me. "Shoot her."

The second big guy pulled out a gun, but Dad grabbed it and started squeezing, hand and all. Really, they shouldn't have stood so close. (But then our kitchen isn't very big.) Now both big guys were on their knees. The first big guy used his free hand to punch Dad, but where could he hit and still hurt him?

Then he pulled out his pistol.

"Mom, lunch!" I shouted, and she understood exactly and slugged him in the head with the heavy glass pitcher full of pureed chicken salad. The guy went out like a light and the puree sprayed all over Mr. Farrar's suit. You could make out tiny pieces of lettuce and parsley. Everything kind of stopped at the sight of it.

"Now get the hell out!" Mom screamed.

Mr. Farrar considered his shirt, which looked like it'd been puked on, and the two big guys, one out cold, the other soon to be due to sheer pain, and Mom, Leo and me, and then my father, standing before him in full leathers, helmet a ball of fire.

"Further violence won't be necessary," he said. "I've seen enough. Young lady, if you wouldn't mind."

I backed up Dad, who didn't let go but dragged the two big guys to the door, where I touched his hands and he opened them. Mr. Farrar and the conscious big guy helped the unconscious one out. They drove off, Mr. Farrar behind the wheel, looking thoughtful in a way I didn't trust.

Leo said, "Did you see the mood helmet? Dad was so pissed!"

After that, Leo kept Dad in his room for a week. I had to leave their meals at the door. Then Leo called a family meeting and asked Mom and me to sit on the couch.

"Mom, Lisa, I want to present the new Dad," Leo said. It was good to see his helmet again. Leo flipped back the visor.

Dad looked out with a kind of neutral expression. He blinked. It was his face.

Mom went, "Oh." I took her hand. It was like the picture on the wall had come to life.

He narrowed his eyes at her. He looked worried. He blinked.

"I installed a monitor," Leo said. "Scanned his ID photo. There's also a tiny camera reading your faces—the same recognition technology they're using at airports. Say something, Lisa."

"Hi, Dad," I said. I waved. His eyes turned on me. He blinked.

"Smile, you're not smiling."

I smiled and Dad smiled back and, oh my God, the tears poured out, because it was his face, *his* smile, like when I got home from another bad day of school, and he'd be sitting at the kitchen table with Mom, and he'd say, "How's my Lisa, staying beautiful?" I kept squeezing Mom's hand, and she let me squeeze real hard.

"I programmed his expression to register his mood. He'll also respond to your expression with an appropriate expression of his own."

"Cool," I said, barely able to breathe. "Awesome."

Dad's eyes got real big.

"What do you think, Mom?" Leo asked. She hadn't really said, and Mom was the determining factor.

"It's amazing, baby, but...."

"Smile, Mom," Leo said. "You'll see. Tell Dad you love him."

The black was draining from Dad's helmet. His video face was going pale, too.

"Dr. W. called," Mom said. "K & K will be back. He said Mr. Farrar will take your father and turn him into a weapon."

"They can't again! Dad'll *weapon* on them."

"Dr. W. said we should say good-bye."

"Just *let* them take him?"

Mom didn't say. She just looked real sad, so Dad did, as well. So we all did, except Leo, who didn't yet understand what "good-bye" meant.

Late that night, I heard Leo talking in his room again. "Yes, sir," he said, and I knew Dr. W. had called and my brother was taking the toughest call he ever would.

Dad so enjoyed that car ride we took about a week later. I would reach over the seat and touch his shoulder and he'd turn his helmet toward Leo and me, and he'd be just beaming, even though he hadn't been looking at us but out the window. It was a long drive, high into the North Carolina mountains, the reception bars on my glitter-pink Cu-T with touch screen and 5-meg camera sinking away one by one. (No loved one of hers was ever going to be out of touch again, Mom had said, and I didn't argue, even though that was the last of the insurance.) We swung off the road and took a couple of tire tracks to Dr. W.'s cabin. He said he would come later. He wanted us to have some time alone.

We parked and walked Dad through the trees, Mom holding the new special remote that had just an on/off button. Leo had built it, but Mom said she ought to be the one to use it. On top of the mountain we found the clearing with the log bench Dr. W. had told us about, where he liked to sit and contemplate. We squeezed onto it and held hands and just enjoyed the view and being together. You really could see for miles up there. Now and then one of us would lean forward to check, and we were happy, Dad's helmet as blue as the sky.

Susan Woodring

Ballenka

As a little girl, I often followed my father to the back of the store and down the thin-carpet steps to snoop among the mannequin parts in the basement. I was very small—barely thirty inches tall at the age of five—and I couldn't see into the green canvas bins. Instead, I saw the bins from below and imagined the broken lines and odd angles of flesh-colored plastic limbs coming out the top, over my head, were the boughs of magical trees. Trees made from mannequin parts.

Once he selected the mannequin pieces, a jumble of arms and legs, middles and heads, he hefted them onto his shoulder and carried them up the stairs to the main floor. I scampered quietly behind, watching as he hauled his load to one of the display windows. He whistled while he twisted and popped the mannequin parts together. The legs screwed into the smooth, bellybutton-less torso which bloomed into breasts, shoulders, then tapered away, the thin, high neck, the bald head, the unblinking eyes. He dressed her, arranging a silk blouse on her shoulders, his thick, freckled fingers plucking at the fabric. He buttoned and smoothed, then pulled a tweed, pink-weave skirt up, over her legs, her hips. He zipped it in the back, turned her around, blinked at the doll under his hands. Stepped back, appraising. Eyes closed, as reverential as prayer. He dropped a wig of glossy reddish hair on her head and fitted her toeless feet with high-heeled sandals, cherry-colored.

He pronounced her beautiful.

Without breaking his gaze, he said to me, Someday, she will be yours.

96

He meant the mannequin, lovely and calm and forever-still, and the store. The whole grand palace. Maybe he also meant Main Street, bustling below, and, beyond that, all the houses, every street, every car trundling along. Perhaps every beautiful thing. The store was youthful and prosperous then, forever fixed-in-place, like the mannequins, and my father believed he owned all of these things. In a sense, he did: for Daddy, beholding a thing was a means of possessing it.

This is heaven, he said. He nudged a wisp of hair out of her eyes. He caressed her shoulder. You, he told her, are a dream.

Behind the department store, downtown Ruby dropped off into a field of scratchy green maintained by the county, and beyond the field lay our house, a shack made of rough-timber and stapled tar paper. Beyond that, finally, the woods. There was a slow, deep creek there, and then more woods—woods all the way to Tennessee, the old ladies said. But I dreamed there was a different kind of woods deep inside. Just beyond what we could see. An unreal woods. One made of plastic body parts, topped with hairy Spanish moss blown in from the southerner climes. The air inside the plastic woods smelled humid and salty and warm, like the beach. The wind whistled thinly through the shiny, flesh-colored trees. When it rained, the mannequin hands cupped the water.

He had always been the display man, years before I or any of my sisters were born. The store was fashioned to look like a Georgian mansion and Daddy put a mannequin, sometimes two, in every one of those windows. From the street, we looked like a house of dolls. It has been this way since the beginning, my mother sighed. She had once been a great beauty, delicate and pink-skinned and blonde. But she had given each of my sisters a portion of her looks, piece by piece, until by the time I, the youngest, was born, there was nothing left for either of us. My mother's face was drained of her beauty, her skin yellow-gray, pebbled, her body too thin, somewhat awkwardly pieced together at the joints.

My sisters, all much older than I, grew up, married, and left, and by the time I was five years old, scampering after Daddy into the basement, there were only the four of us left: Daddy, Mama, me, and Ninny Dee, my father's mother. We each had our designations within the store. Mama tended the cosmetics counter and sold jewelry. Ninny Dee, ancient thing, waddled among the racks of nubby cotton and nylon in lady's apparel. She kept a pin cushion strapped to her wrist and a measuring tape draped around her neck so she could provide on-the-spot alterations. I sold ladies' intimates and kept the gloves display case, hopping on and off and up a system of step stools and rolling ladders, me scrambling up to the counter, punching the buttons on the register. Daddy, the manager and owner, dressed the mannequins and sold shoes.

We were Finch's Department Store, at the top of Ginger Street in Ruby, a college town in the mountains of North Carolina. Our store was the glory of the downtown region. College girls and society matrons came in on conveyer belts, dolls to be dressed. We fitted them in cocktail dresses and ball gowns, pearls. In those days, the old, rich ladies summering in the mountains came in to test our stockings by touching them to their tongues. Real silk, I was told, tasted like dirt, or greenish; it tasted the way tomato vines smelled. We had real, dirt-scented silk. And rounders of airy pastel satin and deep gold and black and red Spanish velvets. We stocked white gloves in every size, every length, from everyday shorts, where finely knobbed wrists were exposed, to above-the-elbow formals. Our ladies' arms were rendered perfect and white, like candles.

It was around this time, when white gloves were still in fashion, when ladies came in wanting Alabama silk—taffeta—and all-weather, space-age polyester, when my father was happy, a renowned display-man genius, when my mother, beauty just vanished, yet tilted her face forward a bit when talking to a man, as if she were offering him something, in the time after my sisters had left, before I grew to be nearly three feet tall, that I, flouncing about in the real woods, discovered my creek thing. My *cetacean* from primordial times. My bright-water, cow-eyed beast.

It happened on a Sunday, when the store was closed. I stole away, as I often did in the rich, busy days of my childhood, and pressed as deep into the woods as I dared. Picture me: small enough to hide in a thicket of weeds, dry, scratchy hair like straw, pink, freckly face. I was rough, like a thing dug from the earth, me the diminutive girl who sold slippery, white underclothes—*heaven*, my daddy had said—tumbling now, unhindered, into the trees.

I came to the gold-bottomed, gray-watered creek, and though I'd been there a million times before, it was now that I saw it. *Him*. My water beast. He was an amorphous dark thing in the water, a liquid thing, pliable and huge; he took the shape of the creek bottom and only his eyes came staring at me from above the water. Startled, I held fast a moment, several steps away, until finally, drawing courage, I took a few steps towards him.

Eyes like sorrow, my monster. Ancient, large and round and hurting. An enormous, sleek, rubbery body, mammalian and ocean-going. Misplaced. My Ballenka cared for me from the very beginning. From that first moment, me, the tiniest, scrappiest, ugliest thing, he loved me. He saw me and loved me and made himself visible to me. Later, he explained it this way: I had eyes to see, ears to hear.

In his soundless way of talking, invisible currents emanating from his tender brown eyes, he said: Sit. I was too afraid to speak, but I did as he told me. I found a rock nearer the water. We said nothing more for a while, and finally, me so curious, only half-scared—I sensed my creek monster was there to love me, those *eyes*—I touched my naked foot to his back. He made his gurgling sound, said, *Ah, child*. And with those words, in an instant, all my fears were dispelled.

I spoke aloud then, whispering into the shivers and sighs of the water trickling through, across the bare-hard cold of the creek-bed rocks. I asked his name, told him mine. He wanted me to keep my toes on his back, barely submerged, he of slippery, sea-mammal skin, purple in the bright of mid-day, deep slate as the sun slipped away. I rested my feet on his thick-skinned coolness and leaned back, into the sand. He said, I am eighty-four million years old. Oh, I said. That is very old. I was a simple-hearted child.

There was a story Daddy liked to tell.

Once upon a time, he was a boy, dirt-poor, riding on a train. The train clicked down the tracks east towards the coast. Daddy slept. He dreamed of the lumpy green mountains behind him rising up, then bowing down, curling into themselves. It was the way of my father's dreams, always. Everything in the natural world shifted in size and shape, everything melted, sprouted upwards, downwards, the sky compressing into an acorn in his hand, the scrubby insects from the dirt swelling into gods rushing through the clouds like the wind.

When he woke, a youngish businessman in a green suit was standing in the aisle of the train at my father's elbow. He was holding a bottle of champagne by the neck, his own hand gripping the back of my father's seat to steady himself against the sway of the train. May I sit? The man asked. My father was fourteen years old, on his way to visit his ailing grandfather, the passing landscape full of timber yards and small towns huddled around the train junctions. Furniture factories burping purple smoke into the air. Backyard clothing lines. Not knowing what to say, he nodded to the man, and when the man settled into the seat and opened the bottle of champagne, popping the cork off into his open hand, my father took a swig. The champagne was in a green bottle with a green label which, in turn, had gold lettering. When he drank it, it was crisp and sweet on my father's tongue. The man was called Mr. Cooley, and he loved the mountains. You're a mountain boy, he said to my father, and my father nodded though this didn't seem necessary. Mr. Cooley wasn't asking him anything. Instead, the stranger settled back into his seat and stared down at the bottle in his hand.

I have a small fortune to dispose of, the man said. My father nodded again, still not knowing what to say. The man cleared his throat, took another drink of his champagne, offered my daddy some more. This time, Daddy declined, and Mr. Cooley chuckled, then asked, What are your ambitions in this world, son?

In that moment—just like that—Finch's Department Store was conceived. Daddy opened his mouth and out it came: I want to own a department store, he said. I want to fill it mostly with women's goods. Lovely things. I want, he told the mythic Mr. Cooley, a character I spent much of my growing up imagining, I want silk and pink chiffon. Where had my daddy, the son of a lumberjack, heard the word chiffon? Silk? What did my daddy know of silk?

But Mr. Cooley, who swallowed the rest of the champagne in a single draught, who slumped down in his train seat and smiled lazily—greasily, my father would later describe the rich man's smile, dark and slick and fleshy—said he could tell from looking at him, my father in his dungarees and best shoes, that he was a man of promise. That Finch's Department store would come to be exactly as my father envisioned it. The stranger, drunk on the champagne, jostled by the train, nodded once then drew his checkbook out of his green jacket pocket.

I returned often, me sitting at the creek, pointed toes stroking his rubbery flesh. I leaned back into the sand, bright sun exploding in little blue zigzags against my closed eyelids. We went on this way for years. For the longest time my creek monster, my Ballenka, asked nothing more of me, only my abnormally tiny feet on his slick, monster back. *This*, he said, is true love. Only that we see each other, only that we touch.

After a number of years of good fortune and easy living, once the store began to thin a bit, to outlive its old glory, Daddy began to worry Mr. Cooley would return. The start-up money, he said, had been a gift, but he couldn't settle his mind, not now that sales were beginning to slip. Mr. Cooley, he was certain, would return to collect on his investment. Daddy fretted, his hands working the air like he was dressing an invisible mannequin. That's how much the store meant to him—he couldn't make himself stop. My mother, who suffered more and more from a number of pale infirmities—

weak blood, she claimed—kept a half-dozen doctors on a string.
They met her in the back room, where the coffee was, and laid
their bare hands on her back to feel the in-and-out of her breathing.
Daddy, still sculpting mannequins in the air, asked me, Who gives
that kind of a gift? Is there anyone who would truly give such a
gift and expect nothing in return?

As I grew, turned eight, nine, ten, every thought I had, near or
away from him, I spoke into the bovine gentleness, the perfect
roundness—just above the dark water—of my Ballenka's eyes.

At the store, that season—fall—the fashions changed quite
suddenly. Overnight, it seemed. One day, open-toe patent-leather
sandals were in fashion, and then, before the season was even
finished, thick-heeled pumps with garish gold buckles, avocado-
and mustard-colored, were in all the magazines. Unearthly orange.
Our customers wore them in from other places, requested we order
some for them. Daddy hated these, said they were intrusive. Too
much, he said, but he obliged his customers, and when it came
time to put his orders in for spring, he ordered coarse blue pantsuits
in wicked cotton. Neck-ties for women. *Cowboy* boots. He had to,
he said. Of course, Daddy, I answered him, and wished I'd held
back a single black velvet dress. For myself, in case I ever grew.
Inside my mind, I told Ballenka: I hate those shoes. I wanted the
red pumps we used to sell, the little black ballet shoes with bows
on them. But they were gone. Obsolete. Also gone: shirt-waist
dresses in periwinkle-blue, frothy ball gowns, velvet capes. Instead,
come April, our windows were full of Daddy's girls swathed in
faux-bohemian batiks. Pioneer-girl calico. Knit plaids. Billowy thin-
cotton blouses. *Jeans.* Never, I told Ballenka. I would never dress
my dolls that way. I meant Daddy's mannequins.

I know, my Ballenka said. *Little whale.* He sighed in his silent
way. He closed his enormous brown eyes for a long moment, then,
rolling back his heavy lids, looked at me. I know, he said again.

In the winter the snow on the streets glowed soft blue under the
moon. Daddy's favorite stillness. Ninny Dee looped purple ribbons

with tiny silver bells attached around the store, the windows, the racks, the jewelry counter. It was only now, in the coldest months, that mama smoked, her standing by her register at closing time to total her receipts, a thin white cigarette gripped at the corner of her mouth. She blinked down at the papers. Daddy swept the floors. Ninny Dee kept watch at one of the windows. Daddy said, The end is coming. Mr. Cooley is coming back to collect.

My Ballenka began pulling his bulk out of the water. Just shifting closer, leaning on his side onto the sand. His broad shiny back glistened there in the weakening sunshine. Big, but not as huge as I'd expected, now that more than just his eyes, the dolphin-ish slope of his head, were exposed. No longer distorted by the way light moved through water. He didn't take the shape and size of the long, deep creek, as I had once believed. Instead, he was like a ballooned walrus. Still: huge, *huge* eyes. The sky turned orange now, just past supper, when I stole away to visit my monster. I lifted my skirt and extended by bare legs across his back, my head back, hair trailing in the dirt. I grew tired, lying there, talking the way we did, our consciouses connected, the sun sinking further down, further away, the earth spinning me and Ballenka and my daddy and my ill, once-pretty mama away from it. The orange going purple, the trees around us dark, and then, finally, everything was black. Often, I slept the whole night out there, my bare legs spread across my Ballenka, his cool slickness growing warm and comfortable beneath me, me sinking into his soft mass.

Ballenka, I told him once late into the night when we were both asleep. Now, at night, it felt that way, like we communicated right through our sleep. My soul meeting his there in the open darkness. The store is in trouble, I said. Ballenka, I whispered-thought, the end is drawing near. No more pearls.

My monster, slow beast, was quiet for a long moment. He had told me how very old he was, how many geological ages he'd survived there, in his creek, undetected. How few people he'd seen over the course of his millions of years, and that I was now the first to see him. He made his gurgly-happy sound: this was because I loved him. I loved him before I knew him. That, he said, is the miracle of you. You love without seeing, my monster told me. You love without *knowing*, he said.

Now, after a long pause, he spoke. No more pearls, he said at last, agreeing with me. He sighed, the heaviest sound in the world, my monster and his sea-lungs. His tremendous, primordial, unknown size.

Before my father disappeared, he and the others—my grandmother, my mother and her weak heart, her clutch of doctors—he told me there was a part he'd left out. Something he hadn't told me about the man in the green suit on the train. The one who appeared just after my father had dreamt of mountains dissolving into pools of dirt and grass. Mr. Cooley, holding that green champagne bottle, everything about him green, everything lush, everything wealthy, prophesied on my daddy's life. He said, You will have five beautiful daughters and one who is freakishly small—as tiny as a thimble. The five beautiful daughters will leave you one at a time, each to a prosperous, handsome husband, but the last, the tiny doll of a daughter, she will stay until the end. When *she* leaves you, everything will be gone.

The man in the green suit had been young and vigorous when he'd sat down, but now, a few hours into their journey, his hair was streaked with gray. There was a long, deep line between his eyes. The aging man frowned. When he spoke again, his voice sounded gravelly and worn. He said, But I *do* see the promise in you, mountain boy. Despite the unhappy end he'd just assigned him. He shrugged. By the time the train reached the coast, where my father and Mr. Cooley parted, Mr. Cooley's words were thin and faintly warbled, as if they'd come whistling through a hollow, reedy place. He bid my daddy good-bye, issued his good wishes, his gnarled, age-spotted hand touching the brim of his hat, and he was gone.

At the end, the university students only came in for Halloween party props and lipstick. To walk crookedly through the racks and elbow each other into the rounders of geriatric cardigans. Seer-sucker raincoats. Broad-strapped mammoth-cupped braziers, still my department. On the streets, we saw them dressed in our old things. What they'd found in the thrift shops and altered, cutting the old, cloud taffeta dresses into vests to wear over their grunge-band t-shirts. They wore the ugly polyester pants we'd sold when I was an adolescent, in shades of brown and mustard, with thick-soled combat boots from Germany. On their ears, the girls and boys alike wore tiny brass chains attached to doll-heads—other castoffs, I imagined—and there were chords of telephone wire wrapped so snuggly around their throats I worried their faces would go blue right in front of me. These were deadly trends, the decapitated Barbie doll heads, the telephone wires. We passed them, my mother and I, carrying the money bag down to the bank at closing time or going out for a quick sandwich, and I sometimes caught the gaze of one of them. Our eyes locked then flicked away. I barely came to their waists; they didn't know if they should look at me or not.

Finally, during Finch's last days, the very old were the only ones who shopped without irony in our store. The blandest and chalkiest of the old ladies, crows picking at the racks, narrowing their peeked little eyes at our goods. They tested the fabric between their thumbs and forefingers; it has always been this way with the old women, with the cacklers, the ancient ones who used to run our silk stockings through their teeth. The same women who, years earlier, had smiled glumly at my father's girls, clucking their tongues at the expensive fashions. They had shepherded their own daughters inside. Pearls, they used to tell them. Your father—though he doesn't know it yet, wink, wink—is buying you a string of pearls.

Once, my father, in a last-ditch effort to keep me, offered to order me a new set of clothes. Silk, he said. Crushed red velvet. A pantsuit, a dress, a robe. Whatever I liked.

He lifted me onto one of the mannequin's pedestals in front of the east upstairs window and took Ninny Dee's old tape measure in his hands. The measure was inaccurate now for the times it had been inadvertently snipped while my grandmother held it across the hems and sleeve cuffs she cut, for the years it had been pulled across so many bust lines, so many waists, its intricate, vinyl-covered fibers stretched. I looked down through the window and into the street. I looked beyond, saw the old dripping mountains of my daddy's boyhood dreams. Daddy put the measuring tape down a minute before starting. He cupped my elbow. He touched my chin with his fingers. I looked up at him and, for an instant, I saw in my daddy's pale-lashed blinking eyes the exquisite gentle intelligence of my Ballenka. We stood looking at each other for a long time, frozen, before I finally jumped down and skipped away, my dead grandmother's measuring tape undone in a limp pile at my daddy's feet.

I sunk completely into my creek monster, my *little whale*. I lay my entire body across his slick, rubbery-purple back, and finally I was completely absorbed. Inside him. We slept that way for years.

When I awoke, rousing inside Ballenka's striated, pink-muscled belly, I put my hands against the spaces around me, testing the boundaries of my balloon-like confines. I couldn't tear my way out, but instead, I pushed up, hard, straining through the bubble-gum pink darkness, and emerged in a hiccup. The fresh air smelled like rain. It smelled the way real silk tasted. I caught a clip of buoyant air and rose. Leaving my Ballenka sleeping there by the creek, I drifted above, across the fields.

I pressed deep into the woods on the other side of the creek, swooping through the boughs of the tall trees, breaking out into the blue. Perfect blue, gold sunshine canopy, and below, there, the forest I'd imagined as a child. It was real now, beneath me: the plastic tree-limb trees, a woods made of mannequin parts, hoary Spanish moss strewn across like clumps of tangled hair. I reached out to touch the shiny, flesh-colored arms legs, the toeless feet, beautifully tapered long-fingered hands, the scratchy, plentiful moss, but my own hand passed right through them. I couldn't touch. I was bodiless, a spirit. I'd left my human body inside my monster, sleeping below as darkly and completely as death. We were one flesh now, unbroken.

My spirit withdrew. I climbed out of the plastic forest, flew east, towards the store. For the longest time, I hovered above, afraid to enter. Already, I could hardly remember my corporal life. My life of changefulness, of nylon panties and, years and *years* ago, of fine white gloves. Finally, I swooped down, glimpsed through the dark windows, naked, half-assembled mannequins inside, my father, fellow spirit, adjusting their poses, dropping invisible blouses over their shoulders, brushing their invisible warm-cinnamon wig-hair. He smiled at the naked, bald-eyed mannequin beneath his hands. You are a dream, he said. It was a moment we'd lived many times before, in ages past. We'd been here, at this window, an infinite number of times. This, my daddy said, is heaven.

I came inside through the window, swept past my father. Mr. Cooley was there, standing a few paces back at my mother's old jewelry counter, the glass top cracked, webbed intricately across, the trinkets inside long gone, only a few errant price tags left, the back of an earring, a dropped necklace clasp. He waved a hand at me. *Hush.* Lifted his gentle, huge eyes at me, my creek monster taking on the liquid shape of a dead man's spirit, said, Child. We were together now, one flesh in the creek, one spirit in the department store, remembering our human lives. We'd repeated this scene a million times, me and my monster. Everything that had ever happened had happened again. The life of the entire planet on a loop, the two of us watching it. I drew close to my Ballenka—he smelled of the plastic forest, of the sea—and together, ghost to ghost, we watched my father piece the parts together. We saw him exhale, touch the shoulder of his newly-wrought mannequin. He stepped back to gaze at her, to take pleasure in what he'd created.

Jedidiah Ayres

The Adversary

And it entered into his body like water, and like oil into his bones.
— Psalm 109:18

Since word of the spread of Tecumseh's scourge, its destination and inevitable path made obvious, panic had seized the wise and charlatanism the foolish. Repentance, as ever, sucked hind teat.

The witch had been holding ceremonies. Sacrifices. Poultry mostly. She blessed and hexed for a fee and she'd send and deliver messages across the Stygian chasms separating worlds. All of her arts were brought over from the Dark Continent and she practiced in the woods under penalty of death by the Law of Moses, which the Reverend Chalfont Avery was charged with upholding now in the face of Armageddon. He had been present at her execution, a willing and enthusiastic participant, but the kicking feet of the blasphemer brought not the warmth of God to his soul, so they torched her home to mirror the flames of Hades and on them he warmed his hands.

The fervor for purging had hit an all time high by Avery's measure and every arcane law of superstition was dusted off and seemed to shine with special relevance to the here and now because where was God? The Northern Philistines were paving a scorched path directly to them through autumnal Georgia; a season of wrath to match any Biblical account and Avery, try as he might to conjure himself Moses descending Sinai and meeting the orgy 'round the golden heifer, could not escape the thought that he was merely Balaam leaving behind his conversant ass and extending a hand of brotherhood to the Angel of Death, I have started without you.

When Chalfont was a youth, and the Apostle Naaman Mosley had first called him into the service of an acolyte, he had felt the Spirit's breath in his own lungs as if awakened from dormancy. The Apostle had recognized the gift in Chalfont, called it out of him and set into motion a great and dynamic ministry. He had performed signs and wonders and prophesied, cast out dark spirits and baptized thousands. They had come to him from a hundred miles in every direction for the words of God that fell from his lips and the touch of power in his hands and Chalfont Avery's name was known all the way from Athens to New Orleans.

But now he was empty.

The authority that had coursed through his speech and actions, that he had eventually mistaken for his own and then behaved in such a manner with encouragement from a silver-tongued politician whose appointment to the state senate Chalfont had helped secure with enthusiastic endorsements and inspired editorials printed in the papers, that authority was null. Once established, the partnership with the government man was influential and lucrative, but in retrospect Chalfont had been intoxicated with infallibility in tandem with the way the sway of his gift had faltered. But no one saw it when he had led a prayer on the battlefield at Chickamauga and thoughts of his own political office would not have seemed outlandish, though by Kennesaw Mountain he was mostly gassy fervor and untethered moral authority.

That untethering had come up in the public rebuke given to his face in front of his own congregation by the Apostle who'd traveled all the way to Athens to deliver it. But by that time his spiritual dipsomania had claimed Avery's senses and he was not inclined to listen to the contrary and jealousy-fueled ranting of the dispossessed and failed. Now, the Apostle's last words to him hung between his ears filling the depression where once the Spirit had resided and spoken an unstopped spring of wisdom for him to translate into language and wield his flesh around. "He has removed his Spirit from you and changed your name to Ichabod."

The Apostle had collapsed afterward. His body dropped like Ananias or Sapphira right there in the sanctuary, and he had taken the voice of God with him. From the pulpit Chalfont had watched him fall and felt closed inside with the void by the ornate, church doors as soon as his mentor had expired. He had known the sensation at once, though it was terribly and utterly new. Soon he would see Sheol and know not the bosom of Abraham. He was a goat now, and would no more be so had he horns protruding from his forehead.

Members of the church had rushed to the Apostle's side. A man named Barnabus had knelt and taken the Apostle's crown into his lap. He had placed his own head near the peaceful face on the floor, then looked up and confirmed to all what was apparent to Avery, The Apostle was dead.

Chalfont had retreated immediately to his hometown of Gilboa sighting grief over the death of his dearest friend and had no sooner arrived than the wrath of God had rained in cannonade fire upon Atlanta and the faithful in exile had changed its significance from New Jerusalem to Babylon in their pleas and railings against the tide of reckoning washing toward them from the north and west.

The territorial Marshal had arrived at his door with a proposition—clear the scrub, dispose of the brush and the fire will not consume us for His judgment falls on the just and the unjust alike, but while Lot's wife became salt, even Nineveh was spared—and Chalfont had been deputized and slain with fervor to catch the neglectful eye of the God of Abraham, Isaac and Jacob, but His jealousy was attached to the Babylonian whore with her mouth round Chalfont, and He remained aloof.

Wrath seemed preferable to indifference and Chalfont had set himself up to be noticed.

On the first morning of the third week since his return, he woke with a start well before dawn, fleeing the same vision that had pursued him through his sleep ever since they'd stretched the African witch. In the dream, she'd addressed him as Simon Sorcerer and not Simon Peter. Worse, he had answered her as if it were his given and accepted name. He woke now, slick with dread, and collapsed there on his knees beside the bed. He cried out to the power of God, but received no deliverance and no answer. He rocked and heaved and hyperventilated in his fervent pleading for a divine word, but none came.

At last he rose, stumbled out of his house and crossed the packed earth to his stable, fed and dressed his mare for light travel. Within the hour streaks of grey had shot through the cracks in the black and he discerned the final crest of the hills that led to the place where she'd lived and died.

The tall grass gave way to loamy pathways from the dismantled livestock pens to the blackened place where the cabin had previously stood. An acrid, smoky smell hung in the air still, held low in the atmosphere as if it were a place that the wind avoided. His horse whined and Chalfont dismounted. He led her to the outermost edges of fence and loosely tethered her there, before continuing toward the tree at the center of the property.

The fire that had reduced the cabin to a collection of charred sticks huddled like spent matches about a roughly rectangular lot had not touched the tree, which stood defiantly an iridescent green even in winter against the scorched, ashen earth and bloody haze of sunrise spreading across the sky. The tree's shade was vast and inky and once beneath, he trembled slightly. Near the trunk, suspended a meter off the ground, the nubs of her feet, ravaged by wild beasts, were just visible.

He remembered now the way she'd cried out upon seeing him. Her bewilderment at the transaction gone sideways turning to stark fear and then bright, black anger, outraged by the devil's betrayal. She cursed him in a dozen heathen languages and licked blasphemy at him betwixt her fingers before he'd claimed her tongue. The posse dropped their pretense and held her down and stripped away her clothes. She'd struggled beneath them, in agony or ecstasy it was difficult to differentiate. Franklin had clapped his hand over her mouth to halt the profanity and he'd looked over his shoulder in hesitation at Chalfont, who'd nodded, then turned his back on her as they'd sawed away at the pale, flapping appendage, finally claiming it in a tug that nearly choked her dead before she could be hung proper. The meat had fallen beneath the spot she'd kicked above while the horse tugged and eventually left her levitating over, angry tendrils atwitch, searching for a suitable spot in which to plant themselves and grow again.

As he approached her now, he caught movement in the circle of yellowing grass beneath her corpse as if the tongue had found purchase and sprouted. What he saw when he was near enough to discern stopped his breath halfway in so that he choked when he remembered the mechanics of breathing again five seconds later. An abominable trinity of cottonmouths writhing there, tangled in a blind sex frenzy. So thick was their lust that they were not disturbed by him and did not yield their ground, and he was forced to kick them with his boot from the spot. They landed in three separate spaces six feet apart and were immediately released from her spell. They slid and slipped away, seemingly ignorant and uninterested in what had preceded. He looked up at her face, eyes gone with the birds, fingers curled into hooks. He took out his knife to cut her down thinking to bury her and end the tormenting nightmares, but as soon as he'd laid his hands upon her body, he swooned.

There was a pressure on his right side so that Chalfont turned his head and beheld the fingers of his hand wrapped tightly around a squirming serpent which coiled likewise around his arm and attached itself by teeth to his throat. A smell as if crimson had an odor crept up his nostrils and lodged in his brainpan and he heard tongues that he could not interpret. He stood atop a hill and saw from the western horizon a spill of smoke rolling over the land and the hungry lick of flames, emissaries of the inferno they announced blacking out the sun. From this advance a sound eventually arrived, percussive and predatory. The beat a rumbling, grinding rhythm like the turning of a great mill that split off into scores of separate swells becoming a crescendo.

* * *

Upon waking he saw that the body lay beside him in the grass and that it was, even then, being fed upon by bold scavengers who took no notice of him. With a start, he rolled to his feet and decided to let the animals claim her. It would be peace enough as her type was likely ever to know and if it brought him a restful night of sleep and a firming up of his bowels, so much the better.

Through the night he slipped under sleep a dozen times and came up again clutching his breast a few minutes later. His attempts to shirk the visions were futile and his efforts with the witch's body in vain. Even if he had succeeded in burying her, he knew it would have been fruitless. He cried in frustration and seethed in anger at his heavenly father who had abandoned him. The day found him limp and spent, gaunt and so pale that he had been turned away by the gaggle of terrified collaborators he led. They agreed he looked like death and they would go the day without a lynching.

He had retired back to his cot where he'd fallen into a more substantial sleep, which produced a dream that he was not able to escape this time.

He stood in the pulpit before his congregation waiting for the Apostle to speak. But his mentor stood mute in the aisle, glaring at him with the perspicacious sight of The Spirit. Chalfont thought to appease him with words, but felt his insides shudder and a weak belch escape his mouth accompanied by a smell like spoiled eggs. The Apostle imperceptibly flared his nostrils and tilted his head. The intensity of his gaze Chalfont could feel on his face like breath. A tickle on his upper lip caused him to touch his fingers to his visage. Upon taking his hand away he studied it, and found that there had begun a nosebleed. He tried to sniff back the trickle of blood and then clutched at his nostrils. He then began to blow trying to dislodge the obstruction inside. After three brief attempts to clear the passage he felt the object work its way out of his airway and pinched it between his forefinger and thumb as soon as it had cleared the orifice. He saw the Apostle drop his gaze and heard the congregation gasp as he pulled the worm from his proboscis.

He held it up to inspect and it began to twist and wriggle in increasing agitation.

Chalfont dropped the creature and gagged. He coughed and spit three pale maggots onto the floor beside the worm. The front three rows of the church stood and the Apostle turned and began to slowly walk out of the room. Chalfont cried out after him, but no words came, only a great slug which he extricated with his hand and cast away with such force that it rocked the wood podium he stood behind. A woman from the flock screamed and the Apostle disappeared through the chapel doors which shut with such certainty behind him that everyone in the congregation had been startled and turned around to regard them.

A steady and increasingly heavy procession of crawling things erupted from Chalfont's mouth and clogged his nose and trickled from his ears, though he remained standing and never stopped trying to speak. By the time a great serpent had slid from his anus and was poking its head out the leg of his trousers the church was in an uproar. Women were crying, men were cursing and some were trying to force open the doors that would not budge.

Though unable to breath for the flow of herpetological beasts from every aperture of his body, Chalfont began to laugh.

It turned to sobbing as soon as he woke.

The witch's house had a Persimmon tree growing right through the middle, a hole in the floor and roof, and Avery wondered at its significance. Set into the woods in no cleared area either by laziness or design, there was a small vegetable garden preceding the door and separated from the forest only by a creaking gate, which Chalfont entered through, announcing his presence to the seer, though he wondered if that were necessary.

He'd left his shiny star at home and worn unfamiliar clothes in an effort to hide his identity. A man of God by reputation still, and a semi-deputized vigilante, he was more concerned with concealing himself from the hoodoo darky for fear she'd clam up and refuse his patronage than that some Christian citizen would be scandalized by his consorting with evil spirits. His desperate need to touch a spiritual dimension again had brought him this low; demons and niggers, but the ethereal plain it would be.

The front door opened while he was yet five strides away, and he beheld the Negress, impossible to say how old, but a handsome woman with a healthy build. She was dressed in rags, but they were clean and her hair was occupied in twisted together ropes and given to adventurous trajectories, around her face and over her shoulders, once sprouted. She tucked her chin and cocked her hip slightly, resting her left hand upon its sturdy form and gave him a look that was part enticement and part challenge. Chalfont stopped his advance and held up his right hand in greeting. She gave him a good once over and glanced about the woods quickly before jutting her chin out and addressing him. "What you want?"

Chalfont reached slowly into his breast pocket and withdrew his wallet, stuffed with Confederate currency and showed it to her.

The African scoffed. "Ain worth shit nohow." Chalfont smiled and pulled out a bag of gold and silver coins from about his waist and tossed it to her. The woman caught his pouch and inspected it disinterestedly. "What you want?"

Chalfont paused. What exactly did he want?

He settled on, "I want to talk to God."

The witch laughed a low and pitying chuckle, and Chalfont felt anger rising in him. "Go home and pray, Christian. Jesus be listen to you." She tossed the coin purse back to him and began to close the door, but Chalfont stepped forward and put his foot in the gap. The door stopped on his boot and she increased the pressure, but he held his place. When he saw her eyes again, the change was marked. Gone was any pretense at demureness, her teeth were bared and her voice was a hiss. "Go away, Christian."

But Chalfont pushed back, "I want to talk to the dead."

The woman continued to push, "Is an abomination, dey kill me for it."

Finally, Chalfont withdrew his foot and the door slammed in his face, but he did not leave. "I want to pay you for it." He listened to the still night. "Please." Suddenly, the anger was gone and it was replaced with desperate fear again. His eyes watered and his breath caught in his chest. "Please, I have to."

The door creaked and opened a few inches. Chalfont stood still, holding his breath. From inside the tiny house her voice came to him as if from the depths of a cavernous space. "Come in, then. Close the door behind."

The cabin did seem much larger inside than out, even crowded as it was with exotic and profane paraphernalia. Pairs of chicken's feet tied together hung from nails in the wall, folded paper parchments of ground spices that he could not name and at least four different types of mossy vegetation hung in cascading formations from pots suspended from the low ceiling.

A modest fire barely burned in the corner, but filled the space with a pungent smoke that made Chalfont's eyes water and his breathing deliberate. "Sit down," came the voice, but he still couldn't place her in the room. He did find a seat fashioned from a tree stump and sat upon it before a small, but heavy wooden table. Chalfont turned his head to find her and saw nothing behind him, but when he faced forward again, she was seated opposite him on the other side of the table. "Now den," she took his hand in hers and the touch was like ice that traveled up his arm and through his torso putting out a fever that he had not even noticed was there. "Tell me who it is you wan to speak wit."

"Naaman Mosley."

If she recognized the Apostle's name, she did not show it, only concentrated on his touch for a full minute. Then she selected some dried leaves and ground them into a powder. She removed a water pot from its place over the fire and strained it through them, making a tea which she offered to him and told him to drink. He did. Chalfont had never tasted anything so bitter, but the warmth of it seemed good in his stomach. He felt a ball of calm, ringed-round with a coat of prickly sensitivity begin to grow inside him. He sprouted goose flesh and an erection after a few minutes.

She sang softly or chanted a mumbly, indistinct parade of sounds that made no sense to him, but held an atonal cadence that he fixed on and learned and went with instinctually, anticipating its rise and fall. She continued repeating her song and watched him closely for some time, and he tried to do the same and hold her steady in his gaze, but she kept shifting suddenly to the far edges of his periphery, slipping the grasp of his gaze, though he was quite certain she was sitting still. Finally, he bent over and vomited a thin, black stream of tea and bile onto the earthen floor and when he sat up again, she closed her eyes and hummed a single low note.

She held that note for an impossible term, increasing the volume and intensity until her eyes popped open to reveal only white beneath her ocular hoods. The humming stopped and she began to hyperventilate with quick, shallow, noisy breaths. And then the voice of the Apostle came forth from her lips.

"Who is calling me?"

Chalfont didn't know what to say. Finally he stuttered, "It's me, Naaman. It is Chalfont."

The witch's face contorted in a mask of terror and she produced a strangled cry, which she held quite independent from the Apostle's voice. "Why have you disturbed me?"

Chalfont quaked and fell to his knees. He pressed his forehead into the floor and cried. "I am so greatly distressed. The enemy advances unabated, sacking and burning and destroying everything and God's spirit has left me and does not answer."

Now the witch formed words of her own with great effort. She hissed at Chalfont, "You have tricked me and come to kill me."

"No," said Chalfont.

"Yes," she said. You are the one murdering mediums."

The Apostle spoke to the woman through her very own faculties. "No harm will come to you on account of this man. He has been brought here to degrade himself by the hand of God."

Chalfont sobbed. "Why? Please help me. Tell me what I should do."

The witch's voice was now merely a faint whine underneath the sound of the Apostle. "You should prepare yourself to die, Chalfont. You have made yourself the adversary of God and He has considered you chaff and delivered you into the hands of your enemy. Tomorrow you will surely die."

Then the Apostle left. The witch's eyes rolled back into her face and she looked at Chalfont with terror and rage. The terror receded some and the rage evaporated at the sight of Chalfont lying on his side on the floor, his head resting in a pool of snot and tears. She got up from where she sat and began to prepare food.

He emptied all his strength to cry in ten minutes and lay quietly awake on the floor until the woman brought him the meal she'd prepared. "Sit up," she said with the gentle firmness of a mother. Chalfont obeyed and she fed him spoonfuls of a brothy soup that sharpened his senses to the point that he finished feeding himself.

When he had eaten enough, she helped him to his horse and once astride, she said, "I'm sorry."

"For what?" asked Chalfont.

"I'm sorry that it wasn't better news."

When he returned home, he did not stable his horse, but set her loose to do as she pleased. He spent that night, his last on earth, listening to the trickle of scout riders passing and prophesying the great current of the devil's flood.

With the dawn came smoke from the fields of his neighbor and the great creeping swarm of Shermanites, their image slippery through the heat. Avery set his own barn alight and strode toward their army with his a pistol in his hands, his bible left to the flames. As they began to separate into distinction and he discerned the countenance of their fore, he called out, "Blessed is he who comes in the name of the Lord," before shooting himself through the brain.

Blood Brothers

I first met Ray up in the mountains at the I-40 rest stop, where I used to go to meet guys sometimes. I found him leaning against a wall, albino-pale, with these watery fish eyes. We messed around in a stall for a bit, and then he told me to meet him at the red truck out by the ravine.

In his truck cab he produced an uncapped light bulb. Below us roared the Pigeon River. "Keeps you up," he said, "as in hard," and I yelped when it burned my fingers. He barked a joyless *heh*. We got to talking: his wife was Sheila and mine was Lisa, and his kids were Ray Jr and Angel and I don't have kids. After we were too high to talk I guess I told him to start driving. Two days and we were in Tulsa. Now it didn't matter if the bulb was hot; the burn felt good. Sometimes he'd smack me upside the head, which we both liked. He asked what I'd do if he broke my arm.

"Go to the E.R."

"But to me."

"Break yours back?" He nodded like it was the right answer. He knew this stuff; so did his wife, who had more sense than to do what Lisa does, which is report me missing. Six days after I'd met him we rolled back into Pigeon Forge to find the cops at my place. "Drive," Ray growls, so I did. Halfway up the mountain he pulled a sheath knife out and held it to my throat. "You've been filming me," he said. "I don't care if it's your wife that called; they've seen the film."

He was giving off this ugly leaden smell, and I could feel blood draining down through me, through my neck. "Thought it was you filming me, Ray."

119

Ray looked behind us as if back toward Oklahoma, lowered the knife, and said, "Makes you jumpy."

"Lisa, she was the one."

"If you're a cop, you're a brave cop."

He motioned for me to face him. When I did, he put the knife to my wrist and cut it open. My yell came out as a *heh* like his laugh. He did the same to his wrist and pressed them together. He said it was a Bowie knife from the Indian Wars and we were blood brothers. I said, "But what about..." and the loons hollered and he said if you catch it, you get the flu, is how you know.

At his house, a log cabin, a girl was jumping on a pogo stick. "Call if you get the flu," he said, but then I left without his number. Back home Lisa ran barefoot into the mud and beat her fists on my chest. "I don't know," I told her as she carried on, "I woke up an hour ago outside the hospital." Next thing I knew I was in the paper, which upset my ma. When I was twelve, she'd had a heart attack, and from that day on she went to church and never smoked. Lisa always told me "you're lucky your ma's so young" but truth is she wasted it on that heart attack. Anyhow she arranged for tests, my ma, and I set off meaning to have them, but on a billboard I saw a girl with black teeth under the words "Meth Destroys." Something gunned in me like a jake brake and I decided to find that girl, get her high. I went to Ray's and he walked out in his boxers followed by his wife. "You slept?" he said.

"That was a week ago."

"So you slept."

"Can I come in?"

There was this Cherokee in their house, and the four of us messed around while a pit bull watched from a cage. Next thing, the Cherokee was leading Sheila and her kids away. "I'll never see those kids again," Ray wept.

I wondered if I'd missed something. "Is there more?"

"You want to be my bitch?"

"What do you mean?"

He reached over, stuffed my balls between my legs, and said, "My bitch." We drove across to Cherokee and played slots until we had cash to start cooking again. He had me wear Sheila's panties when I went out for Sudafed. Law makes you buy just a little at each store but it adds up. So does the money, and we were broke when AT&T offered ten thousand to let them put a tower on Ray's land. They disguised it like a pine and birds nested in it like it was any other tree. Ray would come upstairs with these water bottles and say go for a bike ride. In my bottle cages they sloshed around and mixed up while I tried to climb Mt. Cammerer. Each day I got a little closer to the top. The day I made it, there was a green cloud like an anvil moving across the valley. It hit me with a spray of mist and then I was opening a bottle, offering it my mix. A car sped by and I chased it down the slope and caught it, flipped it off, sped home to Ray.

"Where's the other bottle?" he said.

I seized up: I'd left it at the summit.

"You drink it?"

"Can you drink it?"

"Well, you'll die."

At first I believed I really had. "Guess that's your punishment," he said.

"Don't you care if I die?"

"There's more of you where you came from."

That kind of emptied me out, which he saw. "Just kidding," he said after a while.

"So you think there's more of me."

"Well, just go fetch that bottle."

Folks would come at all hours. There was a deputy who bought five hundred at a time and we would listen to his cop radio. One day, honest, a dude reported his wife had pissed in his coffee. "Call and say we'll report to the scene," said Ray. We piled in, Ray and the cop in front and me behind the grid. The siren screamed as we sped across town. At the man's house Ray told me, "Stay." I tried to get out anyhow but I was locked up. Whole hours passed before they came out chuckling.

"What happened?" I said when they got back in.

"Filed a report," said the cop, and then a look passed between him and Ray. "Did he think you were both policemen?" I asked as we drove off.

"Maybe you should beat him with your stick."

"Replaced our sticks with Tasers."

"Tase him, then."

"Why don't you?"

"Won't fit through the bars."

"I'll pull over."

We veered off onto a dirt path and then Ray got out. "Stand up," he barked at me. A wild boar was watching us from the woods. It had come to protect me, but Ray would tase it too. Stay back, I begged it in my head, and Ray lifted the Taser and at the last moment, as I shook, he said, "Just kidding."

Things got better. We drove to a cockfight and busted it up, then went to another and won some cash. There was a guy the cop said was Dolly Parton's brother. He smoked with us and Ray said, "Where's your big tits," and when he got mad Ray pulled the Taser out and tased him and we took off. Then the cop got to talking about Dolly and her songs. He said she'd written more songs than anyone in history, thousands upon thousands of them. "I admire that," he said. "Me, I've written ten, maybe twelve songs."

I said, "I bet she'd be having fun if she was here with us."

Instantly I got scared they'd tase me for being a pussy again, but they must have liked it, because she got in and rode along with us for a bit. She'd done this deal with the governor called Imagination Library where poor kids get free books. It was on all the billboards, and Ray's kids had read some of those books. Why she was in the car, she'd found out Ray'd stole them from her. I thought to warn him but I looked up and the next light was her road, Dolly Parton Parkway. The cop thought his own fingers were the ones that hit the signal, and I froze and next thing we're at Dale's, but if I tell you we watched Dale screw his girl and took his cash and pistol-whipped him, you won't see how I sat frozen while that bitch stared through me and steered us toward hell. She wanted to show me what happens in hell when you give AIDS to your wife. She had it from her husband and that's what her songs were about. She wouldn't kill us just yet cause it would all be there waiting, come time.

I woke up alone with a note by the bed that said "Call your mom." I drove to my ma's and let myself in to find her at her table, writing. "Knock knock," I said.

"Hi," she told me without looking up.

"You copying a recipe?"

"Where's Lisa?"

"Is it your brownies?"

"Who's Ray?"

"He's my blood brother."

I could see she wasn't meaning to bake brownies. There were some medical instruments lying around—a blood pressure cuff, a stethoscope, a roll of gauze—along with several pill bottles, and I figured she was intending to put Ray out of business.

"Lisa called here not fifteen minutes ago."

"So then you know where she is already."

"She told me she was at Shoney's."

I can't explain. It was like all women were inside her right then, cussing me for not wanting them hard enough. I got to feeling she was a cop. I said if you're so naïve, why'd you have that heart attack? I knew I just needed a hit, so I headed back to Ray's, but no one was home. For the first time I went down to the basement and turned the knob. There he was in a chair, wearing a shirt and nothing else, waiting.

It took me a second to scream. I jumped and hit my head on the low ceiling. "Remember when you told me you'd break my arm?" he said.

I shook my head, stammering *sorry*.

"How would you do it?"

"I know you don't want me down here."

"Tell you what, go buy some whiskey. Here's twenty bucks."

I stumbled over myself running back upstairs. I knew he'd call his buddies, which was too much to bear. I sped through the holler full of dread. I ran over a dog and decided it belonged to a boy who told his dad my license plate so now I'd have to go back the long way while Ray screwed the whole state.

The clerk was a lady I hadn't seen before, with icy eyes the color of blue Kool-Aid. "Back for more?" she said.

"Huh?'

"Run out?"

She was nodding at me, her curls bobbing along with her nods. "Of what?"

"George Dickel?" she said, and I thought, maybe I've got a twin, maybe Ray's doing him right now and drinking his Dickel.

"I'm an only child."

"I'm the youngest of ten."

As she stared through me, I felt more fear than any soldier at war, but she rang me up and let me go. On the way home I passed the tooth girl and tried to count my teeth by feeling them with my finger but I lost count. I recalled finding Lisa on the phone with her friend, giggling about me. She thought Ray was part of her plan but the joke was on her, because I was in love, and I decided right then to help him get his kids back.

I carried the bottle in, unscrewed the cap, and presented it. "Look," Ray said, gesturing out the window behind me. I turned and saw the pine woods across the road.

"You mad about the basement?" I asked.

He shook his head. "While you were gone," he said, "I realized I hate you."

I figured he was joking, so I laughed. "That's what a pussy you are," he said: "I say I hate you and you laugh."

I set the whiskey down and asked what was going on.

"I got you screwed up and screwed your marriage up and never used a rubber and your ma won't talk to you, but you like me."

"So I should hate you?"

"So I should hate you?" he mimicked in the high voice of a pussy.

"What do you want me to do?"

He shook his head. "Nothing. Stay here. I'm gonna go find my wife."

He descended the porch stairs to his car. "Stop," I called out, tearing up, and he pointed at my tears and said, "There's the problem with you."

After that things started to change. I started wanting to lose my teeth out of just spite. Weeks passed. I looked around for the billboard girl and found her in Knoxville. Her name was April and she took me to see some folks. There was a dude that hotwired cars, who drove me to the Atlanta bathhouse. He left after a few days but I stayed on. Your body needs dreams but you can get them while you're awake. Every few days I bought something to eat from a machine. One day I got sick with fever chills, then I got better. When I finally went outside, two weeks had passed, because that was how long my car had been impounded. The bill was twelve hundred dollars, which meant it was totaled. I walked to Big Lots, found a truck, and hotwired it, which was the start of not being a pussy. The sun was rising as I reached Miami. I looked in the rearview and saw the weeks of fasting had chiseled my face, which led me to meet some folks. We drank rum in pools and sang Auld Lang Syne and one day I froze up and realized it had never gotten cold.

"It don't," said Vince, the silver-haired guy I'd been hanging with, but there'd been others before; now suddenly we were alone.

"What month is it?"

"March," he said.

"I had a birthday."

"Well, happy birthday." A grin stretched out from either side of his cigar. I asked if he'd seen my phone. "They turned it off," he said, "remember?"

I felt uneasy as he handed me his. Outside on a deck facing the canal I called the only number I could recall. It rang twice before I got an error message. If I wanted, it said, I could hang up and try again.

"City and state?" said 411.

I had to grip the railing to keep from tumbling into the water. "Pigeon Forge, Tennessee. Dr. Lighter."

They connected me automatically. Each ring was a shock to my chest but I kept holding on. "Doctor's office," said my wife.

I spoke her name. "You're alive," she said.

"Where's my ma?"

"We tried to find you."

"Lisa, come on."

"It was in November, she—"

I threw the phone in the water. The number was on her ID, though. She could give it to the cops. That's what I'm most ashamed of: letting myself think about her ID when I'd just learned about my ma.

I never went back inside. Twelve hours later a sign said *Welcome to Tennessee.* Below those words it said the state was home to Vice President Al Gore, but that had been years ago. I sort of broke down on the shoulder. The cop asked what was wrong and I pointed to the sign. He told me to get on up the road and that's what I did. For months I got up the road to wherever I could. I figured I'd smoke till I died, which would happen when my mind ran out of dreams. All I had to do was quit dreaming. I would drive through the night, and if I started to dream, I slapped myself. One morning I rounded a curve and saw the moon over Mt. Cammerer. It had never risen so late before. I started keeping a list of the things it does. I built up a book of them that could have broken some ground but there was no use so I ripped it up and kept on driving. One of those AM stations was shouting about patience when the preacher asked, What will you miss when you're dead?

It was the stretch where it stops being Dolly Parton Parkway and goes to two lanes. I was overtaking this car. I slammed on my brakes by the sign for Forbidden Caverns. I know how it works in those caves, you go through them together in a group. The whole group gets to know each other and makes friends. What will you miss, said the man, and I looked at the hills and thought, There's nothing I'll miss. Not Lisa, because I can't stand what I did, and not my ma because she's gone. As for Ray, my head sent a signal to my foot just as a semi rounded the bend. I sped up hoping to crash into it. The driver would probably live but if he didn't, I've hurt plenty of folks anyway. I wondered if my ma would be there when I died, shaking her head along with the fucking Lord. I started to cry. My vision blurred and I figured it would keep blurring from there into oblivion, but at the last minute the trucker ruined it by pulling onto some dirt.

That's when I drove to the rest area. I sat there touching myself as families pulled in and their dogs peed and finally a Hummer parked beside me. "You party?" said a fellow in a Braves cap. "I've got tons of room."

His windows had a full tint, so we put down the seats and messed around, nothing special till he pulled a phone out and said, "Know about this?"

"About your phone?"

He swiped the screen and I looked down to see a grid of thumbnail pictures labeled with names. "It's in order of how close they are."

I touched one, and the screen filled up with a guy named Josh. *10 Miles Away*, it said in the corner. "So it knows where I am?"

"No, it knows where *I* am."

"Moon's about to rise." I pointed through the sickly tint of his rear window. Ten seconds later it began to peek above the summit of Mount Cammerer.

"Here's a dude looking for now, and he smokes for sure."

I took the phone and stared down at the inimitable fish eyes of Ray. To appear calm, I stopped breathing. He didn't look so pale anymore. Maybe he'd followed me to Florida.

"Hit 'chat,'" the guy said, and I obeyed. It occurred to me to type *hey*, which floated up the screen in a yellow bubble. Seconds later came the response: 'Sup?'

"Say 'looking.'"

'Nothing,' I wrote instead, and then 'Horned up' chirped onto the screen. The guy grabbed the phone from me and typed with both hands. I watched the moon rise and shrink while my gut did the opposite. "Dude says come over," he exclaimed, and I looked into the future and saw my teeth fall out of me. It would happen that day in 2012 when everyone thinks the world will end. What they mean is the world will carry on, but for each person something important will fall out of him.

"I'll tail you," I said, pocketing the phone, knowing he was too high to notice. I followed him until we came to an exit ramp. As soon as he'd passed it, I swerved off, crossed the highway, and

turned around toward the first clear destination I could recall. I
figured I had until morning before the account froze. The radio
preacher was saying we're made of dust and it won't take much air
for the Lord to blow us away. He said one lung of the Lord is the
size of the world. I pulled into Hardee's and signed on to find five
guys with green dots: Clay, James, Anchovi, Just Lookin, and Kid.
Kid was Ray and his distance was twelve miles. I checked my own
profile: I wasn't the Hummer fellow, but a black guy called Tyrone,
twenty-one, headline reading "Don't fall in love with everyone
you see."

I ordered a hamburger, the first time in days I'd thought of
eating. A long journey faced me. An infinite number of directions
led out from me, and I had to try each one—but suddenly Kid was
eleven miles off. After a minute I hit the button again and it said
ten. I thought of the jack pine and how readily Ray had agreed to
it. He was coming for me and I had no weapon. They handed me
my burger. I thought I might puke, but something in me reached
out and devoured it and I was revved up with gas. I guess that
that's when I began thinking straight. I'd imagined driving in circles,
hunting Ray like a fox, skirting his circumference. I saw now that
the phone was a shield. There were eight miles between me and
his house, and he was eight miles away, but the road twisted in on
itself so many times that it was of no concern to my pulse to go
there.

Back in the car I talked along with the radio to calm myself.
Halfway there the phone said five miles, which was bad, but I
reminded myself it was supposed to feel good not being a pussy.
That's why other guys liked it so much. I gritted my teeth and
pulled up to his house and the phone said seven again. Maybe it
was broken. I used my key and the door creaked open. If he could
see me on his phone I looked like a black kid named Tyrone—
unless he knew to begin with and my mug had a green dot in his
head. That's how it will be in another few years: like now, but in
your head, we'll drive all night just looking for folks in our head.

I felt my way to the basement and plugged in the bulb. It swung
on a cord in front of a mirror in which I saw a St. Andrews cross

and a workhorse. I walked to the closet and swung the plank and there was the knife. Its handle was wood and its blade curved and I'd forgotten what war it came from.

I was climbing the stairs again when my phone rang. Damien Warman, announced the touchscreen, and he said, "Where are you?"

"I'm not telling," I said.

"You two think you can treat me like this?"

I was getting ready to apologize when I remembered this wasn't my phone and a non-pussy would take advantage of that. "Who are you?" I said.

"Screw you, bitch."

"No, I asked a question. If you want to live—if you want to survive another minute of your worthless life, then answer it."

There was a gulp. "Where's Tyrone?"

"Dead. You're next."

"Where is he."

"No, you tell me where you are."

"Downtown Hilton."

"Well, you best get yourself out of that Hilton."

I can't tell you what a thrill it gave me to say these things. I hung up, and then the screen showed the earth in space, the clouds moving in real time. The mountains were inching toward dawn. I guess the camera was on the moon. My blood heated up in anticipation of sunrise. Just as I was about to catch fire, Damien Warman's name flashed across space. To be a pussy was to answer, to say just kidding, so I hit ignore. I found some gin and took a swig and realized the dog should be barking, so I went upstairs to his cage, in which he lay dead.

I had a new message from Kid. "Sup," it said.

"Not much," I wrote.

There was no response, so I looked at his profile: four miles.

I began to feel time slowing down. I went out into the night and ran the knife blade along my finger. It felt intensely strange, and I realized why: I was sober. I pricked another finger, then pricked them all and rubbed the blood on my pants. The cuts all stung. I was so sober I could feel pain. I looked at the moon, which was bisected by the jack pine, and knew on any other day I'd have believed it was broadcasting my thoughts to Ray. I checked the phone again and saw a distance of two miles.

It was curvy those last miles. I had about four minutes. There's a lot you realize when you get sober. It occurred to me to look up "Zeela Tipton 1950-2009" on the phone. I read, "After an illness, Zeela went Tuesday to be with the Lord." I learned she was survived by two brothers and a daughter-in-law. I knew I might meet the Lord soon myself, and I wanted him to know there was some good in me. I typed Lisa's number into Tyrone's phone and wrote, "Ask Dr. Lighter for a blood test."

The noise of a motor faded and grew closer. The phone said 500 feet. I hit *refresh* and it said 700 and then 350, which was about right.

I went in and pulled out the fuses. Through the peephole I watched a single shadow climb out of a car. My pulse was about four hundred. I saw the shadow lurch forward and grow larger. I had read the obituary to help urge myself ahead. I moved from the hinged to the unhinged side of the door. A siren blared for a split second. The last thing before he came in, I looked at the phone, which said zero feet.

The door swung open and his hand reached through the dark. I clutched the knife and plunged it into his arm. It sank easily into his flesh. I pulled it out and saw his eyes bulge as I stabbed again. As the blood spurted onto me he lunged toward me and I held tight onto the hilt. "Sarah," he said as he sank, which is when I knew what that siren had meant.

He contorted away, making gurgly noises. I let go and ran outside. The cruiser window was open, and I could hear cops on the radio. "How do you know a Kentucky girl's on the rag," one of the cops asked, and then they all laughed as the pines heard my phone ring.

I've written ten, maybe twelve songs, I thought.

"Babe?" said Ray when I answered it. "I heard you're back in town."

"How'd you hear that," I managed to say.

"I was on my way to you but I drove into the river."

"I don't live at your house anymore."

"Lisa never answers your door."

"I gave her AIDS. I caught it from you."

"But you never came down with the flu."

"You've ruined my life."

"I have some crystal."

The blue of the light bubble gleamed in moonlight as he told me he was at the S-curve near his house. "I like you," he said, and I told him that was retarded and he said, "I'm trying to say things that I mean."

His front door wouldn't budge. I broke the window with a brick and climbed in and saw the cop sitting up against the door, meeting the Lord. I reached in his pants for Ray's phone. I held it in hand and checked the distance: 2000 feet. A chill went through me then, because Ray had just talked to me on his own phone. It was like Ray had been talking to me from the cop's pocket. I put the phone in my own pocket with the other two. I imagined the phones all talking to each other and to the pine trees. If I was high I might have tried to saw down the cell tower. Its trunk was metal but I'd have made sawdust out of the wrong pine and felt safe.

As I drove the cruiser, I checked my messages: *Sup. Hey stud. Where u at.* One was named Lucifer and he was ten miles away, which I guessed was ten miles down. I passed Dollywood, which is on a back road in a holler, not where you'd expect. I drove deeper into the forest. Finally I pulled off by a precipice where at the bottom of a ravine Ray stood by his wrecked car in water up to his knees.

"There's a way down," he said, pointing to a path.

I left two of the phones on the seat and carried the knife in hand as I scooted downhill. "How are you?" Ray said from across the water when I reached the bank.

"Fine," I told him, brushing dirt off me.

"That's my knife."

"I'll slit your throat with it."

He opened his mouth, then shut it. "The crystal got wet."

"My mom died."

"Mine did too."

"I'm not afraid of you."

"Then get on with it." He pointed to his neck.

"That's the oldest trick in the book."

"Mark's on his way. Call and see."

"Who's Mark?"

"Cop from the dogfight. I made a deal with him: he'll file it as a suicide."

"Why don't you piss off, Ray."

"But it's really what he's coming for."

It was easy enough to look Ray in the eye and still hate him. His eyes were fixed on mine, but that wasn't a problem; nor was I touched by the sound of his voice. I hadn't been prepared, though, for the effect of his breath. It smelled of bourbon and smoke and instantly I was in Tulsa drinking bourbon with him, holding him and thinking he was just a lonely child.

"It's for my kids," he said. "If you had kids, you'd understand."

I guessed there was a fair chance he was telling the truth. "I've been in Florida."

"I like it down there. Took Angel and Ray Jr. to the Daytona 500."

I kicked some gravel into the river. It landed by his foot, and he said, "Remember at the Bristol Speedway, when you thought we were dying?"

I shook my head. "I've never been to Bristol."

"You were lit up back then."

"You were just as lit up."

"But I was aware of it. You, you acted like you were surprised."

I tried to imagine Bristol, which straddles the border of Virginia and Tennessee. I pictured a state line painted down the middle of a street. I imagined fast cars in circles and recalled a race in Mexico where the drivers steered by remote. The cars crashed over and over until I knew the stadium would explode. I dragged Ray out into a country I've never seen. What happened next, he punched me, right in front of the Mexicans. "Now you'll have a black eye for your ma's birthday." He drove me to her house but by then we were in Leo, and she was a Cancer. I staggered inside and found her on the couch with her quilting circle. Those three ladies together weighed less than me, and they sat in a row like sticks of brittle.

"This is my son," said my mother.

I can't account for what came next. I looked down at the quilt, a patchwork maze whose path mapped all that I'd done wrong in her eyes. I saw my house when the bank forced Lisa out of it. I saw her in 2012, dying of AIDS. I saw my ma getting sick and writing in my baby book. It was a list of my firsts, which appeared on the quilt as triangles arranged in a loop. With that loop she was telling me I would never change. "Up your cunt with a plunger if that's what you think," I said, which she must have taken as a response to her words.

I stepped into the icy water and sat on Ray's hood. "I need you alive," I told him, taking his hand, pulling him toward me. He slipped on the algae but I held on.

"You were about to kill me," he said.

"I don't have anyone."

"You've got Lisa."

"I don't want her."

"You want me?"

"You're better than nothing."

He put his hands in his pockets and kicked at some rocks. "That came out wrong," I said, and he looked at the far shore and said, "No, it's true."

Tyrone's phone purred in my pocket. I pulled it out and Ray took it and squinted. "This guy's twelve miles away. Says he's glad I'm online again."

"I wonder what that means," I said.

Ray glanced into his smashed car. "Can you drive?"

I twisted around and looked too. I saw the river roaring around it, flowing into its broken window. Shards of glass from it would reach the Gulf, while others would sink into the ground here. I knew Ray wouldn't change. He took my hand and pressed his fingertips to the holes in mine. The wind blew through me and the river was rising: it was nearly high tide. I could feel the tide even in my blood. That was how sober I was. If the new awareness had ended there with the glass and the blood, I'd have survived it, but I was aware also of being aware. That was the part I couldn't bear. Otherwise I doubt I would have said, "So long as we find a dry bag first." Otherwise I might have gone looking for folks that weren't better than nothing. I might even have told them this story. As it was, I figured I'd keep quiet, because I knew nobody but Ray would have cared to listen.

The Dead Fish at Twenty Mile

I came into Twenty Mile the day Bock Quinn was leaving his store for good. The store was a bait shop a ways down a gravel road that didn't see all that much traffic anymore. The only reason I had even headed down the road myself that morning had to do with Oscar McCullough, because we shared the same last name, and our first names were similar enough that when Oscar was caught having his way with a castrated wild boar penned-up in Colonel Harks' barn in Bodock, Mississippi, on the outskirts of Claygardner County, it was Omar McCullough who was listed in the Wednesday edition of the Bodock Bi-Weekly as being the alleged violator of the animal. The headline read "Backdoor Boar Whore." Or maybe that's what was found the next afternoon spray-painted on the front window of the restaurant where I worked—Mi Pueblo—which specialized in Tex-Mex cuisine, although I was neither Texan or Mexican, but Guatemalan, on my mother's side.

The morning we found the graffiti, the owner of Mi Pueblo, Saul Lopez, told me this wouldn't stand, that he couldn't have folks violating his property like this. I know, I told him. Bueno, Saul said, scratching his double chin, a burly Mexican Jew. He said, Glad you understand, and then apologized for having to let me go as head chef. I reminded him of the fliers the paper had issued that morning clarifying their mistake.

"Si, si, Omar," Saul said. "But see, Omar, my customers don't want even an alleged pig fucker in the kitchen."

I saw Saul's point. Understandably, the last thing people wanted to contemplate when faced with a trio of pulled pork tacos smothered in queso or green chili sauce or both was just how friendly a member of the kitchen staff had been with the hog before the pork made the plate. Had it happened to someone else, I might've understood how the association would cause a restaurant owner to cut his losses. But I was born and raised in Bodock by my single mother, who'd immigrated here illegally to iron shirts and pants for fifty cents and a dollar, respectively, for men like my father, whose surname my mother insisted on giving me, even though the son of a bitch never once had the common decency to acknowledge the result of their affair. Besides being able to crease the hell out of a pair of slacks, about all I knew how to do was cook. Saul was beginning to franchise, starting with a much larger restaurant in the next county. Since I'd been at Mi Pueblo for eight years—started as a bus boy, then a dishwasher, fry cook, and finally settled in as head chef—I was, until "The Incident," as I'd come to call it, the frontrunner to manage the original location. I'd been eight months away from having control of my own menu.

Grief stops being laughable as soon as it becomes your own.

That next night I said to hell with Bodock altogether. There were Tex-Mex restaurants in every direction, some Las Margaritas or Tus Amigos in need of a chef, and so I threw everything I could fit from my efficiency apartment in the back of my mid-sized Chevrolet and covered it with a tarp and headed out. I tried to sell myself on the idea I was pleased with the decision to throw in the toalla: even with control of my own menu, I would never be able to serve, for instance, any variation of my mother's mole sauce on the grounds the dish would read like something the majority of my customer base would use to rid their sod of subterranean rodents.

But it wasn't until I hit the highway well after midnight that I realized I couldn't just go to the next county to find work. Wednesday morning the story of The Incident had hit the AP wires and ran in such regional dailies as the Clarion-Ledger in Jackson and the Commercial Appeal up in Memphis. Back-page corrections followed in the papers' following day's editions, but I'd probably need to go all the way to Bumfuck, Arizona, before any application I filled out, any work history I included, put me right back in Bodock. Barely outside of town and such a profound despair wrapped around me like wet leather quickly drying in the sun or a refried-bean-lined burrito that I began to cry the likes I hadn't since I was a child. First it was just a few tears, but then the water works really came, my body racked with sobs. I alternated between fits of punching the dash and gripping the steering wheel very intensely. So consumed was I in my angry grief that I didn't realize my truck had eased over into the left lane, into the path of an eighteen-wheeler southbound on Highway 54. I remembered the driver bearing down on the horn, my watery eyes opening to see headlights exploding across my windshield like some kind of multi-legged supernova just before I shut my eyes again and jerked the steering wheel towards the highway shoulder in panic.

But before the crunch and explosion of highly distressed steel I anticipated, the horns suddenly ceased. When I opened my eyes again I was alone, swerving back onto the highway from the gravel shoulder just as the sun slowly lifted from the horizon like a yolk falling upwards from a hot skillet. I hadn't slept since The Incident, had obviously and instinctively driven throughout the night and only dreamed the near accident in a brief doze come morning. Not sure how far I'd traveled, I looked at my gas gauge and saw I was running on fumes. Up ahead a wooden billboard announced gas to the left. The station was twenty minutes down the road, and I had to coast the last quarter mile in neutral before easing up to an aluminum shack with the words "Bock Quinn's Twenty Mile Bait Shop" painted on the side.

I pumped the pedal a few times, the brakes ineffective with the engine dead. I was about ten feet past the pumps before the Chevy oozed to a stop. Inside, two men were playing cards. They both looked old, but all I could make of the one with his back to me was the reddish, hay-colored hair and matching sideburns falling from his gray slouch hat. The gentleman across from him was dark-skinned. Not completely black, but mixed. Mulatto, red-boned, etc. He was wearing a white button-down and hanging over the back of his chair was a pin-striped sports coat that matched his pants. A zoot suit much like the ones my maternal grandfather wore in the pictures I'd seen of him in Guatemala. On the table was a fedora with a large feather growing from it. The only other person in there was Bock, seated behind the glass counter. His black hair came to a widow's peak on his forehead and he wore a gray mustache. Even if I hadn't seen the sign outside, I knew it was Bock Quinn because he introduced himself as such.

"What can I do you for?" he asked.

"Need to fill up," I said. A ceiling fan wobbled and hummed as it reintroduced heat and humidity to the place. The shop smelled lightly of dust and old grease. The only light came from the front and side windows, and the few pieces of furniture there announced their presence with elongated shadows cast across the floor: the chair and table the men were dealing cards from, as well as a deep cooler in the back corner I figured the bait was stored in. Some empty merchandise shelves.

"All out of gas," Bock said, "presently."

"There a station further down the road?" I asked.

He looked towards the window, as if there was a billboard out there I'd missed that would announce to us both what I wanted to know. Then, he shook his head. "Not any I know of," he said, directing the fibers of his mustache above his upper lip. "You can always go back out to the highway."

"I'm dead empty," I said and nodded out at my truck.

"My advice then," he said, "would be to hang around for a while. I'm due a shipment of gasoline this afternoon anyway. In the meantime, you're welcome to something to drink," he said and rummaged around beneath the counter, brought up two bottles. "We've got Kentucky bourbon, and rye whiskey, of the Tennessee variety. Some moonshine as well, but it's probably too early for that."

For me, it was too early for any of it. The last thing I wanted to do was get liquored up and wait around here for God knows how long for gas. But it seemed I didn't have another option at the moment. My truck wasn't going an inch farther.

"Wouldn't happen to have any coffee, would you?" I asked.

"I'll get some brewing," he said and squeezed by a half-parted curtain hanging in the doorway to what I could tell passed for the kitchen. This sense of dread settled in on me just then, something that had happened or was going to. To distract myself, I watched the card game unfolding out of the corner of my eye. The half-black guy retrieved a small stack of cards from the middle of the table and shuffled them around with the cards in his hand, then laid them all face up on the table in various sets. They were playing Gin or Rummy or the variation of the two. I noticed then the yellow facings and rank insignia stitched to the sleeves of the old man's coat, which I recognized as mounted infantry only because of the Civil War reenactors who one Sunday afternoon a month would track their mud-caked brogans into the restaurant after a long weekend of recreating Brice's Crossroads or the Battle of Bodock itself or any of the other handful of battles that had taken place in and around Claygardner County.

I was still admiring the reenactor's outfit when Bock appeared from the kitchen then with a cup of coffee in each hand. "Don't worry about paying me," he said when I reached for my wallet. "Been looking for an excuse to make a pot anyway." He pointed at his only customers. "None of them drink it."

The black man pointed at his glass. "Bourbon's better for hangovers."

After I'd taken a sip of the chicory-flavored coffee, I turned back to the Civil War reenactor. "Your uniform's authentic," I told him. "What's the name of your reenactment regiment?"

"My what?" he said.

"Your reenactment regiment," I said. "What's its name?"

"The shit is a 'reenactment regiment'?" he said.

I realized my mistake. The man was obviously a hardcore reenactor, judging by his gauntness and hollow eyes and the antiquity of his uniform. Even the local cavalry buttons on his gray, almost-butternut-colored wool-jean double-breasted shell jacket were tarnished with age, an effect the Bodockian reenactors achieved by soaking the buttons in their own piss all night.

Something about a chemical in the urine oxidizing the metal. Such staunch proponents of history found the term 'reenactor' to be offensive, instead opting for 'Civil War interpreter' or similar designation, if you will. As I was trying to explain my mistake, I saw Bock begin shaking his head in much the same way you do when you want the person talking to cease doing so. But it was too late.

"That is the most goddamn absurd thing I ever heard," the old man said. He turned around in his chair then and, once he was facing me, crossed his legs. His pants were tucked into scuffed black boots that came up to his knees. "What would be the exact point, my boy, of recreating battles when there are more to fight?"

The man was doing a good job staying in character. In Bodock, no one'd ever been able to understand that, while to the unaccustomed eye I might appear part Mexican, I was, indeed, Guatemalan American. When I had tried to explain to my reenactor friends that calling me Mexican was similar to me calling them Yankees even though they were from the South, they kindly informed me such a mistake was a complete and historical inaccuracy. Even then they wouldn't break rank from character while in uniform, except to eat Tex-Mex cuisine in air-conditioning that wouldn't come around for another hundred years or so. But this guy made even those reenactors from the Bodock 155th look like a lot of elementary farbs. I would've been impressed with the authenticity had his tone not made me defensive.

"Because," I said, and looked back at Bock, who just held up his hands at me. "Because who the hell thinks there are Civil War battles left to fight?"

"Well," the black man said, in a thick, Creole brogue. "She-it." He made a slow motion to remove his fedora from the table before sliding his chair backwards.

"The South ain't dead, my friend," the old man said and kicked his own chair behind him into the screen door, knocking the door off one hinge. The chair danced on one leg before toppling over on the porch. Standing now, the man's head was illuminated in the square of light from the front window, and I could see his sock-puppet mouth. He said, "Ambrose Burnside stole these from me—" and pulled at his sideburns "—and so I slaughtered twenty of his men at the Cumberland Gap single-handedly. He saw the whites of these eyes and asked me my name and I told him, 'Michael, the Hand of God Almighty, sent to once again remove the Blue Devil from His gates,' when a stray cannonball from the Yankee artillery ricocheted off the damned earth and found my jaw."

"His name's Leon," Bock said and motioned at Leon with his coffee mug. "Leon Claygardner. Don't worry, he just gets a little worked up sometimes. He cools off quickly though."

As evidence of that point, Leon quietly retrieved his chair from the porch and returned to his place at the table. When I was young, my mother, in an effort to distill in me knowledge of the place I was born, would drive me around Claygardner to show me the historical markers throughout the county. I was familiar then with at least one Leon Claygardner. Colonel Leon Claygardner had founded Claygardner County in the mid-1800s, just before secession. The actual Leon Claygardner fought, among other places, at Chancellorsville, and it was rumored he was even responsible for General Lee's decision to divide the Confederate's already-significantly-smaller brigade against Major General Joseph Hooker's Army of the Potomac, which was twice the size of Lee's North Virginia forces. The man before me was obviously off his rocker enough to honestly believe he was, indeed, Leon Claygardner. But even if I didn't feel sympathetic to him, any further altercation with the crazy son of a bitch I determined should be avoided at all costs. I leaned back and slurped my coffee, prayed wherever the hell that gas truck was, it got here as soon as it could. I had a good mind to wait out in my truck.

"You sure there's not another gas station nearby?" I asked Bock.

"Certain."

"Because you seemed like you wasn't sure when I first got here."

"Really, man, he's harmless," Bock said, arching his eyebrows towards the table. "So what do you go by?"

"Omar." While I'd never been to or even heard of Twenty Mile until now, and while it didn't appear like any of the major daily newspapers got delivered this far out, I still wasn't comfortable enough to chance offering my last name as well. Bock introduced me again to Leon—who touched a finger to the front brim of his hat—and to Leon's card partner, Eshew Eutuban, who lifted his hat slightly off the table. I didn't have a hat, so I raised my coffee cup. Eshew, Bock said, had been a first-generation sharecropper before he ran north to the Appalachians and took up making and bootlegging moonshine whiskey in the seclusion of the hills, exchanging the rotgut in Chicago for Tommy guns he smuggled and sold in towns along the Tennessee-Kentucky border, even as far south as Mississippi, where Eshew had a rather violent and tragic run-in with the Mississippi Mafia.

I looked at Eshew. He didn't look a day over sixty-five, which I pointed out to Bock.

"Did I say first generation?" Bock said. "I meant second. Or maybe third. Do you even know how old you are, Eshew?"

"I'd tell you to check my birth certificate," Eshew said, "but I ain't never received one."

"Hey," Leon said, "you dealing them cards?"

"There's a fourth supposed to be getting back soon," Bock said. "Horace, but he's been out fishing since yesterday afternoon." Bock looked into his coffee mug but didn't drink from it. "Should've been back by now though. Probably just got drunk and passed out on the bank all night, which wouldn't be the first time. He'll drag himself in sooner or later, but without any fish no doubt."

"Not that he wants just any fish," Eshew said, shuffling the cards after Leon had knocked them on the floor earlier. "Just the one—Ole Whiskers—and he ain't never caught the damn thing."

"And not that it'd matter either way," Bock said. "Only thing we got to cook with is the deep fryer in the back, and it's broke."

"And not that that would even matter," Leon jumped in, "as Horace is really only interested in Whiskers in triumph."

"What's wrong with the fryer?" I asked. I was growing impatient and welcomed the subject of something familiar and normal in this place with its conversations of on-going Civil War battles and personified pond fish and ageless half-black men.

"Hell if I know," Bock said. "It's been broke since I took over the shop."

"Tried nigger-rigging it," Leon said, "but it caught fire a little and smoked out the place a lot."

Eshew cleared his throat, stopped re-dealing the cards to stare at Leon.

"Apologies, friend," Leon said.

Eshew resumed his deal. It was nearing eleven then, and I hadn't eaten since the night before. Seeing as the store was generally devoid of any merchandise beyond whiskey and bait I knew, if I had to wait much longer on that fuel truck, I'd have to rummage through the back of my truck for something to eat, which at best would mean cold tortillas and a can of black beans. Homemade chips sounded something delicious just then, and if nothing else I figured keeping busy with the repairs would at least seem to get the gas truck here sooner.

I said, "Probably the fryer just needs to be cleaned is all. At best the filter might need to be replaced."

Bock shrugged and waved me around the counter and directed me into the kitchen. "Knock yourself out," he said and pointed at the appliance. There was a small metal table to one side of the fryer. On the other side of the appliance was a propane tank, its hose running in behind. "Hell, you fix that thing," Bock said, "I'll hire you on as a cook." He winked, patted my shoulder. "Might even give you the whole place."

Bock returned to the front of the store. I shrugged the offer off as a joke. Hell, the whole place seemed like one big gag, and I was just glad to be away from every single one of the crazy assholes in the next room. After I retrieved some supplies from my truck—dishwashing soap, some vinegar, an old cloth, cooking oil, a plastic mop bucket—I placed the bucket beneath the spigot at the base of the fryer. The oil was cold and black and held tan peninsulas of congealed grease and fat around the edges. The oil was only barely draining into the bucket. Settled at the bottom of the fryer would be bits of food charred beyond recognition, clogging the fryer, which would have to be cleaned out by hand. I rolled up my sleeves and the oil clung to my arm like a wet sleeve. The fryer itself was a gas-powered single-floor model in a similar vein as the one we'd used at the restaurant years ago. It all brought back memories of Mi Pueblo. Specifically, the Guatemalan dessert of fried plantains served under a chocolate, spicy mole sauce and sprinkled with sesame seeds. I had perfected the dessert the day before The Incident, and it was one of the first dishes I would've offered once I was managing the restaurant on my own. Now I was back to scrubbing fryers and all the un-goddamn-hilarity that entailed.

When I exited the kitchen to dump the mop bucket full of the same grease I was covered in up to my bicep, I saw a man walking up on the porch. He was red-headed and naked and holding an orange University of Tennessee cap over his crotch. In his other hand he carried a spinner-bait pole and a large tin cooler, both of which he set on the porch before walking in, ever careful not to expose himself. His whole body was severely sunburned, and it was difficult distinguishing where his forehead ended and his hair began. None of it surprised me. I wasn't sure if I would ever be surprised again.

"Where'd you get off to?" Eshew asked, but Horace—I figured—ignored him and walked straight to the counter. Bock brought out the moonshine and poured Horace a slug. Then, another. Horace caught his breath and sat down, wincing as he crossed his sunburned legs so he could return the hat to his head.

"What the hell happened to you?" Bock said, walking the third shot over to Horace.

"Goddamnedest thing," Horace said. He sipped at the shot and continued. "I snagged Ole Whiskers. Damn catfish about snapped my pole as it wasn't nothing more than a old lady's hip bone. But I held on and so did the pole and it took me damn near six hours but I finally got the sumbitch to shore. Swear to God before me it was big as I was. Liked to never drug the thing on the bank. Could've used one of you lazy sumbitches' help but I managed. Whole ordeal completely spent me though and I passed out right afterwards."

Horace paused then and held his glass up for another shot.

Bock handed me the handle of moonshine, and I carried it over to Horace. My hands left a greasy print on the bottle and glass. Horace didn't acknowledge me, just kept on with his story.

"So I don't wake up until this morning, completely naked like you see me now. When I looked around I saw the fish—swear to God, stay with me now—wearing my clothes and standing on the bank of the stream that feeds out into that pond I was fishing from, and it smiles, all whiskers and hotdog bun lips, and waves a fin and tells me thanks. Then, the catfish just hops into the creek there and swims off to goddamn God-knows-where."

No one said anything for a moment. I waited, hoped, prayed someone would call bullshit on Horace's yarn. I couldn't stomach no one questioning the validity of a speech-gifted and self-conscious catfish. Instead, Eshew asked, "So that's it, Horace? You still ain't bring us back no fish to eat?"

"On the contrary," Horace said, and gestured at the large metal pail on the porch. "It was like after I freed the one catfish, I couldn't quit catching them. It was like they was all waiting on Whiskers to show them how to go for a line. Hell, must be twelve or so in that cooler." Horace retrieved the bucket from the porch and removed the top, tipped the bucket slightly to show us his catch. The catfish's slimy gray bodies overlapped one another like one big mass of flexing muscle in the water of the bucket. That's when Horace acknowledged me for the first time. "What do you think about that, new guy?"

"What do I think about that?" I said, and looked at Leon, then Eshew, then Horace, who made a mocking attempt with his hands to cover his crotch, which was still safely obstructed by his crossed legs. "What do I think about that?" I asked and looked back at Bock. "I think y'all're all bat-shit crazy, that's what I think."

"No reason to be rude," Horace said. Then a confused smirk broke across his face and he turned to Bock. "You ain't told him yet?"

Bock was making the same gesture at Horace as he had me when I brought up the end of the Civil War.

"Told me what?" I asked.

"Been easing into it," Bock said.

"You sure didn't 'ease into it' when I got here," Horace said. "You told me first thing I walked through that door."

Eshew said, "That cause you wasn't doing him the favor of taking his place."

"And whose fault was that, old man?" Horace asked.

Eshew said, "Don't blame me for your bad luck."

"Well, who else decides who comes and goes here, E-shoo?"

"Y'all calm down," Bock said.

"What're y'all talking about?" I asked. "I only came here for gas."

"No, you didn't," Horace said. "And since you ain't taking my place, I don't mind telling you that Leon there really did die in the Civil War, Eshew did something so bad before he died he won't tell us but for some reason gives him the responsibility of deciding who gets to come and leave, I drove the goddamn Chevelle I bought with the money my brother gave me to send my boy to college off a bridge into the very creek Ole Whiskers just swam up, and you, man, certainly didn't miss that truck you think you did last night."

"No one's taking my place," Leon said. "Not until Eshew there—" he pointed across the table "—brings Ambrose here—" pointed right in front of him "—so I can hand him his ass."

"Got to beat me first, master," Eshew said.

"He's talking about in cards," Leon said to me. "Not actually, physically beating him. The slaves was long ago emancipated here in Twenty Mile."

It started to become clearer just then: how else would you explain how I'd played chicken with a tractor-trailer in the middle of the night before the truck just up and disappeared and I was flash-forwarded into morning and ended up here, fixing the fryer in the kitchen of a shop where the only customers was a nutcase Confederate reincarnate and a Haitian-descendant slave who was convinced he used to bootleg whiskey for guns that hadn't been made or used regularly in decades, not to mention the red-headed stepchild of Bill Dance who claimed he'd had his clothes taken by a walking, talking catfish?

But I didn't want it to make sense. I wanted the place to make as much sense as it had all day, which hadn't been much. I looked at Bock, whose poker face was not at all convincing. That is, if he wanted to assure me that Horace was playing some elaborate prank on me and that I was, indeed, still among the living, he was doing a piss poor job of it. Instead, he started in on how he made it to Bodock. I tried to pay attention—it had something to do with a lover and cancer and her dying before he could see her again, bed-ridden and under the watchful care of her husband—but it was like the inquisitive look on his face, with the mismatched mustache and head of hair, his damned earnestness, made me remember what I'd done after I was fired. I'd grabbed an aluminum baseball bat from my apartment that afternoon and looked Oscar McCullough's address in the paper, who was still in the county lock-up, for all I'd known. I didn't remember anything about the five-mile drive out to Oscar's house or what I was going to do with the bat once I got there, or if I'd even had a specific plan of action until I saw his Monte Carlo parked in the front yard. By the time I felt someone else's eyes on me, I was standing on the hood of the car, my back to the house, repeatedly taking the bat to the windshield. I had already introduced the bat to the side windows and door panels and clear through a rusted spot on the roof of the car, the rubber of the tires I'd slit melting into the wet yard. When I turned slowly around to locate the source of the eyes there was a girl on the porch in a dress so faded and thin it'd've been a miracle if it survived one more washing without completely disintegrating. I could make out the small brown dimes of her nipples through the material even. At the time her teenage anatomy didn't terrify me, but it scared the almighty shit out of me now, as did what I'd told her when she said her daddy wasn't around because he was off driving a truck for Ashley Furniture: that her daddy, I explained, was actually sitting in the Claygardner County Prison for having relations with a bonafied pig, probably had been having similar such illustrious affairs with other manners of livestock every single time he said he was off hauling love seats and recliners across the country, and just what now did she think about that?

"Looks like you got yourself another deserter, Bock," Leon said as I rushed through the doorway and made the truck in one bound from the concrete slab of the porch. Once seated behind the wheel I fumbled the keys into the floorboard. In the meantime the whole lot had gathered on the porch to watch. Horace had appropriately returned the hat to his crotch, and Eshew was taller than Leon, which I hadn't expected. I got the ignition turned, but the engine only responded with some mechanical grunting. After a couple more attempts the engine finally turned over, only to die once I threw the truck in gear. I left the keys in the ignition and stepped out of the truck and looked down the road from where I'd come.

"Omar," Bock said. "Listen: I didn't get sent here to Twenty Mile because I was screwing some other man's wife," he said. "I got sent here because I was so frustrated over the situation—that the husband got to be with Laurel at the end instead of me—that I drove over to the funeral home after I saw her obituary, told the man to his face how me and his wife would be the ones together again someday."

"Go to hell," I said.

"Already there," Horace said, and held up his shot.

"Shut it, Horace," Eshew said.

I took off running back towards the highway. Behind me I heard someone shout that they wouldn't do what it was I was currently in the process of doing, but when I looked back over my shoulder to kindly yell back that they couldn't be more obvious, the ground gave way and I fell face first into what felt like the embankment of a ditch I hadn't noticed carved across the road.

The next thing I remembered I was back on the concrete porch. Someone had leaned me against a wood column and my feet dangled off the porch. In my hand was a bourbon on the rocks.

"What happened?" I asked. "Was that a ditch? Who covers up a ditch? How the shit did I not hit that damn thing coming in?"

Bock laughed and pulled at his drink. He had taken a seat in a fold-up lawn chair looking down at me, an ample slug of bourbon in a glass sweating in the heat, which still hung heavy even now as the afternoon bled into dusk. The sky held an orange light the likes of which I'd only seen in any number of the techno-chromatic murals of Aztecan gods and goddesses decorating Mi Pueblo. After being knocked unconscious, I felt in a way more dead. Or, at least, more at terms with having died, as if face-planting into an embankment at a full sprint was some sort of rite of passage here. Bock told me Leon had dug the ditch in the event Ambrose would ever be brought to Twenty Mile and immediately attempted retreat once Leon got to whooping him. The ditch worked on some sort of latch that was only activated when approached from the opposite direction of the highway. Bock assured me I wasn't the first person who had tried to escape, that Horace had done the same thing when Bock announced he was dead, which was why Bock'd tried to break the news to me easy. The ditch remained operational, Bock explained, only as a means of saving folks the trouble of running twenty miles down the gravel road only to discover that the road didn't actually lead to the highway if you were coming in the direction from Twenty Mile, which somehow made sense.

"So what is this?" I asked. "Limbo? Purgatory? A way station into heaven?"

"Try hell," Bock said, and followed his delayed wink with a laugh, which I appreciated as much now as when Horace had made the similar crack. It was too soon to joke about such things. "Ah, I'm just pulling your dick. Should've seen your face though. This is," he said, and rolled his hand around on his wrist, as if conducting a church choir, "a place certain Bodockians go who committed some sin they didn't atone for before they died but that ain't so bad it warrants us going to hell neither." Bock pointed at the scar above his left eye from where the husband punched him in the forehead after Bock refused to leave without seeing Laurel's body. "Poor son of a bitch could've gone until he died and never known of his wife's infidelity," Bock said. The morning of the funeral, he told me, he had gone duck hunting to distract himself from trying to return to the funeral home. At some point his waders had filled with water, and he walked clear across the bottom of the pond until he reached the other side.

"'Bout scared the store's previous owner back to death when he saw me emerge from the water," Bock said, "relatively speaking, of course."

I told Bock my story. Hearing it out loud, I still couldn't believe the profound absurdity of it. Had that been what I'd become in that old former life, already moving behind me like that eighteen-wheeler I hadn't avoided hitting? My God, I'd not only, in my misdirected pissy-ness, the lunacy that was me taking a Louisville Slugger to an unassuming Monte Carlo, made a poor white-trash girl's life that much more dire, having to trek now the five miles to town when she once could elect to drive. But I had, in my obsession to not only clear my name even when it didn't matter a damn, exaggerated a truth all to destroy her idea of father. Even the cocksucker that was my own padre only deserved that on my worst of days.

Bock clicked my glass. "Look at the bright side though. At least you've got some experience running a kitchen. Before I got here all I knew how to do was sell insurance."

I smirked. "So what'll you do?" I asked.

"Move on."

"But how're you getting out of here?"

Bock nodded at my truck.

"Thought you said there wasn't any gas."

Bock stood and arched his back until it responded with a string of rapid cracks. "I'll figure something out."

"Well, all right," I said. It made as much sense as anything else.

Late into the night, once I had passed out, Bock would replace my truck with an empty red gas can lying on its side. Under different circumstances I would've thought it a damn dirty trick, but at least the can would be lying next to all the goods I'd brought with me, including the tarp, which would be folded neatly as well. After everything that'd happened, I'd come to appreciate such small courtesies. But just then Bock suggested we get something to eat. I agreed. Even dead, I was starving. Horace cleaned and gutted the catfish, and once I had finished tending the fryer, I filled it with some vegetable oil from the truck. While the oil was heating up, I sliced several packs of corn tortillas into triangles and contemplated setting aside a couple of whole catfish to make a broth for the mole poblano sauce I might attempt tomorrow. Bock used the plastic bags from the tortillas to batter the rest of the whole catfish with my own blend of black pepper and garlic powder and chopped parsley from the herb garden I'd set in the passenger seat of the truck cab, as well as some red pepper flakes I crushed with a claw hammer, all tossed into some corn meal.

We feasted on fish and chips.

Anthony Neil Smith

Bitter Soul

The ghost in my home was supposedly Major Jeremiah Hammeridge, a Confederate surgeon who sawed the limbs off Yankee prisoners of war when they didn't need it— just for fun, no booze for anesthetic. He figured the soldiers would have lost a limb or two in battle anyway.

I had lived in this house on the Mississippi Gulf Coast three years with my wife Joanna and son Alan before someone told us about the ghost. After that, we thought we heard noises late at night: loud belching, fits of sneezing, mumbled curses about "Damn Yankees."

One night I was in the den, sitting on the floor with my back slumped against the couch while reading the Bible. When I was on call for the funeral home, it felt better to stay up than have the phone wake me at three in the morning to go pick up dead folks at their homes or at car crashes or hospitals, drag them into the empty prep room, drain and aspirate them. I would clean up the wounds, fill in the holes with cotton or wax, pump in the fake coloring, Permaglow. Then, dress them up, go home, and try to sleep without dreaming.

But I drifted off and dreamed after all. The ghost came through the wall where the TV had been before Jo made me throw it out. He eased into the recliner, arms stretched, palms on his knees. He was purplish and solid, out of focus. Brutal looking with bloodless wounds on his arms and legs. Dark stained uniform, dusty boots. He had a long thick mustache and pointy beard. No eyes.

"Why'd you get rid of the TV?" he said.

152

I shrugged. "I'm not supposed to believe in it. I'm trying to be a Christian."

"Trying to be? There's is or there's ain't." The Major's voice was high pitched and strained. "There's been a TV in here since nineteen sixty-three. Every family that moved in here after then had one. It's too much—no TV and your wife praying so loud all the time."

"It's the way we are."

"The way she is. You pray like you're scared someone will hear. Well I hear, sir, and I am not impressed."

"How can you see the TV without any eyes?" I said.

"Don't need them anymore. See things differently now." The Major sighed, and dust spewed from his nostrils. The uniform over his chest, stiff and full when he was upright, sank into a concave hole. He disappeared into a dusty outline.

I woke up and needed to use the bathroom. My Bible was open to Ezekiel, chapter eleven, verse five:

> *And the Spirit of the LORD fell upon me, and said*
> *unto me, Speak; Thus saith the LORD; Thus have*
> *ye said, O house of Israel; for I know the things*
> *that come into your mind, every one of them.*

I told my pastor about my dream an hour before service on Wednesday night. Reverend Burtleson leaned his tall-backed chair away from his desk. He crossed his hands together over his bulging stomach. He had a full head of gray-brown hair.

"We know spirits work through dreams," he said, deep voiced and deliberate. "If it's a spirit, I guess we'll rebuke it and cast it out."

"But it's a ghost. And I was just dreaming."

"Don't trust evil, Brother Daryl. Evil lies. What does the Bible say about spirits?"

I didn't know, so he told me, and I didn't get it. I had only been in his church seven months, most of those as a back-row skeptic.

After his explanation, I said, "Then what? Do we go in with Holy Water and splash the place?"

"No, no. That's what Catholics would do, not us. We'll rebuke the spirit in Jesus' name and anoint all the doors and furniture with oil."

"Oil?"

"Olive oil, anointing oil. Same thing we pray for the sick with."

I'd seen that, laying hands on the sick with a dab from a little bottle of yellow stuff. Then the person being prayed for would shake and dance or fall flat on the ground. I had seen it work, too. Saw a flu cleared right up. Sister Margaret had a tumor go into remission after they prayed with her. And he wanted to smear this oil all over my house?

"What's the difference between water and oil? Why not water?" I asked.

"Because the Bible says..." he started, and I tried to keep up but he was a mile past me: Anoint with oil for the sick, for anything you want blessed. (He had a really nice office, lots of space, private bathroom.) And it's not the oil, but the faith we have in the Lord through anointing that answers the prayer. (A nice couch, nice chairs like the one I was in, soft, deep, swirling greens and burgundy. Dark wood desk covered by thick clear coat, slick and reflecting the lamp light.) As it says in Ephesians, we wrestle not against flesh and blood, but against demons and powers and spirits, so dress in the whole armor of God. (Wood paneling, shelves and walls covered with artwork, masks, instruments and trinkets gathered while he was a missionary in West Africa for ten years. I was pretty sure he liked Africa better than he did Mississippi.)

He told me we'd "pray out the spirit" on Thursday night, and he would bring the oil, his wife, and a couple of Prayer Warriors. He said we'd go out to eat afterwards at his favorite Chinese place.

"I could grill us all steaks instead, if you'd like," I said.

His eyebrows flinched up as he said, "That would be just fine."

I should have told him not to mention the ghost to anyone, because he did exactly that from the pulpit, after nearly an hour of jazzy gospel from a band with Hammond B-3, keyboards, bass, and drums. That was followed by a few minutes of screaming from Brother Porter, the assistant pastor. He said the same thing every service, that we didn't worship enough or get into the Spirit, and, "How do you expect God to bless you if you can't get excited about being in His House? You'd yell at a football game, wouldn't you? Well, my friends, this is more important than that."

I aimed my sitting-there-quietly stare at Porter, and he was dying to come out and say, "Brother Daryl, this means you," but Rev. Burtleson wouldn't let him.

The sanctuary had a high arched ceiling. Everything was freezing and echoing and bright. The pastor took his place at the pulpit and dropped one of his favorite lines since I'd been attending: "I'd rather be here in church tonight than in the best funeral home in town." I didn't think it was in good taste.

He spoke of "increased demon activity" in the city fighting against the work of the church. "Why, just before service, a member of this congregation told me about being visited by an evil spirit in his home. Satan's at work, people. Be in prayer tomorrow as we go to cast the demon out of that house."

Heads turned, folks looking for the most embarrassed or distraught face in the building so the gossip circles could get on the phone and dish on the person consorting with devils. I held my lips tight. Jo twisted in her seat to glare at me. She was sitting a few rows up with a friend, and her eyes were tired behind her glasses. She shook her head, and I waved. Alan was sitting across the aisle with the organist's kids, flipping through coloring books. I had forgotten to bring something to distract me and had to work hard to tune out the Bible study, third in the series on "Being A Soulwinning Church In The End-Time Revival."

After the study, Rev. Burtleson invited the church to come pray at the two long padded altars. Most of the congregation went immediately and knelt or stood with their hands raised. Jo stood behind the first pew, reserved as she held hand out in front of her to keep her friend from falling backwards. The friend was dancing, whipping her hair, speaking in tongues. My wife rarely did things like that, but I liked when she did. It surprised me.

Alan came over with his plastic box of Crayons and an activity book, crawled into the pew and handed me a yellow. Brother Porter walked up to us. I stood and shook his hand, but he kept his grip on, leaned over to my ear and said, "Don't you think you should come up front and pray?"

"Not tonight."

"This might be the last night you've got, man. Come up and seek the Holy Ghost. You know you need it." He was sweating through his gray suit. I released his hand, but he grabbed my arm above the elbow.

"I think you need to let go," I said.

"This rebellion isn't going to get you to Heaven," Porter said.

"No, but it will get you punched in the face if you don't let go."

He let go, flashed big teeth and thick gums. "I could take you. Yeah, I could." He walked back to the front of the church, where people were drifting apart. I sat beside my son and kept my head down, silently praying that Jo would hurry up so we could go home.

The Major came back that night. I dreamt I was sitting at the kitchen table finishing a glass of chocolate milk. The ghost fell through the ceiling and floated down in slow motion, writhing the whole way until he landed on his back. He groaned, then sat up and pulled himself into a chair. He was more battered than last time, more pale overall.

"Why do you look like that?" I said.

"Because I'm dead."

"When you die, isn't your spirit transformed into something new, or your injuries taken away?"

The Major shook his head. "I died of a heart attack. Looked fine. Death's a son of a bitch."

I said, "My pastor says you're a demon spirit."

He laughed. "I wish."

I imagined what my soul looked like. Weak, no meat on the bones, mouth sewed up, and a big hole in my side where my liver should have been.

"I'm not going to leave quietly. You can pray and anoint all you want, but I'll put up a good fight," the ghost said.

"How did you know?" I said.

The room got warmer, and his skin suddenly brighter. The Major stared long and hard, didn't answer.

"I've got to take my stand," I said. "Sorry."

He smiled. No teeth. "I know that. I know you'll win, too, if that's what you want. But like I said, I won't go quietly."

He vanished, but left behind an odor like rotten eggs. I whispered, "But I don't want you to go at all." I poured my milk out in the sink.

Jo was sitting on the couch in the den the next night staring at the stereo, against the wall where the TV had been. I stretched across the couch, my head in her lap while she tapped fingertips on my scalp. She was in a pajama tee that reached to her knees, faded drawing of Donald Duck on the front, with her legs curled up on the cushion beneath me.

"What about these dreams?" she said.

"The ghost. He said he won't leave without a fight."

She grinned at that, wiggled her toes against my back. I kissed the top of her knee. I asked, "Is your mom going to keep Alan tomorrow night?"

"Yeah. I'll pick him up after. Mom doesn't agree with Rev. Burtleson, though. She says we should call Unsolved Mysteries and they'd probably pay us something."

"And the whole country would know about our ghost."

"Then he probably wouldn't show up. Ghosts are camera shy."

I laughed and rubbed my chest. Heartburn. Jo's fingers stopped tapping and brushed through my hair. We hadn't been that close in months. I don't know what it was exactly, just things about her going to church so much. She said she wasn't going to cut her hair anymore, since the church believed it was a sin for a woman to have short hair. I didn't mind that. She had nice hair. Then she said she was going to stop wearing jewelry and make-up. Also okay. She didn't need them, as long as she would keep wearing the wedding band. And only long dresses and skirts from then on, no pants or shorts. Whatever she wanted, fine.

But I wondered if maybe our affections would have to be "acceptable" to somebody in a church office somewhere who had a list of marital dos and don'ts. So, I had found ways to keep busy at night, had a lot of headaches. Jo knew the reason but couldn't ask, was afraid to try, and we fought without saying what was really on out minds: Are you still the same person I fell in love with?

"What was that with Brother Porter?" she said.

"He wanted me to come up and pray. I wasn't in the mood."

Jo clicked her tongue. I tried to turn, but she put her hand in the way. I flashed my eyes back and forth.

"I want to believe, I really do, but how can I believe in this if I can't believe in the people who believe in this?"

"Daryl—"

"Porter is a jerk. He said he could take me in a fight. What kind of talk is that from a preacher?" I pointed at her.

Jo pushed my finger down. "You can't keep taking it to heart. You have to learn to get along with people."

"Oh, like Burtleson. There's a friendly one."

She didn't say anything. She was right about me. I found too many faults in nearly everyone except myself, always the first to criticize. Jo once told me her biggest fear about me was that I'd start criticizing her.

She leaned over. I lifted my chin and kissed her, our lips barely touching, shaking. I couldn't move. I felt her mouth go wide in a smile and I bumped her teeth. She whispered, "He's watching us, isn't he?"

"Who, Burtleson?"

"No. That ghost."

I collapsed into her lap and groaned. "Oh, yeah, I'm sure he sees everything else, so he's probably watching us kiss, too."

Jo rubbed lightly against my stomach. "Want to come to bed with me now?"

"I'm not tired," I said.

"Well, it doesn't have to be the bed, then. Right here."

"Then what if Alan gets up?"

She exhaled. Deep sigh.

"I'm just saying 'what if,' you know?"

"Fine." She pushed me up. "Stay here, okay? That's fine by me. I'll go get a good night's sleep, save my energy for this little seance tomorrow."

"Exorcism."

"I thought it had to be inside someone for it to be an exorcism," Jo said. She stretched her nightshirt down. "You're the one having the seances, talking to this demon every night."

"It's not a demon." I couldn't look at her when I said it.

"Shut up. I'm going to bed. Don't wake me up when you get there." Jo walked out of the den stiffly. But I didn't want a ghost watching my wife and me make love.

On Thursday evening, Jo took Alan to her mom's while I fired up the gas grill on our backyard deck. I walked through the house and opened the windows, figured we'd need them open for this thing, even if it meant the neighbors would hear.

Jo made it back and said she had to get dressed, then looked at me and frowned.

"No jeans."

"Yes jeans."

"My God, Daryl, why bother inviting them at all if you're going to wear jeans?"

"He invited himself," I said.

She clenched her fingers towards me like claws and said through gritted teeth, "Fifteen minutes. How can I be ready in fifteen minutes?"

The doorbell rang. I walked to the door and opened it to Rev. and Mrs. Burtleson with Porter and Sister Janet. The pastor was in a print shirt that was too brown. His wife was a head taller than him in a blue blazer and long black skirt. Porter was in jeans, and Sister Janet wasn't smiling. She never did. Her dress was long and severe, with a high collar and sleeves that covered her wrists. I'd heard her say once that she had prayed for people a thousand miles away, and they had seen her walk into their rooms at that very moment. I figured she was like my ghost then.

Jo waltzed out, gorgeous in a khaki skirt and green blouse. I let out a low whistle, but she ignored me and shook all their hands. I flipped the steaks, looked over my shoulder. Porter smiled at me from my favorite patio chair and said, "Could I get some tea, Brother Daryl?"

I shrugged. Jo said she'd get it.

Rev. Burtleson loomed behind me, watching the steaks.

"I thought we'd eat first. These will be done in a few minutes," I said.

He nodded and patted his stomach. "They smell great. I'm not known to miss a lot of meals."

"I'm nervous about this. What if he won't leave without a fight?"

Burtleson grunched his eyebrows. "It doesn't have a choice. It has no power against the name of Jesus."

"He told me he used to read the Bible, too."

The pastor sighed and reached his arm around me, his hand on my shoulder. "Brother Daryl, you're going to have to stop doubting. You've got to trust God. You can't go around believing every evil spirit that comes your way."

"This is my first one."

"Not necessarily. They don't all speak English. How long until these are done?"

"It'll be a while. I just put them on."

"Maybe we should pray first." Burtleson said.

Sister Janet started murmuring "Lord Jesus" under her breath. The pastor asked us to gather inside the dining room. We stood in a circle in the dining room, near the sliding glass door.

"Join hands," Burtleson said. We did. I looked around. Everyone had their eyes closed except Porter and me.

"What about the oil?" I said.

The pastor, eyes still closed, said, "We'll do that later."

They began to pray aloud, Janet in tongues, Burtleson claiming authority by the Word of God and commanding the spirit to vacate the house. His wife was crying, and Porter was abusively loud, jerking on my arm as he punched his accents: "In the NAME of JESUS, al-MIGHT-y God, we will not let Satan set up Hell on Earth before his time."

I imagined the Major bucking on a horse above the dining room table, his mouth open to laugh but he screamed bugle noise at us.

Burtleson's eyes opened. "Now, Brother Porter and I will anoint the doors and windows, and some of the furniture." He turned to his wife, who went to get her purse, came back with two small vials of yellow olive oil, handed one to Porter and one to Burtleson. The pastor shook some of it on his fingers, then walked over to the sliding door and smeared a line across the glass.

Mrs. Burtleson asked my wife and Sister Janet to come pray with her in the den. I shoved my hands into my pockets and watched the ministers, listened to their barely audible chants as they made sure to get a little oil on all my kitchen appliances, especially the microwave. They anointed every doorframe, every window. From the den, Sister Janet was whooping in her rasp, and I even heard some of Jo's prayers, "I love you, Lord," mostly, which was good. Maybe she didn't want the ghost to leave, either.

Burtleson asked if he could go into the bedrooms. I said it was no problem and waited in the hall. Then, Janet stopped making any noise at all, and I heard Mrs. Burtleson say, "Uh oh."

I ran into the den and saw my wife sitting on the couch. Mrs. Burtleson stood over Janet, slumped on the floor in a pile.

The ministers made it into the room just as I went to call an ambulance. While we waited, Jo and I watched as they tried to pray the woman back to life. Then, Rev. Burtleson tried CPR. Nothing worked.

After paramedics took her to the hospital (just in case), Burtleson asked me if I thought the spirit was gone. I felt that the Major was everywhere, watching everything, when I said, "Yes, I think that did it."

Jo looked at me, knew good and well I was telling a huge lie, and she was proud of me.

I didn't embalm Sister Janet, but had to work the visitation, answering questions, setting up flowers around the casket. Many of the church members came, a chance to gossip about how it happened, what we were doing when she died, how the evil spirit killed her. The pastor spent most of his time trying to explain how that wasn't so.

I was standing at the head of the casket when Porter and his wife passed by.

"Just got rid of one ghost, and now you've got another, huh?" he said.

"What are you talking about?"

"She died in your house. Hey, don't worry. Maybe she'll be a good influence on you."

I laughed as he moved away and felt sorry for all the people he would eventually pastor when he got his own church. I thought about planting a Kiss CD in his car to ruin his reputation.

I was shaving Friday morning a week later and nicked my neck. I reached for a piece of tissue, turned the tap off, looked in the mirror at myself again, thought for a moment I saw the ghost's face superimposed on my own.

"Major?"

I blinked. The ghost was gone.

Back in the bedroom, Jo was at her vanity mirror in a slip, twisting her hair into style for the day. "Talking to the ghost again? Kind of early, isn't it?"

"I don't know. I don't think he's gone."

Jo spun around, grabbed the back of her chair and let her hair fall. "What about Janet? She died here. Do you think she'll start haunting us, too?"

"Don't worry about it. We won't see her. She'd be too embarrassed."

I watched a grin rise on her mouth, and her eyes got flirty. "But she can still see us, can't she? Well, there's a thing or two I'd like to teach her, show her what she's missed."

"Isn't Alan going to be late for kindergarten?"

My wife laughed and shook her hair. "Oh yeah. Yes."

I got home from work after five and found a note from Jo: Gone to the store with Alan. Dropping him at Mom's for the night. I sat back in my recliner in the den and pretended to watch the radio news by imagining faces for the anchors. The suit he was wearing, the color of her dress, how fat the sports guy was. Photos, maps, an ambulance drawing with "Fatality" written beneath it in a box by their heads.

I turned off the radio when she appeared in the doorway, two plastic grocery bags in her hands. She tossed one into my lap.

"Look what I got," she said.

"What's in the other bag?"

"Dinner. I'm going to make tacos. Look in that bag." She set her groceries down, leaned against the door frame and kicked her tennis shoes off.

I opened the bag. A pack of Polaroid film and a roll of Kodak 400, 24 exposures.

"I thought we could try to take pictures of the ghosts," Jo said. "Haven't you seen those pictures where it was just a person or a church or a room when they shot it, but when it was developed, a ghost shows up?"

"I thought those were fakes."

Jo pulled off her socks and shoved one into each shoe, then threw them over my head across the room. I hadn't seen her enjoying little things in a long time.

"Go get the cameras," I said.

We started in the den, snapping in dim light first, then bright. Jo had the Polaroid, pulled the pictures out as they came, tossed them down and said we'd get back to them all later. I followed her into the dining room, shot a couple of the space over the table. The flash and whirr made us both trickle with tiny laughs.

As we made our way down the hall, Jo said, "You're not going back to Burtleson's church, are you?"

"No, I'm done with them all." I snapped a photo of the bathroom.

"What if I wanted to keep going and taking Alan with me?"

"Hey, I can't tell you what to do about it. If you want to keep going, fine. I won't complain." But I knew I would.

She pushed Alan's door open, held the Polaroid to her eye, then flashed a shot.

"You really want to keep going there?" I said.

"No, not anymore. But I wanted to see if you'd try to stop me," she said. We were standing outside the guest bedroom, the one we used as an extra closet, had an old mattress on the floor.

"Do you believe in what they teach?"

Jo heaved out a breath and said, "I don't know. But maybe we can go to a different one Sunday. See what's out there."

I looked at her through my camera lens. "Smile for me."

"No, don't." She turned her head, put her hand out in front of my camera.

I snapped a picture anyway and said, "You either get good poses or bad ones. I'll keep snapping."

She arched her back, put a hand on her hip and one on the back of her neck. A big smile. "How's that?"

I clicked again. "Great, good. Have some fun, show me fun."

She spun around, almost fell over and started laughing, her hair strung across her face. She put her hands on her knees. I took a picture. "Perfect."

"Now you," she said.

"Me?" I flexed my arms, strained tight. "This good?"

"No, don't flex. You don't have much to flex. Just be you."

I held my arms behind me, held my chin up, leaned against the wall. "Okay?"

"Yeah, great! I like that." Jo snapped a couple that fell out onto the floor. She backed up until her foot hit the mattress and she tripped backwards with a whoop.

"You all right?"

She was laughing, rolling, flushing in her face. I reached behind me and clicked the light switch off.. Jo was up on her knees, waving her hand at me.

"Come here. No more pictures," she said.

"We haven't seen the ghosts."

"So? Come on." She reached out for my fingers, pulled me down beside her, and I felt her cool breath on my chin. "Maybe they'll see us."

And I thought, That wouldn't be so bad.

Gray Lady, Lady Gray

The corridor was empty. A small mouse nibbled in a corner, whiskers covered in dust, his gray fur nearly translucent in the dark. Preparations were being made below. She could hear them. Scurrying, simpering, slutting. Wood brought in for the fireplaces, which meant the attics would become unbearably hot as the warmth rose from floor to floor. Winter flowers and the deep Scottish weeds tended in the gardens outside, what was left of them, anyway. Balustrades polished, floors washed and waxed, carpets vacuumed, bedding changed.

A wedding, if her long ears didn't deceive her.

A chance.

The lips on her face pulled back from long, taloned teeth in a semblance of a grin.

"Dolon," she called, delighting in the fright it gave the cook, five floors below, who heard the wind whistling through her kitchen and smelled the odor of sulfur on the breeze.

He appeared before her, summoned by her use of his name.

"Yes, Lamia?"

"What have you been doing?"

"Eating the late lambs. They are so succulent this time of year."

She looked closer—her vision wasn't what it once was—and saw the little bits of flesh hanging from his beard, the gray stained black with their blood. Blood. Blood on the corner of his mouth. With sight came smell, the rising odor forcing her to salivate like a rabid dog.

Her loins throbbed.

"Come here, my sweet."

He obeyed, and she flicked a long, pointed tongue around the edges of his mouth, catching flesh and blood and the musk—he'd eaten the lambs from the ass first, the beast.

Just that little bit of essence was enough—Dolon became solid in front of her.

A handsome man, Dolon. Simple, driven by needs not unsimilar to her own, banished to this castle at birth, forced to grow up under Lamia's tutelage. She loved him, in the only way she knew how to love, which was filled with hate and fear and loathing and manipulative desperation.

"That was lovely, darling. Now you must do something for me. It seems we have visitors arriving."

"Yes, I saw. They will have to go to the next farm for the lamb shanks."

He laughed, uproariously. His joke, so simple, so cruel. Just like Dolon.

She ran her fingers along the slick flesh of his forearm.

"Pretty, please pay attention."

"What is your wish, my lady?"

Her tongue curled round her mouth. "Bring me all the information, Dolon. Leave nothing out."

Elizabeth wanted to be a princess.

From the time she was five and grasped the concept of the Cinderella myth—that any woman could capture the heart of Prince Charming—she set herself on the journey to become a princess. She didn't seek a royal throne, no, that was best left to those who would squabble over the scraps and look cross-eyed down their long, nebbish noses at lesser beings like her.

She didn't want a crown. Elizabeth sought the only real path to princessdom. She sought true love.

And she found it. In the form of a wonderful man named Edgar, who looked at her with sunshine and roses in his eyes.

They'd met at a softball game, of all places. Opposing teams. She was sweaty and covered in dust from the pitching mound and a long slide into third, he was sweaty and covered in the dust she kicked up when she slid. They emerged from the cloud coughing and laughing. He'd helped her to her feet, and she'd been lost. Gone. He had blue eyes that sparkled and a strong jaw, not to mention legs like tree trunks and an ass that would make a grown woman cry. He knew how to use it, too. His voice was soft and melodious, and had never been raised in anger toward her. Edgar was an infinitely patient man, one who would bite his lip and walk to another room if she were ever shrill or annoyed. Which wasn't often. He gave her no reason to seek connubial combat.

Edgar, quite simply, made her happy. So when he'd asked her to marry him, down on one knee, a glistening clear stone nestled in a bed of gold extended, she hadn't hesitated. Within weeks, they'd decided to get married in Scotland, at a castle, to fulfill Elizabeth's lifelong quest. Only princesses married in castles, after all.

Elizabeth stood in the parking lot outside the castle keep and raised her hand to her eyes, blotting out the sun. It had been cloudy and rainy since they landed in Edinburgh, but the moment she'd arrived on the estate, the sun had boldly forced its way into the sky, as if it too wanted a piece of her happiness. She stepped to her left so the tower of the castle would help block the incessant rays.

Something moved behind the highest window. The breeze picked up, and Elizabeth's sullen brown hair whipped into a frenzy, then fell limp against her ears. She felt... odd. Filled with longing, her pulse beating hard between her legs. She wanted to bed Edgar, now. She blushed and felt her breath come fast.

"Edgar, did you see that?"

"See what, dear?"

Elizabeth focused on the window again, and saw nothing. She let her breath regulate. Nerves. It was just nerves. She'd been a bundle for days now—the pressure of the trip, the planning, the knowledge she would be binding her life to his forever had her on edge.

"Sun playing tricks on me, I suppose. Shall we go in?"

A small party had been planned as a surprise for Edgar and

Elizabeth. Unbeknownst to them, their wedding attendants had all flown over a day early to have things prepared.

When they entered the long corridor to the castle keep, the hall was lined with white roses and bedecked with ribbons, and a small white sign with a hand drawn arrow pointing down the hall read "This Way." It was quite fetching, and Elizabeth commented as such to Edgar, who agreed, though he was quite preoccupied with their baggage at that moment, and was startled when Elizabeth screamed in delight.

Hands grabbed at them—parents, friends, sisters and brothers, hugging and kissing and showering the couple in rose petals. Elizabeth cried prettily, and Edgar was also moved. To have such love surrounding you is something to treasure, and Edgar wasn't the kind to dismiss strong emotion when it overcame him. He handed Elizabeth a tissue, and took one for himself. Once they were done with the tears, they were ushered into an intimate dining room, seated in the middle of the table, looking toward the window that spread the gardens before them like a fertile green blanket, and tucked in to a light lunch. Elizabeth simply glowed, and he couldn't resist leaning into her begonia-scented aura and slipping in a kiss.

The crowd cheered and clicked their forks against their champagne flutes in thrilled response.

Edgar deepened the kiss, letting his tongue touch hers—so warm, so wet, so perfect. God, he loved this woman. He wanted her. His mind saw her splayed facedown in front of him, legs spread, wide and pink and moist and wanting.

He felt a quick breath of air, fetid and warm, at his right ear, and opened his eyes a fraction. He was a rational man. His mind didn't allow him to see the bearded face, twisting slowly two inches from his own, dark skin rippling with maggots and roaches. His mind allowed him to feel momentarily uneasy, as if something were watching him, or a goose walked over his grave, then he dismissed the smell as old meat left in the sun and put another arm around Elizabeth.

When they broke free, accompanied by hoots and hollers, the

castle staff filtered in and their wedding planner gave them the schedule for the following two days. Edgar did his best to pay attention.

Dolon mounted the stairs slowly. He knew what was waiting for him. Lamia was once a beautiful, cunning woman, sought after by men across realms. But she had become something less than real, something full of hate and spite. He didn't blame her. Not really. He was simply annoyed that he was tied to her, forever. All gray ladies were assigned a demon, for they were unable to leave their earthly rooms without a demon's escort, and needed something that could travel through the air, move through walls, lift into the breeze and delve into the souls that fed her existence to make that happen.

It was just... Lamia was so *old*. Even when she received the essence, became the glorious woman she once was, even then he knew that was crinkled up like an old parchment inside. It interfered with his abilities, it truly did.

He reached the top of the stairs and slid through the wooden door into her rooms. She was asleep in her chair, facing the fire, a fur throw around her shoulders. Her gray skin sagged and a fine line of spit dripped form her hollow teeth. At least she still had them. She would be furious with him for watching her sleep. He slipped back through the door and made some noise in the hall, a warning to wake her. When he moved through the door again, she'd straightened in the chair. The fur throw was in her lap now, and she was smiling at him. Her cataracts made her eyes the color of sludge.

"What news, my sweet?"

"A wedding, Lamia. Just like you thought. Between two very young, very impressionable beings. You should have seen the female when you called to her—she turned red in the face like a baboon's ass. And him, my love, he is strong, but also susceptible. We have a chance."

Lamia leapt briskly from her seat and went to the window. "When is the ceremony?"

"Tomorrow night. Seven. We should have enough time."

"Yes, we will." Lamia turned back from the window to face him, and Dolon could see the vestiges of the beauty she had once been. Even she, old and cruel and severe, could be transformed by joy.

"We will."

The dress Elizabeth wore was simple and elegant. The base had been her grandmother's, a wide bell shaped skirt of thick satin. The bodice and all the lace had been current additions, making the dress modern and sophisticated. It had a cathedral length train, and though it was much too long for their purposes in the small castle chapel, shortening it was a concession she refused to make.

Princesses had cathedral trains.

She swished about in the heavy skirt, feeling the slick fabric mold to her legs. She was rapturously happy. She checked off the list in her head.

She was in a castle.

She was about to marry the most wonderful man alive.

She was wearing part of her grandmother's wedding gown, which brought her back to life, in a way.

She looked beautiful. Her skin was clear, she didn't have her period, her dress fit like a glove. Even her hair had gotten in line and was piled on her head in glorious waves.

That was plenty for one girl's wedding day, she thought.

There was rustling in the antechamber.

"Lizzie, it's time. Are you ready?"

Her father. Tears pricked her eyes. Oh, my God. Her whole life she'd been waiting for this moment, and now, here it was. She took a deep breath.

"Ready, Daddy."

She opened the door and admired her handsome father, resplendent in his white tie and tails. He twitched a bit, uncomfortably humbled by the scrutiny.

"You look gorgeous, Daddy."

"So do you, my dear. Shall we get you married off? Remember, it's right foot first."

There were forty-nine stairs. She counted every one as they went down.

The castle was decorated to the nines. She wondered what mice had descended upon the rooms to make it happen.

Before she had a chance to think anymore, the planner handed her the flowers, a simple spray of white roses and hydrangea, then opened the doors to the chapel.

It all went very quickly from there. The trumpet voluntary sprang to life, her guests rose to their feet, and she saw Edgar, standing at the other end of the room. It was all she could do not to break free and run to him, throw herself in his arms.

She floated down the aisle to gasps of appreciation. She attributed the crawling, goosebumpy sensation to nerves. She couldn't see the two uninvited guests standing at either side of the alter, waiting for her with blood risen.

Her father stopped walking, so she stopped as well. Edgar looked ready to cry. She fought the urge as well.

Words.

Words.

Words.

Her father squeezed her hand. And then it was time. The priest was a homely man with wads of white hair spilling from his ears. *Mwaiwwage...* She stifled a giggle. He spoke in a clear bell voice that snapped her back to sober.

"Elizabeth, will you have this man to be your husband; to live together in the covenant of marriage? Will you love him, comfort him, honor and keep him, in sickness and in health, and, forsaking all others, be faithful to him as long as you both shall live?"

"I will." Elizabeth brushed a single tear from the corner of her eye.

The priest turned slightly with a rustle of cloth as dark as raven's wings.

"Edgar, will you have this woman to be your wife; to live together in the covenant of marriage? Will you love her, comfort her, honor and keep her, in sickness and in health, and, forsaking all others, be faithful to her as long as you both shall live?"

Edgar's voice carried to the back of the hall.

"I will."

"Will all of you witnessing these promises do all in your power to uphold these two persons in their marriage?"

There was a chorus of confident, "We will."

Elizabeth glowed.

"It's time," Lamia whispered. "Their fidelity has been pledged. The moment is ours. Go, Dolon, go!"

His disappeared from Edgar's side. It was easier for Dolon—as a demon he was built to enter the host seamlessly. Lamia, on the other hand, must choke down a potion whose recipe was of unknown origin, one that she'd gotten the chance to make only four times in her existence. She unstoppered the bottle and dropped the contents on her tongue. It was most powerful, only three drops were needed. She swallowed quickly, before the taste of soot and hellfire registered fully, and shut out the voices of the consecrated blood spilled for her formulary that screamed in her head.

She willed it. Willed herself into the body of the girl. Into the sweet nothingness that resided in the girl's blood.

She was getting smaller, her features softening, her hair growing and weaving onto her head her nails shortening her skin smoothing her eyes clearing and then she opened her conscious being and stared into a blue abyss with a slight brownish cast over it. She felt the girl kicking against her liver, drowning in the bile of her body, crying out for release.

Lamia resisted the urge to lick her lips. Her tongue was very long. It might look wrong.

It had worked.

Less than ten hours. That's all she needed.

Edgar took her hand.

"In the name of God, I, Edgar Allen Gray, take you Elizabeth to be my wedded wife, to have and to hold from this day forward, for better, for worse, for richer, for poorer, in sickness and in health, to love and to cherish, until we are parted by death. This is my solemn vow."

Speak, Lamia. It is your turn. Her voice was astonishing, pure and only slightly wavering.

"In the name of God, I, Elizabeth Banks Morton, take you, Edgar to be my wedded husband, to have and to hold from this day forth, for richer, for poorer, in sickness and in health, to love and to cherish, until we are parted by death. This is my solemn vow."

Lamia smiled serenely, and a small red tear formed in the corner of Elizabeth's right eye.

The officiate blessed the rings. There were more words. A single gold band was slid onto her finger, and Lamia felt the power of the metal course through her. She knew she was shimmering, feeding upon this, the love Edgar had for Elizabeth. It was powerful, and good. If she could just make the dawn, sleep and awake in the body of the child, the transmogrification would be complete.

"Then by the power vested in me through the Lord, our God, I now pronounce you husband and wife." The priest leaned in and said quietly. "You may kiss your bride."

Dolon's face flashed through for an instant, a leering grin, then Edgar was back, solemn and steady. He leaned in slowly, savoring the moment, staring into Lamia's eyes. His lips pressed to hers and the flood of innocence brought blood to her tongue.

"To the dawn," she whispered.

Edgar looked surprised for a moment, then smiled knowingly. "To the dawn," he replied.

A cheer went up as they turned to face their new world as husband and wife.

The party went on into the wee hours.

Neither Edgar nor Elizabeth seemed to be in any hurry to get to their marriage bed, instead choosing to dance and carry on. Their friends and family loved it. Seeing their son and daughter, their buddies, let loose, the pressures of the wedding behind them, was just the ticket. The alcohol flowed. The music took on maniacal proportions, going faster and faster until the band members themselves seemed to melt from the sweat pouring off their bodies, yet they continued to play, louder and quicker and more insistent.

Bridesmaids found themselves in dark corners with groomsmen they'd never before found attractive, rolling with wave after wave of orgasm as they were penetrated with all manner of limbs and penises. The whole castle thrummed with a primal rhythm, the bodies and heartbeats bumping in time to the music. And when the music stopped, they didn't even notice.

Edgar even took a quick turn in the bathroom with one of the waiters, and was thoroughly amused when Elizabeth walked in on them and slapped his hand in response.

But at three in the morning, after watching their bacchanalian with an emotion bordered on contentedness, Elizabeth edged up to Edgar and said, "We must go."

They left the wedding party writhing in ecstasy and mounted the stairs. No one noticed them leaving.

This was the tricky part. There were so many conditions on the spell, so many different ways it could go wrong.

Lamia and Dolon needed to exit the bodies they possessed and consecrate the marriage, each to the other, Elizabeth to Dolon, Edgar to Lamia. A very intense glamor was needed to make their appearance deceptive enough. Then each must sleep for one hour in the arms of their lover, and as the dawn broke the sky, the transformation would be complete. Lamia would become Elizabeth. Mortal, for a time. For all time.

Lamia into Elizabeth was the most important. Dolon into Edgar was somewhat of a moot point. Dolon could inhabit Edgar any time he wanted. Dolon, as a demon, could enter bodies and exit them, be them, whenever he pleased. But he was doomed to his fate: nothing, nothing would change him from a demon to a human. But Lamia, having been cast into the role of gray lady nearly fifteen centuries earlier, had a real chance at escape.

She had to trust that Dolon would uphold his end of the bargain. She knew he didn't love her. But she thought he'd want to be rid of her more than he wanted to take revenge on her for his plight.

But demons… they were hard to predict. And Dolon was a stubborn bastard at best.

Lamia tried to focus on the situation at hand and not worry

about what might happen later. She'd only had four other chances like this in hundreds of years, and she wanted this to go smoothly. So far, Edgar and Elizabeth had proved malleable and perfectly willing to be hosts.

She didn't pray any more, but felt a small part of her being lifted up.

First, they needed two separate rooms and impeccable timing.

They'd spent the day creating the identical bridal suites, one on either side of the castle. Dolon was quite handy with the details. She'd never known him to have a flair for decorating before. If this didn't work....

The stairwell was dark. Dolon had unscrewed all of the electric light bulbs. Alcohol would only make their hosts so blind; darkness was needed as well.

Edgar and Elizabeth moved as one up the stairs, the remnants of their possession making them compliant. At the very top, fear began to emanate from one of them.

"Now," Lamia whispered.

A shimmering glow filled the air. Lamia felt the sweetness that was Elizabeth cover her like a gossamer blanket. The glamor was in place. Dolon winked at her as he shimmered into Edgar, taking Elizabeth's hand and pulling her toward the west bridal suit, as Lamia pulled Edgar to her side and continued down the hall.

"Wait," Elizabeth said, but Lamia coughed and made Edgar walk faster.

"I can't wait to be with you," she whispered, running her hands around the front of his trousers.

Edgar laughed, a throaty, drunken sound. "Not going to last long, sweetheart. I think I've had a bit too much to drink."

Lamia smiled her most feral grin. "That's fine, darling. Once is all we need."

Elizabeth woke just before dawn. She was horrendously sore between the legs. She blushed at the mere thought of the things they'd done. As drunk as she'd been, she was willing to try most anything. And Edgar, Edgar had tried most everything.

Oh, God. She had a horrible hangover. Bile rolled in her stomach, her head pounded. But she'd had the strangest dream. Her grandmother had come to her. She wanted her to drink saltwater upon rising. The woman had been dead for twenty years; Elizabeth rarely dreamt of her. But when she did, she always knew to examine the dream, what fleeting bits she could remember of it, then think to whatever pressing question had been weighing on her mind. Grandmother signaled a decision would be made. Sometimes when she didn't even know she was struggling with a question.

Salt water. Yuck. But she'd learned never to question, only to do. She went into the bathroom, looking for a glass. Her grandmother had been a wise woman.

Maybe there'd be salt on the table?

Edgar, curled in the bed behind her, looked exactly like hell. His skin was tinged with green, his hair spiked to one side of his face. He even looked like his beard was growing in. That was strange. Edgar wasn't a heavily furred man.

She spared him one last glance, then went to the window. She heard waves crashing. She hadn't realized the beach was so close. The castle perched on the edge of a cliff, with a long, rickety staircase leading down to the rocky beach below. In the waves, she saw a man swimming.

It looked like… no, that couldn't be. It looked like Edgar. But Edgar was in the bed behind her. Wasn't he?

A strange pull began in her stomach. She heard a voice calling her name.

"Elizabeth. Come to me."

She held her hand up in front of her face. It was transparent. Clear with the morning sun, she could see directly through her forearm and hand to the sill below.

The pull grew stronger. Panicked, she turned to call for Edgar, but there was no one there. She was alone in the room.

She fought her way to the window again, breath coming hard in her throat. There were two men swimming below now, one riding the back of the other in the waves. They were body surfing, two men, together as one. As she watched, they caught a wave and rode it in to the beach, then clambered out of the water. The man was Edgar, and the man attached to him was… Edgar too.

Her breath began to fail. She didn't know what was happening.

"Come to me, Elizabeth. Come now." The voice called again, summoning. She had no control. She looked in the mirror and saw only a wisp of herself as she vanished into thin air. She was gone.

Edgar was exhilarated. He didn't know what possessed him to drag out of his warm bridal bed and go swimming in the cold surf, but he was glad he had. It cleared his head. He felt wonderful. Starving, in fact. And wanted to see Elizabeth. He wanted to see his wife now.

He grabbed the towel and dried off briskly, then started back up the wobbly wooden stairs. He had so much energy. So much power. My God, Elizabeth had done things to him he'd only read about. He had no idea she even knew those things. Saving it for the wedding night, she was.

He didn't think they'd gotten more than an hour's sleep. Then he woke to the note – My love, go for a swim. I'm getting us breakfast – and thought to himself, yes, that's exactly what I'll do. I'll go for a swim.

He bounded back to the castle, up, up the stairs to the bridal suite. He flung the doors open.

Elizabeth was on the floor under a large gray mass. She wasn't moving, but the mass was, sinuously sliding up and down Elizabeth's body.

"What is this?" he demanded, completely uncertain what to do.

There was a deep hissing noise, and he felt the room contract into coldness. Extreme fury pushed at his chest, making him fall back against the wall. A breeze began, one that smelled like sulfur, whipping his hair and drying the last drops of salt from his arms, and he heard the words, falling through the air like the hiss of daggers.

"Dooooollloooooon. Stooooop hiiiiiiiim."

Edgar looked away from the writhing mass for a moment and

saw himself, standing on the far side of the room, arms crossed, a small grin on his face. Enjoying the show.

A small squeaking caught his attention. It was coming from Elizabeth. That thing was killing her.

Edgar tossed a glance at his twin, then threw himself at the thing. He smelled himself on her, his sweat, his semen, and realized he hadn't lain with his wife at all. The thought sickened him.

The thing wailed and fought against him. It was like wrestling smoke. Punches and kicks were ineffectual. Elizabeth's squeaking grew fainter.

With no full realization of what he was doing, he stood and rushed at his twin. Edgar laughed at him, moving out of the way slightly as he drew near.

How could this be? The real Edgar saw a mirror behind the thing that looked like him. Deviating at the last second, he ran smack into the mirror, causing it to shatter in a hundred pieces. He grabbed the largest from the floor and plunged back into the fray, stabbing at the gray thing with the shard.

"Elizabeth! I love you!" he screamed.

A deep, shrieking howl rose from the floor, and blood began to splash. Edgar slashed, and slashed again, until his could raise his arm no more, and his breath gave out.

The scream was earsplitting. The windows shattered. The walls began to shimmy. The bed rocked, and the wardrobe fell over. It was as if an earthquake had struck the room, accompanied by cries of such intensity Edgar felt himself going mad.

And then it stopped.

The silence was deafening.

It took a moment for him to realize he wasn't moving. And another to feel the smallness beside him.

"Elizabeth!" he cried.

She was no longer translucent, but rosily painted in the things' blood. Her eyes were closed, and the parts of her skin that weren't red were deathly pale.

They were alone in the room.

He scrambled to his knees. "Elizabeth, can you hear me?"

She moaned, and his rational mind took over. Blood. There was so much blood.

It had to be hers.

He was rough with her, pulling her body to and fro until he found the shard of mirror wedged deep within her arm. Blood was pouring from the wound; it must have struck an artery. He needed a tourniquet. He grabbed the towel from its resting place on the floor and wound it around Elizabeth's arm. She was going gray.

"Don't leave me, baby. Hang on."

She opened her eyes. "I. Love. You." Her eyes lost their focus.

He started CPR on her, fighting, pushing air into her lungs, pounding on her chest. He didn't know how much time had passed. He just knew he couldn't give up.

"She's gone, you know. You can stop now."

The voice startled him. He looked up, and saw himself standing by the end of the bed. Only this version of himself wasn't covered in his love's blood.

"Who are you?"

"My name is Dolon."

"What have you done with Elizabeth? Why did you kill her?"

"I didn't. You did. You did a wondrous job of it too. Just look at her, won't you?"

Edgar glanced down. Elizabeth's eyes were open. The blood was gone. She was breathing. The horrid open wound in her arm had closed. She started to sit up, and Edgar, lost, bent to help her.

"Edgar, what happened?" She caught sight of Dolon, still looking like Edgar, and shook her head. "I'm dreaming."

Dolon changed forms, just to show them he could, then disappeared.

Edgar rubbed his eyes. He knew he hadn't just seen what his mind said he saw. "I don't know. Something is very wrong with this place. We need to get out of here, right now. Can you stand?"

"I think so. Edgar, you were swimming. And my grandmother told me to drink a glass of saltwater. I couldn't find the salt. I feel awful. Oh, God. Hold on…"

She turned to her right and wretched onto the floor.

When she was able to stand upright again, Edgar searched her face.

"Elizabeth, what's wrong with your eyes?"

"What do you mean?"

"They've changed color. They're gray."

She rushed into the bathroom and looked. He wasn't lying, her beautiful brown eyes had turned a murky gray.

"I don't know what's going on, Edgar. Just… get me out of here."

He was backing away from her, a look of horror on his face.

"That thing… the thing that was eating you, it's inside you."

"Edgar, don't be silly."

"Elizabeth, you died. I saw it with my own eyes. I think… I think I killed you."

"Edgar, I'm very much alive. Look at me. I'm talking to you, aren't I?"

She was talking to him. But it wasn't her. He could tell. He could see the shadows of the woman he'd slept with last night, the details coming back to him in a rush. The teeth, long and pointed, the bat-like ears, the flesh hanging off her body, the vertebrae sticking out like armor.

"You," he said, voice hushed and terrified.

"Me," Lamia replied, her perfect pink tongue caressing her new pink lips. "Let's go home, husband."

I'm Bill Kurtis

Nate had expected the first serial killer. In fact the first thing he'd said to Kelly once their Ford rolled to a stop on the shoulder was, "This is serial killer country. We're finished." She made scaredy-cat eyes and drew a finger across her throat. "Finished," he enunciated. She'd heard his bake before, something to the effect that certain places settled and then maybe recultivated to feel remote—the Wisconsin Northwoods, for example, or parts of the Rockies or, in this case, Dixie Alley— were stuffed silly with the dumped spent corpses that were the nuggets of serial killers' labor. The type needed space to operate. So each tree in the Northwoods doubled as a headstone, each stem of rice out here a memorial, and to hike cross-country through such territory was to traipse condemned through the densest kind of cemetery.

"Do you want me to have a look?" Kelly said. There'd been a gassy whine from under the hood for a minute before the engine cut.

"Just stay here," Nate said, "and lock the doors if anyone pulls over." No headlights shone in either direction of the interstate as he got out of the car. A couple minutes later, after scalding his finger on shadowy motor metal and wondering how to shoot off a flare, he reentered. "She's dead. Call a tow truck."

And so his vigil for their murderer began. Kelly hung up her cell and told him the tow truck would be there in half an hour or so. Or. So. Orso. Tons could happen during that orso. Nate might have imagined that at 30 minutes they would be fine, sitting talking about getting their dogs out of the kennel when they got back to Clarksville, and at 33, at orso, when their kindly tow truck driver got there, they would be going cold and covered in each other's blood, locked in a final embrace. They'd be easy apples for a Son of Sam. Instead Nate's scenarios focused on the appearance of the killer. One time the killer affixed red and blue lights to his dashboard and approached Nate's driver side in the guise of a cop. Another he wore a jumpsuit and presented himself as a well-meaning mechanic just passing by; he kept a gun in his toolbox. Near as Nate could tell they were at the mercy of anyone with a weapon and a will.

Kelly must have seen how much he was perspiring. "Maybe you should stop with the true crime."

"Maybe you should keep an eye on our flank."

Nate kept the lights on for comfort and so any passing motorists wouldn't think what he thought when he saw a dark car apparently abandoned roadside late at night: someone dumping a body. The downside of course was the lights were a beacon for passersby who pleased to slay the innocent for sport.

Orso finally arrived. No one had driven past, so when the tow truck's headlights faded in and tracked to Nate's rearview, he had every confidence that the driver would double as their executioner. The truck eased into position before them. Nate gave Kelly's hand a quick squeeze, stepped out of the car to face their fate.

"Evening, sir," the driver said. He wore his cap low but the smile seemed sincere. "Not your night?"

"Thought this piece of shit had one last run in her." Nate hoped the cuss would somehow make him seem more human.

"There's a decent mechanic just up in Linville. Two exits on. Fair rates."

"There any place to stay the night?"

"Lodge up there's always got rooms. Want me to haul her in?" The man was already appraising the car, crouching down to check the axle. Kelly chose that moment to join them.

"You need me to put it in neutral or anything?" she asked the driver.

"Ma'am, I need to link us up first."

Nate watched for any sign of the man's taking a special interest in Kelly, but the driver's gaze hadn't lingered at all when he answered her. This could have meant he didn't like strawberry blondes or felt it was too risky here in the open or even wasn't a murderer. Nate took it to mean the driver had stalked them for some time, knew his prey. He tried to remain loose and alert at once and thus failed at both. Kelly smiled at him.

Soon the wheel-lift on the back of the tow truck was hauling up their sedan's front fender. The driver called them over to the open door of his cab.

"Just need you to sign here, sir. Then y'all can climb in and we'll be on our way straight off." He turned and handed Nate a clipboard. Nate gave the document only a cursory glance, definitely no more than a second or two, but long enough that he never saw the tire iron that hammered his skull: a short white, a short pain, a long black.

So the only thing surprising to Nate about waking up alone in his own trunk was that he had woken at all. Impressive pain in his head and his hair was a blood-mess that tarred the fuzzy insides of the trunk, but it struck him that the driver's failure to finish him signaled inexperience or maybe just a lucky amateur whom Kelly could outfox or overpower. Kelly. Thinking of her made it hard to breathe. He spent himself kneeing and punching and shoving the trunk door, but nothing, and no phone, and he could tell from the angle that the car was still hooked to the tow truck. Silence outside. The tow truck was stopped or had never started; he didn't know how long he'd been out.

Nate felt like they shouldn't be numbers, like Kelly for sure was more than a number, more than a midseason episode of some true-crime series on TV. He could see Bill Kurtis's face during the coda. "For *American Justice*, I'm Bill Kurtis," said the face. The face said something like that and then they rolled credits on the tow truck murders and previewed the following week's episode about a beauty queen slain in Hawaii. Kelly's eyes seeped into Nate's brain unbidden, like a hacked feed, not her actual eyes but what they were seeing, and not what her actual eyes were seeing but what they might be. He tried to tune out but couldn't. She made out the stars and rice stems and the tow truck driver's face overhead. The face was close and had bushy eyebrows. It dripped sweat on her and later was the last thing she'd ever see as the driver, in this instance, sawed into her carotid. This looped with minor variations: in the truck cab or a nearby abandoned farmhouse or barn instead of the field, and garroting, bludgeoning, or shooting instead of throat slitting. The eyebrows always remained bushy. Sometimes she escaped briefly or fought back with fleeting success, but as time passed inside the ciliate trunk these episodes began to occur to him less and less frequently. Her final thoughts tended to be about Nate, about warmth with Nate and his smiling face, though this is mostly because Nate supposed he would be thinking of her if he were in her place when in fact there's every chance that at the last her flickers were of nothing at all, just the thrashing blank that often petrifies someone near the end, or that images of her mom or a childhood scene back at the lake or even their dogs rather than Nate came to mind and brought such serenity to her face that the killer, the tow truck driver, took pause and visibly went lamb before puzzling loose her bonds—while of course keeping a fast hand on her, except now more the hand of child to mother than captor to captive—and confessing to her as if she were a priest and as if she didn't already know a hell's worth of his sins. Kelly's mind in this turn of events would inevitably turn to what might've been had she made a different face at the crucial moment. Serenity had won him over and effected her reprieve. She could only assume that fear would have made a quick end of her—serial killers relished that sort of thing as she understood it. Defiance sometimes earned a few heartbeats in the movies if for no other reason than that the killer had to take time to wipe the victim's spittle from his face or respond to an epithet before finishing her, but she suspected real killers ate up defiance as busily as fear. She didn't know how zaniness would have been received: she liked to think that a "Hey! Look!" followed by crossed eyes and a protruding crooked tongue would break the tension, create the opening she needed, but then she also couldn't deny that killers seemed to respond to confusion by exterminating the confounder rather than reasoning with her. She hadn't met any other killers so impossible to say where this notion about confusion came from but it felt like simple math. Sadness might have worked, she guessed, because her mere hand on his brow had now reduced him to weepy babble and sobs in soprano that sounded almost more like trills, like singing away bloodlust. This put Kelly in a delicate spot because yes she'd gained the upper hand but things could turn as quick as a look and the wrong word here might still be her last. She looked for a weapon but there was nothing in sight. She considered telling him to go home now or telling him he was absolved or telling him her name but none felt right. So she stood still, hoping they could last like this till dawn, at which time she wasn't sure what would happen except that the sun would come up, expand that skin on her nose and cheeks and suffuse her pores with heat that wicked down through her finger pads into his brow, and if nothing else sooner or later he had to pass out, helpless because, she realized, this wasn't congregant to priest after all but supplicant to god—she was her attacker's god. To calm and burn was her right.

Nate was still stuck in the initial loop, Kelly killed over and over, when he suddenly felt the car start to ease back to level ground, heard the trunk pop open. At first he thought it daytime because of the glare, but it was just another truck parked right behind him, engine idling, a huge semitruck whose headlights blinded him and made an inky boogeyman of the figure standing over him. Then Nate noticed the boogeyman had strawberry blonde hair.

"Can you walk?" Kelly asked him.

"Where is he?"

The semitruck's headlights showed a rent on Kelly's cheek, but the sprays of blood on her shirt didn't look like hers. "The cab," she said.

"You folks need help?"

A man was climbing down from the driver side of the semitruck but Kelly and Nate's hug was so fierce he felt as if his head wrapped around her too, as if it enfolded her and preserved her, so he barely turned it to look at the man.

"Everything OK here?"

"We've been attacked, sir. I think we need the police."

"Name's Trevor. Just one guy? What's his status?" The burly trucker looked ready to mount a charge should the tow truck's door open.

"Just one. In the tow truck. He's dead."

"I can radio a cruiser from my cab. You injured, ma'am? We should get an ambulance too."

"I think Nate might need it more than me." She put ginger fingers to Nate's head as Trevor stepped warily to the window of the tow truck.

He backed from the window wide-eyed. "You're tougher than you look, Nate."

"Not even close." Sad smile.

"Let's get a blanket on you two, make that call."

Trevor motioned for them to come with him. Kelly refused the arm he proffered, but as she turned to walk the blood on her shirt came clearly into his view for the first time. This caused him to stop for a moment. The expression on his face was conflicted, a sort of queasy pity, Nate guessed, but the trucker managed not to look too ill. He composed himself and guided them to his rig. They stood by the road while he rummaged around inside the cab. From what Nate could see they were still where his car had originally broken down.

"Ain't the first time I've seen this, you know." Trevor leaned from the open doorway to hand a plaid wool blanket down to Nate, who wrapped it around Kelly. "Oh, the details are different, but you roll these roads long enough, you're bound to see some things'll keep you up nights." He got on the CB radio; Nate heard some static and Trevor drawling that they had a 10-33 at the nearest mile marker. "You two might be luckier than you think. Usually, something like this happens, they don't find a trace of anyone." Trevor climbed out of the cab to wait with them, scanned the road both ways. No police lights yet. No lights at all. "You done good, miss." He patted Kelly gently on the shoulder, then tomahawked her head into the door of the truck.

Nate could give credit to their first attacker, who had simply been too quick at the crucial moment, but as Trevor's weight flattened Nate on the roadside, as his hands began wringing the oxygen from Nate's windpipe, some small part of Nate felt to blame for this one. It had been slow developing and what in happier times he might've described as a crude scheme. Trevor, he now felt, even looked the part of a veteran serial killer, maw and rage and not a lot else. That they'd just met a predator seemed to Nate a poor excuse for failing to see the second one. He hoped it would go fast for Kelly. As the night faded around him he tried to imagine a way she might beat death again. He failed to see that too.

When Nate coughed himself awake he knew immediately that this time he wasn't in his own trunk. It was level for one thing and squared off and much smaller. He couldn't even move his arms to pound futilely against the metal interior. He offered one meek and agonizing head butt before Trevor's eyes popped into his—the feed again. The nausea that hit at that moment could have been from either his concussion or the headshot of Kelly. She wore her glasses. Tight gag. Soiled leather seat under her head. The glasses were impossible because she'd had LASIK the year before and hadn't even brought them on the trip. Bare shoulders. Purple neck. In this iteration Trevor bundled her body in plastic and heaved her from a bridge, remembering to poke holes in the wrap so she would sit longer on the riverbed. The cycle began again and this time Nate saw Trevor hide her remains in a decrepit silo. He disposed of her in a strip mall dumpster. He left her in the old quarry. He dropped her down a mineshaft, down a well, down a roster of graves Nate had seen on TV or read about, and Trevor never once had trouble unburdening himself of her body and getting away clean even though a mind less distressed than Nate's would

consider the effect of her gentle cheekbones on the truck driver
and know that, though Trevor might pull off, say, tucking her into
an out-of-the-way culvert, it was only then that he would become
a sort of inmate. He'd climb back into his rig bushytailed. Traffic
would be light in the small hours and he'd catch now and then
wide eyes in the mirror, his eyes, not scared but just aware, murder
as NoDoz, and he'd actually try to say something much like this to
himself there in the cab of the tractor-trailer: "Murder is NoDoz."
It was a joke, a lightness anyway, and maybe of note is that he
never shrank for a heartbeat from his act but instead named it
murder in his own mind immediately when Kelly expired, not love
or liberation or the like but murder. Funny thing wasn't the joke
though but the fact that somewhere between Trevor's brain and
the open air of the cab the joke changed into something else entirely
without his even realizing it. He thought he'd said, "Murder is
NoDoz," and as soon as he spoke the words he forgot them, but
what actually came out was, "I killed this pretty face just west of
Linville and shoved her body up a culvert to avoid detection."
With no witnesses present the confession passed without
consequence and before long Trevor's vehicle had slipped back
into its route as if the interruption had been just a bite and a piss.
Trevor whistled at the sunup while his head filled with calculations:
routes, speeds, cargo. He was a professional. He kept his
appointments. Eventually he got on the radio to ask westbound
truck drivers about traffic near the city, intending to call, "Anyone
got their ears on?" over the open channel but instead declaring, "I
killed this pretty face just west of Linville and shoved her body up
a culvert to avoid detection." This time Trevor's words registered
in his ears immediately. He let the microphone slide to the ground
as a string of responses, mostly profanities and 10-9 calls, crackled
through the road hum, and it turns out the dread and disbelief he
felt weren't over the unclaimed confession he'd transmitted into
the atmosphere but over the fog-slick sense that he was helpless
to utter anything else. He tried again, this time aloud to himself.
"Calm down," he tried to say. Instead: "I killed this pretty face just
west of Linville and shoved her body up a culvert to avoid

detection." There were no other words left and he knew in his belly it would be that way from now on. Still eastbound he began planning for life as a mute. First, no more killings. And he'd shed his habit of thinking aloud, even in private. He had no wife but luckily his mother still had good years left. She could see to him awhile, explain his circumstance so that in time town would adopt Dumb Trevor, a sort of mascot and a butt and their own. He'd pretend an innocent smile at the little neighborhood terrors. When Ma passed, an old family friend would show pity and arrange Trevor a sinecure guarding a warehouse nights. They had no old family friends. And one day decades away he'd be abed with nothing to lose, sun stream long on his pillow, but lacking kindred or even pets he'd have no one to talk to except these nurses. His first word would come out a broken croak. Looking down on him they'd urge him to go on.

The clink of metal next to Nate's ear didn't snap him from his trance of seeing Kelly dumped over and over and neither for a minute did Kelly's opening the door of the semitruck's underbody trunk and lifting him out. She stood blood red and strawberry red and solar red, and overlaid on Kelly's live impossible bruise of a face Nate saw Kelly stashed in a landfill and Kelly entombed under drying cement. Kelly vanished up Kelly's nostril. Finally the overlay decomposed but she stayed, staring head tilted with predawn on her shoulder and over it rice to the horizon. Soon the two were hugs and sobs, all reflex, and then Kelly shook her head before Nate could finish whatever question he was spluttering and they just huddled a minute in the shadow of the trailer.

"My phone," Nate said, starting toward the tow truck. "I'll get the police." What he really wanted though was to find the keys and fly, gory windshield and all, dead driver between them or roadside or in the trunk of Nate's dead car.

"I radioed for help." Kelly was hoarse. "Don't go back there."

So he took her up again in the hug of the should-be dead and softly sang her the first thing that came to mind—an army cadence his dad used to do when Nate was a kid. He maneuvered her in a loving hug-shuffle next to the semitruck, passenger side, and put his gray sweater on her. Its color matched the steel of the trailer. "Keep you warm," he said. Murmuring the while about rest he persuaded her to sit with her legs bunched against her chest, reduce exposure. "Stop babying," she said, reeking of blood. Her shelled and sure stare wobbled him.

The first responder to Kelly's broadcast was no state trooper but apparently just a bespectacled Good Samaritan. He rounded the corner of the trailer and initially he gaped at the couple but after a second he held forward a first-aid kit and started saying something gentle about help and harm. His story sounded real. Eventually he started toward them with wide arms and lulling tones that blended with the thrum of the still-idling engine. Nate and Kelly looked quick at each other, and this time they didn't miss their chance: they made a break for the rice. They ran hard and free a moment with dew firing from their soles until as they approached the first row Nate glanced back over his shoulder. Then he stood. The Good Samaritan had begun loping after them but Nate was looking past the man to his vehicle, a white van parked roadside, and the white van parked behind it, and the white van parked behind that, and the white van parked behind that, and the white van parked behind that, and the numberless white vans parked behind that, each with a lone driver waiting his turn, a cavalcade of killers lined up, Nate knew, all the way to the Pacific. Seen from space they'd look like the Great Wall of China, like a trace smile line on the earth's cheek.

Sheryl Monks

Monsters in Appalachia

She hears the dogs coming round now, bugling louder as they draw near, bawling out in unbridled rapture. Their aching bliss, laid plain, bleeds into her like a hemorrhage, and she can hear it, now, too, she thinks, calling them through the woods. Its song the furtive cry of a panther, a wailing baby. The dogs call out again, and somewhere in the quiet depths, he moans with delight as well.

Outside, it is dark as that which plagued Egypt. How the dogs manage in such blackness, she can't say, but they have a scent on their noses and that's how they go, she knows. Still, there are trees and all manner of things to watch out for in the night woods, though she guesses they can scent trees as well as beasts. Anse's Plotts are of an olden breed, the keenest ever was. They can scent things never heard tell of. Trees? Why they must be simple, she guesses. She herself can scent trees, pine rosin and fruiting pawdads, though not at a full tear through the dark.

She wishes it was light out, a whitish day with the dogs scaring up quail from the hawthorn and hedge apples. Retrieving game, not stalking it. She doesn't like the ropes of slobber that hang from their mouths after a chase such as this. Doesn't trust how they pull against their leads so hard and lust for a thing. She can hear it there now in their voices, ringing round the woods. They've treed something or hemmed something in. It is over now. They'll be home in a spell.

She goes to the stove, runs the grate back and forth, shovels out the ash. Then she adds coal and waits till the fire is built up good again. He'll be froze solid when he comes back. She brings clean coveralls into the canning porch, pulls on her coat, grabs the washtubs, and goes to light a fire in the yard. But she is late, and here come the headlights of the truck, dogs still baying, Anse's old Dodge winding out hard to drag the heavy load up the steep drive.

She drops the washtubs under the hemlock and sets a match to the kindling. Anse ties the dogs and goes back to unload his catch. She comes round after him to help.

At first, she thinks it's a bear. But it is not a bear, she knows. Too big. Unless it is a Kodiak, and she's never heard tell of Kodiak round here. Her heart mashes chamber against chamber. "Another?" she asks.

"All that's running," he replies.

"Th'ey God in heaven," she says. "Monsters. It's the end-times."

"Nevertheless."

She hungers for something soft, the sweet, tender things of before. Now it is all hard hide and claw and horns and scales and beaks and necks and parts unheard of.

She looks at Anse. They string up the beast in the hemlock and split it down the middle. Bile rolls out and acid that singes what little grass there is. There is no heart inside it, nor any innard they can recognize, just what looks like a stomach, gut-colored and bloated. Anse pricks it and out comes nothing but noise, low grunts and shushed cries. She grabs it up and throws it to the dogs.

"Look what a taste for it they've got," he says. But she looks away, cannot bear it. "Did you hear it?" he asks. "Hear it wailing? You should've seen it hiss and spit at me. Look at those horns. Have you ever seen anything like it? And those wings."

"It's unclean," she says. "Take it out of here."

"Clean as any other beast," he says. "Why, look, it's an angel."

She steps closer, studies its faceless, floppy form, its veiny, segmented torso, its swine-like hoofs, cat-gut wings. "It's no angel," she says, "but a monster."

"A monster? Yes, you're right," he says. "How many do you suppose there are? What all kinds, you reckon?"

He has counted and killed hundreds. Their mounted likenesses adorn the walls of the milking barn. She has never been to the barn to look, but she knows from night terrors that hell is on the other side. Worse than the monsters themselves is the smell of burning flesh, the sounds of loved ones gnashing their teeth in anguish.

"Try it," he says. "You'd get used to it if you'd just try."

"I don't want to," she says. "I'll do w'thout."

"Very well."

During the day, on her walks, she startles up quail from the hedge apples. "Look there," she says. "There they go. Oh, how I hunger. Lord, don't you know how I hunger? Oh, for the sweet, tender things still in abundance. Look there how abundant."

"I've got a shank left yet in the smokehouse," he tells her, standing to fetch it.

"No," she says, holding him from going. "Not tonight."

"I can heat it myself," he says. "Won't take but a minute."

"Don't bring that filth into my house," she says. "I've had all of it I can stand."

But he is already shaving off strips of black hindquarters with her best pairing knife. "Try a bite," he says. "Look a'here," and he tosses a portion of tentacle, uncooked, into his mouth and chews.

She wonders what it tastes like, how his tongue can abide the fusty butter secreted through its pores without gagging. A yellowish smear of it collects in the corners of his mouth, and suddenly, she wants fiercely to kiss him. At their age, she thinks, cross with herself and the weakness of her flesh. She fights the urge in favor of encouraging him to talk as he eats, so she can catch the faintest scent of his breath.

At night, he sleeps like a hound. She looks at his lips and traces her cracked finger over them. She wets it and runs it over them again. It's all that's left, he'd told her. She looks at her finger, at his lips. She misses him. Who is this strange creature beside her? He looks the same, has the same broken capillaries crossing his nose, the same loose jowl shuddering like a spoon of preserves when he breathes. But something is different. She leans in, breathes in his breath. It's there, she thinks. Inside. She smells it. She looks into his mouth and there, his tongue. It lolls about, wide and thick as a wallet. She sees something, a line, a seam? Down the middle, yes. He smacks his lips and when she looks again, it is split. His tongue forks and flicks and she wakes herself panting.

He begins to capture and cage the monsters. He breeds them, one to the other, domesticates some that till the fields, do the hunting, work around the house. One can speak. It talks to her. Tells her he is the beast, that he does unspeakable things to them. Turn me loose, it begs her. Let me go back to my kind.

But he is a demon and she doesn't trust him. The cages are flimsy. They could all free themselves with little effort if they wanted. No, she doesn't trust them.

Outside, all around, the quail sing from the brush. "Catch me some," she begs Anse, and he sends out the speaking beast, which slaughters two hundred and brings them to her.

"Eat," the beast says. "I will bring you more, all you desire."

But she pushes it away and hides. "No."

He is lying with the beasts now. "Go and look," the speaking beast tells her.

"Get!" she tells it. "Leave me be." But the sounds carry on through the night. She hears his voice above the cries of the beasts. She hears him breathing, hears him humping and moaning. "God in heaven!" she cries. "Why do you let this go on? There is a demon here who speaks to me plainly, but you deny me. Again and again, Lord. Why have you forsaken me?"

He opens a sideshow called Monsters in Appalachia, where he parades the beasts by whip and chain out of the barn and onto a homemade platform built of cinderblocks and three-quarter-inch particleboard. He has identified all the ones from the book of Daniel, but he is missing a few from the book of Revelation.

"This one here," he tells curiosity-seekers, "this one is a silver-tongued devil," and he cracks a whip at the one that can speak until it cries out so that the audience shrinks back in amazement.

Its voice is small now and timid. She listens from the window, hears it say, "Please, master, no more."

She imagines folks leaning in to see if the thing is real or not, or maybe just for a closer look at its injuries. They don't actually believe what they are seeing. They are merely playing along for the thrill of it. Monsters in Appalachia. Foolishness.

She takes down the rifle from the rack over the doorway and sets off for the woods. The dogs have all gone mad with desire. "I will prepare a table in the wilderness," she says and sets out alone in search of quail. She is ravenous waiting on the Lord. She will go in search of Him. He has turned away from the wickedness of this place and may smite it yet, she thinks.

Outside, spectators are clapping and cheering passionately. Carnies sell cotton candy and day-glo necklaces from tents and booths littering the fallow tobacco fields surrounding the barn. There is a lighted marquee dead center of the hayloft on which the Whore of Babylon and her Scarlet Dragon take top billing. Hand-painted banners and sack-cloth signs adorn the walls of the barn, depicting the various monster acts one might see inside. "Hell on Earth!" says one. "Point of No Return!"

The line of those waiting to get inside wraps around the barn. Parents and their children, a group of women wearing pastel-colored uniforms, foul-mouthed teenagers, yuppies, coalminers, housewives, policemen, drug dealers, car salesmen, IT geeks, Bible scholars.

The monster that can speak is talking up the acts. "Step right up. Satisfy your curiosity. Peer into oblivion. Behind this curtain, there is a legion of demons the likes of which the human mind cannot conceive. This is real. You will see beasts loosed on the earth thousands of years ago, bound up now for your amusseement." His voice is menacing, but not so much that folks are terrified. He conceals the pelt of fire and molten cinders covering his body and the bleeding boils beneath with a long black tunic covered in rhinestones.

At the front of the line, there stands a fierce-looking peacock-man, waving his brilliant green-blue wings, the diaphanous feathers of which are elongated and covered in a hundred angry eyes of God. "Depart from this bed of iniquity!" issues forth from a disembodied voice. A quiver of fiery darts is strapped to the bird-man's blue velvet shoulders and broad back, resting in the valley of the creature's poison-tipped wings. People step out of line to get a better look.

"Who is that?" they say to each other, beguiled, sore afraid for the coming of the great cataclysm rendered by the prophets.

"I am the purity of God," the peacock-man says.

The monster howls with laughter. "The purity of God, are you?"

The peacock-man speaks to the beast in harsh tones of another language, a queer bird talk. Then, more plainly, "I am Jophkiel. God will show no mercy, Sumael."

"If you are Jophkiel, the purity of God, why do you take on this preposterous disguise?"

The line breaks and shifts into a sea of onlookers, an audience awaiting a spectacular finale. The peacock-man is awesome, they think. Is it a costume, really? They've never seen anything like it before.

"'It is a wicked and evil generation that looks after a sign. There will be no sign given,' sayeth the Lord."

"Harr!" roars the speaking beast. "If you've no mysteries to reveal. Get back in line." Then he addresses the crowd. "I offer you proof. Beyond a shadow of a doubt. Step right up."

And the line rights itself again peacefully, and one by one, curiosity-seekers step behind the curtain of tinkling, plinkling rhinestones suspended mid-air.

"Did you see them today?" he asks her in bed that night. "The excitement on their faces? The anticipation of something spectacular, impossible, unbearable?"

She does not answer, nor does he care. He is making plans. "Who was that bird-man? An actual Got-damned angel, you suppose?"

"I want a divorce," she says, and he grabs her bony wrist.

"What God has joined together, let no man put asunder."

"I never knew Him," she says.

"I have a vision," he proclaims next morning. "An outdoor drama, like *Unto These Hills*. If there are demons loose on the earth, there must be angels as well. I will find them and unleash them on the demons, and there will be Armageddon."

"Yes," she says, resting her peeling-knife hand in her lap, holding the dirt-covered spud in the other. "It's time to judge the living and the dead." This is what she has been waiting for, what they have all been yearning for fearfully but deeply. Last days, the terrible judgment.

They go together in search of the angel who had shown itself and find it whirling through the trees of the wilderness like a great gust of particle-ized ash.

"Messenger of the Lord," Anse says, falling on his face on the leaf-moldering floor of the forest. "Go and unlock the gates of heaven so that the Creator can separate the righteous from the unrighteous."

At once, a blinding light shines forth more radiant than the sun, and a voice says, "What have you to sacrifice?"

"Nothing," Anse says, black tears burning hot in his eye sockets, leaving blisters on his bearded old jowls. "All that I have and am is misery. My wife there is an adulteress, and I am a sorcerer."

"Even so, the Creator requires a burnt offering. Bring it here and I will intercede on your behalf."

At home again, they sit on the davenport and gaze into the conjure box, which makes light of wars and disease and pestilence plaguing the earth. The weight of their transgressions is made both heavier and lighter now by their confession. She walks to the stove and stares in at the fiery coals. It is good to deny one's self, she thinks.

In the beginning, the earth was formless and void, and darkness was on the face of the deep. And God gave dominion to man, who bore woman of his own flesh. And the woman was tempted by the formless void and the darkness that roamed. So she ate, and he ate what she ate, and they were cast out of the garden forever.

"I have learnt my lesson," she says. "I shall never eat another bite of anything but that what has been bought by the blood of the Lamb."

"Then you sh'll starve, woman," Anse says. "I aim to be fed one way or a'tother." He and the speaking beast sit at the table spread with the meat of their own kind.

"I will never pull up a ch'eer to a table such as that again. Hold my hand to Jesus," she says, clutching a dishtowel to her breast with one hand, lifting the other up to heaven.

"Then you shall perish," says the beast, smiling coolly, "and suffer the terrible judgment."

"I welcome it," says she, unhinging a deranged smile, wringing the dish cloth in her hands. "I give up my whole self, my wretched old body and twisted, black heart. I want nary a piece of it no more."

Suddenly, a form moves beneath the earth and buckles the kitchen floor, tearing asunder the shoe-scuffed linoleum that curls at the walls' edges.

"I would gladly take my place in purgatory but for the terr-ible great judgment of the Lord to come!" She hollers excitedly at the sight of her house being rent to pieces, the windows now twisting and warping and shattering out of their frames.

"I'd cast my own soul into the fiery furnace of hell but for the righteousness of God to be revealed! I'd cast the whole lot of mankind there with me—we none of us deserves no better—but for the glory of Jesus Christ, the gentle Lamb, the terr-ible judge, to rain down His purifying fire from heaven and burn us ever' one to cinders!"

"I would consume the tick-ridden hide of the devil his self to make right what wrong I done," she says, flailing her arms round about her and letting her head flop back.

The little shack crumbles to the mountainside around them,

and now Anse, too, begins to plead to the Heavenly Host to render forth the great ending. "Come, Yahweh, come!"

The blue halo that surrounds the earth becomes gauzy. The sky fills with ice shavings and dust, an astral mirror moving over the face of the waters and the firmament, and over all the herbs that yield seeds and trees that bear fruit, over all the fish that swim in the waters and all the winged birds that fill the air, over all the cattle and creeping things. And the reflection of the whole world is turned upside down and cast up into the sky.

And every eye on the earth and in the ground and in the sea gazes up and looks at its likeness in the sky, and it sees its whole self, from continent to continent, every mountain, every stream, every tree and rock and animal, and between those, every shadow, every dark moving place the eye has ever been tempted by. And beyond that the vastness of space. The blue halo thins further and the sky turns sallow with saltpeter. And a whisper goes out over all the earth, calling every creature by its name.

The Veil

Doc Haskins watched through the kitchen window as the sun skimmed westward across the top of Roan Mountain. The trip to Knoxville was tiring and traumatic, too much for old folks to manage in one day. They were still sweaty from the July heat and a little bit car sick from the ride, but he had insisted that Lorrie try to eat something, as soon as they were home. She had picked at her breakfast hours earlier and hadn't had a bite since.

Lorrie pushed her bowl away, jostled a dollop of stew onto the Irish linen tablecloth. "I can't," she said. She checked the white polka dots on her navy blue dress for splatters, like it was an afterthought, then fingered the pearl necklace Doc bought her years ago. "I'm just not hungry." She stood, started to pick up the dishes.

Doc let his soup trickle off the spoon and dribble back into the bowl. "I'll clean up," he said. He put one of Lorrie's aprons on over his brown suit, then opened, gently slammed, then reopened cabinet doors while he searched for dish detergent. Lorrie retreated to the living room to her rocking chair, to her books.

She had seemed ill at ease with the university doctor. Who wouldn't? He was young enough to be their grandson, but he was so arrogant. Doc didn't expect anything extra, but it galled him a little to hear the doctor call his wife Lorrie instead of Mrs. Haskins.

She seemed reluctant to let him examine her. She appeared doubtful, too, when he claimed to feel a "fullness" deep in the pit of her stomach. He recommended that she see a cancer specialist, predicted that she would certainly need chemotherapy and probably "a little cobalt."

"That sounds bad," Lorrie said.

"There's no such thing as a 'good' cancer," the doctor agreed, nodding grimly, like he was the new sheriff in town. "But you must keep a positive attitude so you can fight it."

Doc recalled Lorrie's image as he helped her don the examination gown. Her backbone looked like knots tied in baling twine. Her skin sagged in loose wrinkles from her weight loss. She wasn't up to much of a fight.

"Even if the treatment doesn't help, Lorrie," he continued, "the information we gather might help your children or your grandchildren someday."

It was a stock phrase, one that all doctors say, one that sounds profound but isn't. Doc Haskins had used it himself in his small town general practice. He felt Lorrie shrink against his arm like something inside her was leaking out.

Doc finished washing the dishes, wiped the table, then draped the apron over a kitchen chair and joined Lorrie in the living room. He loosened his bow tie, unbuttoned his collar, settled in his overstuffed recliner with a pile of unread medical journals stacked on either side.

"I don't see the point," she said.

Was the break in her voice from emotion or fatigue?

"If I don't take the treatment, I die," she said. "If I do take it, you drive me back and forth to Knoxville for a few weeks for some treatment that will make me sicker, and I die anyway."

His craggy face, furrowed as deep as the farmland surrounding Oak Grove, tried to rearrange itself into a smile.

"We're all going to die," he said. "But we don't have to just give in to it." It was another stock answer, one he regretted as soon as he heard the words leave his mouth.

She rubbed his big, knobby fingers with her tiny, chalk white hand, a latticework of blue veins visible just under her skin. "How did you suture with your knuckles this way?" she asked. He once could repair the tiniest cut on the vermillion border of a wrestling child's lip and leave only the hint of a scar.

"I don't know," he said. "Practice, I guess. Doing the same thing over and over."

They sat without speaking, her occasional gentle squeeze on his hand the only reminder that she was still thinking, still formulating words in her mind, arranging her thoughts.

"Promise me that you won't let me hurt," she said. She rubbed Doc's hand, as if to remind him that she knew there was more to him than showed on the outside. "These young doctors don't know there's a difference in living longer and dying slower."

It was a warm afternoon, but Lorrie insisted that Doc wrap her feet and legs in a blanket, drape a shawl across her shoulders, and push her wheelchair to the oak tree in their backyard. They had spent the morning looking at photographs from her summertime travels. He imagined her showing these same pictures to her first graders, offering them her documentary of other people and far-off places as proof that there was a world beyond the Oak Grove city limits.

"This was my favorite place to wait for you to come home," she said. "I've sat here and read for hours."

It wasn't an accusation, but it felt like one.

"I always thought of you when I read Chekhov," she continued. She had a faraway look in her eyes. "Medicine was his mistress, too."

Mistress? That seemed a little harsh.

She reached for his hand without looking at him, as if she could hear his thoughts. "Did you miss me when I traveled all those summers?" she asked.

After their son Zade died, Doc encouraged Lorrie to travel. He wanted her to stay busy, to keep her mind occupied. He immersed himself in his practice, refused to be away from Oak Grove more than a night or two at a time until he was nearly sixty.

"It was like lancing a boil," he said. "Sometimes necessary. Never desirable."

A breeze rustled through the leaves above them. Lorrie craned her head back where she could look up at the tree. "I used to look into those branches and imagine how Michelangelo felt, lying on his back, painting the ceiling of the Sistine Chapel."

Doc looked up. The leaves had changed from green to gold to russet since their trip to the university hospital. He didn't see the ceiling of a chapel. He couldn't imagine how Michelangelo felt. He needed to find out more about Dr. Chekhov, too.

Lorrie reversed her days and nights, blended her memory with her imagination, saw things that were not real, didn't see things that were. He had to move her rocking chair from the living room and replace it with a hospital bed. She wet. He changed her. She vomited. He cleaned her. She hurt. He pinched the skin on her belly and injected morphine.

Her eyes turned a deep orange. Her hands swelled so quickly Doc could barely soap her wedding band off. Her urine turned the same coffee color as the winter leaves on the ground under the oak tree. Her breath took on a sweet odor, one that didn't fade no matter how often or how thoroughly he cleaned her mouth.

"Don't look at me," Lorrie said when she caught him studying her. "I don't like it."

Sometimes she woke and asked questions from nowhere, like she was dreaming a discussion, and when she roused, just continued the conversation.

"What do you think will happen after I die?" she asked.

"I don't know," he said. "I'll ..." He wanted to tell her that he hadn't been able to imagine life without her.

"Do you think there is a place we go, to another life?" she asked. She closed her eyes again, seemed to sleep.

Doc believed death was a biologic fact, the outer boundary to life, that in the universe, there is no change in the quantity of matter, only in the form that matter takes; ashes to ashes, dust to dust. That's all we are. That's all we become.

"A doctor in one of Faulkner's novels said that death only exists in the minds of the survivors, that the actual death is no more significant than a tenant changing tenements," she said, as if he had answered her.

Doc scanned her bookshelves, wondered which book she referenced.

"What do *you* think?" he asked, helplessly pushing the point, dreading her answer. "Do you think there is a place we go to after we die?"

"Oh, yes," she said. "I talk to people who are there. They're waiting for me."

"Who?" he asked, arching his eyebrow. He had always said it was best to humor a delirious patient. Say what they need to hear. Ask what they want to answer. "Who have you talked to?"

"Family," she said.

Doc's mind strayed helplessly to the memory of their son.

"My daddy visited me one night. He didn't say anything, just stood at the edge of my bed and shimmered in and out of the light. He was wearing the suit we buried him in, except he was wearing his hat. I closed my eyes, and when I opened them, he was gone. I thought it was a dream."

"It was," Doc said. He sounded harsh, even to himself. "Maybe, it was," he repeated in a softer voice, hoping she hadn't heard him the first time.

"Maybe. But I never had it before. And if it was a dream, I would have been afraid," she said. "I was glad to see him. I felt safe."

"Have you seen anyone else?"

"Sometimes I see Mom. My brother was standing behind her once." Lorrie's mother died in her sleep decades earlier. Her only brother died in France, during the war. "I guess they're trying to reassure me."

Doc pinched the bridge of his nose, squinted his eyelids tight. He had heard hundreds of tearful stories about death visitations, accepted them as signs of hysteria or emotional incompetence. He had resisted sarcasm, patted slumped shoulders, and said things like, "There now, he's in a better place." He had said these words without feeling them, done these things without believing them, over and over. It was part of the role, part of being a small town doctor.

"So where do you think they are traveling from?" he asked. "And why was your dad still wearing his burial suit? Don't you think it's because that was your last memory of him?"

"I don't know," she answered. "Next time I'll ask."

She said it like their whole conversation was rational, logical, like she knew and he accepted that there was a thin veil separating the dead from the living, one that people could step through, then step back again, at their pleasure, from wherever they are to wherever this is.

She expected there to be a next time.

It was January, bitter cold. Doc had left Lorrie asleep to stand in the darkness on the back porch and cough the stagnant air from his lungs. When he returned, he found Zade sitting on the piano bench, facing the window, looking away from Doc. It was almost as surprising that he was at the piano as it was that he was even present. Lorrie had hopes that she could mold him into a cultured little boy, had tried to teach him piano before he started school, had insisted that he practice a few minutes every day. Zade resisted, much preferred to be in the dirt, kicking a ball, climbing a tree, doing little boy things. Even now, he wore the striped T-shirt, the muddy jeans, the US Keds tennis shoes with one of them unlaced, the uniform of all Oak Grove first graders in the 1960s.

Doc tried to position himself where he could see Zade's face. He wanted to touch the tiny bruise on the boy's forehead, still wanted to understand how a fall from a playground sliding board could cause such a trivial appearing wound yet still be fatal. The room seemed to swivel so that no matter how he approached, his only view was the skinny neck, the narrow shoulders, the perfect symmetry of the round little head with the little boy buzz cut. That much hadn't changed in 35 years.

Memories that had haunted him, images that had roused him from sleep and left him sitting on his bedside with a pounding heart and sweaty palms, played like a movie in his mind once more. He saw Zade's mouth make a perfect circle, watched his head turn toward him with his eyes already glazed over, saw his face soften, heard him exhale a soft whooshing sound like he was blowing out a birthday candle. He remembered how Lorrie perched on a stainless steel exam stool and rocked her body back and forth, how she cried in a high-pitched moan that didn't stop even when she took a breath, how she rebuffed Doc's attempt to comfort himself by holding her. He pictured their pastor in his shiny shoes and cheap suit, heard again his empty prayer that mentioned faith smaller than a mustard seed and mountains to be moved, recalled the way he held both Lorrie's hands in his never calloused ones and told her, "God just let us borrow Zade for a while. He took him back to be with Him."

Lorrie roused, mumbled something. Her breathing changed from quiet and shallow to deep and rapid. Her eyes searched the room, frantic, until they settled on Doc. He leaned over her, put ice chips on her tongue, considered another dose of morphine, then adjusted the moist washcloth on her forehead.

"Zade is here," Doc said, thinking that might calm her. "It's Zade."

She locked her gaze on Doc, magnetized him so that he couldn't look away. Her wide, blue eyes were like mirrors in which he saw his reflection staring back; a tired old man with a halo of white hair growing directly into the scraggle on his face, lines etched deep into his cheeks, a look of sad resignation.

"Zade's here," he repeated. His throat was dry. The words croaked out. "He's over there, on the piano bench."

Lorrie didn't move, didn't change her expression, just continued her heavy breathing.

Doc stood, heaved and shoved the end of the bed to where she faced the piano bench without turning her head. The effort made his head ache, left him dizzy. He collapsed in his chair, rested his head on the edge of her mattress. His breath came in long, ragged wheezes. Lorrie's breathing grew quiet again. Doc lifted his head and stared with Lorrie at the empty piano bench.

Through the window, Doc noticed how the sunrise made a yellow border that outlined the mountain at the eastern edge of town. The oak tree had changed from a black silhouette to a dusky shadow. The yard was foggy, gray, like the darkness had stretched thin trying to reach from dusk to dawn, an extension of yesterday, the beginning of tomorrow.

"He was here," Doc said. "I saw him."

Lorrie stretched her skinny arm toward Doc. He leaned and reached between the bedrails. His gnarled fingertips brushed hers, like Adam's when he reached for God.

James O'Brien

The Man Comes Around

And behold a pale horse: and his name that sat on him was Death, and Hell followed with him. — Revelation 6:8

The man stands on the porch, a jawless hound chained beside him, a slack tether dragging on the concrete stoop. Sam Houck peers through his living room window to eye the man. The dog has no lower jaw. A rough gap wrapped in pale pink flesh runs down below the snout into a deep purple blackness. The dog wheezes and gurgles. Steam clouds from where its lower muzzle once was. Houck remembers the hound's jaw. A snub jaw run with sharp teeth. Gummed in a soft pink, like rare meat. He had felt the beast's jaw around his collarbone, the teeth tearing though his skin and muscle, scraping on his bone. Houck knows the man, knows the hound. He knows they would be coming. But he did not expect them to come today.

Houck walks to his coat closet and pushes through the worn military fatigues and Carhart coats racked there and pulls out a large box of carved oak clasped in brass. He unlatches the box and draws a .357 revolver from the felt lining. Houck runs his thumb along the hatched grip. He snaps the cylinder open and clicks six brass rounds in the chambers and palms the cylinder shut and levers the hammer back. He levels the .357 to his creased eyes and aligns the rear sights with the forward sights. Houck swings the .357 around to the door and sights the man on the porch and the man cocks his head as though he can see though the fogged glass panes. The man inclines his chin as though occupied with a small creature.

The man stands as if he waited as if he had been there for a long time and will remain as so until he desires elsewise. The man wears a long white trench coat that snaps at his heavy boots and a matching fedora banded in red cloth. His lean eyes stare out from behind thin-rimmed silver spectacles and his hard cheekbones whiten in the cold. But the man's lower face is what Sam Houck remembers. The man's jaw is a deep, mottled red, the color of wine, and the skin there seems to ache and pulse in small ripples, as though it moves in a manner unto itself. Hard ridges of pale skin rim the edges in a continuous ragged slash as though his lower face had been branded with an ill-made iron. The scar covers the left side of his face, reaching below the eye down to the chin. Houck knows the man will not depart until he has got what he wants. And the man, today, wants Sam Houck.

Houck walks to the door and stands along it slantwise and hides the .357 behind the frame. He opens the door just enough to see the man and the hound and the snow covered path beyond. He sees the forest and his Jeep parked under the eaves of the forest and snow mounting on all things. But the man has no snow on him anywhere. Nor does the hound. Houck feels cold. Cold down deep into his fingers, then his organs. They feel as though suddenly frozen.

"Didn't expect you to come today," Houck says. He tries to remain composed. He straightens his back as he had when in the Marines. He evens his brow and clenches the pistol.

"You should have," the man says. He doffs his red-banded fedora and holds it before his pelvis. "You should have expected me this day the same as any. All days, all places, all lives I call my province." The man tugs on the halter and the dog looks up at him as though considering. Their eyes connect. The man says, "I have come to see if an opportunity to reenter business partnership with me might be befitting to your current sentiments, or, if a business partnership would not be at the utmost appropriate give our rather troubled history that at least you might consider the temporary lease of your services to my organization."

"So you want muscle," Houck says. The wind gusts and the snow rattles from the tree branches encircling the house.

"I want a killer."

"Then you don't want me."

The man smiles. His teeth are very white in the front but browned in the crevices between. One of his canines is missing. "I know what I want," he says. "Do you?"

"I was thinking about you getting the hell off my porch," Houck says. He taps the .357 behind the door frame.

"Before you act upon that desire, or before you draw your iron on me, consider this proposition: There is a certain man, a man with whom you are not acquainted, who is in need of fatal punishment. This man has committed certain transgressive acts against the interests which I so represent. These acts do not matter. That he committed them alone is your concern. The interests I represent demand he be judged by ancient law. Fire and steel. The interests I represent have endeavored to bring this man in question before the appropriate authorities. Our authorities. They have failed. Our messengers have failed. You will not."

"You're saying I got no choice."

"You have choice. There is always free will. But do you fail to act upon the concern of my interests your life will indeed be forfeit."

The man stands there quite still despite the wind. He might smile. He cocks his head at Houck and sets the fedora on his brow. He says, "I knew you before you breathed, before you took the breath of others. That is your job. The task to which you alone have been appointed. None other may succeed. Seek me and you will live. Do not and you will die. Do you wish that?"

"I don't think about it too much."

"You will. Find me where you need me," the man says. "You remember the place, I am quite sure."

Houck nods. He remembers the vacant lot in the city's iron district, remembers the toxic haze and sulfurous odors spewing from rusted stacks. He remembers the boarded houses, the discarded lawnmowers warping in dead lawns. He remembers meeting the man there so many times. He remembers killing after that. He wants to level the .357 at the man's scarred face and shatter it from mouth to nape. He wants to empty his chambers into the man's dead chest. He wants to beat the hound's mangled skull until it runs in crooked chunks, stains the snow a deep red. He wants to kill them both, to kill the man and the hound, to kill the memories of death and murder and pain they brought upon Houck's life. But Sam Houck cannot kill them. Not yet.

"Maybe you need some time to consider the offer. To weigh your own soul against those of others. These matters are substantial matters. Consider them as so," the man says. Then he goes. The jawless dog turns and looks at Houck. He imagines it might growl. Then it too turns and leaves.

Houck slams the door and padlocks the gauge. He walks back to the door and peers outside. The man is gone. The hound is gone. Only his jeep occupies his drive and the woods around his log-serried house. The snow has fallen and covered their footprints and as though they had never been.

Late that morning Houck sits upright in a lacquered chair facing the house's front window and wonders what he is to do. If he should see the man. If he should wait for the man to come to him. Then, he decides. Sam Houck walks to his closet and draws a mauve holster and belts the clasps to his waist and holsters his .357. He fumbles in his Carhart pocket and unslings a buck knife and sheath and he stuffs the buck knife to his right boot. He goes to his bathroom with the gun and the knife and reaches under the sink and draws a zinc-plated .38 snub nose from the piping. He pulls a roll of silver duct tape from under the sink. He stands in the mirror and duct tapes the .38 snub between his shoulder blades and lets it rest there, hard and cool.

He eyes outside and checks for the man but sees nothing. He watches the snow powder his blue Jeep. He exits to his driveway and he pulls his jeep into his garage. The woods around, all oak and eastern ash, tall, scrape against a gray sky that seems to hang close to the earth. The trees stand stiff, their boughs sagging under snow, backlit by the white wash. Holly stands green in the low scrub, and here and there a ridge of gray rock run through with dun iron striations jut from the snowpack. Occasional headlights girdle the roadway below, and now and then Houck hears a distant airhorn, a far wail in the valleys. The snow pushes through the Catoctin Mountains, their smooth ridges nothing more than a mottled white and brown shear. Snow piles to his window sill, still, unconcerned. Houck fumbles through a toolbox against the wall and clasps a sawed-off shotgun and sets the sawed-off shotgun to the right of the Jeep's driver's seat. He reaches in the glovebox and pulls a thumb knife from under his registration and tapes the thumb knife to the outside of the steering wheel. He goes inside and draws the blinds and locks the doors. He pushes trunks and bookcases against the frames.

He cooks a Boca burger in a black iron skillet, the bottom crusted with old grease and a lanyard around the handle. Houck does not eat meat. Cannot abide it. He hates its iron tang. He hates the thought of flesh sizzling in its own juices. He does not love animals. He just hates the meat. The meat reminds him of the peoples' faces after he shot them. The rifle jumps, slams back against your shoulder, and, through the scope, the world jolts. And, for that second, you forget what you have just done. Then, it falls back to where you aimed first. A chest. A forehead. A throat. You see it decimated. The skin shredded and the muscles and brains scattered in small wet flecks. Teeth on the dashboard. A lung displaced.

When he sees deer cross his property Houck will run outside with his .357 and fire shots into the air. He lashes aluminum pie pans to the surrounding trees to keep starlings and crows from roosting. He sprays his windowsills with insect repellent. He tries to live without sound, without disturbance. But mainly, Houck waits. Houck waits for the mail to arrive. He waits for the cars to pass below, nothing more than twin beams cutting through the gloom. He waits for the sun to rise and fall. For the rains to blow from the south. For the storms to tear from the North. He waits for time to pass, for his back to cinch and bend, for his heart to slow and his synapses still. He waits for that bleak senile gray that awaits every man. He waits to forget.

Houck has many things he wishes he could forget. His father's tight fists. His first shot of whiskey. That unsure year after graduating high school. Enlisting in the Marines. The faces of the men he has killed. The man.

Houck met the man after returning from the first Gulf War, or, rather, the man met him. Houck had recently returned from Iraq. There in that blank desert land full of wind and heat and ancient words Houck had been a Marine serviceman, his head shaved to the bone, his arms run with blue veins. He was a good shot. One of the best. Houck had almost gone special forces. Almost. He never missed a target. Not once. And that, the man said, was how he found Sam Houck.

Houck had been sitting in a bar drinking down his hazard pay and trying to concentrate on football. He had been out of work for some time and his money was running low. He did not care about that too much but he needed to. So he sat alone in the bar trying to figure out what he should do about not caring and not having money. He cared about the buck heads and bear heads and stag heads stuffed and hooked to the walls. They reminded him of the shootings, of the desert. He went to urinate in the stall and when he returned the man was sitting there in the seat across from him with the hound by his hip. Houck thought he had forgotten where he was sitting, but when he saw the tumbler of well whiskey and lime he knew the spot was his and he walked over, wobbling, and sat down.

The man was the first to speak. He said, "Samuel, you are a man of vast talents, great talents, talents that many would pay to have."

"I can drink alright," Houck said. He downed his tumbler.

"No. No. Not that. You can kill. Kill well. I have seen your files. Those from the military."

"How'd you find them?" Houck said. "What you want with me?" Houck said. He stood up and began to back over the rough wood floor.

Then, the man explained. The man explained many things. He told Houck how he could make money by working with the man, and Houck had agreed to work with the man. He did not care who the man worked for or what the man wanted him to do. Houck only wanted to do something and to be paid for it. So he did.

Houck did not know if he liked the man or if he did not like the man. It seemed that liking was something you could say about most people but the man seemed beyond that. Like it was too simple for him. The man did things and that was that. You could not say if you liked him or if you didn't. The man was polite, and that was something. He made you feel comfortable, or tried to, Houck thought. But that was not good enough. The man made him uncomfortable, made his skin feel like it was slowly peeling off and exposing his muscle. But for endless years Houck worked for the man, killing the men he said to kill, and being paid for it.

Then, once, Houck had had to kill a man that he did not want to. He had been told to kill in the usual way, but things got messy and the target had to be killed in front of his own family. Houck had left the man's employ after that, changed his name and moved as far away as he knew he could go. And he had lived there, alone, in the deeps of the Catoctin Mountains, biding his time, remembering, fearing, and waiting for the man to come around.

Now, with a red-run evening striating the distance, Houck sets a bolster under the sheets on his mattress and draws the covers high. He unscrews a lightbulb from the socket above his bead and breaks the lightbulb and tosses the shattered glass on the hardwood floor. He reclines in his tub with the sawn-off shotgun in his lap and the .357 on the porcelain lip. The .38 snub's sharp casing gnaws his backbones. The duct tape's glue runs down his spine, thick, gelatinous. He tries to concentrate on the house's small sounds. The radiator ticking. The frames creaking. The windows rattling. This is how his live has been for years, but now, with the man in his mind, Houck thinks it all feels more punctuated, sharper, like a whetted knife. Sometimes snow crashes with a soft thud in the pack outside, and Houck starts, clawing for the shotgun grip. He thinks he is getting old, getting tired, that somewhere in the darkness of his younger life a malignant mass has formed, overriding him, dropping his eyelids, weakening his limbs.

At night in his dreams the dead reanimate and loom. Fire rains. Molten ore crashes to a desert ground. All life clamors for purchase on barren rock. How the flame hisses to the earth. How the earth buckles and splits. How the mantle cracks and roves apart to a great void. And from that void the voices of the dead do rise. The old voices. The pained voices. Houck hears them cry. He knows not what they ask of him but their asking cuts like thistleblades and shocks like pure voltage.

These dreams are nightly dreams. Houck knows them. He wanders through them. He sees jagged mountains sawing the red sky. Smoke chokes him. From the pits a figure crawls. A faceless form, deep in burning. The flames sear to the muscle and boneblades. Houck sees the entrails roll in a hollow torso. The figure rasps and totters and reaches forward.

Houck wakes thinking he is on fire. He snatches the sawn-off shotgun from the enamel lip and fires its double bores into his ceiling. Plaster and tile rattles to the floor. Houck blinks. He recharges the shotgun and holds it close to his chest.

The next day Houck decides to meet the man. He packs his guns in the jeep and padlocks his door and drives from the mountains to the city and nears the low red-brown brick blotch. He drives under enclosed walkways, rusted bridges, the paint worn into the burnt brick walls, the windows fogged with gray spray, half-lit store signs saying, come and see. These were places he could have been, could have worked towards. Telecom offices. Diners. The road buckles, now and then. The city enlarges. The pedestrians distance. The car engine's metal hum seems buried under stone. Houck feels as though floating, riding on an asphalt surf. He forgets in that moment where he has been, where he is going, and Houck likes things that way. Likes to feel the jeep rumbling under his seat. Likes the motor's continuous purr.

He comes to a district of iron and cinder. A haze rests on the smokestacks and rusted roofs and he passes the shattered lot where he knows the man will be waiting. He parks his jeep two blocks away. He rests the sawn-off shotgun between the door and the seat and stows the .357 under the passenger seat. He checks his .38 between his shoulder blades and the buck knife at his ankle. Houck walks down the street and around the block with his coat pulled close against the cold.

The man and the hound stand in the center of the rubble, crushed cinderblocks and tormented piping charred and rusted and rent to bestial forms. They claw from the barren ground. They moan in the wind. The snowfall has blown in drifts to the windows of the warehouses around, a perfect flat bowl, as if a meteor struck that exact spot.

Houck hunches in his Carhart coat against the cold and the wind. He walks through a drift to the man and the hound. The man's scared face seems especially dark, almost as though it's color shifted with the cold, and Houck thinks it seems to move like a spider along a log.

"Won't you come inside?" asks the man. He points to the warehouse and its yellow windows barred in metal rods. Snow scatters from the corrugated eaves. Houck thinks the warehouse looks warm, pleasant. The man turns, the jawless dog leading, and walks through a heavy door. Houck follows. He crosses through a shadowed loading dock stacked with towering boxes. The room smells wet, soaked, as though the cardboard boxes have begun to rot. He hears small ringing sounds somewhere in the dark. Then he goes on.

A frame of light radiates from the far wall, the outline of a door. Houck walks to it and opens it. The man sits with his legs crossed at the ankle and his back to a slight bend. Red carpet runs the office and the walls are of composite wood paneling. The room smells of old fumes, gasoline and meat. The jawless hound sits quite still, its open throat pulsing now and then with its breath. The hound wheezes. It curls against a thick desk carved with strange animalistic figures. A Bunsen burner and a manual type writer sit on the desk and behind the desk run a series of dented file cabinets chained and locked. The man removes his coat and sets it aback the chair. He rests the red-banded fedora on his lap and scoots his chair to the hound and strokes the hound's broad brow ridge. The hound's upper canines are chipped and flecked with deep gouges as though it has strived with many things. The hound stretches and his paws scrape the chair's broad feet cut as lion's claws.

The man draws a small bag from his trench coat and unzips it. He picks a snifter of bright red meat from the bag and pushes the meat into the jawless hound's tracheal throat hole. The hound might whimper. Houck sees the beast's throat working downward and he thinks of frozen meat and ruined skin. His stomach aches.

"He never stops eating," the man says. "Such a beautiful glutton." He zips the bag shut and stuffs it in his pocket. He pulls a tissue from his pocket and cleans his fingers and tosses the tissue to the ground. He adjusts the fedora on his lap as though it will fit an appropriate place, obscuring something.

"He just stopped," Houck said.

"Did he stop or do you think he stopped," the man said. The dog's gullet seems to be working still, inching the flesh down its throat.

"I just said he stopped," Houck said. "The hell you want with all these dumbass questions."

The man smiles. His teeth are white as his trenchcoat. "You merely perceived that the beast quit, that his muscles ceased working. You have judged this as so based on apparent vestiges, the passing permutations of skin and bone, and these are nothing but anatomical masques to a larger chaos." The man readjusts the hat on his lap. "And yet in that manner you may be counted as ostensibly correct. Permit me to expound on the matter—"

"You never did shut up," Houck says.

The man cocks his saurian head. "This too is relative," he says. "But your task—that is not. Your task is quite clear. Come and see."

The man opens a file drawer and flips through a series of folders and pulls one from the stack and hands it to Houck.

"You must forgive the antediluvian nature of this atavistic

communiqué. You see, computers make our work complex, and, when complex, our work invites mistakes," the man says. "We do not want mistakes. But then, you know this I am sure."

"I know it."

"Prudence, then."

Houck opens the file and sifts through its contents. Several black and white photographs detailing a large man are paper clipped to pages of notes and maps. Houck studies them, memorizing the face, the address, the house.

Houck slides the file across the desk. The man switches the Bunsen burner high and rests the file on top of the grill. The stock paper browns from the center in a spiral and then opens from there as though blooming. The photographs burn in a cool blue flame, green around the edges, and here and there Houck sees shreds of the images twist and curl and blacken and vanish. The man looks at Houck and says, "Goodnight."

Houck drives back through the town and turns south to take the highway. The mountains diminish behind him, and the trees flex and bow in his Jeep's headlights as though pained. Soon, the snowfall tapers to scattered flakes, and occasional cars pass by. Other men and other women commuting to work. Houck tells himself that his work is no different than their work. That he too is just on his way to a job.

Houck passes Washington in a wide circle, turns off at a stunted exit a few miles south of the city, and takes the truck route farther south. Through the Jeep's canvas topper Houck smells the marshes, the Chesapeake, the salt and mud and methane, all of it slow rot, bodies decomposing.

Houck's stomach tautens. He feels as though he floats roadside. He has not eaten since the Boca burger. He wants something, anything, to fill him. He stops at a gas station grafittoed on the side and buys a ham sandwich and pulls the meat from the bread and folds the bread over and eats. He goes on. Night falls. Buildings rarify. Their lights infrequent, just occasional specters glowing through the trees.

Houck turns where he has memorized to turn and the trees knot and bend into a high arch above him. A marsh glimmers in slick blue strands to the left side of the jeep. Cattails reed the opposing side. Houck parks his Jeep in a turnoff down a narrow road and backs the jeep behind a stand of cattails. He unslings the sawnoff shotgun from its fitting and holsters his .357 and presses his back hard against the seat to secure the .38 between his shoulders. He checks the buck knife at his ankle and strips the thumb knife from the wheel and tapes it to his left wrist, just below the sleeve line. He pictures the maps and addresses and photos the man had shown him and orients himself. He needs to cross the marsh to get to the target's house. The house where the target eats and sleeps and lives. Houck tries not to think about that. Men eat and sleep and live. Targets do not.

Houck primes his weapons and crosses through the marsh in the cold air and his footsteps crush through the thin ice. Water runs to his calves. Burrs and thistles tag his jacket. Houck picks at them. He imagines the night as a sliding thing, slowly slipping away, a snake maybe, a black king snake twisting and cutting and dodging through low scrub. An owl hoots and Houck stops, considering. He could go back, could run and hide from the man, could be more ready the next time the man comes around. But there is no escaping the man, Houck knows. And now, he needs to do what the man has told him to.

He walks on. The mud and the frozen water suck at his legs then numb them. He counts his toes. His breath clouds. The marsh steams as though diffusing. Cypress rattle above him. He thinks they smell like the pine in the mountains. That evergreen tang. But sharper, alcoholic almost. The juniper berries.

Then, lights drift through the cypress. Disembodied lights. Like candleflame beheaded. A manor looms behind a hedgerow. The manor the man showed Houck. The manor stands two stories high. Soft brick wraps the house, like meat, Houck thinks. A sleek sportscar, lacquered a grim black, is parked near the triple garage. Needle-spindled rims, high-gloss zinc, same as the .38, glimmer in the night. Small gardens and low hedges cross the lawn. A small rowboat rocks at warped moorings down the marshway. This is where the target will be.

Houck crosses through the lawn crouched low. Security lights flicker on as he passes but he passes quickly and gives no thought to them. He stands around the garage's corner and eyes the well-lacquered sportscar. He eyes the zinc rims. He pulls his .357 from its holster and aims for the gas tank and fires.

The car erupts. Houck saws back at the explosion. A pillar of pure light sears the dark night. A zinc rim, now oxidized black, rolls to Houck's feet. The car burns there, the frame backlight black and ragged and wholly engulfed.

A door slams. The target comes running from the manor with a hunting rifle butted in his armpit. Houck swings from behind the garage verge and draws his sawnoff shotgun and crouches and aims through the fire. He shoots the target in the stomach. The target doubles back over. Houck sees his belt flash a silver-yellow. The rifle clatters somewhere in the shrub. Houck stoops and picks up the shell casing. He finds one, fumbles through the grass for the other. The target moans. Houck draws his .357. He feels the weight. The coldness. The target has crawled on his back to the front driver's side wheel. His suitjacket is ripped to scorched tatter. The shotgun pellets glitter from his ruined abdomen. Blood wells deep from the center. The spleen might be outside his skin.

"He sent you—the man," the target says, wheezing.

"Don't matter who sent me."

"He sent you," the target says, "It could be him alone and no other. I know where he sleeps. I know his name."

Houck tries to trigger the .357. But he cannot. He watches the target's entrails writhe atop his tattered flesh. Houck thinks of sausages. His head feels as though bored through with rough screws.

"Tell me," Houck says.

The target tells Houck everything about the man. The man's history. His name. His dwelling place. When he finishes telling the target's face has gone palm-white and he lays there rasping on the gravel. Houck shoots him in the right cheek with his .357 and the target stops rasping.

Now, Houck knows the man's name. It is an old name. An ancient name. Houck drives he repeats the man's name over and over, letting it roll in his mouth like cool soda. He turns his radio on and listens to old country songs about duels and the devil. He mumbles through the lyrics he knows and hums the bars when he cannot remember the words to a song. He drives to Washington's low outskirts singing and humming and repeating the man's name. He passes columned mansions and deep lawns cast blue and strange in the night. He crosses shopping malls and brick-walled project housing. He turns through small ramblers and littered streets and looks about him to check the addresses and slows and passes the house that is supposed to be the man's. The house is small. Brick, maybe a deep red, runs the place and inside a warm light glows. Houck rounds the block and parks his jeep and primes his shotgun and checks his .357 and his .38 and his knives and walks through the snow and around the house.

He walks though a dead garden and crouches near the back window. He rests his arm on a wound hose. He looks through the window. The man sits at a card table stained in brown circles. The jawless dog sleeps underneath the top. The man is setting ham and bread and cheese on the table. He is shirtless. His stomach sags. Brown spots fleck his loose torso. His shoulders hunch. He fumbles for mustard as though his eyes are poor. Houck almost wants to hand the man his glasses. Almost wants to lead the man to the refrigerator. The man pats his leg and the hound rises and heels. The man mouths something to the hound and the hound leads the man to the counter and the man pats the counter and slides his glasses on his nose's long bridge. The man tears the ham into strips and pushes the strips in the hound's throat hole. A gas stove burns blue behind the man, the flame roiling there and the methane diffusing, some concoction boiling above it. The man sits on the table and presses his sandwich together.

Houck rounds the small house in a crouch. He turns his heels in from the outstep so they will make no noise on the snow. He scrapes more snow from the ground and puts it in his mouth to cool it, to prevent steam from rising. He unholsters his .357 and cocks the sawed-off shotgun and holds each in his hands. He steps on the back stoop and saws back on this thighs and shoulders against the door. The door buckles and splinters but the lock remains clasped. Something scrambles inside then the lights flicker out. Houck charges again and the door gives and he tumbles to the linoleum floor and tucks his legs to keep rolling. The .357 slips from his grip and the sawed off shotgun unlashes from his wrist and the guns skid along the floor and Houck reaches between his shoulder blades and rips the .38 from his skin. Two shots wrack the darkness, small and slow almost.

Houck lunges through the wide arch and shoots doublehanded to the corner and hears something fall. He kicks at the darkness and the darkness seems to give. The only light comes from the blue burner. Everything seems in a cool sheen. Houck sees a pair of low eyes glimmer in half crescents. The eyes rush him. The hound launches at Houck and Houck feels a series of dull pricks. The hound's upper canines work at Houck's jeans. Houck knees the hound in the head and the hound crumples and in the blue moonlight Houck sees the card table snap shut and collapse on the dog.

Houck scrambles for his sawnoff shotgun and grabs for the butt and pumps the two rounds off into the blackness and hears a moan. Houck stands and fumbles for the lightswitch and turns the lights on.

The man lays there in the corner, his sagging chest open. A pistol, some ancient revolver arabesqued in twisted grooves, sits some feet away from the man. The man claws at the ground and Houck kicks his arm. The man's scar looks redder than his blood. Houck can see some of the right lung contracting and expanding. The man curls in on himself. His face tightens. He sighs.

"Don't kill the dog," the man rasps. "Please, be so kind."

"I'll kill what I want."

"I made you."

The dog noses the man and the man lifts his arm. The hound gurgles. The hound seems to whine.

"I'll end you."

Houck raises his .357 and shoots the man in the jaw. The pistol recoils to his tendons. That hard familiar snap. Houck shoots the man in the face and his lower jaw clatters against the far wall in fragments. The hound darts to the corner and cowers. Houck shoots the hound through the brow and the hound's brains splatter into membranous chunks against the floor. They sit there like they had been destined to fall there. Houck crosses the room and kicks both bodies and stares at them for a while. He looks at their dead eyes, their mangled faces. He looks at the pattern the blood and flesh had made. He sees how the blood webs from the floor to the shadows beyond. How it vanishes there as though selfsame. He looks at it for a long time. He sees in those rude mazes some memory. Some past. Things he does not know. Cannot know. He feels them. Sips of sweet wine he had never drank. The lush smell of far fields. The dew rising from them in a damp dawn. He sees faces. Sad faces. Their eyes cinch to taut wrinkles. Their jaws low. Their tongues churn. Howl. Mothers and fathers and children and friends. He feels the breath pass from those dead to his dead, and then into him.

Dawn breaks outside. A soft yellow burn. Houck girds his weapons. He walks to the kitchen. The stove flame has evaporated the concoction and the concoction burns in a thick smoke. Houck lets the concoction burn. He cocks the other dials on the stove so the methane gas hisses from the valves. The ham sandwich sits there on a cracked plate stained brown where forks and knives have scratched it. Houck looks at the meat, thinks about killing, and takes a bite, chewing the meat, the flesh, letting its slick juices roll down his throat, letting the meat ball with the soft bread, letting it slip down, deep into his stomach, deep into that internal dark.

Like a Feather

Layla finds a monster while digging holes in the backyard. She runs with mud-caked shoes through the house and up the stairs and bursts into my home office.

"Daddy, lookit!" She yells with one arm holding the tail of it and shaking it toward my face. The monster has thick brown hair everywhere but the underside of it, big yellow owl-eyes and two horns—one on its nose and one on the top of its head. It smells like radishes and wet dirt and it sticks out its green bumpy tongue in deep throated pants.

"His name's Feathers. Can I keep him, can I keep him?" Layla begs. My wife, Tess, walks in to check on the commotion, sees the thing and screams out, throwing herself back against the wall. It, Feathers, screams too, like an old woman who's been smoking cigarettes since she was nine.

Feathers has opposable pads on his hands and feet. He can crawl about two feet up the living room wall before gravity and his belly gut force him back down. Layla, Tess, and I sit at the kitchen table while Feathers roams through the living room, sneaking under the sofa and then trying, once again, to work up the wall.

"I wanna keep 'em! I never get to have any pets!" Layla cries.

"Layla, honey, you're allergic to cats and dogs, remember?" Tess says.

"But it's not either! And I'm not allergic to him."

I sneak a glimpse at Feathers in the living room. He's sitting on an end table pawing at the lamp, but he's also looking dead at me.

* * *

I rummage through the garage for a medium sized box and some old beach blankets for Feather's makeshift bed. When I turn around he's there, propped up on his hind legs watching me with his head cocked to the side. He breaths heavy, like that girl from the Exorcist movie, and reaches out for his new bed. I hand it over to him. Feathers pierces the bottom of it with his horn and then walks back into the house, balancing it on its head.

At night, Feathers snores like I imagine a barge would sound, dragging down the Mississippi. Walter, who lives next door, calls to complain about the noise. I don't know how Tess falls asleep but by her twitching and pulling against the bed sheets I think she's having a nightmare. I think it's a nightmare about Feathers.

After school the next day, Layla commands a small army of kids lining up outside the front door to see Feathers. It's her whole second grade class. Layla and I both know her mother doesn't get home from work until about seven so she can get away with parading the monster to everyone. I sit back in the living room recliner to supervise, make sure the kids don't provoke Feathers to do God-only-knows-what. For most of the afternoon Feathers and I trade slow gazes at one another, sizing each other up.

Feathers seems to like children but it's me and Tess that put him on guard. He stops whatever he's doing when Tess looks at him and gapes open his big mouth and green tongue. Tess' eyes are bloodshot and the skin underneath them is darker than usual.

I can't sleep at night with Feathers blaring through the house. Walter calls again and threatens to call the police. I take a pillow from the linen closet and stuff a corner of it into Feathers' mouth. That dampens the snoring. The little monster's chest fills and lowers with air as he eyes move rapidly underneath his bumpy eye lids. For a second the thought flashes through my mind that maybe with enough force behind the pillow, and maybe, if I hold his nose and pinch his nose horn, just maybe Feathers could die in his sleep. We can tell Layla it was natural, maybe even that Feathers was an old man monster. Then tomorrow I can scrub his stench off all the floors and walls and we'll be free.

Feathers coughs once, and then a second louder time, like he's purposefully getting my attention. I pull the pillow back from his mouth and he glares at me, the giant man standing over him with a pillow in the middle of the night. He blinks his dome eyes at me.

"You snore." I tell him. He coughs.

When I slip back into bed Tess screams from her sleep and grabs my throat.

"Oh my god, I'm sorry," she says, "I thought you might have been that thing."

We find out that turning Feathers over face-to-blanket at night goes a long way to keeping the noise down. It also vibrates the house a little and none of the family photos hang straight anymore. For a few days children would surround the house before Tess got home from work, trying to sneak a peek of him. Some high schoolers ditched class and asked if they could take a picture of Feathers for their yearbook but eventually the hype faded. The Keegans, three blocks over, installed a water slide for their pool and even Layla started to lose interest in Feathers, who abhorred water of any kind.

Tess and I let Layla run down to the Keegans one Saturday and as soon as the doors shut, Tess' eyes go wide.

"Where is it?"

"Where's what?" I blurt back, and then say, "Oh, Feathers!"

Tess runs to the kitchen and fetches a knife. "We can bury it, deep, deep in the backyard. Layla won't have to find out or better! The county incinerator, they don't ask questions there—they don't care."

"Honey, you're talking about killing it?"

"I can't," she says, putting the knife in my hands, "you do it."

"Tess, I—"

"Do it!" Tess hadn't screamed like that since she was in labor with Kayla. "I'll be waiting in the car."

I pull out the couch and find Feathers laying on his back with his bulb eyes dilated.

"Feathers?" I say. He coughs. The monster's breathing deep and pathetic, staring up at the ceiling. And he looks familiar then, like Layla the day was she born—wrapped in a round pink blanket and nestled in basket box with all the other new ones, staring just in front of them.

"Nasal strips. Feathers, can you try nasal strips?"

He coughs again.

I sigh, "We'll go to the store."

Nik Korpon

Eyes That Melt Wings

J immy finally turned up today. They found his body in the parking lot across from the Oyster, wedged between the dumpster and buckets of fried chicken grease. He was burnt from his toenails to eyebrows, hair singed into clumps. His skin, about the same as blackened tinfoil. Dental prints IDed him, though the medics had to take a leap of faith over the missing teeth, just assume they had been there. For a dope fiend, he had a surprising number of chompers. They cleared the scene a while ago and the forensic guys have been sweeping it ever since. Shame that cops have to work on a Sunday.

The thing that really got us though, and what we've been muttering into our glasses all afternoon, is that Jimmy never drank at the Oyster. Avoided it, even. He always said there was something off about the place. Makes me ill at ease, were his exact words. And he never saw Sofia's eyes, either.

Then again, apparently no one else did.

A drop of condensation slid down the can of Natty Boh, only to be sucked up by the bandage around my thumb. I was under the bathroom sink in a house we'd been rehabbing down Sandtown, and Stink called my name right as I was shortening the pipe. I'd commented that the floor looked like a Pollock painting, all blood, sawdust and iron shavings. Stink only grunted.

Bert was relaying some supposed conquest from the weekend—which we all knew was basically a montage of Bert's midget porn, but felt obliged to humor him—flapping his arms all over the place.

His obscene watch threw tiny orbs of light around the bar like a disco ball. He wouldn't take that watch off, during a job or washing his hands and I'd bet even when showering. Underneath the band, we knew his skin was the color of pale moss. Out of the range of Bert's arms, Slim fed coins into the Wurlitzer like it was child support, drumming the chrome edges to the rhythm of the song in his head. A sweaty voice dragged itself through Memphis bars and fast food parking lots. I ordered another drink.

A sharp tapping cut through the song. In the stool next to me, Stink clinked his high school ring against his glass. Faint sunlight slanted off the scarlet center stone and made it shimmer like a rabid eyeball. He was giving the death-glare to a herd of guys hunkered over a table in the corner. They'd been high-school football rivals or something. It was all Aramaic to me; when they were trading insults and ass-slaps on the field, I was under the bleachers trying to see Jenny Franklin in her underwear. But me and Stink came from the same neighborhood, and rivalry don't abide by zoning bylaws, so I was grouped with Stink and the lot. So goes Baltimore.

Besides cheap liquor, I liked the Oyster because it sat across from a Gothic church and I could catch glances of it in the mirror behind the bar. My old man was a deacon, so I was never into the Church—with a capital C—but the structures themselves, the symbolism and mythology that went into the design, that was what inspired me go to school to be an architect, to create that sheer power and awe with just bricks and glass and steel. Then—well, then things happened, and then I started laying pipe.

Moose, the bull of the rival herd, stood up from his table and crossed the floor, all slow and Spaghetti Western. Fistfuls of dust kicked up behind him. He leaned back on his heels and ordered a round for his table, dagger-stares straight down the bar. I could feel Stink's hackles rise, and debated whether to finish my beer in the bathroom or butterfly my blade and swing for glory. Then the front door opened. Chunks of dust seemed to freeze mid-air when Harbinger came in, a girl with hair like an oil slick cupping his arm.

She was on the young side for me. With her red and white checked shirt tucked into some jeans the same shade of nothing as her hair, she looked so acutely displaced—like she'd fallen out of a Dukes of Hazzard comic book or something—that I laughed to myself. I gave Harbinger a psychic high-five, figuring he'd finally broken down and bought some Viagra.

They sat on the other side of me. The tension in the bar evaporated, but up my back I felt like someone was playing Guess What I'm Writing with an acetylene torch. I took a sip of my beer and checked her with haphazard glances in the mirror. Stink grunted at Lauren to order another beer and nodded towards Harbinger and the girl, one for them as well. I took the Zippo from my pocket, rolled it over my knuckles and snapped my fingers to light it, then did it again. Her eyes were heat lamps on me. I started to sweat.

She caught me glancing after a few minutes, bit her bottom lip to play coy and not smile. I flipped my Zippo like a quarter, snapped my fingers and made a flame, then turned to her.

'I'm Steve.'

She was looking down at the bar, self-conscious or extending the game, I didn't know which. My heart beat more than a few times before she raised her head. Her mouth opened to tell me her name and probably accept the offer I was about to give to take her out to dinner and a movie, then get a drink or some coffee and sit by the harbor's edge sharing anecdotes about bad relationships and how easy it is to get sidetracked from future aspirations until the background music played us away. But Bert barged over and spilled their drinks over the counter. It dripped into puddles around their stools. Lauren cursed him and smacked him with some drink shakers. Sofia sat frozen-frame, as if nothing had happened.

'I'm Sofia,' she said, more into the hand covering her mouth than me. She giggled and looked up.

Her eyes, damn, her eyes. Even now, they still seem impossible. To start, they were almond shaped, but not like the almond-eyed beauties in melodramatic novels. Longer, and thinner. They were almost as wide as my pinkie is long, but depthless the way you can get lost in the background of a Dali painting. Her pupils looked cut from diamond, and oblong like a cat's, but all the light that would've reflected off anyone else's had been sucked in by something behind her eyes. Really, colorless diamonds don't do it justice: Sofia had black holes for pupils. And all surrounded by a cornea the milky yellow of malaria.

But those eyes, they were sunk into something that couldn't be carved by the most talented hands in all of ancient Greece. Standing next to Sofia, Venus de Milo was a gonorrhea-scabbed harpy, and Helen of Troy, well, fuck Helen of Troy. Alabaster cheekbones and lips that could turn a man sterile. Her breath smelled like a wind-swept field on a summer's day. Even her laugh was more a symphony of accentuated breaths than a spasm of her diaphragm. And when she smiled, her cheeks rose and eyebrows dipped, and they covered those sulfuric blights in the middle of her face.

At the job site the next day, Jimmy was jonesing again, shifting from foot to foot and scratching his neck. Branching blood vessels obscured the whites of his eyes, but that pathetic junkie stare burned through. He would've hopped into the hole where the stairs were going if Stink hadn't grabbed him first. Bert was scheduled to build the steps that day, but never came in.

Lying on my back underneath a dual sink, I pinched the bridge of my nose until I saw static, Sofia wearing a path through my head since she left the Oyster the night before. The thought of her made my gut twist itself into grotesque origami. I got twice as much piping done just trying to stay occupied and not think of her.

'Just twenty, man. Just twenty.' Jimmy's whine reverberated through the pipes above my face. Across the house, Stink laughed. 'I need to get my phone turned on.'

'You ain't had a phone for three months.'

'How am I supposed to call my woman if I can't get my phone turned on?' A trickle of blood on his neck from scratching. He didn't seem to notice.

'Use a payphone,' I said.

'Jimmy, I got your damn phone.' Stink cleared his throat and spit something orange on the floor. 'You sold it to me last week for six bucks, and that's only because I ain't let you blow me.'

Between his whimpers, the damp stench of charred insulation and the migraine Sofia's phantom steps were giving me, I toyed with the idea of kicking him down to the basement.

'Here, you goddamn loser.' Stink hung a twenty out. 'Get going. You're making me anxious.'

Jimmy snatched the bill from his hand and bounded away. I gave the pipe an extra hard twist and breathed a long sigh. Definitely stripped it. 'He's never going to clean up if you keep helping him.'

'I ain't enabling him.'

'Just don't do it.'

'I saved him a broken neck, is what I did. I was about to throw his ass out the window.' He laughed and took off his tool belt, sat next to my feet and lit a cigarette. 'Forget him. What's up with that girl last night, is what I want to know.'

'What about her?' I unscrewed the pipe and looked inside. Threads were beyond gone.

'Don't know. You were the one talked to her all night.'

'She seemed nice. I introduced myself, that's about it.' I walked to the window and tossed the angled piece into the carcass of the shop next door. They couldn't keep up with the payments and rather than have squatters and needle-jockeys take over, they set it aflame. The pipe landed with a muffled echo, a cloud of dust rising. 'I wouldn't call it all night.'

He blew smoke through his nose. 'You two seemed pretty cozy.'

'You notice anything about her? Anything about her eyes?' I leaned against the window frame, saw her face in wood knots, her eyes in the ringed burns where nightwalkers dropped their crackpipes.

Stink raised his eyebrows. 'Noticed a lot about her, none of which I reckon would be proper discussing with you. And speaking of—' he stretched his arms above his head, flannel shirt revealing part of a faded tattoo under the hair on his gut '—bout that time, I think.'

A nauseating wave of déjà vu swept over me.

* * *

Thirty minutes after Lauren served us, I was still nursing my first
and Stink had already killed a half-dozen. The earlier incident with
Jimmy might've touched something deeper in him than I'd thought,
but either way, it didn't bode well for the evening. He rose to go to
the bathroom, steadying himself like he was sailing the high seas. I
stared at the patterns in the particleboard floor, watched chunks of
grey ash blow away when the door opened. I peeked up without
moving my head. Moose came in, his boys filing behind like ducklings.

Lauren snapped her fingers in front of my face. Her bleached
ponytail swayed when she moved.

'You seen Bert today?'

I shook my head, asked why. She pressed the phone to her
shoulder and said it was his wife. I called across the bar and asked
Slim, just as drunk as Stink and holding himself up on the jukebox.
Again. The urge to smack myself welled in my arms, to wake from
what I hoped was Dream Purgatory.

'When she sees him, tell him I'm pissed. There's a ton of work
he was supposed to do today and if I have to haul my crap up that
ladder one more time, I'm going to run him over. Then pop it into
reverse.'

She smirked. 'I'll relay the message.'

I lifted the beer to my lips and a hot-wax sensation spread over
my skin. I didn't need to turn around to know Sofia had walked in.
She sat to my right, smelled like the air before a lightning storm.

'Fancy to see you again.' Her tone was somewhere between
you drink too much and I was hoping you'd be here, so I just smiled
back and waved to order two more. Sofia caught Lauren's arm and
asked for a Manhattan instead. That Memphis voice started playing
on the jukebox.

'Christ, Slim,' I groaned. 'Can't you put something else on?'

'Fuck you and your college-boy music.'

'I just said something else. How is that college-boy music?'

Slim wobbled, muttered something and smacked his fist into
his palm. 'Go write a book report or something.'

Lauren set our drinks in front of us. I turned to Sofia. 'I did go to college, just so you know.'

She arched an eyebrow. 'Okay'

'Sometimes things happen that you don't expect and it changes things.'

'So change them back.' Her corneas contorted and swirled, the surface of twin suns separated only by a delicate nose. 'Or are you waiting for them to change more favorably?'

My skin burned with some invisible fire. 'Do you ever feel like you know exactly what's going to happen tomorrow, because it's exactly what happened today?'

'I never wonder about anything.' She leaned towards me, her hair falling in ringlets like manicured tornadoes. 'Don't tell anyone—' she licked her lips, and in a flash, her tongue was a shimmering indigo ribbon '—but I'm psychic.'

'Do you have a hotline?'

'A psychic is different from a helpline, but I'll see what I can do.' She nestled a cool finger against my lips—shhh—and closed her eyes. Her lips twitched and from her expression, a ghost might've been giving her a massage. 'I see in your future, that you will finally do something with your life.'

'What's that supposed to mean?'

Eyelids clamped and moving like they held writhing centipedes, she said, 'You'll need to make a choice, and that choice will change your life.' Her finger drifted from my lips.

I took a long sip of beer and held it in my mouth. Moose sauntered over towards us, swirling a bottle in his hand. He leaned down, forearms resting on the chipped bar top. His whisper was dried leaves blowing down an alley but I couldn't make out any words. She took two long sips from her drink. The entire time he spoke, his eyes never left her chest and she stared at some point invisible to the rest of us. In a parallel universe, possibly.

When he finished making a pass at her, she turned to him. I yawned, and in a sideways glance at the mirror, saw her tongue shoot out like a snake's and lash his face. Her jaw dislocated as if she was about to consume him whole, two fangs glistening with venom. I gasped, blinked, and she was breathtaking again, laying her hand on Moose's chest, whispering an inch from his face with honey breath and a complexion to make him weep. His face distorted, so aroused he was ready to dissolve into a pile and let the wind take him. She took the cherries from her glass, put them in her mouth, then, still facing him, reached her arm behind her and placed the stems, square-knotted, in my palm.

'How in god's name did you—'

Stink's biblically loud voice cut me off. 'What the fuck are you doing talking to his woman?'

Moose straightened like someone hit him in the spine with a cattle prod. A shatter, and light reflected razors off the brown glass littered over the bar. Two bangs and Stink was howling, blood leaking between the fingers clamped against his cheek. Slim locked Moose in a wrestling hold, hands behind his back. I didn't even see him come over. Lauren sprang from behind the bar, stained baseball bat in hand, and hit Moose, his collarbone cracking like a fresh carrot. I grabbed a handful of napkins and rushed to Stink. His blood made my fingertips sticky. I turned to tell Sofia I'd be back in a minute, but her seat was empty. Her glass, full.

It took fifteen minutes and half a roll of paper towels to stop the bleeding. An empty bottle of superglue sat on the ledge of the mirror. His face looked like a cheap Halloween mask.

'What the hell were you thinking?'

'I was defending your territory.' He touched the gash—now early-morning grey under all the poor-man's-stitches—picked off a flake and rubbed it between his fingers. 'Keeping that damn vermin from your woman.'

'Hey, Fucknuts.' I smacked the back of his head. 'At least look at me.' He turned, still staring at the glue between his fingers, edged with pink. 'She's not my woman. And besides that, she left because you two started playing slice-o-matic out there. So you ruined what you were trying to save, and now you have a vagina on your face.'

'Oh,' he said.

'That make any sense to you?' I thumped him on the forehead with my palm. 'Next time, let me ask for her number first before you try to go bonecrusher on someone, okay?'

'Sorry, brother. My bad.' He touched his face again, like it might be ancient parchment. 'How's it look?'

I told him it wasn't great, but at least he wouldn't leave splatters every time he looked down at the sidewalk. He opened the door to leave. Sofia's stool was still empty.

I washed the flecks of blood down the sink, scrubbed my hands and splashed water on myself. My face was a rain cloud. With every drop came an uttered promise to re-enroll, draw more often, go to the gym, eat more salad; I grabbed a handful of towels and dried off. I fished in my pocket for the Zippo like a nervous tic. Something metallic and cool touched my fingers, but not a square lighter. I pulled it out, held it in the light.

Bert's watch.

On the inside, small patches of something green. Like pale moss.

Stink bailed on the job the next day—Bert, too—leaving only me and Jimmy to do the work, which basically meant me. I figured Stink was recuperating from the bottle wound, so I called Slim for extra help.

Jimmy skittered from one spot to the next, stopping and starting like someone was experimenting with a film projector. Slim almost cold-cocked him, just to get him to stay still for a minute. Before he could swing, I snatched the wrench from his hand. I went to put it inside my toolbox, and sitting on the latch were two cherry stems, tied in a square knot.

I told Jimmy to go home, slipping the stem-knot into his pocket like a voodoo doll. Maybe it would ward the monkey off his back, scare needles from his arms. Slim and I went to the Oyster. In the corner, Sofia sat statuesque with her perpetually full Manhattan and I knew, despite my best efforts, I'd inevitably drift to her like Icarus. Her eyes threatened to melt my wings.

Slim flapped his lips for a long time, alternating between the pros and cons of Johnny Cash and Shooter Jennings, and interrogating me about the alleged torrid affair with Sofia. Everyone was talking about it, he said, you and that smoking hot bitch. He said he'd trade his wife and refurbed Charger just to smell her panties.

'But her eyes! Don't they freak you out?'

'What're you talking about, eyes? Brother, did you see those mammaries?'

I shook my head and kept sniffing the inside of my shirt. The hint of gasoline clung to me.

At some point, one of the other regulars came in. He said he'd seen Jimmy creeping around an alley. Supposedly, he'd ripped off his dealer.

All I could smell was gasoline.

The job had fallen a week behind, but I didn't bother to call Slim for help.

Pink fingers of morning knitted across the sky, the sun burning away the overnight fog. All across the city, church bells rung out in an accidental symphony, the tones overlapping and harmonizing with each other. A blue jay perched on a stud, watching me work. Two blocks down, a bakery turned on their fans and covered the neighborhood with the aroma of fresh bread.

And still, the only thing I could smell was gasoline.

I sliced open my hand twice, trying to move too quick and keep my mind occupied. Her face came to me in jagged pieces and soft pulses. Cheekbones and lips and a forked tongue. Jaundiced eyes with swirls like hot lava. And every time her image assembled itself, my stomach knotted the way it did before I asked Jenny Franklin to move away to college with me. Then the swirls in those eyes sunk their claws and my body crumpled from the inside. It was Jenny saying no all over again.

A robin joined the blue jay on the stud. I tore bits of crust from my sandwich and laid them on the frame, creeping slow to not scare them away. Outside on the street, I half-expected to see Jimmy slinking along, peeking over each shoulder before coming inside and trying to bum twenty from me. A woman with wrinkled charcoal skin held the hands of her two grandchildren, dressed in Sunday best. The boy picked up a chunk of brick and hurled it through the remaining window of the shop next door. The birds pecked at the bread.

After I ate the rest of my sandwich, I hunkered under the pipes to finish the work. Or as much as I felt like doing that day. Some junkie had snuck in during the night and ripped out twenty feet of copper to sell. They might've been smacked out when they did it, and hadn't bothered to look underneath the tarp in the corner. I pulled two lengths of pipe from underneath. Something fell out alongside, a grommet or something. I bent down to pick it up. It was two cherry stems, tied in a square knot.

Hot electricity shot through my body and I threw the stems into the street. I tossed tools from the box Stink had forgotten, hoping to find a pack of smokes. No luck, and I paced for a few minutes, chewing on my thumb. Another bird landed on the stud. I watched them watch me, calming myself. Eventually, I slid back under the pipes.

There'd been a problem with the main drainage. Too many traps, and whoever had set it angled the long section upwards, so the water just sat there festering. I undid the valve, careful to not spill anything. Still too far up, so I got a rubber mallet. Gentle hits at first, they became harder and harder. The dull thump vibrated through the pipe. After a dozen wallops, it started to tip down. I leaned on it, thinking body weight would help it, and something red flashed on the ground but before I could grab it, the pipe cracked and I tumbled down, thick black water pouring onto me. It coated the cracks of my eyelids and the inside of my ears. I rolled away from the rancid fountain, scraping my hand along the floor for a cloth. Stink's jacket, the one he forgot two days before.

The pipe calmed to a steady drip. Fluid covered the floor like chunky tar. I choked back the gag reflex. The smell of gasoline wafted through all the sulfur and rot. I looked up and the birds were gone. Couldn't blame them. Church bells rang. I coughed something up and spit in the water, then a flash caught my eye again. I swept it with my foot. An oblong chunk stuck to the bottom of the red flash. I swallowed, picked it up with only my fingertips. Bile rose in my throat. To my side, I felt for the jacket and dropped the chunk in it. I cleaned it off—that feeling in my stomach again—then peeled back the cloth.

The flash, a scarlet center-stone, like a rabid eyeball.

Underneath the stone, Stink's finger, down to the knuckle.

'Double Turkey, Lauren.'

Like a reflex, it appeared in front of me. Two other regulars, facedown, at the end of the bar. I swallowed it without a breath, slammed down the glass.

'Another, please.'

The reflex.

Beside me, Sofia materialized, seemingly from vapors. She caressed my side with frozen clawed fingers, slipped them into my front pocket. Her breath lapped against my neck in faint currents. Church bells rang, funereal tones trudging down the street.

'Lauren, one more.'

One of the crime scene cops kneeled down, picked up something from the pavement. He turned it over in his hand, eyebrows furrowed like he was deep in abstract thought, putting pieces together. After a minute, he waved to his partner. They conferred, exchanged a few rebuttals.

Fingers so cold they were hot pressed into my back. I curled my hands around the edge of the window to get a better look. Sofia whispered in my ear but I couldn't understand. Or didn't want to. I turned to tell her and her crazy fucking eyes to fuck off and never manifest in front of me again, but caught my arm on the rusted nail where the regulars hung their keys.

I looked up and the cops were a few feet from the front door. I assumed my stool, slumped against the bar and sipped at the drink I thought was mine. A blast of humid air when they opened the door. A static voice exploded from a walkie-talkie. Lauren gave them a curt nod. In the distorted reflection on my glass, I could see them survey the place.

'Steven Forster?'

Dead silence fell over the already quiet bar. Only the squeak of Lauren drying a glass.

'Is there a Steven Forster here?'

Someone grunted. Out of the line of sight in my glass-reflection and I had no idea who it was, but a hand fell on my back. Hot wax spread over my body and I felt Sofia's skin on mine, her sunstorm eyes warm my blood and melt my wings. Her cheekbones caressed mine, teeth scraped my neck and tongue licked my jugular. The cop's hand spun me around in the stool.

'Mr. Forster, we're going to need you to come with us.'

For Housekeeping

J uli used her housekeeping master key to open room five-eighteen, looking up and down the hallway to make sure she wasn't noticed by some guest who might wonder why she was working so late. She'd never quite believed what Raoul, the housekeeping supervisor, had told her when she'd started at the hotel a month earlier: that she would be as good as invisible to the hotel's guests.

"No one wants to know who's scraping the toothpaste and short hairs off the bathroom floor," he'd told her. The sudden twitch of his right eyelid might have been a wink. She liked him fine as bosses went, but Ana, who had helped her get the job, had warned her not to be alone with him any more than necessary.

As the door clicked closed behind her, she kicked a bright yellow ball that had rolled into the room's entryway so that it skipped back into the living room.

The Mason family, who had been living in the suite for more than three weeks, were dead on a highway in the Allegheny mountains, some hundred miles away. Raoul had told her that afternoon, just before her shift ended.

She'd been in the suite that morning to clean, and the room had been as it always was. Maybe a little neater. There were often a few toys scattered around, and, once, a bright green pacifier with smiling ducks painted on it lying on the edge of the bathtub. In the bedroom, Juli kept up with the small, careless piles of clothing belonging to the children's parents, folding the clothes and leaving them on the room's single chair. If there were dishes in the sink, she loaded and ran the dishwasher. Nearly every morning she found a pair of slightly sticky wine glasses, one with a lipstick-smeared rim, on the coffee table. There were always two or three fresh bottles of wine among the vegetables, cheeses, and meats in the refrigerator.

The Masons were a mystery to most of the staff. No one—including Juli—ever saw them come and go. But each morning when she came in to clean, there was a note for her on the skimpy hotel notepad, with a couple of dollars or a lottery ticket lying on top as a tip. Not many guests left tips for housekeeping. Sometimes Juli did feel invisible—just as Raoul had described—pushing her heavy cart through the silent corridors, disappearing into the rooms on her list. But she was sure the Masons were different from the other guests. They knew she was there, and how hard she worked for them. She'd even won five-hundred dollars with one of the scratch-off tickets they had given her. They never acknowledged the pale pink rose in a vase that she'd left for them as a thank-you for the winning ticket, but she was sure they'd liked it—especially the little girl. When, almost two weeks later, it was still in its place on the coffee table, petals curled and brown, leaves brittle from want of water, she'd thrown it away herself. If she felt a little embarrassed, it wasn't their fault. The Masons were busy people.

It was the first time she'd played the lottery. At home, where she'd lived with her aunt since she was five, games of chance weren't allowed. Juli wasn't the sort of person to argue—at least not with her aunt, who had never given Juli any kind of reason for her prejudice against gambling. Not religious, not moral. It was a rule. A simple rule.

The two of them lived simply, on simple, healthy food. Her aunt wore simple clothes of natural fibers and had always bought the same for Juli. They both wore their ash blonde hair simply, straight and parted down the middle, and used very little makeup. There was no drama, no yelling, no hateful exchanges between them, as there was among their neighbors. Juli had taken the job cleaning rooms at the residence hotel for the summer because it had simply presented itself by way of Ana, whose backyard opened onto the same narrow alley as her aunt's. With her pierced tongue and trio of elementary-school-aged children, Ana was one of the least simple, and strangest people that Juli knew. Also, Juli needed the money for college because her parents hadn't left her a dime, and her aunt considered any kind of investment besides a plain bank savings account decidedly un-simple.

This evening, Juli was tired. Her head and limbs felt weighted, ungainly. Ever since Raoul had told her about the Masons, barely looking up from the papers spread over his ugly metal desk, she'd felt like her body was moving against some kind of punishing current. *Hit by a semi that came over the median—total shitstorm, he'd said.* She'd pressed him for more information, but that was all he had to say, except that they were going to have to contact someone about picking up the Masons' stuff. *Their stuff: the toys, the yellow fleece bunting lying on top of the dresser, the crayons, the little girl's pile of stuffed animals, the woman's hairbrushes and makeup, the husband's worn brown slippers, the small pile of sports magazines.* It all belonged to someone else, now. Or no one.

She'd been loading clothes into the washer at home after her shift when the idea came to her to go back to the suite. Her aunt would be at work until eight, and wouldn't miss her. All she could think about was being close to the little family—or at least close to their things. They'd been so thoughtful. So generous. She'd imagined that one day they would meet, and maybe they would even have liked her enough (of course they liked her! they'd given her so many gifts!) to hire her to take care of the two Mason children. Many times she'd wished that they'd kept family pictures in the suite. She'd worried that someday she would see them, and not recognize them. That they would remain strangers.

When she'd arrived at the hotel for the second time that day, Raoul wasn't at his desk. The staff entrance—which all staff were required to use—ran past his office. If she were caught coming in one of the guest entrances she would be written up. Three write-ups in a month would get her fired. She had a story ready, about accidentally leaving her cell phone in her locker. The first couple of times she'd gotten tips from the Masons, she'd mentioned it to

Raoul, and he'd told her she was lucky. But she knew he would want to know why she was there at night. She knew he would be suspicious.

Already there was something empty and cold about the suite, a feeling of other-worldliness that made her wish she'd put on the cozy pink hoodie she kept down in her locker. It wasn't just the hotel-sparseness of the furniture, or the dull beige walls hung with soulless pastel prints of flowers. The suite was too quiet. Even the highway sounds that usually bled through the thin outer walls had disappeared.

Startled by her own image in the full-length mirror just outside the largest of the two bedrooms, Juli stopped. Inside the Masons' suite, she looked paler than usual, as though a little bit of life had drained out of her since she'd come into the hotel from her car. Even her hair, knotted loosely at the nape of her neck, seemed to glisten with new white streaks nestled among the ashy blonde. Leaning close to the mirror, she fingered the hairs close to her scalp, finally singling out one of the white ones. Gripping it, she jerked it out, bringing a brief, pained look to the face of the girl in the mirror.

She hurried to the bathroom where, that morning, she'd paid extra attention to the scuffed tile floor, and looked at the hair beneath the harsh light of the fluorescent bulbs.

Sure enough, it was stark white. Not even gray, or any other color at all. It was white and fat, and the bulb at the head of it bore a tiny drop of blood. Repelled, she dropped it into the garbage can, where it settled, coiled in the can's shiny, stainless bottom.

The woman was blonde, just like Juli—Juli had wiped the long, pale hairs out of the tub many times—but her clothes were a size smaller than Juli wore. Her makeup was all fair, and she used expensive moisturizers and sunscreen. She was careful about her appearance.

The husband? Athletic and surely handsome. There was a tennis racquet leaning against the closet wall. The dress shoes lined up on the floor were shiny, and looked expensive. Maybe even new. One morning Juli found a tiny lens-cleaning cloth and a bottle of artificial tears in the bedside table, and guessed that both belonged to him. She pictured him in chic, wireless frames that showed off his bright green eyes. The little girl whose stuffed animals covered the bed, and the baby who slept in the portable crib would have his eyes, but their mommy's fair hair.

The clothes in the closet were substantial and real, proof that the Masons had existed. Proof that there had been people living there who liked her. The woman might have even let her borrow one of the dresses—no matter that she didn't have anywhere to wear such lovely things except to church, where she hated to go because everyone knew her aunt, and immediately assumed that Juli wanted to be there. They thought she was there to make friends, when nothing could be further from the truth. She didn't want her aunt's kind of friends.

Juli turned on the bedroom's overhead light and opened the closet.

The dress she chose was sleeveless, pale blue silk, pleated at the bodice with a slender pencil skirt that reached just to the knee. She took off her uniform and shoes, and put on the dress, careful not to damage the fragile fabric. She went back to the mirror in the hallway. Maybe the dress was a little tight and too old for her, but it made her feel pretty. Grown up.

In the kitchen, she checked her Timex against the clock on the microwave. Would the police be coming? She thought that they might. But they wouldn't know her, wouldn't know that the dress she was wearing didn't belong to her. And there was the story about the cell phone.

Thirsty, she opened the cabinet to get a glass for some tap water. But her hand rested instead on one of the sturdy, hotel-issued wine glasses.

Juli carried a glass of wine and a plate holding a chunk of imported cheese, some crackers, and a small steak knife from the kitchen to the table in front of the living room's picture window. She was surprised to find the barrel-shaped chair beside it so comfortable. How odd that she'd never sat in it before! She'd always thought it looked stiff, and uncomfortable. Of course, she'd had no time to sit. She settled against the chair's deep, upholstered back, and looked out at the glass and steel office building across the highway. Red and gold waves from the setting sun bathed the glass in warm color. Below, the traffic was light. Silent. She could only hear the hum of the suite's air conditioning. She still felt sad, but couldn't ever remember feeling as peaceful as she did in that moment.

The first drink of the wine was tart on her tongue, then sweet, like fruit candy. She licked her bottom lip, catching an errant drop. At church the wine was red and bitter, and she only took it when she went to Saturday mass, without her aunt. Her aunt had made it clear that wine-drinking was not a question of morality, as the Baptists thought. It was simply not necessary to a simple, healthful life. She told Juli not to believe the reports about French people who lived longer because they drank great quantities of red wine. Her aunt didn't trust the French.

The cheese was bitter, the crackers fragrant with rosemary and garlic. She chewed slowly, the way her aunt had always encouraged, so that she might savor every unusual bite. She was careful with the crumbs, brushing them from her lap, into her hands, and back onto the plate.

By the time she prepared the last cracker (who knew death would make her so hungry?), the building across the street had returned to being its cold, glass-and-steel self, and she was feeling a little drunk. Not drunk like someone who had spent the whole day drinking beer in a bar—that was for people who had no self-control. *No class*, as her aunt would say. She felt happily drunk, like someone who was on holiday. Someone who was celebrating. Even though she was here to be close to the dead, she couldn't help herself. She looked down at the pale blue dress, now also gray in the twilight. When was the last time she had celebrated something? Maybe her birthday? She and her aunt had gone to The Coach House, where they had ordered shrimp cocktails and New York strip steaks. There had been dessert, but no singing by the waiters and waitresses. In fact, hadn't she been relieved that her aunt hadn't mentioned that it was her birthday? All that attention on her. The thought of people staring at her paralyzed her with fear. It was too much.

Walking across the darkening living room in search of another glass of wine, she stepped on a plastic toy pony. It dug painfully into the pad of one foot, and she stumbled. The words that came immediately to her lips weren't curse words, but once those words were out of her mouth, she threw a loud *son-of-a-bitch!* after them, and felt better.

Sometimes, in the quiet of her own bedroom, she cursed in front of the mirror, whispering the words she heard the men on the maintenance staff use. *Asshole. Dumbshit. Dickface. Shithead. Shithead* was her favorite.

"Shithead," she said. The sound of the word melted into the beige walls of the living room. As it disappeared, she smiled. She picked up the offending pony by its satiny blue mane and put it on the table where it couldn't hurt her, again.

In the bedroom, she put her newly-filled glass of wine down so she could more easily take the woman's other clothes from the closet. Grabbing hangers with both hands, she piled the pants, dresses, ruffled blouses, and fashionably short (but not too short) skirts on to the bed. When all that remained were the man's clothes, she started on the woman's dresser drawers. There were only two. She worked more slowly here, letting the satiny panties slide through her calloused fingers onto the pile on the bed. How wonderful they felt against her skin!

Picking out a pair of pink silk panties trimmed with matching lace, she stepped out of her own simple cotton briefs, and slid them over her knees, then thighs. They felt like a whisper. A tickle. They were the kind of panties she saw on the heavy-breasted mannequins in the Victoria's Secret windows at the mall as she hurried past, anxious that someone might step out from that temple of sex and sensuality and ask her if she wanted to come inside. To *indulge* herself.

The panties were romance itself against her skin. Standing in front of the mirror, she lifted the dress and posed, noting how slender her hips looked.

What had the woman looked like in the panties? Had her

husband thought she looked pretty? And what did she look like now that she was dead? Had she been thrown from the car, or had she been crushed inside?

Juli shivered.

She sat down on the edge of the bed, and leaned back on the fragrant pile of clothes. They smelled of lemon—probably verbena, like the leafy plant her aunt grew in the tiny square of garden at the back of the house—and of detergent. Her hand rested on something soft—a scrap of velvet—that felt just as wonderful as the silk panties. She thought about the baby, and how it might have liked the feel of velvet on its tiny face.

She got up and took off the blue dress slowly, and laid it on the bed. Undressed down to the panties, she downed the rest of the wine in her glass.

The velvet gown she'd pulled out of the pile of clothes was a rich emerald green. It looked like Christmas. She lifted the gown so that it fell over her head, down past her arms and shoulders, and, finally, covered her whole body. She struggled with the zipper, but when she finally got it, she found that the gown wasn't too small at all. Its satin underskirts rustled as she hurried to the closet, where the wife had kept her jewelry bag inside one of her extra purses. Juli had found it one day when she'd taken the purses down to dust the shelf. It was a terrible hiding place. The woman might as well have just left everything out on the dresser. It made Juli sad to know that the woman hadn't trusted her even after the several weeks she'd spent taking care of them.

The dress embraced her like a friend, as though the Mason woman herself were holding and reassuring her, and she realized she'd been wrong. It wasn't that the woman had mistrusted *Juli*, but any other person who might have come to clean in her place.

Juli clipped on a thin gold necklace whose only decoration was a small, apricot-and-cream cameo. Looking in the mirror, she saw a princess.

Juli woke on the couch in darkness, desperate for breath. Something heavy lay on her chest, her mouth was smothered.

Pulling back as far as she could, she saw a man's laughing face in the scarce light from the window. Her lips felt slick and wet and she knew with a sick certainty that it was his saliva.

"Hey, she woke up." A woman's voice.

For an all-too-brief moment, Juli was convinced that she was sleeping, dreaming. Never in her waking life had she been so afraid. She squeezed one hand tightly so that the nails dug into her palm, to force herself awake. But there was only more pain, and she knew it was all real. She shoved at the man, trying to roll him off of her, but he was too heavy. And he was laughing. The man leaned close again, and licked the side of her face.

Now, the woman was laughing, too.

"Raoul, you're freaking her out," she said. "You better get off."

Raoul snorted. "What the hell do you think I was trying to do?" But he came up off of Juli all the same, and moved awkwardly away to sit on the coffee table.

Juli struggled to sit up. She could still feel the alcohol in her blood, but the sense of peace, of celebration, had vanished in that hideous moment of waking. *Raoul. Ana.* They were here with her. Only they felt familiar. Everything else felt strange.

Ana, who held a half-full glass of wine, came to stand over her. Her bright orange lipstick, usually so carefully applied, had smeared onto the skin around her mouth. She wore a white jumpsuit that Juli had never seen before. Even in the relative darkness, Juli could tell that it didn't suit her. She looked half-dead. Washed out. The leer in her eyes didn't help the way she looked. Juli remembered telling her aunt that Ana was tall, and rather pretty. Ana was no longer pretty.

"Nice dress," Ana said.

Juli was finally able to rise to a kneeling position, and gathered the deep skirts of the gown around her.

"I fell asleep," she said, her voice shaking.

Raoul laughed again. "Just like Goldilocks."

"I guess that would make you Papa Bear, huh?" Ana said.

He didn't answer Ana, but leaned in closer to Juli. Waves of his sour breath told her that he'd been drinking wine as well. A lot of it. He fingered the green velvet skirt of the gown, and gave a low whistle.

"This is all very unprofessional, little Juli," he said.

Juli wiped at her mouth with the back of one hand. Although Ana had been the one to tell her not to trust Raoul, Juli hadn't liked him from the hour he had first interviewed her. But she had never imagined that he could be so coarse. So vile. She could still feel his bulk on her chest, the prodding thing between his legs that he'd jabbed against her clothed body. In the darkness, she colored to think of it. It wasn't that she didn't know what he was doing to her, or that she was even that inexperienced. It was that she'd felt so powerless beneath him. Stunned.

"What are you doing, here?" she said. "You and Ana." They shouldn't be in the Masons' suite. Of course, she knew that she shouldn't be there, either. But she belonged in a way that the two of them didn't.

She could tell that they were both very drunk. *What about her? She had drunk the Masons' wine without their permission. Her hand dropped unconsciously to her lap. What had she done?*

"We saw you, silly," Ana said, dropping to the sofa cushion beside her. "Here, Rolly. Get me some more wine. I bet there's some in the fridge." She pouted, and Raoul rolled his eyes. Still, he got up.

On his way to the kitchen, he flipped on the overhead light, causing Juli to squint.

"You shouldn't be here," she said, quietly. She still felt shaken by Raoul's attack. She'd never thought about how big he actually was.

"*You* shouldn't be here," Ana said. "So, we're even. Rolly didn't see you at first. But I saw you on the security camera letting yourself in. It's awesome, isn't it? They're dead, and we get to be in here." She glanced around the room with comic exaggeration as though the Masons might still be hiding somewhere, watching with disapproval.

Juli didn't like the idea of Ana being in the suite, let alone the idea of her talking about the Masons. *Dead. They were dead, and they were her friends. Or they would have been her friends. Maybe even her family.*

"You could be in real trouble, honey," Ana said. She put a hand over Juli's. It felt damp and hot on Juli's skin. "Like with the police." Ana had a very slight lisp from the piercing in her tongue.

Juli hesitated, wanting to explain. But what would she say? She didn't have an explanation beyond a sense—a certain sense—that she belonged here. Then she saw the mocking glint in Ana's eyes. She jerked her hand away.

The tiniest of smiles flitted across Ana's lips.

"I just don't want you, or Raoul, to get into trouble," Juli said.

"Trouble?" Raoul carried Ana's glass of wine ahead of him. Juli noticed that he was wearing a different shirt from the gray uniform shirt that he usually wore. This one was the color of cranberries and made his dark eyes look darker, almost like two dark holes in his face. His face was fleshy, with the five o'clock shadow beard that always appeared by three in the afternoon. He was a good two inches shorter than Ana, but he walked with a small man's swagger, as though daring the world to tell him he wasn't actually tall, or good-looking.

"Who's in trouble? You're not talking about me..." His words cut off with a cry.

Ana gave a little shriek as Raoul tripped, and the wine glass flew out of his hand. Its contents splashed Ana's hair and dress. She held her hands out in front of her as though she could ward it off, but it was too late.

Raoul's face contorted in surprise as he fell to the fell, his arms spread wide so that he banged one hand on the coffee table. He made an "oof" sound as he hit the floor.

Juli's initial instinct was to jump up and help him. But she thought of his weight on her stomach and chest, and the way he had smelled, and she shrank back.

"What the hell?" Raoul lay breathless on the rug.

"Damn it, Rolly!" Ana said.

He stared up at her, irritated. Petulant. "I tripped over that damned toy," he said. "It wasn't me."

Juli saw the plastic pony with the long blue mane and tail lying on the rug behind him, its painted purple mouth grinning aimlessly at the ceiling. It was the same toy she had tripped over, the one she remembered putting on the dining table.

"But it's pink wine," Ana said. "It will never come out."

Unsteady, Raoul got to his feet.

"Go get yourself cleaned up," he said.

Ana didn't answer him, but stalked off toward the bathroom at the back of the suite, her drunkenness dissipated by her anger.

"You," Raoul said, sitting down heavily on the chair by the window.

Juli didn't want to be in the same room with him. She'd had to sit in his office, waiting, while he put her off by talking on the phone or doing paperwork. He'd seemed to want her to sit there until she became truly uncomfortable, just as she was, now. It came to her that what he'd done to her while she was asleep was some kind of joke to him. He hadn't been planning to rape her as she'd feared when she first realized he was on top of her—he had just wanted to torment her. To make fun of her because Ana was there. Ana, who was no longer her friend. Had she ever been her friend? Juli wasn't sure.

"I'm not going to ask you what you're doing here," he said. "I think I already get it."

"I should go help Ana," she said. She started up, untangling her legs from the skirt of the gown. Despite the awkwardness of what was happening, the gown was gentle on her skin. It had begun to feel like a part of her.

"Sit down, Juli," he said.

Juli stopped, and sat down.

"You surprised me," he said. "I took you for one of those bleeding hearts. One of those women who get all sentimental when some bad shit happens. You put in twenty whole bucks when you heard James's kid needed new glasses for school, and you hadn't even been here a week." He shook his head. "Now you're up here in some dead people's suite, wearing their clothes, drinking their liquor. I'd bet you dollars to doughnuts that didn't come in here with you."

He pointed to the necklace she was wearing. Self-conscious, Juli wrapped a hand around the cameo.

"Why are *you* here?" Juli said, feeling bolder. Strangely, that he misunderstood her didn't bother her at all. She just wanted him to leave.

"Why wouldn't we be here?" Raoul said. "The creep-out factor is pretty high. Ana said she'd get off on it, and I hate to disappoint Ana." His smile was grotesque.

All the bad things Ana had said about him...maybe she'd just been trying to keep her away. As though Juli would ever want anything to do with him.

Then he was serious. "So, is that all that's worth anything? Is there more jewelry?"

"I didn't steal it," Juli said. "She would've given it to me!"

Raoul laughed. "That's a good one," he said. "They leave you a few tips and you think you're the new heir to the crown jewels? You've got balls, I'll give you that."

Juli was suddenly afraid, as though she'd spilled some kind of secret for which she'd be punished. Raoul and Ana didn't know what she knew. They could never understand what the Masons had meant to her, and she to them.

"You're right. None of us should be here," she said, trying to sound calm. "The police are going to come, aren't they? We should clean everything up."

"No. No police," Raoul said. "I don't think they've even found any next-of-kin, yet. They found their room keys from here and our address in the GPS. We're it."

While Juli was weighing his words, trying to figure out how to get Ana and him to leave, Ana wandered in from the back of the suite. She carried a stuffed pink dolphin under one arm, and was wearing the blue silk dress that Juli had left lying on the bed. Ana was skinny—skinnier than any other woman Juli knew—despite the three kids she'd borne. The dress didn't flatter her at all. She'd left the pleated bodice of the dress unbuttoned, exposing the broad valley between her tiny breasts. She looked like a skeleton playing dress-up.

Ugly, Juli thought. *Ugly as sin.*

But it was more than that. What Ana had done—stealing the toy for one of her little brats, and putting on the dress—was a violation that was worse than a sin. She didn't belong there at all. She'd brought Raoul into the suite for disgusting reasons. She'd violated the Masons' sacred space, the place where they ate and slept and took care of their children. The place where Juli took care of *them*.

Juli didn't think about picking up the steak knife or about crossing the room. She didn't stop to wonder at how Ana's smile slowly disappeared as she got closer, or how Ana's face blanched with fear. She simply struck before Ana could move, burying the knife in the hollow space beneath Ana's collarbone, close to her right shoulder.

Stepping back, Juli watched as Ana grabbed, dumbstruck, at the hard plastic handle of the knife, trying to pull it out. But she screamed louder with each tug, until she crumpled to the floor, exhausted and terrified.

Behind Juli, Raoul was frozen, watching. Then Juli stepped aside, not wanting to be close to Ana and all the blood running from her wound. It had already blackened much of the blue silk dress and now was spreading to the rug.

"You crazy bitch!" Raoul finally moved and shoved Juli farther aside, so that she stumbled against the bright yellow ball that she'd earlier kicked into the room. This time, it rolled all the way into the kitchen.

"Why?" Raoul screamed. "Why in the hell would you hurt Ana?"

Juli didn't answer. She didn't really know the why, other than that Ana had been wrong. Ana had gone too far. Ana had pushed.

But Juli felt calm. Almost elated. The celebratory feeling she'd enjoyed before she'd fallen asleep had come back. She didn't want it to go away, again.

It was the yellow ball that showed Juli the way.

With Ana and Raoul finally gone, she was happy. Raoul had picked up the unconscious Ana and hurried out of the suite. By then, a crowd had gathered in the hallway because of all the screaming. They, like Juli, had heard Raoul shout that he'd thought he was just going to have to fire her, but now she'd have to deal with the police. Also that he thought she would probably get the death penalty. Julie knew he was being ridiculous. There was no way that Ana was going to die. The wound hadn't been that deep.

She began to tidy up the suite. Ana and Raoul hadn't been there long, but they had brought chaos: Ana's shattered wine glass, the blood, the displaced furniture. In the bedroom, Ana had strewn most of the woman's clothes around the room, searching for something. It annoyed Juli that they had both chosen to wear the same blue dress.

She was in the kitchen loading the dishwasher when someone knocked on the door. It was a timid knock, not at all like the knock of a policeman or fireman or some other official who wanted to take her away from the suite. If it had been, they would have gotten a surprise because she was never going to leave.

Juli pressed her face against the door, listening. She thought maybe she could hear someone breathing, but when she looked through the peephole, she saw nothing but the stretched out triangle of wall and carpet that the peephole always revealed. Nothing moved. No one was there.

Something jostled the thick skirt of the gown, and she looked down to see the absurdly cheerful smiley face that was painted on the yellow ball. It stared up at her, the white-dot centers of its eyes focused tightly on her own.

The ball gave a little lurch, and began to roll. She followed it with her eyes until it rolled past the coffee table. Then she went after it, smiling herself at the whimsy of the thing. *Whimsy.* It was a word she loved. A word she could never hear or say enough. But she had a feeling—a happy, comforting feeling—that she was going to be more familiar with that word than she had ever been before.

When the ball reached the wall between the table and chair beside the window, it stopped. Then it rolled back and forth a few inches, hitting the wall, acting as though it were trying to get out. To knock down the wall, and make it disappear.

Juli understood.

She opened the window, sliding the glass aside. There was no screen between her and the outside.

It was no longer night, but the mellow light couldn't properly be called daylight, either. The cars, the highway, the tall buildings that usually stood like tall, stone and steel creatures that were always just beyond her reach were gone. In the murky distance, she saw a face emerging. A child's smiling face. As the girl came closer, Juli could see that she was smiling shyly. Her halo of blonde, wispy hair held the light of both sunshine and stars. She held her arms open to Juli.

Juli bent down and picked up the ball, her thumbs at each corner of its goofy painted grin. She tossed the ball to the girl, who caught it like small children will, with not just her hands, but her forearms as well. She clutched it to her and turned away, laughing. Julie thought that an angel's laugh couldn't sound more beautiful.

The little girl ran into the gloaming, toward the man and woman waiting for her. She glanced back every so often, and Juli knew that she was looking for her. Waiting for her.

Juli followed.

Josh Woods

He Who Fights with Monsters

... should be careful, lest he thereby become a monster.
—Nietzsche, *Beyond Good and Evil*

He sits studying his hands front and back, those limbs wrapped and taped as solidly as casts from fingers to forearms, the wrapwork bulging grotesquely from the brass knuckles underneath, an advantage that doesn't really bother anyone in the crowd, or anyone in the promotion, or even anyone in the other corner for that matter, being that he fights living breathing monsters in this underground circuit and that his own human figure squared off against such beasts makes a thing like using brass knuckles seem excusable, even expected, yet his hands seem distant somehow, not doing any good in his effort to remember just how it was he got himself to this point in life.

These days, the fighting is just for the cash. These monster fights have been big money so far, and tonight's fight against a thing they brought in from Germany will be the biggest purse so far. They billed it as, "Man VS Monster, Real UFC Vet Ivan Troupes Fights Terror of the Black Forest—The Doppelganger!" His handlers, who have been saving up his money for him, tell him that this fight tonight will be against a very familiar body-type—in other words, it'll be a fight against a creature with a mostly human anatomy. And a win tonight should be enough cash to get him far away from all this, away from this concrete fight-pit, away from this burnt-out bourbon distillery and its foul crowd of cash-waiving hillbillies and gun-toting bookies, far away from eastern Kentucky. It'll get him off of this canvas cot, where

257

he has recurring nightmares of what seem to be formless terrors from the deep past, and it'll get him out of this dark, dank, cell of a room. It'll be a chance to become a completely different person, which he wants so badly that he sits, a pugilist at rest, searching the weird sight of his hands for some reminder who he really is and must have been.

He remembers, surely, his fighting in the UFC in the early days, before they had the phrase "mixed martial arts," before they had the cable channel deals and the reality shows and the preponderance of rules such as being forced to wear gloves or being penalized for striking the groin. Well, he remembers at least watching the videos of himself fighting. His tale-of-the-tape read, "Ivan Troupes, 6 feet 3 inches, 218 pounds, 77.5 inch reach." Thick-shouldered yet slim-chested, a bearded face but a hairless body, he could have hailed from the Bronze Age. He studied the fight videos of himself skipping sideways around the cage and then switching his trajectory as swift as some airborne thing, shooting in for the clinch, locking up the other fighter despite wild struggles, like Menelaus to Proteus, and then lifting for a skull-first slam into the mat. He was good. His current handler says that if the UFC hadn't cut him over his refusal to take a dive for the sake of the bracket setup and for pay-per-view overrun time, if he hadn't been forced to fight in the even shadier promotions in Japan where he finally got blacklisted, the once-great Ivan Troupes could have been a legitimate belt-holder. His name could have been in the Hall of Fame with Royce Gracie and Ken Shamrock and Dan Severn and Oleg Taktarov the rest of the old-schoolers. Instead, he has ended up in an illegal racket fighting all manner of unnatural beasts, which he needs no videos to recall clearly. His first fight here, as he remembers well, had been against a troll from Wales.

The Welshmen had kept the troll covered with an army-green tarp, which must have functioned like some sort of hawk hood because the troll seemed to be doing nothing under there except breathing calmly, despite all the noise. The crowd roared and spit and cursed; the announcer bellowed from his bullhorn, something about this troll hailing from under the second oldest bridge in Britain, something about its steady diet of children. Ivan just bounced on his toes, side to side, thinking only of a quick, sharp knockout so he wouldn't have to grapple with that monster. It wasn't until the other men cleared out of the concrete pit and yelled "fight," not until they yanked a rope to withdraw the tarp, did Ivan worry about what the troll looked like.

It crouched on its haunches as if it were a primitive third-worlder by a fire, and its features were impossibly swollen. A nose like a butternut squash, ears like fleshy pink manta rays, its bald head covered in liver spots, it was as if someone had decapitated a nursing-home giant and had attached that head to some corpulent baboon body, connected at the shoulders by a lion's beard. Like the rest of its limbs, its feet and hands were fur-covered, and they were as wide as suitcases, the troll's fingers dripping with its own spit and snot. Its eyes glowed blue, but they weren't enlarged or piercing like he would have expected of a monster, not wicked or searching. They were close and small, too much so.

Ivan decided to wait on his side of the concrete pit and to keep hopping, to stay loose, so that the troll would have to move first and reveal how it went about attacking things. Soon it slouched forward, helping itself walk every few steps with its hands. It seemed to approach Ivan as if he were a passive meal set out for easy consumption, a steak for a gator, and when it reached out slowly to take Ivan by the skull, he slid out, circled the troll before it could lumber around, and launched a flying knee into its spine. It fell forward, and it lay there hacking and wheezing.

The crowd cheered. Ivan raised his arms. Even if he hadn't ended the fight just yet, he knew at least that a win was inevitable. He was simply too fast for it, and he wondered for an instant if monsters like this one had aided in the evolution of the human body millennia ago, requiring it to become the fastest of the apes.

The troll, still coughing and hacking, turned toward Ivan. It had its arm down its own throat, elbow deep. Bile leaked down its fur and spilled on the floor. It kept hacking and reaching deep into its own guts; then it withdrew its arm and, in its hand, held out the severed head of a young girl. Her face had been wrenched in a perpetual cry, silent yet full of pain, her skin having been turned a weird gray from digestive juices, her long, curled hair soaked but otherwise golden blond. The troll threw the head at Ivan, who was so shocked by the sight of it that he stood unmoving and was hit right mouth.

He fell. The little dead girl's skull had hit him like a bowling ball, busting his jaw and cracking his teeth. The taste of its fluids twisted his guts. The stench was yellow. He rolled on the ground wiping his mouth, and spat, and shook his head to regain his wits.

Then the troll was upon him.

It lay heavily on him and tried to corral his arms and legs, perhaps in an effort to roll Ivan up into a shape that would fit easily down its throat. It made the huffing sounds of a pervert, a rapist, and it grabbed at him just as eagerly. Ivan writhed and kicked. On his back, he managed the semblance of an open guard, jiu-jitsu style, and he arm-dragged the troll off-center just enough to create an escape for himself. He slid away and scrambled up to all fours, his hand clutching a mess of golden curls. Then he stood with it and felt the weight of the little girl's head hanging at the end of its hair like a medieval ball on a chain. He grinned.

The troll roared and turned slowly to him, ready to pounce now, ready now to attack full-on.

Ivan rolled his grip and twisted the hair one turn tighter; then he began swinging it, bringing it faster and faster into a deadly swirl. He stepped carefully, checked his distance with the other hand outstretched, then he whipped the little girl's head down onto the troll's face.

Something split. Blood sprayed centrifugally. Ivan twirled the girl's head back to full velocity and, again, struck.

The troll curled up now, and Ivan stood one foot on the beast, beating it over and over. When it was no longer clear which flying chips of bone belonged to the dead girl and which to the troll, when the head at the end of its hair no longer looked human, when the troll had ceased twitching with each hit, Ivan stopped. The crowd wailed with delight. Both sets of cornermen and handlers and equipment shufflers and managers rushed in and lifted Ivan aloft, men's hands reaching up to him in apotheosis. Someone cried, "I can't wait to see what they make him fight next!"

And he did continue to fight. He fought a chupacabra, a giant Chinese caterpillar, a were-cow from India that they billed as a minotaur, and, the worst of them all, a goblin. That goblin, the furry little sucker, was supposed to be a cushion fight, something to get folks feeling safe enough with putting money on the winner that they would gamble on the length of the fight, or on the manner in which Ivan would finish it. Instead, as soon as they opened the goblin's cage, it climbed out of the pit and took off into the crowd, attacking the on-lookers, lacerating their skin, slicing achilles tendons, leaping from one set of shoulders to the next and biting plugs out of their scalps, latching onto their crotches and chomping away. The crowd had torn loose. It was pandemonium. The bookies fumbled with their decommissioned assault rifles and took pot-shots at the goblin, but they wounded only the people who ran and swarmed in every direction, arms flailing, unable to find a working exit.

Ivan climbed into the crowd and shoved his way toward the ever-moving sprays of blood until he caught up with the nasty little thing. It was busy cleaning its way through some guy's shoulder, its teeth digging as fast as a ban-saw, the guy screaming and dancing in a helpless circle. Ivan loaded up for a heavy right hand, waited for the victim to swing around one more time, and he knocked the goblin senseless. Then he pulled it down to the ground by its leg, stepped on its neck, and gave that leg a sharp tug. He felt it snap. He lifted the lifeless goblin up like wild game and yelled to the crowd that he got it.

All those who were free of serious injury cheered wildly for him. Even some of the wounded uttered cursing thanks. They had paid him to be an entertainment, and he had done that. They had wanted him to be ruthless and fearless, and he had been. When, in need of a hero, they wanted him to save them from their own monster, he had. He could be anything they wanted him to be.

So Ivan stops searching the strange sight of his own wrapped hands because the men tell him it's fight-time. He stands, shakes out the tension in his limbs, pops his neck, and follows his handlers through the corridor. They lead him between the crowd held back by sawhorses, and down into the fight pit through a hatch opening in the newly constructed cage dome—a creaking, metalwork, web-like structure which the promoters understood now, after the goblin incident, to be necessary. As awkward and as makeshift as that cage dome looked, it seemed strong enough to keep out all but the most unimaginable terrors, those of his nightmares, which would never be put in the fight-pit in the first place.

Ivan doesn't want to bother looking toward his opponent, the monster, because he's seasoned, because he now knows that first impressions don't end up affecting the fight, because if it's going to be a surprise no matter what—as it always is—then anticipating nothing will make him invulnerable to surprise. He doesn't even want to bother listening to the announcer or to his own cornermen or to the opposing cornermen. But their noise gets in his ears anyway.

"In this corner, what you've all been waiting for." The announcer screams through his bullhorn. "Real-life UFC veteran Ivan Troupes!"

He bounces on his toes side-to-side as he always does, looking down at the filthy concrete beneath him, trying hard to think nothing, to hear nothing, to see nothing.

The crowd's cacophony is all static.

"And his opponent, the terror of the Black Forest, the mirror of fears, the monster you all know too well: the doppelganger!"

Ivan can't help it. He looks up to the far side of the fight pit to see the monster. And he sees himself. It is him. It's exactly himself in every way: the build, the face, the side-to-side bounce. It's face looks just as shaken by the uncanny sight as his own must, the only difference, a slight one, being that it looks older, not the younger face so familiar from his old fight videos.

And that's when the realization hits him, and it sends his head reeling, a flash of a thousand lost thoughts, a sudden upside-down feeling, like the snag of a net in a dark forest.

The men clear the pit and call a start to the fight, but he stands inert in shock. The other Ivan Troupes rushes to him and batters him with immediate hooks and overhands and looping kicks. He covers up and crumples. He receives the blows despite his attempt to shield himself from them, and they hurt, but a deeper anguish overwhelms him. He feels betrayed and, in that instant, indignant. He can hear the humans screaming for Ivan to kill the doppelganger, and he knows now that they mean him, and he knows now that it is true.

And he can feel his suffering taking hold of his body, changing him. He feels the real Ivan Troupes halt his attack and back away. He feels himself transforming into something far worse than any here have ever seen, into something from the recesses of history, from the old abyss, giving form to an ancient terror these men have forgotten.

Julia Patt

Hunting the Pigwoman

Hunting wasn't the kind of thing we did together but it happened anyway—one February night I followed Steg Johnson into the woods on the other side of town. Him with his prized Remington slung over one shoulder and me with my daddy's Model 500 tucked into the waistband of my jeans. "Dumb way to carry a gun," Steg'd said when he saw me and smiled a little, but that was it. He walked into the growing dark between the trees; the failing sunlight snagged on the rifle's muzzle like a beacon. And I went in after him, my boots sinking into the winter wet. I squeezed my jacket closer with one hand, pulled the fabric tight.

Keep that night air out, as my mother would say, would have said if she'd seen me slip out the back door, Daddy's gun in my jeans, our big metal flashlight in my jacket pocket. But she hadn't seen me and Steg's mother hadn't seen him either. We wouldn't have been out there hunting the giant feral pig if they'd known. It'd nearly gored two people by then, a park ranger up by Dalton and a hiker on the Appalachian Trail before that. Night, both times, and neither of them could say much about the thing except, "Big, real big." But there'd been no trace of it for over a week, even with everyone looking for the next "Hogzilla."

But Steg had seen it in a dream two nights ago—or so he'd told me after gym.

A big guy, Steg probably had sixty pounds on me, so I flinched when he caught me coming in from the track, me still clammy with sweat, him slick and pink all over from the showers. Then, that gut-seizing moment when I thought he would hit me for some reason I didn't know yet. He never talked to me in public otherwise. So I froze, waiting for the punch.

Instead—"Cole, you still got your daddy's gun at home?"

He was dripping on me. I wiped the water off my face and shrugged. "Sure, yeah. Of course," I said. My mother never threw anything out, least of all something of my daddy's.

He lowered his voice. "I know where it is. The pig, I mean. I saw it."

Saw it, the way Steg saw things sometimes in the middle of the night, though not many people knew that about him.

"I'll go with you," I said, though he hadn't asked. He wouldn't and he didn't need to.

A night bird trilled in the trees above me, calling on the dusk. I'd fallen in step with Steg, a few paces behind him, our shoes making hungry noises in the muck. Every now and then, he paused, shook his head one way and the other like a hound, and adjusted our path. The air had gone soft and blue with evening around us; it all glowed. We walked deep in, probably crossing the state park line though it was impossible know out there where private property ended and the parks began. No one much cared either.

Eighth grade, Steg and I were bunkmates at camp, before he got tall and well liked and I didn't, before my daddy, before everything. That summer Steg dreamed about Libby Trevor and a big black snake in the weeds and whispered down to me what he'd seen. His trembling rattled the bed. And about a week later it happened—Libby sallow-stiff on the ground and rushed away in a yelping ambulance. Steg shaking under the canoes by the lake, me talking him through it.

He'd dreamed about my daddy, too, I knew it from the way he didn't talk to me that spring or for a long time after, even to push me around the way he did sometimes for show in school. I never asked him about it. What he saw. And then, that night in the woods I didn't say, "How do you know where we're going?" Instead: "How much farther, do you think?"

"Not far," Steg said. "You got that flashlight, right? Keep it pointed at the ground."

I walked in his wake, as if drawn along by some unseen line from his broad shoulders to my ribs, my daddy's gun a bumping weight against my hip. I'd never told anyone about Steg—all of what I knew about him. That even when he didn't see things in his sleep, he talked, usually nonsense but once the chorus to "Try A Little Tenderness." And that he was no great athlete and he knew it but he worked hard. That he almost always pulled his punches and wouldn't take money from the other kids, though his friends did. That he wanted to be a forest ranger or a veterinarian if he ever got out of Gaulver. Yeah, I knew Steg, better than most people did really, but neither of us would ever say it.

"Cole," Steg said.

I didn't see the pig so much as the space around it, the impression it made in the world, the twilight clinging to its mass. It must have stood six feet at the shoulder, been better than ten feet long, the whole of it solid in the way that nothing is solid, not houses or cars or anything made by people. It was solid the way the Angel Oak is solid or Sassafras Mountain is solid—heavy and unyielding as bedrock itself. I could smell it in the cool air, the rich, meaty stink of it, the tons of flesh, rank and rubbed deep with earth and sweat.

Steg. I didn't say it out loud. Steg. Don't.

He had the Remington up on his shoulder, was taking aim when the thing screamed and charged. A sow, I saw it late, the low hanging teats swaying as she ran. That scream. Not-white tusks in the dark. Did the ground shake? It must have, for a hog that size, but I didn't feel it.

The Remington cracked the night open but the pig did not stop. And after: Steg sprawled in the wet leaves; his split side grinned black through his shirt. The gun flung into the undergrowth.

Wet bloomed under my knees and cold washed up and down my bare arms, as if I'd jumped into the lake. I balled up my jacket and pressed it against Steg's torn-open side, trying to keep everything in where it belonged. Both my hands on that jacket, the flashlight lying in the dirt, lighting up the dead leaves.

"Steg." I said it this time; the final consonant caught hard on my teeth and strangled me. "You alright?"

"Cole." His voice steady. Of course. "Where'd it go?"

"I—"

"Cole," he said. "Get your gun out."

I fumbled at my jeans with one hand, keeping the other on my jacket on Steg, and found the weight against my hip in the dark. My daddy's gun, not that it had helped him any, stowed in the glove compartment on Rte. 76 when he stopped to help a nameless man with a flat. I took off the safety, cocked it.

A noise behind us, something stirring, a gentle noise. Too small to be the pig. I grabbed the flashlight.

She was barefoot and gray-colored, her breasts and belly covered by an old piece of hide, her shoulders left naked in the cold. Her hair matted over her collarbone, its original color lost to dark and dirt. She was probably taller than me, maybe taller than Steg, and she was big, her breasts drooping low under the hide, her thighs heavy. Calves and feet swollen pale and bulging in the night. Next to me, Steg made a dry sound. I raised the light, shining it on her face; her small eyes snatched the glow and threw it back at us. Her chin and lips were smeared wet and deep red. She bared her teeth at me and snorted—a challenge.

"That one," she said. "He's mine."

I raised the gun in her direction. "No."

She blinked at me once before I fired. The shot went off somewhere into the trees and the sound of it echoed and bounced around us. She came over to us then, crouched next to me and Steg, put her hand on mine, the one holding the gun, and lowered it. I could smell her again, that same rank, meaty smell and, if I'd wondered at all before that, I knew then what she was.

She pulled the jacket from his wound, exposing that slashed open mouth on his side. She lowered her face to it and sniffed. Extended her long tongue and took a taste. Steg made a thick noise and I grabbed at her, meaning to push her away. She shoved me down hard in the leaves next to Steg. The air went out of me. "Please," I said. "Please don't. Just let him go."

I had replayed this conversation countless times before, brought it back out of the deep time and again for months before that. But

it was not the pigwoman and it was not Steg when I thought of it.
If I had been there to say something. If I could have. "Please just
let him go. Please."

She did not respond, instead plunged her hands into the dirt at
her knees. She began to fill Steg's wound with it, the handfuls of it
alive with earthworms and beetles, shifting and moving in her
cupped palms. She pressed them into Steg and he cried out—high
and thin. "Cole," he said. "Cole, please." My hands fell at my sides.

There had never been stories about the pigwoman though there
should have been, I thought, as she pushed the soil in, packing it
in tight like she was planting a crop under his ribs. Of all the
stories of the mountains, she had slipped past us, unnoticed,
growing big and hungry in the dense trees, finally driven out of
state forest—by what? Someone must have disturbed her and her
litter. They were probably hungry without their mother. And I saw
clearly what she intended—to drag Steg back half alive and
squirming, to toss him into her nest for them to feed, for them to
open him up with their developing teeth, pry the fingers from his
hands while he howled, to suck the meat from him, cartilage
crackling, organs hot and slippery soft in the still-bright night.

And again, after they picked him clean, someone else. In her
pigshape, no bullet would worry her. As a woman, no man would
think to shoot her.

But that night, she wanted him. Steg, who'd known my father
would die on a lightless highway cutting through the Carolina Blue
Ridge and not told me. Who'd carved our names into a bedpost at
camp and pushed me into a locker two years later, his friends
laughing behind him.

"Cole," he said. Steg, who had crowded me against a wall two
weeks earlier, his eyes very close to mine, breath softwarm on my
face, *Cole*, hands planted on either side of my head. About to say
something before he pulled away, I didn't know what.

The pigwoman was busy with her work, had sealed the wound
up with muck and leaves and wiped her filthy hands on Steg's
shirt. She grabbed him just above the knees and turned, preparing
to drag him away, to make a furrow across the hillside with his

body, to take him to her young. And only me—never strong, never brave, not Steg, who was full of dirt and worms now, not my father, who had leaked his brains out on a dark mountain road. No one would know. No one would thank me.

I raised the gun.

Pig Hole

Pig Hole dropped off one hundred sixty-three feet into the earth. The height didn't get under Hew's skin, or the thought of the pig bones at the bottom that gave the place its name, animals that had fallen in and died screaming on snapped legs. No one knew how many had starved to death down there during the decades before the iron grate had been riveted over the mouth of the cave. First timers picked out a jaw or a hollow vertebra as a souvenir when they reached the bottom.

It was a free drop. He wouldn't touch anything all the way down—no rockface to push off, not even a waterfall pouring freezing muck over him like in Murder Hole—total cave darkness all around. The thought of it made him ache. As long as he could touch stone, touch something . . . Hew stood over the grate as Molly unlocked it. He tried not to watch her ass. When she'd suggested this trip at the cave club party he'd been in the smooth whiskey haze that came before the anger. The invitation had prolonged his buzz, elongated it and helped him avoid the usual fights and shuttered memory. In the half-light on the terrace her teeth had shone, perfect ivory squares. Hew held his own hand in front of his mouth or tried to keep his dead gray incisor covered with his upper lip when he talked.

Hew had done every technical cave within seventy miles aside from Pig Hole: Yer Cave, Stay High, Unthanks Cave and Loco-motive Breath among others. Wall-drops, free climbs or squeezes were no problem. The millions of tons of rock overhead felt like that moment during sex when he lost track of his limbs. In

Salamander Cave he'd wriggled through a passage so tight that he couldn't get his arms past his shoulders. His face lay in muddy puddles as he'd scraped through an inch at a time. When the namesake salamanders had begun trying to climb into his mouth while he'd panted, the only way to get them to stop had been to bite them in half. He spit most out but the largest and most insistent had wanted to be swallowed. That's what it had seemed like to Hew. The bitter crunching had not stopped the creature's movement right away. He'd felt a twitch as he forced the masticated mess down. It had made him pause and he almost choked with the salamander plugging his throat like Hew blocked the passage.

Molly tugged the padlock open and lifted the bars. The grate opened silently. If he offered to help she'd snap at him. Every male in the club had learned that.

"Are you going to start building the anchors or stand there playing with yourself?" she asked. She brushed her short dark hair out of her face.

"Sorry," Hew said. He retrieved the duffel with the technical gear.

They were breaking the rule: at least three members on a trip. Molly said she'd invited others, but only the two of them had shown up on the steps of the student union at dawn. Hew did not mind in the least. Before last night she'd hardly spoken to him. Every semester she had a different boyfriend. He'd noticed that she usually dated a man right before he was about to leave: graduation, the military. It made Hew nervous, because he had no plans to go anywhere. He'd dropped out of school four or five years ago to work as a groundskeeper at Tech, but still hung around the cave club. They couldn't exclude staff even if they wanted to. He had the feeling that if he stopped showing up to meetings or parties no one would notice. The students seemed to get younger every year.

"I filed a log," she said.

Hew nodded. Another rule: a written report left in the cave club "office," the grimy closet where shared gear hung, outlining who had gone where and when they planned to return.

The nylon webbing lay in neat rows inside the duffel. He pulled the end of a daisy-chained bundle and it unspooled in his hands. The water knot seemed to form on its own. How many had he tied? Thousands, millions . . . or one large knot that never ended. Hew made a y-anchor using a nub of rock above the entrance to the hole and the front hitch of Molly's truck. Against the rules again. No tying off to anything that moved, but the closest solid second anchor point lay thirty feet away. Molly sat on the rope bag to pull off her boots. She stepped into her coveralls. Her body was tight. Not model skinny, but small and strong, with high breasts and a firm stomach that flowed down into the V below her hips. Hew had tied a harness for her once out of a single piece of webbing when she'd forgotten hers on a rock-climbing trip. No one else in the club knew how. The nylon loops he'd made had passed around her thighs and circled her waist, supporting her, tying her up. When she'd climbed Hew had watched from below.

It was almost time to drop. Focus. He could smell last night's whiskey in his sweat. He turned away to fetch his own gear from the truck: coveralls, harness, helmet and carbide lamp. He dribbled water into his lamp's chamber, then slid a protein bar into one zippered coverall pocket and a spare flashlight into another. His small pack held a headlamp—the required third source of light—a water bottle and a dump can for spent carbide.

Hew tightened the leg loops on his harness. He "put all the furniture in one room" by rearranging the crotch straps so they didn't cut off circulation to anything important. The waist belt he cinched last, folding the tough webbing back against itself and through the buckle to lock it in place. He chose jumars and foot loops from his rack for the long climb out, added prusik knots, and finally his figure eight for the descent. All but the last went into the pack. His hands shook as he pulled on his leather gloves.

While he'd gathered his gear Molly had tied one end of the rappelling rope into the anchor and then launched the coiled remainder into the hole. She stood at the edge of the grate, looking down into the abyss with her head cocked to one side.

"We're down," she said. It meant she'd heard it hit bottom.

Finding a snarl halfway down would have been a problem. The kernmantle rope ran over the old piece of canvas at the lip meant to reduce friction and disappeared into the dark as if sliced off.

"Ready?" Molly asked. She knelt at the lip of Pig Hole, her skin radiant in the morning sun. "I'll follow you down."

He reached for his lamp to open the valve. She stopped his hand with a touch. He could feel the heat of her skin through the thin hide of his glove.

"I've dropped in the dark," she said. "It's like flying. Wait at the bottom and I'll come down dark, too."

Black all around without the warm glow of the lamp. He wanted to scream. Hit her. Kiss her.

Hew stepped up to the lip and took the rope. He made a bight on the line, a kink, and passed that through his figure eight, then snapped the device into the locking carabiners hanging from his harness's tie-in loop.

He stood with his back to the hole and began to lean. The anchor rope running through his left hand took up his weight. The free end he held behind his right hip to provide friction. His helmet ground against the rock on the opposite side of the lip, and he walked his feet down to fit through the hole as he eased up on the rope and let it slide slowly. Three steps. Then nothing. He dangled at a thirty degree angle. Daylight above him formed a jagged crack. It seemed to float. Molly's head hung dead center in it. He wondered if she could still see his face.

The dark touched him. He felt air creep past him and fall into the depths. Caves breathe. Mile-long rock lungs expand for hours then contract in slow increments, perhaps one breath over an entire day. Differences in air pressure. The miasma of cave breath might smell of rust or rot, but sometimes it held a sweet undertone—rain, the scent of a playground—impossible smells that made Hew want to crawl in and wait for the entrance to seal up.

There had been no sweetness for a time. The caves that riddled the long ridges around Tech gave out only damp vapors, or at best were silent. Something seemed to have climbed up out of them to stalk the valley. First the mute shooter in the classroom killing dozens, then the student who'd hacked off his girlfriend's head in a crowded coffee shop at the union. The last, perhaps the worst, the murder of a young couple who had parked not far from this spot. They'd been engaged to be married. Both bodies butchered, literally, with pounds of meat carried away and never found. Thighs cut to the bone: hams removed, shanks, calves and all. No witnesses, no motive, no clues even a year later. Hew had always heard that the perfect crime would be to kill someone you didn't know, for no reason.

His arm shook with the effort of holding himself motionless. He needed to tie off or drop.

The light fell away from him.

Darkness. Not the absence of illumination but its inverse. True dark—forget the mild star-filled night that passed for it half the time above ground. No moon, heat, life. Hew felt it touch him under his skin, through it, the molecules of black in his spine threading into the blood passing along the arteries, tearing holes in the walls. Without the rock for him to hold onto it could surround him, seep into him, burn Hew hollow. All caves had been burned out of the ground. Rain drained through limestone to form a weak acid that melted off an impossibly thin layer wherever it landed. The rock was eaten away but replaced by darkness as heavy and thick and impossible to pass through as the stone. This was his terror. Drop. The drop. Falling on a rope. Feel the rope in his hands, the taught anchor stretching up and beyond, still attached oh lord jesus please still firm and threaded through his rig, singing against the fabric of his coveralls and away and down into the dark.

Hew couldn't shake the feeling that he wasn't moving. The rope pulled up and away. He stayed in one spot and the cave orbited around him. The floor did not exist.

How far? Falling was thirty-two feet per second. Half that? Three seconds, five, forever. Hew relaxed his grip on the free end and dropped faster. Friction heat grew in the palm of his glove and he resisted the perverse desire to let go, to shake the cramp out of that hand and let it cool while he fell.

Then it was empty.

Shit. No rope. No ground. Hew jammed a thumb in the figure eight's hole to trap the line, but too slowly. The rope end had whipped across his thighs and snaked through and free of the rack. The left hand spasmed against the sliding sheath of polyester. Nothing to grip. Gone.

The fall.

After the end of the rope had passed through both hands it seemed natural and peaceful. Now he would float. Eyes open or shut, no difference. Hew hung in mid-dark, safe. Then he hit the rock, heels first then tailbone, spine. Pain like colors without tone or edge, shades of the dark. It felt as if he gulled down through the rock like a bird hitting the water. Glints of mica and quartz swam past his head in schools. The rock held the warmth of the earth. He buoyed gently back up into the broken body afloat on the cave floor.

He felt loose. Things under his skin had shifted, lumps and growths that he had never noticed before. Hew couldn't tell how many arms he had. Moving made a moaning bubble up from somewhere near his chest, and a grinding at the point where he used to have hips, like rock on bone or bone on bone. His own bones, or pig bones? He might find enough of them to put himself back together. He couldn't feel the rock underneath himself to tell which way was up.

A task remained, but grasping it felt like catching a flame. Rope. Molly. She must have dropped the hundred foot rope instead of the two hundred footer. She would follow him down. Had to make noise. That train of thought derailed when the snakes landed on him. He managed a hooting sound. It felt like snakes or tentacles, cold and sliding. Molly had figured it out and dropped the right length of line. She should stay up and call for the rescue team, the litter, the winch. She should cradle the sun and bring it down to Hew.

The rope thrashed on him and small boots landed on either side of what had to be his own head. Something knelt next to Hew in the dark. He wondered how tall he would be after the operations.

"Oll," he managed to say. His mouth filled with blood. He'd bitten off the end of his tongue.

He heard her unclip her descender rig and felt the ropes slide off as she pulled them away from his body.

"I am sorry," her voice said from close by his face. "The thing is, I get so hungry."

Hew turned those words over in his mind as someone slit the front of his coveralls open. He felt the perfect hard edge of her teeth and sighed. He screamed, yes, but it contained a sense of his relief. He knew now where he was . . . where up lay in relation to his body. The teeth were up. They touched him again, tearing loose a mouthful of what he'd been in the light. He felt that tiny morsel lift away from himself and be swallowed. Wherever the teeth reached, that was the way out.

Marilyn Moriarty

After the After

H ow do you like it up here?" Armando sat back in the chair beside his mother-in-law and kicked one leg over the other. Sitting up there on the edge of a precipice, Asunción looked down and saw everything, time reduced to a single point. Blue skies bulked in a mass like the ocean, airwaves billowing and cresting, swelling here, there into thunder-clapped mounds. Only poufs of white clouds blossoming like buttercups in a field reminded her that the world still turned. Everything moved deliberately save for Armando's kicking leg.

"You are so restless," Asunción observed. She felt her arms. There was no breeze but she was comfortable.

"I can finally drink coffee the way I like it. All those years with that lousy heart . . . ."

"It ran in your family."

"Everything runs in a family. A disease. A passion. They all come up again in the blood."

"Everything sure ran in your family," Asunción said, mentally conceding some good looks, though Armando's son, Sebastian, made the better deal with nature. Still, Armando appeared to Asunción as when he had come as a man of thirty, straw hat held over his heart, to court her daughter. Even his linen suit remained perfectly creased.

Armando nodded to the panorama below. "There she is again, trying to move the pots."

Searching for the house in the abyss, Asunción placed both feet on the ground, perching on the edge of the chair. Her sandals

277

were fastened with slender leather straps, light almost buoyant, so different from the scuffs she used to wear.

When she leaned forward, her back rippled like water, smooth and easy, old arthritic vertebrae become liquid, a physical grace that came as remembered and renewed. Unlike her, the old lady down there hunched over, her body like shoes too tight for feet. When the old lady's head dissolved into the shadow thrown by the house, Asunción squinted to keep her in focus. She wavered like a mist of water on a hot road, but, with Asunción's concentration, the figure grew stable, as if someone had drawn a circle around it.

"Your daughter is an unhappy woman," Asunción said to *Abuela*, the old woman below. "She drinks the coffee grounds."

"She can't keep a man," the old woman said back. "Except her son."

At first Asunción thought she was watching the house like watching a play.

"She can hear me," Asunción said to Armando, surprised.

"It is nothing," he said. "She thinks you are a ghost."

"Old lady," Asunción called down to the woman in the yard. "You can move the pot yourself. You can drive your daughter crazy if you try to move it. Tell her, Armando."

Armando bent over, cupped his hands to make a megaphone, and leaning over the precipice, blew his words like wind: "*Abuela*, I am dead. They don't tell you. But you got it straight from the horse's mouth. You can do anything you want. You heard it from me."

"Armando, I miss you," she called back at him.

"She misses me," he told Asunción.

"Of course. I would miss you too."

They laughed together with the irony only the dead know.

"That poor old lady, always in the house, always in the yard. . . I'm glad I'm not there." Asunción spoke of her material double, for the old lady below was her when she was alive. She loosed a bobby pin that dug into the nape of her neck, and her hair fell, silky like a living thing.

"But you like to watch," Armando said slyly.

Asunción exerted her will to sharpen the focus on the panorama below. Bearing down inside her mind, she performed an isometrics of concentration, making a thought wave strong enough to break bricks. Karate-chop. She tried to draw her ears together on the inside. She squeezed her hands palm-to-palm, and when her knuckles turned white, a lacey band of thought dissolved into particles like azalea petals.

"Let me help you." Armando tilted his head, raised eyebrows winglike over his hawk-nose. His beam of thought turned blue and smooth, merging with hers to bring the house below into view— first from afar, like a bird turning circles over a nest, till the red tile roof came into focus. Thought took the roof off the house enabling Asunción to see on the inside, like a ghost from the rafters, what was happening below.

Inside, the dust mounted with the insistence of geologic time. Every day, *Abuela* fought it with her broom, sweeping it out, taking out the garbage. In a million years, the drips of water staining the white porcelain sink would have turned the bathroom into a crystal cavern, water-spiked stalactites and stalagmites grown to the height of a man. In a hundred years, the dust from kitchen would have left sediment deep enough to measure geologic time. But *Abuela* would have none of that. She mopped the floor. She scrubbed the sink. She cleared the drain, pulling strands of slimy, black hair out of the trap.

In the yard, everything grew against her. The grass, over and over—she couldn't keep it cut. Also, the citrus trees in what Sebastian called his orchard. One day, a tiny bud eased its arrow-tip out of the branch; the next day, a blizzard of limes made drifts in the backyard. Flowers blossomed and died before she could clip them. Leaves fell everywhere and then blew away before she could rake them. Taunting palm trees flipped fronds in the air like mermaids tossing sassy hair. It was a contest against nature she was destined to lose.

"Attack, attack," Asunción shouted to *Abuela*, who worked in the garden, tangled in morning glory vines, their tendrils around her ankles.

Asunción's fingers closed around Armando's arm. She was no longer a lobster with hands that were claws. Her skin glowed, translucent like amber. "Look, there is Sebastian taking away her hoe. He stops her. Why can't he let her work in the yard? Why can't he let her be happy?" "

"He's just trying to help . . ."

She waved her hand to pooh-pooh him. Would Armando now tell her lies, like the ones Sebastian and Mercedes continued about his death?

"She sweats a lot for an old lady but she has the energy. I remember that plant. The stinking bugs came to it. I hated it. Little flies. Then they would come in the house and buzz over the garbage. It made me sneeze. She is smart to move it. Ho, old lady, you are smarter than you know!"

Armando said, "Asunción, stop it. You want to kill her?"

"But she doesn't know, does she? Let's help her. We can do it, can't we? Reach your hand down there, Armando, help her with that pot. Oh, help me do it."

Below, *Abuela* was in the back yard moving pots, waist-high ceramic pots filled with geraniums. Although *Abuela* was very thin and eighty-four years old, she possessed the tenacity of a thousand men. Her arms were clinched around the top of the pot, and she grasped the lip between her thumb and forefinger. Then she bent her legs and raised them, using her legs to rock the pot back and forth. When it seemed the pot would tilt over, she pushed it in time with the rocking motion. The pot moved.

"*Abuela.*" Sebastian, the grandson scolded as the old lady melted into a twisted human gargoyle shaped from terracotta, six geraniums swaying above her head. "*Abuela!* Stop it. You are too old to do this."

Sebastian seized the other side of the pot, freezing it.

Asunción had never implored Armando so. Her eyes burned with the light of many lives. "Help me," she repeated. Dimes of silver appeared on his wrist where she pressed her fingers. "Help her."

"It's against the rules." Armando pulled his hand away, and rubbed at his wrist.

"What rules?"

The panorama below dissolved. Aha, so now it was night! Like a snowball smashed against a windshield, the stars in the sky exploded into brilliant shards. The constellation Scorpio blinked red giants, and the double stars in the Big Dipper turned cartwheels.

"The rules of this place."

"I don't see any rules." Asunción looked from right to left and reverse. There was not even a place or thing on which to post rules. Not even a billboard with the Ten Commandments or a "no smoking" sign.

"That's why I am here. To tell you."

"Tell me what."

"The rules."

"Are they written?"

"Everywhere."

"I don't see them."

"Like the law of gravity—it's written down. But before it was written, it was built into nature. So even though it's a law, 'law' just means that someone named it. It was a law before it was a 'law.'"

"So, there's no way I could break the rules, is there, since they are more than written?"

"Exactly."

"You can't break the law of gravity, can you?"

Armando laughed.

Asunción returned to her task. She brought the wide beam of her attention into a small range, narrow as the light from a flashlight. This time she opened the image in view from her own power. "*Mira,* she is fighting the war with garbage cans. The plantains are full to the top."

"You can't change anything down there," Armando told her. "That's a rule. For once, stop arguing. You are a stubborn woman." His scolding was gentle, but he meant it.

"But I can talk to her, can't I?"

"That does seem to be possible," he observed cautiously.

"*Mira.* Mercedes told Sebastian the old lady peed in her pants. Look at Mercedes' face. *Abuela,*" she shouted down, "what lies your daughter told you!"

"I didn't let her sit in it," Mercedes told Sebastian as he climbed out of her new chair, a blue recliner with magic fingers that massaged the back. Mercedes eased herself back into its embrace. With time, her body would leave its mark on the chair so no other would fit it. "Listen," Mercedes said deliberately to Sebastian, the massage mechanism silent. "Don't say anything to her, please, but I think your grandmother is getting too old. She can't hold her urine. She is, what do you call it . . . ?"

"Don't do it," Armando begged. "Please. It was her only happiness."

"Do what?"

"You know."

"Know what?"

"What happens after."

"After what?"

"Forget it. Oh, dios mio," he said, "I forgot what they forget."

"How do I forget what I don't know?"

"Armando," *Abuela* implored from down below.

Abuela wandered the house nights looking for Armando. She paced as if her steps might, by accumulation, add up to a journey that would lead to him. "What's wrong with her?" Sebastian asked Mercedes. Mercedes said, "Old people don't sleep good." *Abuela* wanted to make the house special for him when he returned from his job in Guatemala. She shifted the step ladder to the kitchen so it would be ready, first thing when she awoke, to climb. For him, the ceiling must be painted. For him, the house must be made new. For him, the floors must be sparkling. She invoked him, in a worn photograph attached to the refrigerator with a magnet: "Please come home soon."

"*Abuela,* some espresso?"

"Why don't you do something?" Asunción asked.

"Technically, she is not talking to me. This is a general wish."

"If she knew she was talking to you, then . . ."

"Then it would be different."

"She is so tired. She suffers for you. She waits. She sweats. There's a drought now in Florida. You are not there. You were never there."

"She was a nice girl, that Yvonne, wasn't she? I would have liked to meet her." Armando took a cigar out of an inner pocket in his coat, held it up to his nose, and sniffed it through cellophane.

"Everything is so dry. The old woman tries to keep the grass alive. She waters everything."

"Yvonne would be nice even to me, the bad guy in the house. Don't you think she would like me?"

"One lightning strike is all it would take."

"I often gave Sebastian advice about women. He never listened to me." Armando peeled the cellophane off the cigar and balled it up. It crinkled like heat lightning.

Asunción whispered down the gap so softly that Armando could not hear, but *Abuela* heard her while she was sweeping the sidewalk that led to the front door. She raised her head, holding the broom stick in two hands, and nodded her head up and down as if she understood. Then Asunción parted her lips as she leaned forward in her chair. She pointed her index finger down below, directly at the house as if she were Zeus hurling a thunderbolt.

Armando tried to grab her arm before she could do anything. He cried, "Stop it, Asunción!" but by then, it was too late.

It was a mystery to all the day that Mercedes came home and found her blue recliner in flames on the carport. Tongues of fire leapt up from the footrest, in the raised position. The seat was black but the massage mechanism, the Magic Fingers, made whirring noises. A charcoal odor seeped through the neighborhood, into the houses of people down the block.

"It was the power," Sebastian explained to Mercedes as she watched her chair dissolve into smoke. "The electricity from the lightning bolt. It activated the Fingers' mechanism."

The neighbors watched until the fire department came and put the flames out with one whoosh of water. "Did you see?" Mercedes moaned to Sebastian. "Even the people from the drug house came out to look."

"You don't know your own powers," Armando said.

"My first experiment," Asunción said.

"Well, it doesn't make any difference in the long run. Mercedes gets fatter. Sebastian lonelier. Without us for them to hate, they have nothing in their lives."

"We can make changes. Look at her chair. I blew it up."

"Hard-headed woman, the changes don't stick."

"She didn't get a new chair."

"That's not what I mean."

"Armando, the poor old lady. She wants you to come home for Christmas. All her life, she has been moving, and now, she sits. She rocks waiting for you. Can't you do something? I can't stand to watch her. I would not do this for you."

Asunción's batted her lashes at him. Her eyes glittered as if they were plugged into an electric outlet or possessed an independent power source. Her dark hair tumbled down around the embroidered collar of an off-the-shoulder blouse. Her bare, tight skin made her beautiful, she knew. "She is so alone without you." Asunción's breath carried the scent of peppermint. Her touch on his sleeve was like the touch of an angel. "For me?"

Armando fidgeted. He reached into his vest pocket, took out a piece of paper, and then returned it to his pocket. "You are not her. She is the body. You are the spirit. You could have a different body."

He still had it, she knew it, that weakness for women. It did not desert him even in the next world, or this world either, for that matter.

"I can't do anything, my dear. I can't go down there again," he said, as if pleading. "I've been back twice already. Nothing changes. The flesh commands the spirit. We can't resist it. You might think we can, but we can't. Besides, we have to do something else. We must decide where we will go next. We must make another choice."

"I'm not ready yet. I want to do something. For them. For my family."

"All right." He sighed. "What can I do?"

"Help her move the pot."

"I can't."

Asunción sulked.

"Are you hungry, *Abuela*? Do you want to play croquet?"

"I want to do something . . ."

"Thanks, God."

"Where is God?" She looked around. Wasn't he supposed to be in charge?

"He delegates," Armando said.

What then were the limits of this world? If Armando, the son-in-law was the fool that God delegated, he could easily be tricked.

"I want to drive a car. Sebastian's car."

Asunción stood up and stretched. Nothing around resembled traffic. "Tell me where I get lessons."

"Remember how you died?" Armando asked.

"No."

"See. You don't even remember."

"Please tell me."

"I won't. See, you need me."

"Tell me."

"You always were a flirt, *Abuela*."

"Armando, as you are my son-in-law, I demand it. By the law. The law which is not written. The law of this place."

He cocked his head to the side, folded his hands over his knees. He studied his sock when the cuff rode up his calf. At the anklebone, a cherub made an emblem on his sock. "Silk," he said. "It carries over. Becomes one with the glorified body."

"Armando."

"*Abuela*, forget it. We must move on. That's a rule. Think about your next life. You can pick any one you like. Any time. But I'm not going back to the same old life. If I came back as your husband, I would die too young and never know you when you were old. Old, you were the best. My son, that's a ride never to be taken."

"We can come back in ourselves?"

"I have been myself twice over. When I was tender to you, it was the tenderness of two lifetimes. Every touch of my hand had twice the love from other lifetimes behind it."

"You were a good son-in-law."

"What about Yvonne? One day you will come back as her. Think you would like her life?"

"She had a nice body," Asunción said.

Down below, *Abuela* was a good spy, peering through the shutters at Yvonne where she slept naked in Sebastian's bed. That girl could have many children if she wanted.

"You can go back any time." Suddenly, he jabbed his ear with a finger as if a bee had climbed in. He shook his head side to side as of trying to shake it out. "You can start over from the beginning is what I mean."

"Nothing changes?"

"Nothing."

"Why did you try to stop me with the chair?"

"I don't know. It was a thought, that's all. I had a thought."

"So," Asunción said bending over and squinting hard to find the right place in time. "We are allowed to have thoughts in this shithole place where you can't do anything for any one you love?"

Asunción still needed more practice at locating the points, but she always had eyes like a hawk. She searched for something familiar in time, in space.

"Whatever you're doing, don't do it," Armando said.

Asunción rested on the balls of her feet, her hands on her knees as she crouched over the edge of the precipice.

"I can see it now," he complained "You will come back as a cell, a shitty one-cell cell. If you are lucky, a tick. With grace, maybe a plant. You are ruining yourself, and do you listen to me? No." He sighed. "I will be demoted. For this mother-in-law, I will pick a good life, but I will wake up fucking in the streets, pissing on trees, a dog. You will be the tick I scratch."

He grabbed her by the back of the neck and pulled her away from the edge. "Stop it. Stay put, *Abuela*. Listen, Asunción, we can go to the next level." He grew frantic. "There is a higher level, higher. All spirit, no matter at all. There, all are one."

"Don't touch me," she hissed. Just what she needed, another man like Sebastian telling her not to move, trying to stop her from doing what she knew she had to do.

He pulled his arm back abruptly.

Below her, the cosmos swirled, a vortex of stars spilled out against black night. Now where was that little blue world in all those stars, the one dressed in a swirl of white clouds?

"Where's the world?" she asked. "The pretty one."

"The pretty one?" he snorted. "You mean the dirty one, where the horizons have gray clouds, where the oceans cook rotten fish in oil, where there are cigarette wrappers on the beach? You mean the dirty little world that stinks like a rotten orange."

Asunción looked around. "Does anyone around here drive? I always had to walk. Traffic, I like it. Where is everybody?" she asked.

"Who else do you want to see?"

"My father. My mother. My brother."

"They're down again. Starting over."

"They couldn't even wait till I got here?"

Armando was silent.

"Only you waited?" she asked.

He nodded and his leg moved in time with his head as if a string had connected his chin to his knee.

"You always were a good boy," she said. "My daughter. She had a good heart. She was vain and fat, but her heart was good. Even the chair, I understand. She wanted something for herself. I miss her already."

"The real love here," Armando sniffed deeply, "was with Sebastian. And his mother. They had that intimacy, you know, of spirits—like us. They ganged up against *Abuela* with their lies. Their world is full of order, but it is also full of accidents. Every time I go there, I make the same mistakes. I get married to the same person. I find the same mistresses. I deserve to be demoted."

"She was my daughter, Armando. She came from my body. She did not deserve someone like you."

"I understand. But that is who she got. Over and over. Don't ask me."

"You should come back as her."

Asunción made this a pronouncement, but Armando acted as if he hadn't heard her.

"If you went back as you, it would be the same thing. The village in Spain. Your trip to Cuba. Your trip to Miami." He bit the end off the cigar and spat it out, his teeth white and even. "Nothing changes."

"The same mistresses?" she asked.

"What?"

"So, you found a whore more than once in the same life, too, eh?"

"Please, *Abuela*."

"How many would I see if I looked in your life?"

"You aren't allowed."

Asunción kept trying. She hooded her eyes and squinted.

"This isn't hell," he said.

"I was the cleaner in that house," she said, remembering.

Mercedes' sorrow was recorded in the house. Walking the halls in search of Armando's spirit, *Abuela* stumbled upon Mercedes coming out of the bathroom. Mercedes' face was pink where she had scrubbed the makeup off, white half-moons swelled under her eyes. *Abuela* found a towel so wet with tears, it drenched everything around it. Mercedes cried in private, but her grief left its image imprinted in the steam of the bathroom mirror. *Abuela* went into the bathroom, flushed the toilet, and ran all the faucets to wash it down the drain into the sea. She wanted to yell at her daughter, "Empty yourself outside," because the furniture soaked up her sadness. When Sebastian sat in a chair, he said, "This chair feels gooey. Did you wash the furniture, *Abuela*?" Only the house knew the magnitude of Mercedes' disappointment.

All of a sudden, Asunción understood. The dust was not nature—nor the yard growing, nor the stains in the sink. The house was flooded with her daughter's misery. *Abuela* knew because she was the cleaner. She swept out sadness every day.

"Don't you think she wanted to be loved?"

"I couldn't help it, *Abuela*. I can't explain it," Armando said, lighting his cigar. "Here, these are the best you can find." He inhaled deeply.

"She was always my daughter," Asunción said.

"What?" Armando asked, tossing a match down into the funnel of time.

"My daughter. You betrayed her twice over."

"Flesh has its own nature. How can you fight your own nature?"

"Mercedes was my nature."

Armando inhaled, sucked cigar smoke deeply into his lungs.

"I thought you would like it here," he said. "No suffering. No pain. Infinite possibilities. The future open before you to do anything. Shit, I asked to be assigned to you."

"Tie me up," she said. "You want me to be happy, tie me up."

"Oh, *Abuela*."

"Or teach me to drive."

"You are driving me crazy," he said. He muttered, "A dog. Pissing in the streets. A cell."

"You are a useless man," she told him. "You were a pretty boy but a useless man. Armando, I waited for you all my life. Even though your spirit was gone, I waited. Even though I thought you were dead, I waited for you to come back. Why didn't you tell me there was no choice?"

"It was only the body. Here we have a saying, 'Write in flesh, write in stone.' I am happy to rest for a while. Don't you see, it is only matter that divides us?"

He waved at the air, as if brushing aside flesh as a matter of trivial nothingness. He pointed around to the cosmos, the heavens, his hand circumscribing a whole new world that Asunción might have explored.

"What about tears?" she asked him. "What about grief? What about cooking for someone?"

"They are gone now," he said. "You are too beautiful to cook."

"Sorrow always lives," she said.

"The soul knows no sorrow," he said.

Asunción stretched out her hands, and then ran them over her shoulders and stomach. Was she a soul? She seemed solid. Maybe her hands were made of the same substance as her body. Perhaps energy could touch energy. If she was a soul, why would she worry? Maybe this was a dream. She looked at her son-in-law. She knew his face. She knew the man. But something was wrong here. Pah, everyone in her family lied to her: him, Mercedes, Sebastian. Why should anything be different in the afterlife? And Armando had touched her. She had touched him. They must be made of something, not air, not clouds, not ether. Did Armando have a girlfriend around? Was he having sex after death, even though his wife was destined always to mourn for him?

"There are tears. There is pain. And waiting." She pointed down to the place where sorrow lived.

"We are spirits. We are glorious. Life is so short, it means nothing."

Asunción jumped from the rocking chair. Armando jumped in time with her. "What are you doing?" he asked.

Asunción raised her hand to strike him, and then she punched him on the jaw with the force of one past life. Even though they were immaterial, the blow made him quiver like a character in a flickering movie reel. His cigar, struck from his mouth, fell through eons, leaving behind a trail of crumbling, red cinders, which, at the North Pole, raised gasps at the Aurora.

"So fresh from the grave," he mumbled

Gathering her skirt around her legs, she planted her feet at the edge of the precipice. With arms outstretched at her side like wings, she dived down, headlong into a thick blue sky, headlong back into life.

"No, stop," Armando called after her, rubbing his jaw. "You don't know all the rules yet," he shouted, but he saw only a twisting vapor trail like that of a comet. He stood where she had jumped and looked down, his eyes following after her.

Where *Abuela* landed, there was a ripple in time until time closed up after her.

Sophie Littlefield

What Goeth Before a Fall

A unt Git always said my sin was Pride. She had a sin for each of us. My little brother Bullet's she said was Gluttony. That was hard to argue, him larded heavy with fat till he got to junior high when he shot up clear of all that. Lydia's was lying all the time.

Mine was Pride. Git with her Bible on the porch on Sunday afternoons when us kids were too full of dinner to chase each other around—Git had lots to say. My punishment, she said, was I was gonna have to carry big stone slabs on my back for all eternity. Bullet would go fetch some big rock and I'd stagger around the yard with it on my back, all of us laughing to bust a gut.

I took some satisfaction on account of Git said Pride was the worst sin of all. It was kind of like being the best at something. But we all agreed lying was worse, even Lydia—even though lying wasn't even a deadly sin. Git didn't know the punishment for lying but she said if it was up to her it would be to have your mouth sealed shut, the lip skin fused together. Lydia said maybe they oughtta do it to Bullet so he couldn't stuff his face, but Git said no, Bullet would have to eat rats and snakes in purgatory, that was his punishment. But we didn't pay her hardly any mind, we all had our mouths clamped shut making "mmm-mmm" sounds like we were Lydia struck with her punishment.

I didn't think Pride was my problem, just I was a little too pretty. Everyone said it. I'd been pretty since I was a baby, so how could it be my fault? Besides, I wasn't afraid of purgatory or even Hell.

Someone like me, that everyone liked, that was everyone's favorite—I was going to Heaven, no doubt about it. And I'd just bring Bullet and Lydia with me. They'd let me, they'd have to. I'd say I wasn't coming in unless they did.

If Git had to go to purgatory, that was okay with me. She wasn't even a real aunt, just my mom's old cousin who didn't have any other kin. But we'd miss making fun of her.

Git was old, but by the time I married Mitchell Stancyk she was bent-over old. She sat in a chair Bullet dragged around for her all afternoon so she could be right where everyone else was. For our wedding gift she gave us a Bible—what else?

My bridal portrait stayed up in Holt's Photography's window for two years. Mr. Holt gave me ten percent off my album, in exchange for me letting him put my picture in the window, blown up huge.

When people found out me and Mitchell were expecting a baby, it was like the whole town had something to celebrate.

Now maybe you think I had it coming, what happened to me. But the thing is, I never asked to be pretty in the first place.

Git hung on almost nine more years. By the end she didn't know anybody, didn't do nothing all day but rub on her blanket with one scrabbly old hand.

Lydia and me went to see her a few days before she died, a hot day in June. They said the end was coming soon. We were sitting on chairs we pulled up close to the bed and we were whispering, I don't know why because it wasn't like she could hear us or anything.

All of a sudden Git makes this suck-in sound and her head lifts off the pillow a little and her eyes flutter and then she's looking right at me and her lips move around like she's trying to say something, and my heart went crazy pounding, and Lydia and me jerked back away from the bed.

I don't know if Git was trying to say an actual word but a sound came out...it was kind of like "haaaaaahhhhg." She looked at me the whole time she said it and I backed up, scraped my chair across that shiny linoleum floor trying to get away from her.

She settled back down slow, like that little spark of life that was in her was slipping out, her lips going loose and her eyes rolling back.

I don't know what made do what I did next, with my heart slamming around like it was, but all those years of being scared of Git—and then this last thing, it was too much.

I got out of my chair and I leaned over Git like I was gonna kiss her cheek and I heard Lydia behind me go "Jeannanne, don't," and then I said in Aunt Git's wrinkled-apple ear:

"There ain't any such thing as sin!"

Then I grabbed Lydia's arm and pretty much dragged her out of that room. Not that she didn't want to go. I think she was shocked at what I had done but I also think she didn't like to leave it like that with Git. Maybe she knew this would be our last visit. I guess I knew it too, but I didn't care.

I knew what I did was wrong. I even felt a little bit bad about it. But mostly I was still angry. It never stopped ringing in my ears, the way Git used to talk all the time about sin, making lists of all the sins she could think of, and their punishments, and reminding us which ones were ours.

Mine being Pride—that was the biggest hurt of all, now that the years had worn down my shine. I didn't have any pride left. I put on weight with the babies and I didn't fuss over my makeup and hair any more. Mitchell turned out to have a temper and he couldn't hold a job more than a couple of years at a time before he'd piss off his boss, and we were in a shitty rental house and I spent my days in dirty sweat pants with my girls, eating Stouffers pizzas and ice cream to make the time pass.

Git died soon after our visit, and there were less people at her service than I can count on both hands. I tried to work up a few tears but I didn't have much luck. Neither did anyone else. They put her in the ground and I think we were all relieved.

Candy and Jorry Rayburn showed up a few days later.

Around four on a warm afternoon, I was out pushing the mower around the yard. The girls were drawing on the street with chalk. Here comes this car, a long shiny red one, and I hollered at Gloria and Cheyanne to get back on the lawn.

The car's coming real slow, and I see this woman leaning out the passenger window with her long blonde hair blowing in the breeze. They pull over in front of our place and I go and say hi.

The woman says hi in a real friendly way and this brown-haired strong-built man leans out his side and says they're moving in down the street, and he was the kind who makes you forget what you had in mind to say. Great looking, with a smile that looked like he meant it. They had a boy in the back, cute with short brown hair like his dad, and he piped up and said hello. The man said wasn't it nice, their Cole was about the age of my older girl. I look over at my girls and Gloria's got snot trailing out of her nose and Cheyanne's got dirt around her mouth and I know she's been eating it again.

I took the Rayburns a pitcher of lemonade while they waited for the moving truck. We sat on the front porch steps and talked while the kids played in the front yard, Cole sharing the toys in the backpack he brought in the car.

I knew they got the Muller place for a steal. The bank foreclosed on it when Erwin Muller took off and left his wife and she let the bank have the place and went back to her family. I'd wanted for me and Mitchell to put a bid on it, but we couldn't scrape together the down payment. Candy said with the money they saved they were going to have the house painted inside and out and put down new carpet.

Jorry was working at the WalMart auto center. He said he'd been with the one up in Cavern Springs, and they wanted him to come down to Chester. I said that was nice and he said yeah, it was a big step, he was going to manage the place. That shut me up: he wasn't any older than Mitchell, and Mitchell was back at square one with yet another construction job. Mitchell wouldn't ever manage anything, not with his temper and all.

Candy said she was excited to be in a new home, a new town.

She said she loved to do yoga in the living room and go for walks in the mornings and why didn't I join her.

When Mitchell came home I told him about the Rayburns. About Jorry's job and how Cole had nice manners and how I might start walking with Candy. Mitchell said it was going to take more than just walking to get my ass under control. That made me crazy mad. But not just at Mitchell, at myself, too. When I bent over my stomach made folds, thick rolls of fat. My tits were sagging flat too. And my face had gotten puffy. I hated that, hated it worse than the rest. In pictures I didn't recognize myself.

There's no way I can say this next part without sounding bad. I'd say I was sorry about that, if I didn't figure I'd been punished enough.

Here it is: when you've been beautiful your whole life....not just pretty but beautiful, and then one day you wake up and realize you're just ordinary? I can't tell you how much that burns. It's like losing everything you knew about yourself.

The next day I took brownies over to the Rayburns and in the evening Candy and Jorry and Cole walked over to return the plate and you should of seen how Mitchell's eyes just about fell out of his head when he saw her. Candy had me beat and then some. Don't know what she birthed Cole out of but her stomach was still flat and smooth and she looked good up top too and it was plain she liked to show it off. She had on a tank top with tiny straps, and as she walked up the drive with the plate in one hand she tugged on her shorts with the other, they'd rode up some but I couldn't make out any cellulite on her. Tan skin and gold bracelets and no chips in her nail polish.

I talked my fool head off, saying to Mitchell wasn't it nice how Jorry did the management training program. Jorry smiled and told a couple jokes and when he left he clapped Mitchell on the back, said let's watch the game sometime, hey? When they were gone I stood in the kitchen, looking out the bay window and watching them walk away, and I didn't know it then but it was already starting. I watched Candy's gold bracelets all glinty in the sun. I watched Jorry put his hand on her back, lean toward her while she said something that made him laugh, his arms rippling muscle, and I felt pure want in the hollow of my gut. I could have had a man like that once, but not anymore. Candy had him, Candy had everything I wanted, and my skin tingled and itched and I rubbed at it but rubbing didn't make it feel any better.

Candy called the next morning and said come for dinner, just casual. They were all moved in and she wanted to celebrate. I must of tried on four different outfits. I had an allergy or something, my eyes had been tearing up for a couple of days, and that morning I'd woke up with them crusted shut. I thought it was just pink-eye, but when I took a hot wet washcloth to my face, it wasn't just yellow pus came away but also some sort of black strands, spiky short things that jabbed at my eyeballs and left them sore and red.

All day my eyes streamed and I had to keep wiping off the pus and the little strands. I thought maybe it was my eyelashes coming out and I looked real close but the strands seemed to be coming from the rims of my eyes, where the little tear ducts were, and I thought about going down to the clinic but we were between insurance until Mitchell was six months on the new job.

And there was something wrong with my skin, too. I thought maybe it was related, some sort of virus going through me. It started out itching but it wasn't an itch so much as kind of a numb cold feeling. My cheeks were turning pale and when I put my fingers to them, the skin was hard and chilly. It was worst around my face but I could feel it down my neck and chest and even along my arms.

Mitchell got home late and sure enough he'd stopped for a beer with some of the guys. He barely even looked my way when he came in the door. I said you're not going in that, he had on this old shirt with sweat stains under the pits. He said why not and I thought of Jorry with the nice pressed golf shirt, the way his shoulders bulked up the sleeves and his I could see the outline of the muscles in his stomach.

There was a time, not so long ago, when I would have flirted a little with a man like Jorry. And a little would have been all it took, they ate it up. When I married Mitchell they said there were a lot of hearts broke that day.

But as I got dressed in my old denim skirt and a loose top to hide my gut, I realized that Jorry hadn't looked at me that way when we met. He hardly looked at me at all. And why should he, when he had Candy to come home to?

Mitchell came out in a different shirt but he didn't look much better. But in the kitchen where the light was good he looked at me and said holy fuck, what happened to you and I put my hands on my face, kinda scared now, but what came out of my mouth was if he could keep a Goddamn job maybe I could go to the clinic and get it looked at.

Mitchell didn't say anything for a minute and I figured he was getting ready to really light into me but then he looked at me closer and said what's that in your eyes so I had to go back in the bathroom and pull out more of the little black things and put on more concealer.

By the time I was done, we were half an hour late to the Rayburns.

First thing I noticed was they'd had new bark put in all the flowerbeds and planted some little baby trees. I told the girls don't you run in them flowerbeds.

But what Mitchell was looking at was the car. He whistled and told me how it's a forty thousand dollar car with the options they got on it. Sunroof, spinners, like that.

Mitchell put out his hand like he was going to pat that car and then he pulled his hand back and I saw that he was afraid to touch it. Like he'd put a mark on it or something. Like we weren't good enough, that's how it made me feel. And that tingle on my skin stretched out down to the ends of my nerves.

Candy came to the door before we could even knock. She had these Capri pants on that had sailboats on them. If I wore those, I'd look like a cow, but she was so thin they just looked cute. She had a red halter top that showed off her shoulders and I saw the way Mitchell looked at her.

Suddenly everything I'd thought of to say seemed stupid. I just gave Candy my plate of cookies and followed her in. Inside the house, I had to take my sunglasses off, though I would have liked to keep them on all night, the way my eyes looked.

Jorry came into the room smelling nice and fresh, just out of the shower with damp hair, and I saw him look at me and lose his place for a second. I knew what I looked like but at least the itching was gone, in fact I couldn't feel much at all, my skin was numb and getting number. It was all the way down my arms now and down my back and starting down my butt and legs. Jorry said can I get you folks a glass of wine and I said sure before Mitchell could ask did they have any beer.

Candy's dining room set was the nicest thing I ever saw, made out of dark wood. There were curlicues and flowers carved in the legs and the chairs had cushions covered in pale pink silk. I said didn't she want to put something on the chairs in case the girls spilled their juice and she laughed and said no, she didn't believe in saving things for special occasions. She said life is too short and she liked to use her best every day. It made me think how when me and Mitchell got married we got just one place setting of our china from our cheap-ass families, and how we said we'd buy a little every year but we never did.

Jorry called down the hall for Cole to come on out, they had company. His hair was combed down with gel and he had on a neat striped polo shirt. Cole came around and shook Mitchell's hand and said hello, Mr. Stancyk it's sure nice to see you. He turned to me with his hand out to shake and then he looked at me and his eyes got all big and he said, What happened - and then he smacked a hand across his mouth like he knew it wasn't polite. He looked at me about knee level and nodded his head once and walked out of the room fast.

Candy just about started crying, she was working so hard to apologize for Cole, and Jorry filled up my wine. Mitchell just stood there looking around with his hands in his pockets and it was him I was angry at, for some reason.

After that I knew the night was ruined.

Candy put out this appetizer that had layers of red and green and white stuff, I don't even know what-all was in there but Mitchell couldn't get enough of it. I said let me help when she went in the kitchen to put dinner on but she said no, no, you're the guest, relax.

I went to use the bathroom. But when I got to the hall I saw that I could look around a bit and I peeked in the other rooms. They had nice furniture in every room, nothing looked hand-me-down. Their bedroom suite was light wood with iron trim, right out of a magazine, with pillows and curtains and everything all matching, even the shower curtain in their bath. I peeked in Candy's closet and you wouldn't believe all the clothes she had: jeans and pants folded over hangers, and tops sorted by color. And shoes: twenty pairs easy, all lined up on shelves. Even her sneakers were practically brand new, white with pink trim.

I went back to the bathroom but I squinted so I wouldn't have to see myself in the mirror. The numbness was in my scalp now, and down to my fingers; I could barely work the zipper on my pants. When I smoothed down my hair it seemed like a lot of it came out in my hands. I didn't want to put it in the waste basket where Candy would see it so I rubbed it into a ball and flushed it.

Around my eyes I knew that more spiky strands had poked through the rims, because I could feel them brushing against my eyeballs. I knew it ought to hurt like hell but the numbness was almost everywhere now. I could feel water leaking from my eyes but couldn't feel it on my cheeks. I took some toilet paper and rolled it up and pressed it against my eyes and rubbed the rims. When I pulled the toilet paper away there were two of the little spikes on it, and they looked blacker and thicker than before. I knew there had to be more still in my eyes but I couldn't bear to look in the mirror.

I had to get to a doctor. I knew that. Tomorrow was Saturday, though, and the clinics would be packed. And I couldn't go to the emergency room, not when we were still paying for Gloria's stitches from a swing set accident two years ago.

So I splashed some water on my face and tried to act confident when I came out of the bathroom.

Dinner was so pretty, even if I'd had an appetite I don't know if I could of ate it. Chicken stuffed with something green and sliced in little pinwheels, tiny buttered potatoes. A salad with nuts and cherries on top. Jorry lifted his glass and said Here's to good neighbors and good friends and then we all clinked glasses, the girls and Cole giggling at the little card table Candy had set up for the three of them.

I tried to eat. I did. I chewed up a few bits of each thing and swallowed, but it was like I couldn't even taste the food, like I could barely even feel it on my tongue. And then I looked down at my plate and there was this little piece of something lying there, like a corn flake, but gray.

I pushed at it with my fork and tried to think what it was and if I was supposed to eat it when another one drifted down. Smaller, with a little white in the center.

An awful thought came to me and I put my fingers to my face and what I felt there gave me a shock. My skin had gone all loose and crumbly, and what had fallen on my plate was a piece of it. I could feel dry feathery edges where the skin had come loose, places where other patches hadn't come all the way loose yet but were holding on like when you have a sunburn and the skin's shredding and working itself free.

I looked down at my arms and saw that they had gone almost totally white, but there were spots of gray here and there. In one or two places the gray was almost black and the centers of those areas were cracking and separating, and I knew that it was just a matter of time before the skin was going to come loose from there too.

The other thing was that my vision had a black line across it. One of the spikes must be sticking up right in front of my eye. I had to get it loose, but I didn't want to do it here. I had to get out of the Rayburns' house.

It had been a mistake to come here, looking like this, when the Rayburns were so perfect. I thought about my picture in the window at Holt's Photography, how people used to stop me on the street and wink and ask me how was that honeymoon going. How everyone loved me. If only the Rayburns could have seen that picture, I thought—but then I realized that Candy was every bit as pretty as I ever was, and maybe even prettier. That she had her fancy dishes and furniture and the car and Cole probably got perfect marks at school and Jorry brought her flowers just because he missed her during the day, and it made me feel so empty inside it was like everything that I'd once been had been scooped out and I'd been filled up with black bile instead, and now the poison was leaking out of me into my skin and my eyes and I pushed my chair back, practically knocking it over and I said I don't feel well and I pretty much ran out of there and back to our house.

I picked up the phone and called Lydia, finding the numbers more from feel than sight because more of the black streaks were in front of my eyes and I don't know what I said exactly because I was crying but she said she would come, just stay put and she'd come as fast as she could.

I looked at my arms and the gray patches were turning black so fast that it was like watching storm clouds come in. One of the patches had come loose on the way over—a chunk of my skin had fallen off and was probably lying in the street, dead and black. Underneath was not the shiny pink raw look of what's under a bad burn, but yellowish and globby. I lay down on the couch and laid that arm carefully on top of my stomach and prayed hard for Lydia to come fast.

I prayed but I knew that no one was listening. I'd said there wasn't any such thing as sin. Said it hatefully to Aunt Git practically on her dying day.

I didn't think she'd heard me with her rattling stinking breaths in that awful room, but I was wrong.

But Git had been wrong, too. Pride wasn't my sin.

My sin was Envy.

As I lay there waiting for my sister, I remembered Git's voice on those warm lazy Sunday afternoons:

"Envy," she'd say, sighing and rubbing the worn cover of her Bible. "Punishment for Envy's havin' your eyes sewed shut with wire. And submersion in freezing water. Forever. You cain't ever get out."

She recited her list of sins with trembling awe, but they floated away like dandelion fluff on the breeze, and I never paid any mind because I was the prettiest girl in Chester and everyone loved me.

Gregory Wolos

Interstate Nocturne

I'm driving down Interstate 81 into the blackness of well past midnight. Driving alone, to keep an appointment I have in Knoxville tomorrow morning at 9:30 with a man I barely know about some numbers I've compiled concerning his liquor business. The figures are in a briefcase in the trunk of my car; I haven't thought about them in miles. The car's a rental, a white Honda Civic, 6138.7 miles. I wouldn't dare drive my own car on a long trip, especially late at night. I know too much about what could go wrong, what has gone wrong. I picture us—the car a lifeless chunk of metal, me hovering beside, dumbfounded, while traffic whizzes by at speeds that threaten to suck me off the shoulder through the holes they smash in the air.

I'm smashing my own hole through the star-freckled night, nothing around to be sucked into my trail except a few small animals that trickle out of the humps of forest the highway splits. They squat on the pavement, transfixed by approaching headlights. Assuming that only humans can contemplate their own mortality, I imagine the deaths of these creatures for them. The radio wrings only static from the air. I have no CDs for the CD player, but its slot reminds of the black boxes salvaged from the wreckage of downed aircraft, the mystery of "what happened" locked within them.

The engine hums through the night air. My headlights cast an apron of light that extends my isolation only about a hundred yards against infinity. The broken white line flashes from the darkness like grains of rice. With each slight bump the blue digits on the clock trace a blur in the air.

Without warning, I am weightless—falling or flying. The humps of forest have collapsed, and the chill black sky is now beside and beneath me. Balancing on the broken white line as if it's a high wire, the Honda carries me from stripe to stripe. I flatten the accelerator, desperate to cross a bridge I can't see. The hairs at the back of my neck tingle at the rumble that follows me. The car and I dive for land, and the forest's solid darkness embraces us again. I'm convinced that the bridge I've crossed has disappeared.

"FFFF . . . ." A sigh of relief from the figure in the passenger seat—the ghost of my mother. Occasionally she joins me for stretches of time along the night highways. The bright numbers of the clock frosts her in blue. She clutches her sweater to her throat.

"These bridges, Jackie," she sighs. She is wearing one of her better wigs. "When are they going to stop frightening you, hmm?"

"I don't know, Mom." I sigh too, partly out of relief, partly at having to admit my fear to my mother. I don't know how her ghost winds up in my car. Strictly speaking, it couldn't be her ghost, since she's not dead yet, which may be why her appearance never frightens me. She doesn't acknowledge these nocturnal visits when I see her and Dad three or four times a year "Why don't you fly?" she asks then if I complain about my lonely drives. My mother's ghost would never ask such a question. Flying is even more frightening than crossing bridges—it's a long, long trip over a bridge of air.

Ghost Mom is wearing her glasses, the wig, and a wool suit she reserves for special occasions. Together we glide along the highway.

"Nice car," she says. "When did you buy it?"

"Never," I answer. "Rental. You know I rent for these trips." She's got something else on her mind, I can tell.

"Of course you rent, dear. That just makes you a little harder to find is all." I don't ask why.

"It's chilly in here." She gathers her sweater more tightly about her with bony fingers worn so smooth they reflect the clock's blue glow.

"Air conditioning, Mom." She and Dad hate air conditioning.

They claim it makes their noses run. "Do you want me to shut it off?"

"No, no. Don't make yourself uncomfortable on my account." I turn off the air conditioning. I roll down the window, and the blackness slops in, splashing onto my lap like warm ink, puddling around my feet and the pedals. Darkness pours over my crotch, and the puddle rises over the edge of my shoes. My legs become sluggish. Mom dabs at her nose with a lace handkerchief.

"Aunt Anna died," my mother says. I barely remember my mother's aunt. When I was a child she was already so old that I was more annoyed than embarrassed about accidentally walking into the bathroom when she was on the toilet. She'd already stopped counting, even to children.

"She was 97," my mother says. "Died in the nursing home. They say she was senile." My mother speaks the word in a whisper, rhyming it with "kennel." Mom mispronounces many words that make her uncomfortable, like "gynecologist" and "semen." "Isn't it a shame she couldn't have lived another three years?" Mom asks. I don't answer. The question feels like a trap.

Black air rushes through my window and down my neck and chest. The tail of some slippery night creature smacks my jaw, flops in my lap, and joins its mates below my knees. Now and then one rubs against my calf like a cat.

Outside, the dotted line penetrates our apron of light like a cartoon gamma ray. Inside, my mother's glasses absorb the clock's blue light. Her legs stir the deepening night; it splashes faintly against her door.

"Your father read me an article to me about a bridge," she begins.

"Mom, come on . . ." My hands crowd midnight on the wheel, fists together, index knuckles targeting the pulsing white line.

"Now, dear, there's nothing to cross between here and Marion, for goodness sakes," she says. Then, comfortingly, "Don't I feel what you feel, honey? And please don't roll up the window. The air feels nice. I really don't know what air conditioning does to my sinuses."

The black tide rises above my seat and leaks under my thighs, soaks my butt cheeks and edges up my spine.

"Some major highway somewhere—not too far away, I don't think—" Night, warm and tasteless, lolls beneath my lower lip; a swell covers my mouth, and another takes my nose and ears. Finally, my eyes. Submerged, I peer at Mom, who's also under, all but the very top of her wig. She glows blue in the night air. Tiny bubbles of light shimmer off her lips when she smiles.

The white line, now blue, strikes relentlessly. Gliding shapes leave trails of iridescent bubbles about my face. Everything seems soft and comfortable in the night air.

Mom settles into her story, I think of the books she read to me when I was little, how I recognized the letters and studied the pictures, but only her voice gave them meaning. Something like that is happening now.

"There was a bridge, an overpass, above a little stream. With all the rain, the stream swelled and weakened the supports that held the overpass up. Then, just like that"—she snaps her fingers with an explosion of bubbles—"the bridge collapsed! Just dropped straight down, maybe 50 feet, right into that flooding stream." The lenses of her glasses throb with blue light.

"Right off the bat, about ten cars drove in, nine cars and one tractor trailer. Seems like only one car tried to brake; only one set of tires left marks."

I am inside each of those cars, falling, wondering, screaming.

"Somebody watching from a local road down by the stream—it was just about a river now, roaring right along—he saw what happened and rushed up to the highway and started waving at traffic. On his way up he saw two cars plunge in."

I see a heavy man in a plaid shirt and worn overalls waving at me from the side of the road, and I worry at how desperate he looks and I consider stopping to help him, but I don't.

"The troopers took days to find the bodies because the water was moving so fast. They're still only "reasonably certain" how many victims there were."

I see pictures, as if from a children's book. The cars are vintage, red and blue and mustard yellow. The truck is a moving van driven by a man in a neat uniform who a few pages previous would have carefully packed a worried child's teddy bear in corrugated paper. The warning man is a round faced farmer whose grandson and granddaughter, waiting safely on a high bluff, had earlier in the day learned about chickens and milk cows and who will, by their story's end, receive the kitten of a farm cat to take back to their suburban home.

"The police waited to get word of missing people—folks who didn't get to where they were supposed to or return from wherever they'd been."

A slender blond woman wearing a blue apron holds a telephone to her ear. One of her penciled eyebrows arches. A blond, pink-cheeked girl wearing an identical apron frowns at her mother's side. She holds a blond, blue-aproned doll under her arm.

On the facing page is a bald man with a black mole centered on his forehead. Bristles protrude from his wide nostrils. His upper lip sweats. He also holds a telephone and glances through thick glasses at his wristwatch. Beside his desk are boxes marked with the brand names of vodka. The headline of the newspaper on the desk has a single decipherable word: "BRIDGE."

"Your father said it was a good thing the bridge didn't go down at night. Nobody would have seen the stream then, so there wouldn't have been any warning. Cars from both directions might have kept driving off until dawn. Your father said that after a while the cars would have piled up so high that maybe folks would be able to drive right over them instead of falling in. Isn't that a terrible thought?"

"Mom," I whisper, "that's enough."

"You're probably wondering about the police," Mom says. "Your father thought about that too—if this had happened at night, I mean. Maybe the toll collectors would have noticed that nobody from past a certain point was coming through, and maybe they'd call the troopers. So a few police cars from either direction would be sent. And they'd fall into the stream! When they weren't heard from, a few more would get sent. Same result. Then so on and so on until morning, when someone finally noticed."

The round-faced farmer and his grandchildren stare at a glittering mound of automobiles towering over the level of the absent bridge. Cars spill onto both sides of the highway. Here and there men and women jut out form the wreckage, unbloodied, Xs where their eyes should be. A few wear police caps.

"Oh, it's just your father's morbid story—something to pass the time." Mom's sweet, youthful voice reaches me in popping bubbles. The steering wheel squirms out of my grasp and loops around my wrists. I squint against a blue glare. My mother is no longer visible. I feel her, though, as if I'm an egg waiting to hatch. We fly backwards on the highway: the car spits blue-white dashes into a single beam. My eyes close. I'm floating. My knees bump my forehead.

"Mom!" I cry, "What about Aunt Anna?" But I lie in the soft curve of time's arm, my words lost in a baritone lullaby, and I am one rock-a-bye away from sleep.

Brad Green

Until Shiloh Come

Therefore they commanded the children of Benjamin, saying, Go and lie in wait in the vineyards; And see, and, behold, if the daughters of Shiloh come out to dance in dances, then come ye out of the vineyards, and catch you every man his wife of the daughters of Shiloh, and go to the land of Benjamin.
— Judges 20-21

This is like the flood that happened during Noah's time, or the destruction of Sodom and Gomorrah! We ARE being punished for our sins! The dead are rising, and Judgment Day is upon us!
— Reverend John Hicks, from *Night of the Living Dead*

Few things were known save they arrived enraged. The first of Dinah's children—if one dared name them as such—started with the red antler of a cramp, some sense within that change was unfolding and wouldn't be stopped. That the child dropped from her dead and yet moved but would not die again could not be disputed. And though the tribe shunned her, the Benjamite did not. He continued trying to make something pure with her, failing each time. The pain of the latching in every conception charged her with hope, though. Perhaps this child would be the one to come and cleanse the world of the others she'd wrought. Hope is the great deceiver, Dinah learned, but still she'd lift her robe in front of the Benjamite's beaten copper mirror, hoping that bump swelling under her palm was a ravenous seraph inbellied. Woe to the wicked, she'd whisper.

Dinah was to go dancing in the vineyard, her and her sisters, all the unwed daughters of Shiloh, and she suspected nothing. None of the daughters envisioned what was to befall them. What Dinah remembered most was the smallness of the stars as she whirled bare-armed around the crackling fire unaware of who crouched in the dark, and she remembered the wine, how it plied from her the concerns of her home and her father's illness, his shrinking fingers and stumpy feet, the leprous swellings on his face. He was her father and Dinah was loyal as the Lord commanded daughters to be, but to see her once-strong father toweling his rash and boils with a cloth moistened from the same bowl where she washed her face made her shudder and touch her own cheeks with trembling fingers. It was wrong of her to shrink from him that way, but allowing the images of her father's wrecked skin to fall from her mind was a private bliss, as was the loss of his deep moan through the night as he failed to apprehend why the Lord punished him.

"I'm a faithful child of Israel," he'd tell her. "I went up against Gibeah with Judah to revenge the Levite's concubine. I kept my oath to give no daughter as wife to a son of Benjamin and yet I'm stricken and shunned?"

Dinah had no answer. She held cups of quivering water to his lips and watched strength seep from his limbs till the night he commanded her to dance in the vineyard.

"Go with the others," he told her, waving his bandaged hands. "Go. Dance. Be young and free from the tribulation that I am."

And he would hear no word from her other than yes, and though she was sorrowful in her belly at leaving him alone in the tent, Dinah also harbored a secret glee at the thought of dancing and feeling the fire's warmth on her skin while she and the other girls escaped, if only for a short moment, from the toil and concerns of their homes.

She remembered all this each night the Benjamite came to her huffing, his neck sweaty and his feet red and hot from hours of herding. She remembered the shouts of her friends reaching her slowly through the wine-fog as she danced, how the Benjamite's hands had been hard against her biceps and how his fingers tasted of goat dung as they clamped over her lips. The stars whirled and at first Dinah thought she'd fallen, but then she heard the clatter of the Benjamite's cold armor and saw how the moon stretched long and distant as a reflection down the length of his blade. And then Dinah saw the other Benjamites boiling from the dark, those wifeless soldiers hidden long in the rocks of Rimmon after the sacking of Gibeah, their faces haggard with want. And Dinah saw the Benjamite soldiers gathering up the maidens of Shiloh and taking them away as wives. This is the way the tribes of Israel reconciled?

In the Benjamite's tent, his shadow loomed blackly on the wind-whipped fabric as he told her softly of his sheep and goats and how heavy the sword had been to his arm, but Dinah did not believe him because that same hand's thick thumb pushed redly under her knee's tendon when she made to leave and she knew the horror he'd done to the Levite's concubine that night in Gibeah, so Dinah was made to lay with the Benjamite and she became his wife, shuddering quietly afterwards with both her hands pressed between her thighs as she stared at the smoky congestion of hair on his chest, wondering why the Lord had allowed this tragedy to befall her and wondering, most of all, why the Benjamite's breath smelled like cabbage when his habit was chewing clove. She knew her father had given her up, as had the other fathers of the other taken daughters, for if the girls were taken, then no daughter had been given over to the sons of Benjamin and no oath had been compromised. Dinah knew this and felt her heart harden against the Lord and the men of all the tribes of Israel.

Each time her child-cramps quickened, anger tightened Dinah's belly with black bands. That's when she knew the child would be wrong. Dinah knew the Benjamite desired her to birth Shiloh, the one who was promised to publish peace amongst the tribes, but such foulness had taken up camp within her belly that her children were changed into sons of Belial, more wicked than the Benjamite himself had been in Gibeah.

As Dinah covered her feet one afternoon, a familiar cramp bent her form to its will. Her elbows speared her knees, toes clenched white in her worn sandals. No, this wasn't a sacrifice.

That was the word the Benjamite spit from his throat thick with baggy flesh. No, this was punishment for him and the men of the tribes of Israel, punishment for her father and his deceptive attempt at reconciliation. This making was supposed to unite the tribes of Israel, but it had only brought pain and ruin and Dinah laughed into her sleeve each time she saw the Benjamite's face stricken with woe. There was no King, and each man did as he saw fit to the women of Israel and they all suffered as her children consumed them all.

Dinah heard the frail splash before she felt the leaving. Straightening, her elbows left hopeless pink ovals on her knees.

She would not look. Though she was still hardened against the Benjamite, regret loosened her heart at everyone else for the death her children had caused. All twelve tribes had been devastated. Men, women, and children, all turned and once turned they began to feed on those not yet stricken. Word had reached them that Dinah's children were everywhere now, but perhaps there was hope for salvation after all? She thought that in this last latching there had been the genesis of a warm bump, a verifiable and alive presence contrary to the cold lump she'd become accustomed to carrying, but this child left her early like the others and felt just as sloppy in its departure as those that came before. The Benjamite would accuse her of using cotton root bark, but she'd long since given that up. Nothing she did to help or harm changed the outcome. Didn't he understand she wanted these makings to stop now, that not even her wicked heart wanted this doom? There would be nothing left but empty tents and sand if her children did not die. No sliver of bark steeped in water, no prayer, no spear thrust into their chests lacking breath, no wishful hope ever stopped them. If only she hadn't followed the others into the vineyard that night trying to escape her father, she might not have been made unclean. Birthing Shiloh was her only escape now. The Benjamite looked to her for that, but she didn't know why. What made him think her heart was any less wretched than his? For Dinah knew all their hearts had wrought this woe, and the tiny flame of hope

she harbored in hers threatened to whither each time a new black
monster rose from beneath her robes.

She spread her knees and pulled up her robe to peer into the waste
hole, but then clamped her thighs together. To look upon the face
would be too much to bear, another cloth snarled with red snot,
looking the same as the other ill-latched redeemers. She could cup
her hands in the bloody water and scoop it out but it would lay
lifeless in her palms for an hour, maybe three, before its worm-
slick skin trembled and began to grow. She'd seen the transformation
many times, how the death dropped from her slack and sick, how
the teeth then pushed snapping and wild from the black, mucky
mouth even before the gelid eyes uncrusted red and warbled loose
in their sockets, the arms and legs splintering forth too quickly till
her child wobbled up on its own with a grunt and stalked the
earth, possessed with terrible violence. So little of the world was
left now. Her children had destroyed it all. Everywhere one looked,
one saw their black presence, their lurching limbs, that slow, rolling
moan as they hungered for clean flesh. Through its blood, the first
had become a hundred, the hundred ten thousand and now all that
Dinah knew and saw was reduced to the Benjamite's mud walls.
For all she knew, the tribes of Israel were now utterly gone, or
turned into the beasts that her children made of men. She listened
to her water trickle away through the trench and though she'd left
many of her dead children there to wash away, each one had
crawled back. Each of them made more black brothers as they
chewed and tore through flesh their way back to her. They each
racked their bones and rotting skins now against the walls the
Benjamite constructed to keep them out while he waited for her
to fulfill his hope and birth something pure.

An inch of light under the tent flap stuttered from the Benjamite's
shadow. Dinah heard his mumbling through her children's howling
din outside the wall. *Unclean girl, you condemn us.* This she knew too,
and well. Befouled, she had been given away to this. Her father's
illness was within her and she'd been taken from the stars to destroy

the world with God's wrath. This was the only explanation. If the Benjamite had killed her earlier the world might have been spared her children, but hope had driven him to keep trying. It was hope Dinah cursed the most because hope is what damaged them all. Hope is what caused her to bring her father water, let his fingerless hands touch her cheek and watch his tears fall upon her smooth skin. If she had shunned her father and cast him out, she would not have been made unclean. Shadow swelled into that bright undertent inch as the fabric was pushed aside. Dinah squeezed shut her eyes, knowing the tribulation to come. The Benjamite would lay her down again soon, his hairy mass shuddering over her as he spilled his seed between her thrust-apart legs, laboring to make the world a better place and failing each time. Yes, it was better to meet her fate blind. Though she thought herself ready for him, his sound was different and her breath caught when she heard the click of his scabbard and the hiss of his sword drawn forth.

Pinckney Benedict

Damselfly

> *And the shapes of the locusts were like unto horses prepared unto battle; and on their heads were as it were crowns like gold, and their faces were as the faces of men. And they had hair as the hair of women, and their teeth were as the teeth of lions. And they had breastplates, as it were breastplates of iron; and the sound of their wings was as the sound of chariots of many horses running to battle.*
>
> – Revelation 9:7-9

A t just past four in the morning, with the false dawn brightening the eastern sky, Nimrod Nickel once again found himself wide awake. He sat in the place where he'd watched the sun rise every morning for a week or more: perched on a hard wooden chair turned backward, arms crossed on the chair's rigid back, staring out of his open kitchen window, praying for a breeze. Anything—a sigh, a whisper, a kiss. Anything but this apparently endless doldrums. The suffocating summer's heat and the constant droning of the seventeen-year locusts had bored their way deep into his brain, and he felt like at any minute he might go mad. At any moment, he might explode into flames. He might scream. He might hurl the kitchen chair through the screen door that opened onto the back porch. He might even do a worse thing. Give me something, he thought. His voice no more than a whisper, he said, "Anything."

Out in his back yard, not far from the old smokehouse, something moved. It was slight and pale and it walked upright.

Nimrod squinted. Sweat dripped from his furrowed brow into his eyes, and he wiped at it. A child? A girl? The salt of his sweat stung him, and his vision momentarily dimmed and swam. The pale figure—pale wasn't the right word for it, exactly; it seemed luminous, it seemed almost to glow—crossed the bottom of his yard with its flitting, light-footed gait and, quick as a wink, brushed open the door of the smokehouse and slipped inside.

For a moment, Nimrod imagined that the glow he had seen—a blue luminescence as pure as light refracted from the faces of a diamond, as calm as the rays of the late-afternoon sun glancing off the surface of a cool, deep lake—outlined the heavy wooden door of the ramshackle smokehouse. How bright must that radiance be, to shine through the gap around the door that way? Inside the smokehouse, which hadn't seen any proper use since his grandfather's time, it must be blinding, he imagined. Nimrod closed his smarting eyes and held them closed, and when he opened them again, his vision had cleared. There was no figure, no girl, no glow.

Pharaoh pharaoh pharaoh, cried the locusts in their unnumbered millions. Pharoah pharaoh pharaoh: the locusts' two-syllable mating chorus, endlessly repeated from every tree on Nimrod Nickel's place, from every tree in the green little valley that lay beneath the looming shadow of Nickel's Ridge, and from every tree and shrub and bush on the ridge. It was as though the trees themselves were crying out.

The only trees that had been spared the locust infestation were the ones covered in caterpillar cocoons. These trees stood shrouded, silent and ghostly in their white silk garments, amidst the others. Apparently the caterpillars and the locusts had an understanding between them. But the other trees: they were cloaked in the whirring, creeping, buzzing carpet of locusts. Pharaoh pharaoh pharaoh. Nimrod Nickel's mother had told him when he was a little boy, when the unrelenting cry of the seventeen-year locusts had frightened him, that they made that sound to remind the world of the fate that had befallen the magnificent Pharaoh of Egypt when he hardened his heart against YWHW, the Lord God of Hosts. The eighth plague, followed by darkness, followed by the Destroyer.

The crushing heat had continued unbroken for better than a month now, not a breath of wind since the day in early summer when the locusts had begun boiling up out of the ground (repulsive, to watch them pull themselves free of the earth, like dead men clawing their way out of their graves; and yet he hadn't been able to look away, fascinated for hours as his land bloomed with this weird, alien crop), and the humidity made him feel weak and woozy and sick to his stomach. He knew he needed to drink water to stay healthy, he had learned that much as a boy and had relearned it during his time in the desert, but still he couldn't bear it. On his tongue, the metallic tang of the tap water—drawn by electric pump from an ancient limestone aquifer four hundred feet below the surface—made him think of blood. He felt his gorge rise, just imagining it. He had grown up in that house, drinking that water, and it had never bothered him before this summer, but now—now it didn't bear thinking about. Like the locusts bursting from every inch of his property. Unbearable.

Needless to say, he wasn't eating well (You're going to waste away, his plump, pretty wife, younger than he was by several years, said to him at every meal—Don't you care for my cooking anymore?) and he'd begun losing weight, his jeans hanging loose from the sharp angles of his hipbones, his workshirt when he put one on in the morning draping over him like some kind of a caftan. He'd had to punch two extra holes, first one and then another just a week later, in the wide leather belt that he wore, the one with the heavy brass bull's head buckle. He hadn't slept through the night in weeks. He was beginning to see things, movement in the corners of his vision, cobwebs where there weren't any cobwebs, moving shadows when there was no light to throw a shadow and nothing moving to cast it. And now—had she been naked?—a girl. A girl had drifted across his yard and gone into the smokehouse.

He'd had visions like these before, seen things that weren't there. In the desert. There too, the heat had seemed likely to drive him mad. The endless patrols. The Dexedrine to get himself up for combat, the Restoril to get to sleep again, go, no-go, in an endless, hallucinatory, ever-tightening spiral. He knew he had killed people on some of those patrols, because he had seen the pictures of their sprawled, awkward bodies on the bright screens of his squadmates' cell phones. They had clapped him on the back, his fellow soldiers, and declared their admiration for his fearlessness. Nimrod, they had said to him, you, sir, are a warrior. All of his people, all of the Nickel men, had been warriors, from the very first one of them, who had fought the Shawnee in this very place. Still, he was damned if he could recall any of it with clarity. The visions, the voices, the glowing girl at the end of his yard—those were clearer than the things that had really happened to him.

He knew that if he went out to the smokehouse, if he threw the door open, the little eight-by-eight cell, with its impossibly thick walls, iron-hard oak log piled on oak log and cemented together with viscous, greasy bitumen—he knew the room would be empty. Some trash and leaf litter in the corners, a few spiders creeping along their silken webs high up among the rafters. Those, and the ghostly pong of curing meat, residue of long-gone salty slabs of bacon and monstrous sides of beef and the muscular loins of whitetail deer, sweating blood, and the rounded forms of ornate pheasants, their feathers gleaming slickly, ripening as they hung by their necks, waiting for their glossy bodies to drop away. "That's when you know the meat is ripe." He heard his grandfather's voice, as though the old man were speaking into his ear. "When the body falls away from the neck." Nimrod cupped a hand over his mouth, queasy again.

All of these things he remembered from his boyhood, his grandfather sweeping open the door and gesturing young Nimrod (how old had he been? Eight? The age of his own son?) through, showing him the richness of the interior. "So long as this smokehouse is full, you'll never know want," Nimrod's grandfather had said. His face, the old man's face, had been seamed and pocked, the flesh loose on the bones beneath (as though it might fall away, as though it might finally be ripe), and even his grin, full of pride at the sight of all that high meat stored up against an uncertain future, had seemed frightening to young Nimrod: you grew old and you stored up aging meat in a small wooden house in the

shadow of Nickel's Ridge, and you yourself were aging meat hidden
in that selfsame shadow, and that was what the future held for
you. That was what the boy Nimrod had taken away from that
little expedition. That, and a taste for store-bought victuals.

As a man, he had never once put meat in the smokehouse. The
smokehouse had stood empty through the years that he had owned
the place at the foot of Nickel's Ridge. And had he known want?
From time to time he had, his family had, but he had always staved
it off in one way or another. Mostly by working for other men on
their land, because Nimrod Nickel was strong and handy, and it
was only with his own land that he seemed to have no luck. For a
few years, by joining the service and shooting people in a far-off
place, which hadn't paid as well as you might think it would, but
which was a trade the men in his family had always followed and
in which they had always found success. Thus he had staved off
want and, having put it at bay, had returned to his own house, the
original house of the Nickel family. That house was a rambling
collection of rooms tacked on, at various times and in various
styles, to the stalwart log cabin, not so much bigger than the
smokehouse, and not so different in its construction, that the first
of the Nickel men (another Nimrod, who had spelled his last name
with two Ls, Nickell) had, in the mid-eighteenth century, erected
in this place among the Shawnees, as a trading post and, more
often, a fortress.

Nimrod had been mulling over an offer as he sat on the hard
kitchen chair and listened to the incessant thrumming of the locusts
and prayed for a breeze (was it too much too ask? Just a slight
movement of the air, one of the blessed drafts that so often flowed
like water from the shoulder of the ridge and down into their little
valley) and looked out the window at the log-walled smokehouse
that his grandfather, who had also been named Nimrod (Nimrod
was a great hunter before the LORD!): the offer he was considering,
and which had come to him as a complete surprise, was a rich one:
an offer for the ridge itself and for the precious seam of soft black
coal that lay hidden beneath it.

The Monongahela Consolidated Coal Company would purchase

the ridge, if Nimrod agreed, and they would dynamite its top, throw the vast mass of it down into the valley, they would bury this valley with its rambling old house that had belonged to one Nickel and then another and another, generation after generation, great hunters before the LORD, hunters of men, and the land around the house itself, as well as the thick-walled smokehouse (was it empty? Had a girl—a naked girl—dashed in there a moment ago, as light on her feet as a deer or fox? So light that she seemed almost to float over the ground?), and the ancient twisted old oak trees with their burden of chittering, remorseless locusts. They would help the Nickel family to move—where? elsewhere—and they would decapitate the ridge and they would scoop out its valuable heart, they would fill the valley with rubble, and then they would be on their way again, on to the next place. And what of the Nickels? What would become of them?

Yes, there had been want. After this one last sale, though, there would never be want again.

Pharaoh pharaoh pharaoh!

Nimrod's wife didn't seem to have any trouble sleeping. Their son, who was genial and nervous and bucktoothed and bespectacled and skinny as a whippet, constantly grinning at nothing in particular—he didn't seem to have any trouble sleeping either. They were both asleep right at that moment: Nimrod's wife lying on her back amidst a warm tangle of sheets, slightly damp with sweat, in their bedroom next to the kitchen; and the boy atop a thin mattress on the floor of the sleeping porch at the far end of the house.

Even the dogs slumbered, flattened against the floor like hairy rugs. The heat had rendered them unconscious. In that household, only Nimrod Nickel had difficulty staying asleep. He thought for the millionth time of the vial of Ambien that stood on the porcelain of the bathroom sink, untouched since his wife had procured it for him, when he had complained to her about his sleeplessness. He thought of it, and of the Restoril and the Dexedrine, of go and no-go, of the photographs of the twilight killings that he couldn't even recall; and of the things that fluttered nastily in the periphery of his vision: the terrifying six-winged angels with their burning faces, the hump-backed thick-hided beasts that cavorted and battled and rutted just out of his sight. He wouldn't go that route again.

Maybe it was an escaped prisoner in the smokehouse. They got away, every now and again, from the federal women's prison (the camp, they called it, the administrators there—how precious!) ten or so miles away, in an otherwise uninhabited valley to the east. They were mostly city girls inside there, almost all convicted on drug charges, and when they broke out (broke out? When they walked away from the place, because there weren't walls or even fences, really, not of the sort an actual prison would have), they usually followed the highway or the railroad tracks until they got picked up by the state troopers a few hours later. By then they were hungry and tired and ready to go back to the camp.

Sometimes the more ambitious among the escapees tried to follow the river or, setting out cross-country, got lost in the deep woods, and when they were finally found, sometimes after a few days, they were footsore and covered in poison oak, hypothermic and half-starved, dehydrated and babbling about the beings that they had seen among the lonely, abandoned hills, yammering on and on about the things the stealthy hill-creatures had said to them, the liberties they had taken.

A few of those ambitious ones, he recalled, hadn't been found at all, and Nimrod figured their bones were scattered on the floor of the forest, their skulls home to rodents and snakes and beetles. So maybe this was one of those pitiful ones, huddling inside his smokehouse, hoping—like a little kid—that someone was going to come and find her and take her back to a place where there was electricity and air conditioning and hot nourishing food and television, and where the sound of the locusts didn't surround you and drill into your head and drive you mad.

He stood up from the chair, considering for a moment whether or not he ought to take the little double-barreled coach gun out there with him. There were two possibilities, he figured: either the smokehouse was empty, or there was some girl—if there was anybody at all, it was someone quite small, and he was a large man, in his physical prime—from Detroit or Fort Lauderdale or some other urban shithole, and she would probably thank him for discovering her and ask to borrow his phone to call the feds to come and get her. He flexed his muscular arms and decided he wouldn't need the gun.

As he threw open the screen door, one of the dogs stirred in its sleep. He waited a moment, to see if it wanted to come with him on his errand, but it subsided, whimpering slightly, back into its dreams. The door slapped shut behind him, and Nimrod stepped out into his yard.

Into cacophony. Inside his house, he'd at least had the sense of human belongings around him, of a human arrangement of objects and spaces, of a place that had been planned by and that made sense to the human brain. Out here, though—out here he understood that he had stepped into the insect world, and his mind reeled. As he made his way toward the smokehouse, the discarded husks of locusts crunched under his feet, and their shrilling song— Pharaoh pharaoh pharaoh!—filled his ears, ten times, a hundred times louder than it had been when he sat within his own walls, within the ancestral fortress of the Nickel clan.

The locusts hopped and burrowed and ate and winged their noisy way from tree to tree. Blindly, they batted against his hands and his face, and he struck out at them, even as he understood that there were too many for him ever to rid himself of them. The could not be driven off, so they must be borne. He remembered a teaching saying, in some long-ago junior high science class, that, if you were to put all the people on the planet into one great big garbage bag, and all the insects on the planet into another, the bag containing the insects would weigh several hundred times more than the bag containing the humans. Until this moment, he had always found that statistic difficult to believe.

Even worse than the screaming locusts, though, were the trees— silent, ghostly—that had been shrouded by the tent caterpillars. At least the locusts were life. The caterpillars were death, mantling the trees they had chosen in thick webs and then consuming them.

Nimrod listened closely and heard, under the shrilling of the locusts, a ticking, clattering sound that came from within the caterpillars' canopy, and he knew that it was the sound of their droppings raining down within the veils of their cocoons. The hidden caterpillars were converting his trees to shit. He peered at the nearest of the tented trees and thought that he could make out, under the white blanket, the creeping shapes of the caterpillars as they went this way and that on the doomed trees branches. It was difficult to tell if it was a million caterpillars in there, or just one vast being made of a million undifferentiated creeping parts.

He had meant to burn out the caterpillars at the beginning of the infestation, had even devised a clever propane wand, a torch with a hissing eight-foot flame, that would have served the purpose handsomely. He had meant to save his trees. But then the locusts had come, and the whole place had been overrun, and there hadn't been a point to it anymore, it had seemed to him. Now, of course, it was too late: he'd have to burn the whole place, set fire to the whole ridge, the whole forest, to get rid of the caterpillars.

He laughed a little. What will you do, he thought, when Monongahela Consolidated buries you? What will you do then, you killers, you ravagers, you obscenities?

And he found himself at the door of the smokehouse. The wood of the door, the logs of the walls, were thick with locust casings. Nimrod examined one of them that clung to the door at the height of his eyes. It looked, he found, precisely like the living locust that had abandoned it. It was perfect in all of its parts: its nimble legs, it delicate thorax, its bulging eyes; but it was empty and dead. He took it between his thumb and forefinger and tried to pull it away from the door, but it clung fast. Only when he twisted it so that its legs snapped did it come free. In his large palm, it was tiny. It weighed nothing. It gleamed like bronze. He tossed it onto the ground, and when it fell he could not tell it from the ten thousand similar shells that lay there.

He had stood outside doors like this one before. In combat. He had blown doors like this off their hinges and tossed grenades into the rooms inside. He had entered the rooms, M4 chattering in his hands, hot brass shell-casings clattering and spanging off the walls, falling in bright cascades to the floor. He did not recall it, but he knew that he had done it. He was Nimrod Nickel, and the Nickel men were warriors.

Feeling more than a bit silly as he did so, he knocked on the door of the smokehouse. Shave and a haircut, two bits. "Is anyone there?" he called. His voice sounded weak and thin to him, nearly drowned out by the shrieking of the locusts. There are so many of them, he thought, and, truly, so few of us. What is to be done? He thought briefly of the makeshift flamethrower in his garage and knew that his instinct about its futility had been correct. The infestation was here. It was in the land, it lay deep in the earth. It had gestated there for years, blind and squirming. It had been there before him and his kind, and it would be there long after them. It could not be overcome by the artifices of man, no matter how clever. And soon, it would be the problem of Mon Consolidated. They could crack open the vault of the earth if they liked and come to grips with what lay hidden there. "Ready or not, I'm coming in," he called.

No more stalling. He swung wide the smokehouse door, knowing full well that the little outbuilding was empty.

And saw her.

Slender as a young birch. Long-limbed, her posture holding the promise of a superhuman litheness. Narrow, supple waist, surprisingly full breasts. Wide eyes, impossibly wide, and lidless. Nude as the day she was born, and her skin shone like the surface of a pearl. He felt himself drawn to her, more strongly than he had ever been drawn to a woman before, and he felt at the same time the strangeness of that attraction. He was disgusted by it and helpless in the face of it. She smiled at him, and there were things— glistening, mandibular things—revealed by her smile that no human mouth should ever contain. He wanted to flee, but because he had never beheld something so awful and so beautiful before, he stayed rooted to his spot before the open door. She seemed to sense that her smile was disconcerting to him, and her expression became somber, the wriggling mouth-parts hidden behind moist lips.

She was a nymph. That had to be it. And it was nymph, wasn't it, that they called the final form of the locust, the one that came up out of the ground? There were other forms too, conjured through a multitude of moltings: larva, pupa, imago—it seemed preposterous to him, somehow, that something as simple as a locust, something not even as big as his thumb, should have so many different forms in the course of its life, and that the great bulk of that life should be lived out in utter darkness and silence, buried in the ground beneath the Nickel place; and that the rest of it should be carried out in his trees, shrieking and shrilling in the great universal competition to find a mate.

Many insects, he recalled from that selfsame science class, from some antique film strip replete with grainy images of burrowing beetles and horned, carapaced things that burrowed in the dirt and ate the flesh of the dead—many insects, perhaps most, had forms that were called nymph.

He could almost hear the stentorian voice of the film strip narrator as the images flowed past, a phantasmagoria of a myriad fluttering, buzzing, translucent, venous wings; jewel-like eyes with a thousand depthless facets; spiked feelers and feathery antennae; obscene proboscises furling and unfurling; intricate, wicked appendages; and gleaming, chitinous exoskeletons:

"The nymphs of aquatic insects, as in the orders Odonata—" A cricket click to indicate that the teacher should advance the filmstrip, and now on the screen there stands the image of a dozen multihued dragonflies hovering over a patch of cattails at the edge of an algae-covered pond.

"—Ephemeroptera—" The cricket click again, and a clutch of mayflies whirls through the air, alive for only perhaps a score of hours and then gone forever.

"—and Plecoptera." Click, and a swarm of primitive-looking stoneflies clusters thirstily just above the sparkling rapids of a clear, swift-flowing stream.

"The nymphs are also sometimes called naiads," continues the narrator, "which is an ancient Hellenic name for the race of mythological water sylphs which would, through the use of their considerable feminine wiles, lure unlucky, unwise or unwary men to their dooms."

"Am I unlucky?" wondered Nimrod. "Or am I unwise?" Aloud, he asked, "Who are you?"

It seemed at first as though she would say nothing, and he felt foolish, having asked her. Could she understand him? It seemed unlikely. Then: "Daphne," she replied, revealing again, but only for a moment, the horror that lay within her beautiful mouth. Her voice was light and tinkling, pleasing to the ear, and it cut easily through the uproar that surrounded them.

"Daphne," he said.

"Yes," she replied, making a little curtsey toward him before she turned away, as though she were embarrassed; and that was when he spied her wings. She had four of them, two pairs, and for an instant when he first saw them he thought to himself, She's a seraph, but then he thought, No, the seraphim have six wings: one pair with which to cover the face, one pair with which to cover the feet, and the third pair with which to fly. And eternally they cry, Holy, holy, holy is the LORD of hosts; the whole earth is full of his glory!

She was not an angel, could not be, not in this place where there would never be any angels. She must be an insect. But what sort of an insect was she? The dim light of pre-morning spread vivid color—red, orange, yellow, green, blue, indigo, violet—across the gleaming surface of her wings. Like stained glass, he thought. Like the windows of a cathedral. For a moment he glimpsed his own face reflected there, submerged in the shimmering colors, and he was shocked by the mixture of terror and desire he saw written on his features.

He tried, in an effort to combat the macabre welter of emotion that was rising up in him, to think clearly, categorically. They lay vertical along her back, the wings, and for a moment this fact puzzled him. She was, then, not a dragonfly—what his grandmother had called "the Devil's darning needle"—because the wings of a dragonfly do not close against its back but are horizontally outspread. What was she, then, this delicate four-winged creature that stood so demurely before him, her gaze (her eyes possessed a thousand facets, and they were set at a ghastly distance apart from each other, nearly on the sides of her head) fixed intently on his, her body turned slightly, modestly, to the side, her slender hands covering (or were they caressing?) her womanly breasts and the fuzz on her pubic mound? What was she, if not angel or dragonfly? And then—he almost snapped his fingers in relief as the thought came to him, because he, like most of us, hated almost but not quite to be able to name something—he had it: damselfly.

"Yes," she said, Daphne said, the nymph said, as though she too were relieved, as though she had somehow read his mind and realized that within him some internal struggle was over. "Damselfly." Her sibilants were thick and ungracious, as though whatever language she spoke natively did not make use of them. She took a step toward him on her slim, delicate feet, two steps, three, she was almost upon him, and her hips undulated deliciously as she walked. Her wings whirred with her excitement, throwing shards of light across the dark walls of the smokehouse, and Nimrod could feel the breeze that they made as it caressed his sweaty face. How he had wished for a breeze, back in his kitchen (it seemed like a lifetime ago, but it must have been only a few minutes, a few minutes to rise and leave his house and cross his yard and throw open the door of the smokehouse), back on the hard seat of his chair, his dogs asleep on the floor, his family resting comfortably in their beds. And now that the breeze was here...!

The wings stopped their motion, and he wanted to cry out because the breeze had stopped. The heat enveloped him again. He took a step toward her, toward the great damselfly. He thought that she must have been there with him on the battlefield, when in his delirium he had killed and killed and killed. He did not have the memory of those deaths, but she did, and she approved. She was prepared to accept him, Nimrod Nickel (Nimrod was a great hunter before the LORD!) as one of her own. How could he refuse such an offer? How could he possibly refuse such generosity? Her delicate face was tilted up toward his, her expression almost merry, her attitude inviting, her lissome arms outstretched.

Outside the smokehouse, the locusts went quiet. Even the numberless tent caterpillars seemed, for the moment, to have ceased their crawling. His family would miss him, Nimrod knew. His wife would sign the rich contracts (she was no fool!), and nothing could afterward stop the destruction that was coming. They would be wealthy, his wife and his son, and this place would be destroyed, and they would be far far away, in another world altogether, when the end came.

He, though—he had asked for the breeze. He had begged for it, prayed. And here it was, in these wings, in the wings of this creature that stood before him. He took her in his arms, and she was abominably light, the flesh of her lush body as unyielding as cold-rolled steel. He was shocked by the unthinkable strength of her. He was more than twice her size, a hundred times her weight, and he understood that he didn't possess even a fraction of her power. She grinned, a spectacular grin, a grin full of mandibles and palps and other damp unspeakable things. He lowered his face to hers, and she wrapped him in her fierce embrace.

Once again, the locusts took up their shrilling call. Pharaoh pharaoh pharaoh! they cried. On and on, endlessly.

Alexander Lumans

Before I Offer Myself
to the Birdmen

The birdman comes to the farm in the morning. One per household in town, too; dozens in all. His legs are the pink of cow tongues, his beak long enough to swallow saplings. He spits, but only when he speaks. And when he stands up straight—a rare thing—he is as tall as a chimney. We're not supposed to stare into those melon-sized eyes; we must wear cooking pots on our heads and look dumb doing so. In our yard, our birdman beats his white wings while my wife and I hurry to his clawfeet with our small, bundled offering. The giant, malformed stork commands, "Feed us your softest child."

You would think he'd eat the child right then and there—but he never does.

At first the birdmen returned every two years. We gave them our runts, the sickly, the most misbehaved children; we took the visits as a blessing. The Great Claiming, the town called it. Then, the Claiming came every year. If you moved away, they found you. But all the songbirds still left. Ducks and hawks, too. Only the crows stuck around. We kept our good sons and daughters hidden. We stopped naming the ones we sacrificed; it made the whole thing easier. And now that it's twice a year—every March and October—we risk our own life and limb to keep up.

"Two weeks," my wife says.

"Which one should we hand over?"

It's evening. In the garden we are raising the scarecrow before nightfall. From the front I pull the rope tied around the cross and the hanging scarecrow. My wife pushes the cross from behind. The tallest, oldest children usually help instead of her, but there are none left. The smallest ones—the only ones—stay in the house.

"Don't say it like that," she says. "'Which one,' 'Hand over'; you make it sound like a gift."

"We have to choose."

She groans while she tries to push up the cross. Even with me pulling hard, the scarecrow barely rises. "I can't do this," she says, and lets the cross rest down on her shoulders. She has always been a strong woman—inside and out—but that won't last much longer. Even now, she hunches over in great huffs, rubbing her broad hands together and staring down as if a bird might appear therein.

"We've done it before."

"Doesn't matter," she says. "It gets harder every time."

"Here." I drop the rope. I come around to her side. I hold her hands and place them high on the cross's vertical beam. I take a lower position on the same beam. "Is this better?" She nods down to me. Then we both push.

Slowly, the cross rises. Once it stands too tall for her to continue pushing, I nod her away, but she hunkers down alongside me and adds her hands to mine. We push like this until the cross drops into its posthole. It stands tall enough in the sun's last light to cast a shadow all the way to the back door's flagstones. I hold the vertical beam steady while she fills in the hole.

I say, "See? That wasn't so hard."

"I wasn't talking about the scarecrow." When she looks up at me, concern passes across her face, and I think it's gone as quickly as it's come—but there it is again, perched in her damp eyes and in the downed corners of her mouth. "I just want to know when it's going to stop." Still on her knees, she glances toward the house. A small head disappears from the window.

She needs my help to get on her feet. I don't have any good answers for her, but I want one as badly as I wanted her to be my wife, and then a mother. All I can do is guide her around to the scarecrow's front and give her a chance to admire our work.

She says, "Thank you," keeping hold of my hand. Even when things are darkest, she is kind. "But you forgot the face."

The head is a cornmeal bag stuffed with straw, completely vacant under a wide-brimmed hat.

"It doesn't need a face."

"Just wait," she says. "The birds'll come."

I fix the scarecrow's leg where the straw sticks out. She squeezes my hand.

"Two weeks."

"And more."

Once, I tracked the birdmen to their swamp home, but when I found what they were building there, I had to turn back.

"How can you build a wall out of babies?" my wife asks after I describe what I'd seen. We eat soup and bread in the afternoon before the light in the house is too dim. Her red hair grows stiff like pine needles—all the town women resemble her: hardened to the chore of birth and love and flight. Her hands are so broad that when she molds this wall in the air between us, I can feel the air blow on my face. Then she pushes the invisible wall toward me. She is used to giving things away.

"It's easy." From my plate I tip breadcrumbs into my palm. Sprinkle them into my other palm. They pile up. Then I nudge this pile into a jagged line. "This is the swamp," I nod, "and this is the wall. It's strange. Can't be scaled or burned."

"Those are crumbs."

"No, they drop the bundles when they fly over the wall." I turn my hand over and the crumbs fall to the flagstones. "I saw this."

"Leave it to you to reduce the children to food." She kicks the crumbs toward the door. "I never did appreciate your sense of humor."

This has me laughing. It has been a long time since someone's accused me of making anything other than sacrifices. But that's before Plan B occurs to me.

On the first try, Plan B fails.

Our birdman announces from beside our garden, "Feed us your softest child." Without looking at his face, I place some blanket-wrapped straw in his pointed beak.

He spits the bundle out. The straw scatters everywhere. The blanket blows away.

Our birdman shouts, "Feed us your softest child!" He clacks his bill. It echoes over and over inside the cooking pot on my head. In recompense I must give him our last—the four-year-old we've been secreting in the root cellar.

While she stacks kindling in the furnace, my wife says, "You shouldn't have tried to trick them."

"I'm sorry," but I am not.

She lights a match. "We don't want to end up like the Bremlers."

At the mention of our old neighbors I shudder. Harriet and Bin. I can still see Bin's hands curling around the orange beak as he was carried off; word is, his wife was infertile, and at the first Claiming he'd tried to pass off a wooden doll as their own. He'd had no real child to replace the doll in the birdman's beak, so the flock took him instead.

Plenty of husbands have been scooped up for making the same mistake, but you always remember the first. Just like I remember our first child—Helen with the rich, ruddy face—and how many coral snakes she and her mother would catch by the stream, how heavy she weighed in my arms the morning I delivered her to the birdmen. Should my next bundle be refused, I don't have any other cellar boys or attic girls to keep me from being taken.

The birdmen never came for Harriet, nor any of the wives. They must not care for them. We're becoming a town of widows.

The match in my wife's hand burns out. She's been thinking about the Bremlers too. In the dark I notice for the first time how she sniffs and wheezes and gives herself little time to rest. This life's hard on her. She stacks more kindling, then lights strips of newspaper. After she cups her big hands and blows until the heartwood catches, my wife turns to me and says, "Still, it was a clever thing."

Next October, I make a son.

I shape him out of mattress foam with a knife. I fill his insides with wax for weight. I draw a face on the head, bangs and all.

My wife sees my work. "You think our children are smiling when they're taken away?"

At once I wipe off the mistake and redraw the mouth: a jagged line that resembles the swamp horizon over which our family has disappeared. Out the window, the red sun sets behind the scarecrow watching over our garden. Even without a face, the scarecrow has done well.

The birdmen come later that week.

Our birdman squeezes the tightly wrapped bundle in his beak, and I wait for my son to be spit out at my feet.

When nothing happens, I steal a peek at his face, though I shouldn't. His large eyes are bloodshot, as red as mine are in the mirror after every Claiming. Then our birdman nods to me, clacks his long bill, and takes off toward the wall in the swamp.

I make love to my wife that very night, and for many nights after.

From mattress foam to wool sweaters filled with pebbles to corncobs wrapped in muslin: I experiment. I draw different faces on the heads with jagged lines for mouths. But I don't give them names.

The townie couples say, "Never," when I ask if they want lessons in homemade children. "We remember the Bremlers." But when my homemade child is carried off with their real ones, they discover their own recipes. The milkman teaches me about molded cheese.

It's firm, yet yielding. It's easily carved. And it is delicious. I go to town for more rennet and milk, and the townies smile at me for the first time ever. The alleys are filled with the sounds of children stoning stray cats.

But my wife, whose stomach has grown measurably with a new child on the way, does not smile. She goes to bed earlier, stays in bed longer. October is coming, she tells me, then March, and then October again, every year in the same terrible order. She never leaves the house anymore. And her hands never leave her belly. Yet when I ask to feel the child kick, she retreats to other rooms.

She holds the wall when she walks, which is only into the kitchen for milk and onto the porch to call me in from the garden. "What is it?" I ask, my arms limp at my sides from picking squash all day.

"I need you to cook potatoes," she says, breathing heavily as if she had just run from town with Helen and their bag of snakes. "Use fresh rosemary this time."

"Now?"

"Right now." As the pregnancy advances, my wife needs me more and more.

I understand this. I cook the potatoes with fresh rosemary, and we eat them while she keeps the furnace stoked. We need each other, we always have. But all this work—both hers and mine—could be for nothing, too. Instead of asking politely for food or not asking for help at all, she wavers in doorways and at windows. She claims she hears their clacks outside. When I ask her when it will hurt the most, she says, "Tomorrow," and when I ask what I can do, she tells me what I don't want to hear.

I've seen in town where the widows walk. Had long dreams about them. They dowse with copper rods for water or unmarked graves. In black, they walk slowly, without sunhats. No boys or girls pull them faster down the alleys to the river. They slip; they flag. They eat early and alone. I have not seen Harriet Bremler in over a year, but last Tuesday the smoke still climbed high from her chimney. It blew west, toward the wall. All of the women stare west. But unlike the rest of us, the widows don't duck their heads when shadows pass across their faces, be it kite or crow or nothing at all. They are seers, dreamers—these widows walking through town.

"It's a boy."

How does she know?

"The widows read me," she says. "They spun their long rods over me."

Tomorrow is the next Claiming. For a week the bundle has sat in the corner, nearly complete, but that's not the child I'm nervous about. All day I mouth boy names. While I turn over summer soil, I carve them in the dirt with my garden tines.

During our squash dinner by firelight, I ask, "What do you think of 'Ivan'?" The back door's open to blow out extra smoke. And the furnace spits sparks that die in these cool drafts. "Isn't that a good name?"

My wife says, "I-van." Between bites she adds more kindling to the furnace.

I say, "Our little Ivan."

"I miss Helen." Her fork scratches the plate. It makes the sharp cry of a bird, or a small child's shriek. We both expect the faceless bundle in the corner to suddenly move. Then she continues eating while I consider if our new son will live longer than us.

"She was a lot like you." I hope this is what she wants to hear.

"You always make boys." She takes another bite, swallows, sets her fork on the table. "Why is that?"

With the light dimming, I kick the furnace to shake up the logs. "I don't know."

"It's sad."

"That I don't make girls?"

"That we are who we are now," she says. "That we'll be hiding like this forever."

She used to believe differently. She used to believe all this Claiming would one day stop.

"The widows are wrong sometimes." I point my fork at her large stomach. "This one could be a girl, like Helen."

"It's not."

"Would you like me to make a Helen?"

"I would like to be excused."

While my wife is gone from the table, I study my son in the corner beneath the cooking pots on hooks. He is not an Ivan. His face is still blank, like the scarecrow's. When I imagine him in our birdman's mouth, our birdman is Bin Bremler. He is taller and older and covered in gray and white feathers. I remember how our birdman had once nodded to me, as Bin used to from his window, and I remember that the only time I ever looked into our birdman's eyes his were as bloodshot as mine. The birdmen are still men. They could be the husbands from our town and other widowed towns, men who've changed in the swamp and now try to keep their own flock from dying out.

I tell my wife this when she comes back an hour later. She calls that absurd, which says how right I must be. A cooler breeze flutters the fire again. When she sits down, she holds her belly and sniffs. Her cheeks and her eyes sag red in the smoky light.

Then my wife announces, "I want to keep this boy."

"You can."

"I want him," she says, squeezing her belly tightly before letting go of it completely. "But we're going to have to give him up. You know that, yes?"

"No."

"Our birdman is not dumb. Just like the crows learn that we're not always in the garden." Shivering, she breathes into her hands and rubs them together over and over.

As if on cue, a crow lands in the doorway. It pecks at crumbs between the flagstones. My wife hides her face from the bird until I chase it off with a saucepan. As I stand in the doorway to make sure it's gone, the garden scarecrow moves. By the moonlight, ten, maybe twenty crows preen on the dummy's arms. She's right: the crows aren't scared at all. How much they remind me of the widows. They look safe in the garden. "We belong here," they caw. "We belong."

From inside: "What is it?"

I come back in and shut the door. "It's nothing. I'll take care of it." I pile cold squash onto her plate. "You should eat more. For the boy."

She pushes the plate away. "I'm not hungry."

"You were an hour ago."

"If I eat even crumbs this late, I will have bad dreams."

"No different than this," I say. "No different than now."

She looks at me with that same jagged mouth I've drawn so many times. "I am old." And those hard lines now run down her chin, around her nose, out from her eyes, all in the wicked shape of large birdfeet. My wife is right about this, too. She is old. This will be her last child.

I tell her, "Go to bed, then," putting my hand to her large belly and waving to the boy inside. She rubs her eyes. She nods once to me, and that is all.

I finish my dinner, then hers. I stare into the heart of the fire for an hour.

When the birdmen take me tomorrow, it will be for the best. They won't come back for her. And they won't come for him. She and Ivan can stay and catch snakes and raise the next scarecrow together. I will go, knowing I've done this. I will grow old among the birdmen.

Before the fire dies, before dawn is here, I pick up the bundle. I carry it into the backyard. I lure the crows from the garden with small pieces of cheese until I have nothing else to offer.

Cover artist **STEPHANIE BRACCIANO** was born and raised in
rural Michigan and has always had an appreciation for
nature and wide-open spaces. She began her photography
career in 2003 at Washtenaw Community College in Ann
Arbor, Michigan. There she was fortunate to have great
professors who helped her transform and grow as an artist.
In 2007, she earned her A.S.S. in Photographic Technology.
Also that year, she won an emerging artist contest at the
Ann Arbor Street Art Fair for her complex photomontages.
In 2008, she was awarded a Presidential Scholarship to
attend the Savannah College of Art and Design in
Savannah, Georgia. In 2010, she graduated with high
honors and received her B.F.A. in Photography.

Contributor Biographies
& Story Notes

Jedidiah Ayres lives in St. Louis. His fiction has appeared in several books, magazines and electronic journals including this one.

Story note: The Adversary is an update of one of my favorite ghost stories found in the Old Testament (1 Samuel 28.)

Pinckney Benedict grew up in rural West Virginia. He has published a novel and three collections of short fiction, the most recent of which is *Miracle Boy and Other Stories* (Press 53). His work has been published in, among other magazines and anthologies, *Esquire*, *Zoetrope: All-Story*, the *O. Henry Award* series, the *Pushcart Prize* series, the *Best New Stories from the South* series, *The Ecco Anthology of Contemporary American Short Fiction*, and *The Oxford Book of the American Short Story*. He is the recipient of two Transatlantic Review awards, a Michener Fellowship, and the Nelson Algren Award. He has received grants from, among others, the West Virginia Arts Council, the Illinois Arts Council, and the National Endowment for the Arts. Benedict is a professor in the creative writing program at Southern Illinois University Carbondale and in the low-residency MFA program at Queens University of Charlotte in North Carolina.

Story note: I've long been fascinated by animals whose calls take on the sound of human words. The drunken bullfrog that calls out for his "jug o' rum" (though ancient Greek frogs apparently cried, "Brekekekex koax koax!'); the barred owl that asks continually, "Who cooks for you? Who cooks for you all?" and the cicadas (often mistakenly called locusts) that call out, perhaps as a warning to the long-ago ruler of Egypt to let the Hebrews go, "Pharaoh pharaoh pharaoh!" This attempt on the part of animalia to communicate with us, which is of course in reality simply our imposition of human patterns onto something with no human content whatsoever, seems to me very much like our storytelling impulse: the human desire (or more precisely, the human need) to project order onto chaos, or what we take to be chaos. This story, then, concerns a man whose world has been tragically disordered by war, and who subsequently hears the relentless prophetic call of the locusts: "Pharaoh pharaoh pharaoh!"

Laura Benedict has published two novels of dark suspense, *Isabella Moon*, and *Calling Mr. Lonely Hearts*. Her writing has appeared in *Ellery Queen Mystery Magazine*, and numerous anthologies such as *Thrillers: 100 Must-Reads*, and *Noir at the Bar*.

Story note: There's a strange bond of unintentional intimacy between hotel guests and the people who are paid to take care of them. I feel very self-conscious about having strangers touch my clothes, wipe down the bath, or make my bed. I want to know who they are, and what they think about. What they want from their lives. But, really, they're just there to do their jobs, and the rest is none of my business. So I feel free to make it up.

Rose Bunch, a native of Arkansas, spent the last year in Bali on a Fulbright Scholarship in Creative Writing, and returned to the United States to take up residency as a MacDowell Fellow for the fall of 2011. Her work has recently appeared in *Tin House* as the New Voice in American Fiction, *New Letters* (winner of the Dorothy Cappon Prize in Nonfiction), *The Greensboro Review*, *Poem*, *Memoir*, *Story*, *River Styx*, *Gulf Coast*, and *Fugue*. A two-time Pushcart Prize nominee, she has also received third prize in the Playboy College Fiction Contest and an Honorable Mention in The Atlantic's College Nonfiction contest. Her latest fiction is forthcoming in *Speed Chronicles* (an anthology from Akashic books), concerning the effects of the methamphetamine industry on America. She received her MFA in Creative Writing (Fiction) at the University of Montana, and will complete her PhD at Florida State University in 2011.

Story note: This is my first attempt at a fictional story about ghosts. I say fictional because my nonfiction essay about ghosts (entitled, originally enough, "Ghosts") won an honorable mention from *The Atlantic* and was published in *Fugue*. I grew up around haunted places, and have been troubled by the nature of what haunts us as living individuals as well. Add to this a rather gory versing in sanctified religion and, to me, nothing is scarier than the concept of resurrection. I always envisioned it as a kind of zombiehood. Living in Indonesia when I wrote this, where ghosts and spirits are an everyday part of life, I started to also imagine what a ghost might bring back with them if they were resurrected. Kind of a reverse version of what is buried with someone to take into the afterworld with them in ancient Egypt. What if they came back with everything they killed off in their former life? What if they came back hungry? Multiple cultures, including the Balinese, teach that ghosts are appeased by what they most desired for their corporeal bodies in life. Food, drink, and even cigarettes. Offerings are laid out daily around my house. I imagined a woman, much like several I used to know back in Arkansas, burdened with a traditional country marriage to a demanding husband (an everyday monster of sorts), who then came back demanding even more.

Robert Busby received his MFA in Fiction from Florida International University in Miami. His stories have appeared or are forthcoming in *Cold Mountain Review*, *Arkansas Review*, and *Stymie*. The former fiction editor of *Gulf Stream*, he now lives with his wife in Memphis, Tennessee, along a strip of parkway that, back in the day, was the premier spot for drag racing horse-drawn carriages.

Story note: The bait shop in "The Dead Fish at Twenty Mile" was originally based on a similar store my great uncle owned and operated on a gravel drive connecting the main road with the farmhouse he grew up in with five other brothers. As a kid, I remember the old men gathered around tables smoking Winstons and eating Nabs and generally shooting the shit while drinking from Coke cans probably spiked with various types of whiskey, although I wasn't aware what went on in those cans at the time. Perhaps the place was frequented with at least a few Bill Dance types, haunted by walking, talking catfish or not, I'm not sure. I am certain no broken-jawed Confederate colonels or Jazz-era bootleggers ever darkened the doorway of my uncle's store. Which is to say, once I entered the fictional world of "Twenty Mile," the place—with the help of its motley crew of inhabitants—grew quickly and organically into its own licensed stamp of soil. In the five years since I first drafted "The Dead Fish at Twenty Mile," it has become the story I didn't know I had been trying to tell all along, which I guess is a sort of fable that incorporates a part of the American South and its history in a New South context while establishing a mythology for fictitious Bodock, Mississippi, and its founder, Col. Leon Claygardner. Yet, at its best, I would like to think the story makes an honest attempt to get at that part of the human condition where, perhaps even dead, we're alive enough to regret allowing the worse parts of our nature to get the best of us.

J.T. Ellison often finds herself cowering under her sheets late at night after the most fantastical nightmares. Some say she's touched in the head. Others say she is the bestselling author of the critically acclaimed Taylor Jackson series, with novels translated all over the world. Is she crazy, or a former White House staffer who moved to Nashville and began dreaming up horrific stories? Regardless, she has worked extensively with the Metro Nashville Police, the FBI, and various other law enforcement organizations to research her novels and feed her overactive imagination. One fact: Ellison lives in Nashville with her husband and a poorly trained cat. Visit http://JTEllison.com or follow her on Twitter @Thrillerchick.

Story note: I spent several months of 2010 researching and writing about a castle in Scotland. The castle itself was fictional, cobbled together from multiple visits into Scotland, brochures and obsessive Googling of haunted castles. But it came alive for me on the page, as did its secrets. My castle, you see, was haunted.

In the way of all haunted castles, there are multiple tales, legends, sightings and horror stories that accompany the structure. In a country whose history is so bloody, it's fitting to have remnants—echoes—of those battles seep onto the page, whether between hundreds on Culloden Moor, or simply one on one, when bared, softly skinned throats are slit in silent stone-walled bedrooms.

Are the legends true? Are the castle ghosts of Scotland real? All I know for sure is I would sprinkle salt across my threshold and along my windowsills before I'd spend a night alone in Dulsie Castle. They say there is a gray lady who lurks in the attics. Her name is Lamia. The questions is, who, exactly, is she? And what does she want with you?

I'll never tell...

Originally from Pennsylvania, **Mark Fleming** has called North Carolina home for more than 20 years. He met his wife Angela working in a Greensboro mental health hospital, and he's taught writing at UNC-Greensboro, Elon University, Guilford Technical Community College, and High Point University. His stories have appeared in regional and national journals, including *Cities & Roads*, *Full Circle Journal*, *O.Henry Festival Stories 2003*, and *Night Train*. He has two children, and he's seeking a publisher for his novel, *The Nun, the Alien, and the Amish Boy: Gospels*.

Story note: "A Father's Place" stems from a bit of brain drift I experienced before falling asleep one night. The image of a father wearing a black motorcycle helmet, with digital readouts instead of a face, came to me and stuck for some reason. Well, at the time, my kids were about the age of the kids in the story, and I remember worrying about how I fit into their lives, what purpose I actually served. This might explain the silent, faceless automaton in the role of dad, a kind of Franken-father.

Brad Green lives in North Texas with his wife and three children. He's an editor at *PANK* magazine. Find him online at http://about.me/bradgreen.

Story note: "Until Shiloh Come" originally started out as a 300-word piece of domestic flash fiction about a housewife having a miscarriage. It never really worked so I filed the story away. The day I read that *Surreal South '11* was opening submissions, I took this story out again and decided to let go of my preconceptions. The moment the housewife became a woman giving birth to zombies was the moment the story finally breathed. Of course, the setting had to be Biblical. After all, nothing else would make sense.

Reuben Hayslett is currently studying his MFA in Creative Writing at Fairfield University. His works have appeared in *The Splinter Generation* and *Orgeon Literary Review*. His lives in Austin, TX.

    Story note: "Like a Feather" is a part of a collection-in-progress inspired by funk music.

John Hornor Jacobs has worked in advertising since the mid-90s. He began writing, seriously, in 2007. *Southern Gods* (Night Shade Books, 2011) is his first novel. He is also the author of *This Dark Earth* (June 2012, Gallery/Simon & Schuster) and the YA series The Incarcerado Trilogy, starting with The Twelve Fingered Boy (Carolrhoda Labs, 2013) followed by *Incarcerado* (2014) and *The End of All Things* (2015). He is represented by Stacia Decker of the Donald Maass Literary Agency. He is also the creative director and co-founder of *Needle: A Magazine of Noir*. His dance card is totally full.

    Story note: "Old Dogs, New Tricks" was written in 2007 and was my first attempt at combining Southern crime fiction with supernatural horror. It's one of my most polarizing stories among friends and pre-readers—while most have no problems with me doing all sorts of horrible and nasty things to my human protagonists, there are a few who cannot handle any sort of cruelty to animals, even if fictionalized. I've never been to a dog fight—though I did attend a cock-fight in Belize once—and this is just what I imagine one to be like. *I am not a monster.*

Michael Kardos is the author of the story collection *One Last Good Time* (Press 53, 2011) and the forthcoming novel *The Three-Day Affair* (The Mysterious Press). He grew up on the Jersey Shore, played the drums professionally for a number of years, and now lives in Starkville, Mississippi, where he co-directs the creative writing program at Mississippi State University.

    Story note: Over a couple of summers in high school—this was the mid 80s—I worked at a seaside haunted mansion that, unfortunately, burned down. I wrote about the place in a 2002 story called "Behind the Music." Eight years later I wrote "The Castle of Horrors." By then, my story collection-in-progress had become a lot weirder. And it seemed wrong to write about a haunted house without there being an actual ghost to, you know, haunt it.

Nik Korpon is the author of *Stay God, Old Ghosts* and *By the Nails of the Warpriest.* His stories have ruined the reputation of *Crime Factory, Shotgun Honey, Out of the Gutter, Dirty Noir, Speedloader, Warmed&Bound, Black Heart Magazine* and some others. He lives in Baltimore. Give him some danger, little stranger, at nikkorpon.com.

Story note: I was sitting in a bar one night, trading ghost stories with a friend. I waved to someone across the room and when I turned back, my friend had disappeared. This creepy feeling passed over me, like we'd unwittingly summoned something from the depths just by talking about it. Turned out, he reached down to get something out of his jacket pocket and had slipped off the stool. Regardless, the memory of the feeling lingered, and I wrote this story from that.

Ron Lands is a member of the teaching faculty in the Department of Medicine at the University of Tennessee, Knoxville campus where he practices and teaches Internal Medicine, Hematology and Narrative Medicine. He has work published in the collection *Breathing the Same Air, an Anthology of East Tennessee Writers* as well as *New Millennium Writings, Branchwood Journal, Wind, descant, The Distillery, Washington Square, Fourth River, Nassau Review, RiverSedge,* and the *Big Muddy.* He has published essays and poetry in the *Journal of the American Medical Association, Annals of Internal Medicine, Journal of the American Geriatric Society* and the *Journal of Palliative Medicine.* His work has been nominated for a Pushcart Prize.

Story note: I've been writing "The Veil" for the past fifty years. I sat behind a boy during the first grade who died of a ruptured appendix over the summer break. My only real memory of him is the perfect shape of the back of his head, his fine brown hair and his multi-colored striped T-shirt. When I was a little older, I heard my mother and her sisters talk about how my grandmother came to breakfast one morning in December 1944 and told the family that her oldest son, serving somewhere in the Pacific theatre during WWII, had stood at the foot of her bed in his dress uniform all night. A few weeks later, they were notified of his death at the battle of Leyte. Now, I work with people who are near the end of their lives. Some of them tell me about conversations with family and friends that I find out later have been dead for decades. I spend my days trying to see through the veil that separates the dead from the living, one that some people can step through, then step back again, from wherever they are to wherever this is.

Sophie Littlefield grew up in rural Missouri. She writes the post-apocalyptic *Aftertime* series for Harlequin Luna. She also writes paranormal fiction for young adults, most recently *Unforsaken* (October 2011). Her first novel, *A Bad Day for Sorry*, won an Anthony Award for Best First Novel and an RT Book Award for Best First Mystery. It was also shortlisted for Edgar, Barry, Crimespree, and Macavity Awards. The third in the series, *A Bad Day for Scandal*, was released this year. Sophie lives in Northern California.

    Story note: I was a serious child, sensitive to perceived injustice, and I spent a lot of time sitting in church thinking about how unfair the seven deadly sins were. How could God punish people for things that were out of their control, like pride and envy, especially if they kept the thoughts inside and never acted on them? This story revisits that sense of unfairness and my early rebellion against conventional concepts of sin.

Robert Hill Long is the author of *The Power to Die* and *The Work of the Bow* (Cleveland State, 1987, 1997), *The Effigies* (Plinth Books, 1998), *The Kilim Dreaming* (Bear Star Press, 2010), *The Wire Garden* (Arlo Press, 2010) and *Walking Wounded* (WordTech Editions, June 2012), in which the current *10x3* poems will appear. He taught creative writing for 20 years, and is now a faculty research administrator at the University of Oregon.

Story note: "Out of the Whirlwind" is a 1000-word monologue by a velvet painting inhabited by the ghost of James Dean, delivered to a pompous Indiana redneck car salesman, in a flea market one Sunday afternoon.

Alexander Lumans hails originally from Aiken, South Carolina. He graduated from the MFA Fiction Program at Southern Illinois University-Carbondale. His fiction has been published in or is forthcoming from *Story Quarterly, Black Warrior Review, Cincinnati Review, Greensboro Review, The Versus Anthology,* and *The Book of Villains,* among other magazines. He was a Tennessee Williams Scholar at the 2010 Sewanee Writers' Conference and he won the 2011 Barry Hannah Fiction Prize from *The Yalobusha Review.* He was also recently awarded a MacDowell Colony Fellowship. He now lives, teaches, and eats in Boulder, Colorado.

Story note: It started with this word: "birdmen." Some knuckle-dragging amygdala of mine just spit it out one day. Nothing about it ever sounded amiable or charitable. It's the kind of word that I could picture people being frightened to say too loudly for fear of what it might suddenly conjure up or call down. This is probably because I'm obsessed with large birds—hell, I received a hawking glove for Christmas. Up close, they command so much awe. They're not too many mutations away from turning into insatiable tyrant-storks; and what better creature to take away human children than the one that supposedly delivers them in the first place?

Josh McCall (joshmccall.com) is the author of *The Blackout Gang* (Razorbill, 2006) and has had his fiction and nonfiction published in the *Surreal South '09, The Southeast Review Online, The Florida Review, Southern Humanities Review, New Plains Review,* and *The Dallas Morning News.* He lives in Texas and is married to the poet Jennifer McClanaghan.

Story note: This piece began from a desire to tell a metamorphosis story. In fact, I wanted to do something much more specific than that: I wanted to retell Julio Cortazar's "Axolotl." But what metamorphosed most was the narrative itself, and in its final version, "The Easy Payment Plan" is a ghost story in which the narrator is haunted by, among other things, his own desire.

John McManus was born in Knoxville and raised in Maryville, Tennessee. He is the author of the novel *Bitter Milk* and the short story collections *Born on a Train* and *Stop Breakin Down*. His stories have appeared in *Ploughshares, Harvard Review, The Oxford American, Columbia, Tin House, Night Train, storySouth, Grist, Surreal South '09,* and other journals and anthologies. He lives in Norfolk, Virginia, and teaches at Old Dominion University's MFA program, and also at the low-residency MFA creative writing program at Goddard College.

    Story note: I wrote this story after I began to imagine Grindr (the iPhone GPS-based gay dating app) in the hands of depraved methheads in the Smoky Mountains. It maintains the intensely subjective POV of a severely sleep-deprived methamphetamine addict who hallucinates that Dolly Parton is speaking to him from billboards and who blacks out whole weeks of his life. My intention wasn't to portray my protagonist's hallucinations as literally real events, but they're real enough to him that he can't discern otherwise when they occur.

Sheryl Monks holds an MFA in writing from Queens University of Charlotte. Her fiction has appeared in *RE:AL, Backwards City Review, Southern Gothic* online, *Surreal South '09, Fried Chicken and Coffee, Night Train,* and *storySouth*. Her story "Justice Boys" was named a Notable Story of 2009 in the storySouth Million Writers Award competition. She teaches English and Humanities at Wilkes Community College in Wilkesboro, North Carolina.

    Story note: "Monsters in Appalachia" came from a dream I had about an old woman wishing for "the sweet tender things of before. Now," she said in the dream, "it is all hard hide and claw and horns and scales and beaks and necks and parts unheard of." It took a couple of years to re-enter the dream awake and finish the story, but eventually it came about all on its own.

Marilyn Moriarty teaches literature at Hollins University, in Roanoke, Virginia. Her work has been published in *Faultline*, *The Kenyon Review*, *Mondo Greco*, *Nimrod*, *Thema*, *Peregrine*, *Quarterly West* and *Relief*. Her book *Moses Unchained* won the Associated Writing Programs Creative Nonfiction Prize.

Story note: Two things were on my mind as I worked on this story. 1) What does the idea of reincarnation imply about our normal idea of time? If you believe in reincarnation, certain assumptions about the nature of time are suspended. If those assumptions are suspended, why should material, lived time be linear, always moving forward; couldn't a *next* life go into the past? You could meet your self in another incarnation. You might be all the people in your life. And the ghost in your house might be you in the afterlife, looking down, trying to help. 2) In answering a related question—what is the purpose of life on earth if heaven exists?—I always come back to Robert Frost's poem, "Birches": "Earth's the right place for love."

"After the After" is from an unpublished collection of interconnected short stories called *'Flight' is the Name of a Goddess*.

James O'Brien attended Iowa State University's MFA program in Creative Writing, graduating in Spring 2011. His work has appeared in or is forthcoming from *The Colorado Review*, *The Portland Review*, *The Collagist*, *NY Tyrant*, and over a dozen other publications. He can be found online at www.thedevilsthroat.com and contacted at jdobrienwrites@gmail.com.

Story note: One morning in February I woke to snow drifting against my window. The world outside was covered and white. I decided I wasn't going to walk out in the storm, so I sat inside watching it from my living room, listening to Johnny Cash. Few people passed. Those who did seemed spectral and half real. The snow kept falling and blowing, and soon I could see little at all. Strange shapes formed in the snow before me. It was all similar to the way that you'd lie on your back in warmer weather and name the things that clouds appeared to be. And that was when the Man came around. The first thing I saw was his dog. The Man followed.

Then Houck. Throughout the day I found out more and more about them and what they wanted. I wrote that down. By evening the snow had abated and I had a few pages written. Storms blew through throughout the week. I had little to do other than write the story. And that's what I did.

Where the story came from I'm not sure. The jawless hound is especially mysterious to me. The Man is more than anything influenced by Dracula and *Blood Meridian*'s Judge Holden, in that he embodies a distant and formal sort of malevolence. Houck is the traditional "lost boy" who wants to be better than he is, much along the lines of his namesake. That's Huck Finn. But largely it was the location that kept impressing itself on me as I wrote the story. It's set in the places where I grew up and lived as a college student. Certainly the grit and the cold of those places loomed in my mind throughout writing the piece. And Johnny Cash. Always Johnny Cash.

Julia Patt hails from Mitchellville, Maryland and is consequently on the fence about her Southerner status. She studies creative writing in the MFA program at UNC-Greensboro, where she's also getting an education in porch sitting, jalapeño cornbread, and sweet tea. Her work has recently been featured in *The Dead Mule School of Southern Literature*, *The Medulla Review*, and *Bards & Sages Quarterly*, and her flash fiction, "Fall 1970," won the 2011 Stymie Magazine Trading Card Contest.

Story note: "Hunting the Pigwoman" is an amalgamation of sorts—a collision of unrelated stories I'd been writing and rewriting for a while. The two boys in the woods with guns, following a vision. The pigwoman, from my native Maryland. The mania for "Hogzilla," which was introduced to me by one of UNCG's poetry faculty, Rebecca Black. And then one night, it all connected with this question of hunting: who is hunting whom and why? It became a story about wildness, of being out of your depth in the natural world. It's easy to forget, I think, that there are still places in the country where we feel lost and helpless. And that's what monsters do; they occupy the places we don't want to go. Thing is, those places also exist inside of us, the aspects of ourselves we don't want to consider, the dreams we don't want to remember. So the most frightening monsters are also part of us, part human—even if we only glimpse them at dusk, deep in the woods where there's no one around to tell us if what we saw was real.

Victor Schultz is a copyeditor for a trade journal near Chicago. His fiction has appeared in *The Acentos Review*.

Story note: This story's origins are in the hypnotic voices of narrators on true-crime shows, in the ways we tell ourselves about the worst sins, and in the flatlands I pass through during my annual drive from Chicago to South Texas, where much of my family lives.

Anthony Neil Smith is the Director of Creative Writing at Southwest Minnesota State University. He is the author of *Psychosomatic, The Drummer, Yellow Medicine, Hogdoggin', Choke on Your Lies*, and the forthcoming *All the Young Warriors*. He's also the publisher of the noir ezine *Plots with Guns*.

Story note: Still recovering from my eight years in the Pentecostal church, I wrote this ghost story as a way to get myself "right" again—what better than an anachronistic ghost telling the protagonist that this church of his is nuts? Since the Pentecostals are heavily into the supernatural with miracles, speaking in tongues, dancing in the spirit, praying for instant healing, and a constant stream of apocalyptic talk, it made sense to pit the believers against the good Major in what they saw as a fight against good and evil, even though it's more a fight between dogma and free will.

A.K. Thompson is a fiction writer and musician who lives in a cabin on a pond in Makanda, Illinois, where vultures descend each fall. She sings the part of a ghostly banjo on the album *Long Term Plan* by The Whistle Pigs. She holds a Master's Degree in Writing and Consciousness from the New College of California, as well as an MFA from Southern Illinois University—Carbondale. She served as Assistant Editor for the *Crab Orchard Review* in 2009-2010. She has been published in *The Smoking Poet, The Chiron Review*, and writes a monthly column, "Dirt Church," for *Adventure Sports Outdoors Magazine.*

Story note: "The Taxidermist" came about after a series of bona fide surreal events, of which I took note as they haunted me to the very core. The story was demanding to be written and with little regard for my mental health, but a writer has got to listen to the other-worldly when it comes to such things—that's what good fiction is all about—an almost demonic possession by angels. After seeing a series of dead dogs, seemingly dumped, or in my interpretation offered up by the wild blue yonder, at the side of Route 51 over a number of years, and always south of the same small town, I began to speak, in what almost bordered on tongues, into my tape recorder, and went from there. The occurrences were so evocative to me that I had to make sense of it—and the page was the only place I could try and manage this huge task. During the writing process the haunting continued when I noticed a deer mount in my kitchen begin to "sweat." So I built an altar, crowned her with owl feathers, and told her I'd get the story right come Hell or high-water. Quite literally I felt the ghosts of these animals were trying to communicate with me. Something far larger than my earthly understanding was speaking to me, and by the last revision she had returned to her forever un-dead normal. The writing process took a lot out of me, but in the end gave me something every writer dreams of—a story that lives and breathes of its own cryptic accord.

Anne Valente's fiction appears or is forthcoming in *Hayden's Ferry Review, Bellevue Literary Review, Unsaid, Annalemma,* and *Hobart,* among others. Her work has been twice nominated for the Pushcart Prize, and is also included in Dzanc Books' *Best of the Web 2010* anthology. She currently lives and teaches in Ohio.

Story note: This story developed when I was very much missing my grandparents, wondering at times if they were ever watching me, and if they were proud of the choices I'd grown up to make. Though the story bears no autobiographical resemblance beyond that, I did include a few details from my own childhood with them—

swimming pool floaties, pogosticks, and grappling hooks made from pine twigs and twine. And the rest: my own fascination with ghosts, and with the blurred, indistinct line between real and not-real.

Jim Walke grew up in Michigan and still has near-freezing Yankee lake water in his blood. Following college he was a stage actor for a decade or so, living in and touring dozens of states while getting paid very little to swing swords and kiss pretty girls. Gravity, advancing age and the promise of health insurance have finally dragged him to a halt in southwest Virginia close to the Appalachian Trail. He received his MFA from Queens University of Charlotte in 2010. His recent work has appeared in *Ampersand Review*, *Gulf Stream*, and *Jersey Devil Press* (nominated for Best of the Web 2011). www.jimwalke.com

Story note: "Pig Hole" feels like cheating because nearly all of the elements were handed to me on a platter. In the years since the Virginia Tech shootings, Blacksburg and the surrounding mountains have been affected by one odd tragedy after another. That strange background intersected with a physical location when a hiking buddy asked, "Jim, you want to do Pig Hole next weekend? Hunnert-sixty-foot drop, total dark." All I had to do then was write it down.

Gregory J. Wolos's fiction has recently appeared or is forthcoming in *Storyglossia*, *Prime Number Magazine*, *elimae*, *Apple Valley Review*, *Underground Voices*, *Prick of the Spindle*, *Gulf Stream Magazine*, *The Fiddleback*, and other journals. In the last year his stories have earned recognition in several competitions, including a 2012 Pushcart Prize nomination. One of his stories was selected as winner of the 2011 Gulf Stream Award for fiction, and another won the 2011 New South Writing Contest. He lives and writes on the northern bank of the Mohawk River in upstate New York. His website is: www.gregorywolos.com.

Story note: "Interstate Nocturne" was inspired by the collapse of a bridge—an overpass over an Interstate, as in my story. Caused by flooding, also as in my story, the collapse occurred at night, and cars headed south drove into the gap until daybreak. When I read about this, the notion haunted me, and still does—every night-time bridge over which I pass becomes susceptible to collapse. My story tries to capture some of the psychological terror of these night-time journeys, as the doomed protagonist is drawn back to the womb, through a transformed midnight, guided by the ghost of his mother.

Susan Woodring is the author of a collection of short stories, *Springtime on Mars* (Press 53, 2008), and a forthcoming novel, *Goliath* (St. Martin's Press, 2012).

Story note: I have been playing around with a story about the demise of a tourist-mountain-town department store and the family that owns it for the last few years. I couldn't quite get the thing to hang together until I dreamed up the store owner's dwarf daughter and her love, a creek monster named Ballenka. I wanted to create a monster that was entirely dear and lovable, and yet also dangerous and huge. I worked to pit the monster against the store owner, a deeply deluded man, yet a good man, but I wanted to save the story's power for the girl.

Josh Woods is editor of *The Book of Villains* (Main Street Rag, 2011) and of *The Versus Anthology* (Press 53, 2009). He worked with Pinckney and Laura Benedict as Associate Editor of *Surreal South '09* (Press 53, 2009) and was also an Assistant Editor of *Crab Orchard Review* (vol.14 n.1, and vol.14 n.2, 2008 and 2009). His fiction has won in the Press 53 Open Awards, and his work has appeared in the fiction anthology *XX Eccentric: Stories About the Eccentricities of Women* (Main Street Rag, 2009) as well as *The Press 53 Open Awards Anthology* (Press 53, 2008) and *The Susquehanna Review* (vol. 1, 2001). He has also contributed fiction to *The Book of Villains*, *The Versus Anthology*, and to *Surreal South '09*. He graduated from the MFA program at Southern Illinois University Carbondale and is currently an Assistant Professor of English at Kaskaskia College in Illinois.

Story note: This story was an opportunity to combine two of my favorite things: fighting and monsters. I've been a fighting hobbyist since the late '90s, and I have wanted to be a monster for far longer than that. In fact, I'd trade all of those countless, sweat-drenched hours of jiu-jitsu rolling and muay Thai sparring for the slightest chance to have big claws, lots of fur, and a staggering howl.

As for the "southern" qualification, I'm from Kentucky, and I set the story in the vaguely eastern part of that "dark and bloody ground," where things like this might actually happen. As for the "surreal" part, this story takes the existence of its monsters at literal face-value, so I'll call that surreal enough. As we all know, trolls live under bridges and eat children, so that's the tradition of this troll. The goblin was inspired by an impossibly mean little dog in my neighborhood, but also by the movies *Gremlins* and *Lilo and Stitch*. I figure doppelgangers can be duped into thinking that they are actually those whom they double, and I don't see why even an ancient, shape-shifting, god-like thing can't, for a time, forget what it once was. Maybe this story is about finding yourself, even if you are an unspeakable horror. Also, the name "Troupes" is an anagram, a word that has shape-shifted.

www.ingramcontent.com/pod-product-compliance
Lightning Source LLC
Chambersburg PA
CBHW032228010726
47494CB00002B/396